z^2

a novel

by

Sherrie Cronin

DEDICATION

To my boyfriend Kevin with whom I have shared thirty-one years of marriage, three children and the greatest friendship of my life. I thank him for treating my passion for writing as if it is perfectly normal, for feeding me so well while I write, and most of all for being someone strong to hold onto while the howling noises and twirling lights run circles in my head at night after I shut off my laptop

and

I wish to thank a lady named Mrs. Jacobs who once taught the lyrics to "The Sounds of Silence" in eighth grade English at Hays Junior High School and who wrote across the top of my first science fiction story that I should write more. If anyone finds her, please tell her that she created a whole new timeline for me that day and that the universe I have inhabited ever since has been so much more interesting because of it.

This novel is volume three of six in the collection
46. Ascending

 First Edition. Published 2013
by Cinnabar Press, Montgomery, Texas 77316

ISBN-13: 978-0-9851561-4-5

Cover design and illustration by Jennifer FitzGerald of www.MotherSpider.com

A note to my paperback readers

This book was originally designed to be read on an electronic reader and it included up to a few links per chapter that led to photographs, news reports and opinion pieces designed to enhance a reader's enjoyment of this novel. Obviously no such links are possible in a paperback book.

Please be assured that these links were always supplementary material and the book itself stands alone and requires none of them. In the interest of avoiding confusion, I have removed the underlines and occasionally a few words referencing the link. A curious reader can still find the complete URLs listed at the end of this book and as live links on the book's website at http://www.zsquaredblog.org.

The electronic version also contained references to nine songs, intended to be a sort of soundtrack featuring some of the favorite music of Alex, the main character in the novel. I have removed the references to the music, but both the songs and their context within the story can be found on at the website given above. Interested readers who do seek these out are encouraged to support the referenced artists, news outlets and websites.

You may notice that the characters in this book turn to the Southern Poverty Law Center for up-to-date information on hate groups and their activities. This is a real organization. Please consider supporting them, but also know that if you paid for this book you have contributed already as ten per cent of the author's proceeds from z^2 are being donated to the SPLC.

You may contact the author at alex.zeitman@gmail.com. If you enjoyed reading this, please look for x^0 and y^1, novels about other members of the Zeitman family. Also watch for c^3, the story of youngest daughter Teddie, which will be available in late 2013.

Finally, for those whose love of math is meager, allow me to explain that the number of total possible outcomes at the end of the day is equal to 2^z if z is the number of meaningful choices you make that day and if every decision just has two possibilities. Alex knows very well that this formula would have made a more mathematically accurate name for his club, but for his own personal reasons he prefers to name his organization z^2 instead.

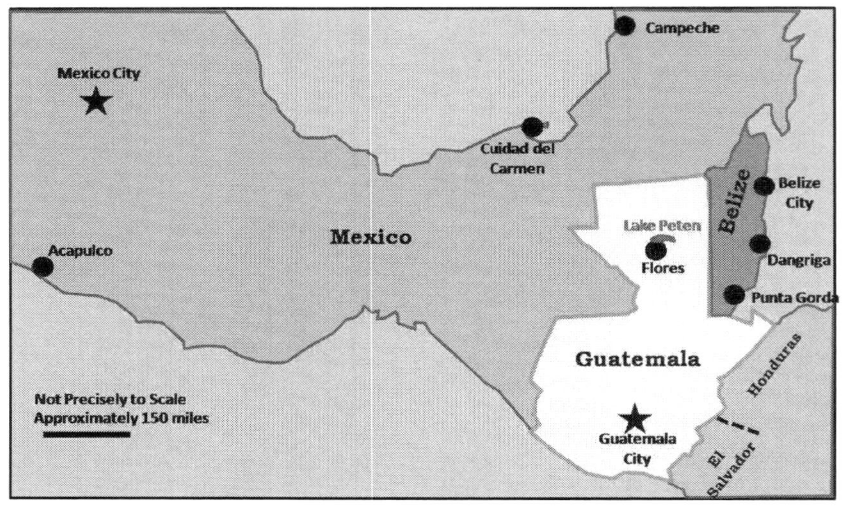
Campeche
Mexico City
Cuidad del
Carmen
Belize
Belize
City
Mexico
Lake Peten
Acapulco
Flores
Dangriga
Punta Gorda
Guatemala
Honduras
Not Precisely to Scale
Approximately 150 miles
Guatemala
City
El
Salvador

Before
Chapter 1. December 1696

When the time came, she knew it, just like her father promised her that she would. She saw the signs as her rulers became friendly with the strangers, and she listened with fear as they became ever less cautious. Nimah watched with her own horrified eyes as the singers and priests of the others were finally allowed to walk brazenly into her city and she cried as her neighbors welcomed the invaders.

Of course, the strangers' warmth disappeared quickly when they did not get their way. When Nimah's king would not convert to the new religion like they had so clearly expected, the strangers responded to the fine hospitality of the Itza by sending soldiers to convert them by force. The Itza fought back valiantly.

"The day on which you must act will not be long after that," her father had cautioned. So in the months since that attack, Nimah had been actively preparing herself and her two sons for today. At twenty-six, Nimah thought of herself as responsible and mature, one who took her obligations seriously. She had learned well her people's history and religion, and her people kept fine records, so there was much to know.

She knew that she was part of the Kan Ek, the ancient race whose rulers were descended from the Gods. She knew that once, more generations ago than there were days in a moon cycle, her people had been far more structured. The lands were bigger then, with many more families, and there had been many cities and giant gatherings where customs were shared. There had been much more wealth and, some had said, much more greatness. But Nimah thought not. She had also learned that lives had been more stringently controlled back then and that there had sometimes been cruel penalties for those who failed or wandered astray.

Many people of that time appeared to have believed that the greatness of the Maya would go on forever. Nimah knew, she had studied their texts. But, over hundreds of years, the carefully recorded famines and droughts and wars had brought an endless string of hard times to the seemingly invincible people. Nimah had studied how, over time, her people had been forced to huddle closer together for strength and how the resulting battles for food and water had shrunk her world. Finally, her own people's realm encompassed only the area around Tayasal itself, the beautiful town built on the remains of the great old city of Noh Peten.

Now her people, those of the majestic Lake Peten Itza, were free to develop their own rules and more flexible ways. Nimah personally thought that they had evolved, that they were now an older race, one filled with more enlightenment and compassion. So Nimah was glad that she had been born when she was, not at the time when her kings ruled over the most amount of land, but at the time when her people themselves had never been better.

Outsiders were of three types now. There were those who were Maya also, but who hailed from the other surviving communities that had fought with the people of Lake Peten Itza many years ago. These outsiders would travel to the low flatlands of the Peten Itza region for trade and for news. As they were no longer enemies, they were welcomed and cared for. Goods and information were exchanged before these visitors returned to their homes.

Then there were the Xiu Maya, from the Northwest, who before Nimah was born had grown weary of fighting off the others and had instead joined forces with them. They were not to be trusted and were never welcomed.

Finally, there were the strangers themselves, the new people. Not so new, really, Nimah thought, seeing as they had been here before her great-grandmother. They called themselves Spaniards. At first they mostly came looking for gold and other treasures, although over the last generation or two they had been increasingly eager to take land and cities as well. For years now, they had been sending more visitors, showing more interest in the land and in the towns of Nimah's people.

The Itza response had been to lay low. To appear to have nothing. To tell the strangers very little. That had worked well for over five generations as the Spanish sought their riches everywhere else. But it looked like they had finally run out of other places to look. Soon, they and their ways would be here and before that happened Nimah had to act.

It was too bad that her husband had been taken by illness five years ago. She could have used his strength on this day, in more ways than one. But luckily, in the intervening years, her two sons had grown larger and stronger. Now at twelve and ten they were close enough to men, and Nimah was confident that they were ready to assume their roles in this family obligation.

She woke her boys and gave them a simple breakfast as they went over the instructions. Today, the three of them would take the largest and heaviest of the three boxes and would hide it carefully in one of the small caves on the other side of the lake. Nimah had found the perfect place months ago, and had spent weeks preparing both the hiding spot and the document that she would place in the box.

Tomorrow she would say goodbye to Ichik, her dear oldest child, and send him off towards the rising sun. He was larger and he could better carry the heavier of the two remaining boxes. In that direction were flatlands and friendlier people, and Nimah thought that the boy would have the easier journey. This would be good, because for all that she loved Ichik she knew that he was just a little bit lazy. He had a calm and somewhat meek animal spirit guiding him. It was just a fact that he would never make much of a fighter. She needed him to keep walking until he reached the sea, and Nimah had no idea what the boy would find at that edge of the earth. Nimah hoped fervently that it was not something that would require him to be fierce.

On the day after that, Nimah would send Balam, her second son, off into the setting sun with the smallest box of the three. This boy was still slight in stature, but fierce in spirit. Nimah would also tell him to journey all the way to the water, to make a home there, to hide and guard the box he had brought for as long as he lived, and then to ask his sons and their sons to do the same.

Thus each boy and his descendants would keep safe a valuable piece of the puzzle, just as Nimah's father had asked. Nimah, now alone with her eight-year-old daughter, would devote the rest of her life to protecting the biggest box, left behind in the cave, and to guarding its secrets. And her daughter and her daughter's children would do the same.

One day, Nimah's father had promised, all of his descendants would be freed from this burden and all three boxes would be reunited. When it was time.

Few other family members knew about Nimah's task. Those who did assumed that her father had entrusted her, a daughter, with this important job only because she had such a clever mind for puzzles. But Nimah suspected it was for more reasons than that. Underneath her love of riddles, Nimah was a self-disciplined woman, one who knew better than to dread or to ignore the inevitable. She, among all her father's children, could take instructions and follow them through to the tiniest detail. And she would. She did this not only to honor her own father, of course, but for the sake of her own descendants and the descendants of all of the Maya. She even made this sacrifice for any others who were not as greedy or cruel as these Spaniards.

The day was particularly hot and muggy for December as Nimah and her two boys made the short hike to the cave while Nimah's daughter was left to watch the house. Nimah knew that the boys were hiding their fears and doing their best to stay strong. She had never been more proud of them then on this day when she was about to say goodbye to them both forever.

They helped her carry her burden, and watched silently while she opened the thin, beautifully carved obsidian box that she had spent so much of her adult life designing and then years more creating. Inside the box, there was a paper made from the fig tree, carefully prepared and soaked with her best preservative. Nimah gently smoothed the paper as she looked at it one last time. Neither boy spoke until her oldest son finally read the words at the top of the page, and started to laugh.

"The greatest treasure ever?" Ichik said raising an eyebrow. "Don't you think this perhaps exaggerates a little, mom?"

"No," Nimah shook her head firmly. "I don't. I don't think so at all."

Chapter 2. February 1981

When the 23rd annual Grammy Awards began on the night of February 25, 1981, Alex Zeitman wasn't watching them. He was sitting on the bench mostly, itching to get put into the game. It was his senior year, dammit, and one of the last games of the season. He'd had a good run playing college basketball, and had been a starter for much of his junior year as a solid contributing point guard who tended to pass rather than shoot. Okay, so he wasn't a phenom at scoring, but when Alex had a good night on the court, his team always played a fine game as well. And the coach that had recruited him to this small college outside Austin, Texas had known and appreciated that fact.

But the new coach this year hadn't been as fond of Alex's style, preferring the flash of a sophomore point guard who scored often and who had the added charm of being worth grooming for the next two years. As Alex's senior year unwound he found himself spending more and more time on the bench, and his once reasonable hopes for a few years of playing professional ball abroad were starting to evaporate.

"Just let me out there," he muttered under his breath, but there were only four minutes left in the game now and his team was down twelve points.

"Zeitman!" Alex jumped up when the coach called his name. Three minutes and fifty-three seconds. *Okay.* Alex thought. *Let's see just how much good I can possibly do in such a short time.*

As he hustled on to the court, the noise of the crowd softened in his head. Alex focused instead on the sound of his own heart pounding slowly. He moved into position as the rhythm of his heartbeat kept a constant time, like a metronome, while the play of the game itself seemed to slow down around him, as it always did. He began to match his movements to the rhythm of the sport that he loved so well. Dribble. Pass. Catch. His hands, always soft and capable, had a magnetic attraction to the ball tonight. Jump. Pivot. Turn. His feet, usually light and happy, almost danced on the court, their quickness defying his size and bulk. Alex could feel the energy grow and he knew that tonight, now that he finally had his chance, he was going to be on fire.

Then he had the ball. He took the inbound's pass down the court and penetrated the defense with his dribble. There was an open teammate on his left. Alex made a perfect pass. Score. His teammates pressured the ball in the backcourt. Double-team, deflection and Alex had a steal. He saw a man open down court. Pass and score. Time for more pressure. The ball was loose on the floor, and squirted out from the bodies around it. Alex grabbed it, took two dribbles and scored again. Two minutes and fourteen seconds left and now the Panthers only trailed by six points and the noise level was rising. Alex grinned. *Should have taken me off the bench sooner, buddy.*

A wildly thrown pass came his way and he jumped high to get it. An opponent charged into him while Alex was twisting in the air. He felt time slowing down even more as he fought to recover his equilibrium and land squarely on both feet. And he would have, because he was good at recovering—uncommonly good at not getting injured. But in the split second before his right foot touched the ground, a teammate crashed into him hard from behind. The surprise force of the impact twisted him as he came down forcefully on the inside of his right foot. His leg bent fast and wrong, folding under him. As the rest of his body hit the ground, the searing pain in his knee let him know that his evening was over. *Shit, shit, shit*. He crumpled onto the floor and nausea from the pain overtook him before the agony itself made him black out.

Later, leg elevated and packed in ice, he was taken to a local emergency room. Several other players came along and tried to lift his spirits before the doctor saw him, before the doctor told him that it was likely that more than his evening had ended. His anterior cruciate ligament, commonly called the ACL, had been ruptured quite badly, and he was absolutely out for the short remainder of his college basketball career. The coach was sympathetic enough, even though Alex suspected that the man was mainly relieved that it hadn't been a sophomore or junior who had been injured.

The hospital staff settled him into a room, having insisted on keeping him overnight for observation. The last of his teammates left, not knowing what more to say. So as he waited for the new pain medication to kick in, he morosely watched Christopher Cross receive a Grammy for song of the year on the tiny television. Alex had nothing against the soft rock song "Sailing" that seemed to be sweeping up the awards that night, but frankly being in a sailboat wasn't an image that moved Alex much. All that sitting still. He would much rather have seen Pink Floyd win best album. And for best song? He guessed he had been rooting for "Fame". It was catchy. With a beat. The way Alex preferred music.

Did you really think that fame would make you live forever? he laughed at himself. Of course not. Alex thought about his hopes and dreams for playing some pro ball before he got older and had to move on to something boring but acceptable like coaching high school ball. The doctor had just counseled him that a lengthy program of rehabilitation would help him recover eventually and that surgery was of course possible. But Alex had to face the fact that there was no real excuse for devoting himself fulltime to his own recovery. With no professional team to pick up the expense, it wasn't likely that he or his folks could justify all the money for the sort of surgery and rehab it would take to get him back to where he had been. He just hadn't been that good. And, even worse, he'd still be prone to knee injuries for the rest of his career. It just didn't make sense.

So twenty-two-year-old Alex Zeitman lay with his sandy-colored head on a hospital pillow and sadly watched the end of the 1981 Grammy Awards as he let go of a dream. Crowds wouldn't cheer as he flew down the basketball court, or be amazed as his sturdy, lightly freckled hands performed spectacular physical feats that would, maybe, have had people remembering his name, at least for a day. He would not play basketball for a living after all.

The only problem was that he didn't really have anything else that he wanted to do. But even at twenty-two, Alex had a sensible streak. He knew that while at the moment tomorrow seemed horribly bleak, sooner or later he would figure out another plan. The good news, he supposed, was that things could only get better from here.

The future had never looked brighter for senior Stan Drexler, as he stared at the acceptance letter in his hand. Unbelievable. Grad school. With a full ride. Four, five, maybe six years learning from some of the greatest experts in the field, studying the one thing that for whatever reason had fascinated him ever since he was a small boy.

He was actually going to get to travel to Guatemala and to spend years looking for undiscovered Maya artifacts in the Lake Quexil area. No, he wasn't just going to be allowed to do it. He was going to be paid to do it. And at the end? They were going to call him "Doctor Stan Drexler" and probably pay him even more money to keep doing it.

This was almost too good to be true. Stan hoped that he wasn't misleading himself about how wonderful this life would be and how much he would enjoy his work. Because even at twenty-two, Stan had a sensible streak. He knew that while right now tomorrow seemed like it couldn't be more perfect, sooner or later there would be problems or drawbacks. There always were. And unfortunately, things were so good at this very minute that it seemed like they could only get worse from here.

Chapter 3. February 1993

When Dr. Stan Drexler saw the shiny black corner of the stone box twelve years later, his heart skipped a beat. For over a decade now he had unearthed dozens of clay pots and hundreds of shards of pottery from a variety of small excavation sites near the town of Flores on Lake Peten Itza. Some had been informative, a few finds had even been mildly interesting, at least to another anthropologist. But nothing, not a single goddamn thing, had ever lived up to his hopes and dreams as a young grad student who had been driven to truly discover something new and fascinating about the civilization that had, once upon a time, so thoroughly mesmerized him.

These days, of course, he held less lofty dreams as he supervised grad students of his own, letting the willing young men and women dig into the muck, watching them sweat hard as they swatted at bugs while they dug into the earth.

"Careful," he would caution them. "Slow down. That pottery shard is my next publication and your next research paper." And they would chuckle along. Because, of course, none of them ever struck something truly worth celebrating. Until today.

They had been just about to pack up and leave, having already stayed an hour longer than planned. He was tired, and he knew that the students with him were exhausted and hungry. But excitement grew as his two most eager students, Nelson and Shelby, brushed and dug and finally gently wriggled the artifact free from the earth. Stan thought it had probably been deliberately buried, as the remnants of what must have been a protective cloth fell from around it, part of the muddy rotting material landing on Shelby's right shoe. She instinctively flinched as it landed on her, then winced when two of the boys laughed at her.

Stan gave the two boys, Jake and Kyle, his best "grow up" look, then moved in to inspect his prize more closely. It really was a thin box, but it turned out to be shaped almost like a triangle. Odd, actually. One end of the triangle was cut off, giving it four sides and making it technically a, what, a trapezoid? It was about the size of a modern coffee table book. Stan's trained eye immediately put it at post-Classic Maya, so at least after 1200 A.D. It was made mostly from shiny black obsidian, and carved with incredible detail, but it had several places on the top and sides where small pieces of what appeared to be jade and agate and other stones had been worked into the finished product. The rich colors were becoming more visible as Nelson, for once hushed and not trying to show off his knowledge, gently wiped the dirt off with a soft cloth.

"It's so beautiful," Jennifer gushed. And it was. The more Nelson cleaned it up the more it became apparent that elaborate hieroglyphs and designs adorned all four sides of the box and the lid. As the lid wobbled a fraction of an inch under Nelson's touch, Jake, his chief smart ass, turned to Stan hopefully. "Can we open it?"

"That is why we are here," Stan chuckled at finally hearing genuine amazement from the boy. Maybe he would make an archeologist yet. Nelson tactfully stepped back to let his professor do the honors.

But in spite of the wobble, the lid was stuck. Stan suspected that the box had not been disturbed or opened since it was buried several hundred years ago. He tried loosening it carefully with his fingernails and finally pulled out his pocketknife and pried very gently.

The lid gave way, and Stan had to steady his own breathing as he lifted it off and gently laid it aside. In complete silence, Maya expert Dr. Stan Drexler and his five best graduate students stared at a piece of light yellow paper the size and shape of the inside of the box. It was the proverbial message in a bottle, sent from an unknown Maya hundreds of years in the past.

"Do you think it is part of a codex?" Kyle asked softly, alluding to the few remaining pieces of actual Maya books displayed in libraries around the world. But this paper appeared to be only a single sheet. The Maya were known, of course, for their advanced ways of preserving paper. This page had fared well and was absolutely covered in hieroglyphs. Stan suspected it was made from fig wood and coated in some sort of preservative, just like the coda themselves. He studied it carefully. He would not have dreamed of touching it.

"What's it say?" Shelby asked.

"I have no idea," Stan lied. "I think it is very late post-classical, and it's not a dialect I can read easily. It will need to be analyzed very thoroughly, but you know that this sort of thing usually tends to be about astronomy and about their gods."

Shelby nodded mutely and squinted harder at the document.

Stan carefully replaced the lid and laid a large canvas bag over the box to protect it. In a bright, end-of-discussion tone he said, "Okay, enough excitement for today and then some. We are already in overtime. We'll leave the box *in situ* and, like the good archeologists that we are, we will not disturb it further. Tomorrow, we will inventory and photograph and describe in excruciating detail. It is going to be a good day. Tonight, I'll make some phone calls and get some more experts down here as fast as possible. Congratulations boys and girls. You've probably just been part of one of the biggest finds of your career or, for that matter, anyone else's."

"Great," Kyle had laughed. "It's all downhill from here." And with a sympathetic shrug back, Stan herded his students towards the two trucks.

As Stan stood outside the cave while his students packed up the gear for the day, he had no trouble imagining why the owner of the box had chosen to bury it here. It was a beautiful spot, on high ground above a stream with a pretty little waterfall made all the more lovely by the surrounding lush greenery and rocks. He considered briefly posting two of the students as guards for the night. Which two? They all needed dinner and sleep.

Then he had another thought. They'd been digging at this site for over a month and no one in the area had been the least bit interested. Perhaps guarding the site might be the worst way of raising suspicions. No, the best idea was certainly to leave the box just as it had been found. He needed every one of his students alert tomorrow, and the wonderful artifact was probably at its safest if they all treated it as one more boring find.

Ixchel worried that her choice had been a poor one, even

though it had seemed so sensible a few weeks ago. Women eight-months pregnant should not fly. But, of course, women eight-months pregnant also should not make an eighteen-hour journey in a car. Yet, as an only child whose parents clearly needed her there, what was she supposed to do?

In the end there had been two deciding factors. One was Raul. Fly alone and she would certainly make it in time, only to face her father's death and her mother's grief by herself. Drive, and Raul would have to take her. He would be there to hold her hand and hold her mother's. She wanted him there.

And then there was the second reason. Her secret reason. In the best of cases, Raul and his dependable van could become a vehicle of mercy. For if her father could be made comfortable enough for long enough, Ixchel had every intention of persuading her own mother and her new husband to do the unthinkable. She wanted to check her father out of that horrible cancer clinic in Houston that had only sucked away her parents' life savings and provided no cure, and she wanted to simply put her father in the back of Raul's van and drive him home. There he could die in his own bed surrounded by all of his loved ones. There her mother could be comforted and held in her hour of need by her family. And there her father's body could be laid to rest in its proper plot, buried by his pastor, near to the bodies of his parents and ancestors, as the man surely deserved. And none of that would be possible if Ixchel had flown from Mexico City to Houston.

She didn't know much about the legalities of transporting a body, but after all the money that the treatments had cost, Ixchel doubted that her mother could afford to fly her father's corpse home. And Ixchel strongly suspected that in the U.S. one wasn't allowed to just drive off with the deceased. But, for absolutely free one could drive off with the nearly deceased, now couldn't they?

In fact, she realized with a sigh, her poor dear father didn't even have to live through the journey home. He just had to live through getting discharged from the hospital and making the very short journey into the van. After that, getting him from Houston to Brownsville would be easy either way. Eight hours on a good highway. Then crossing the border back into Mexico should not be a problem. Officials were on the lookout for live Mexicans coming in, not dead ones going out.

The ten-hour trek to Mexico City would be more difficult, hot and on bad roads, but she would join her mother in rosaries while Raul drove. It would calm them all, and be good for her unborn baby to hear her pray.

She had not, of course, mentioned this plan to either her mother or her husband. No sense stirring up agitation until she looked her father in the eye and knew that this is what he wanted. If it was, and Ixchel was certain that she would be able to tell, then she planned to persuade all.

Only here they were in Matamoros, halfway to Houston and spending the night at a cheap hotel before crossing into the U.S. in the morning. And she was sure that she was having labor pains.

Raul had the television blaring. She wanted to scream at him. Maybe it was just nerves. What did they call early labor? Braxton-Hicks contractions. Ixchel closed her eyes, did her best to shut out the television, the couple yelling next door, the baby crying down the hall. *Breathe,* she told herself. *Breathe.* You have a fine plan and it's all going to be okay. *Breathe.*

Unfortunately, no matter how slowly you breathe, both birth and death are notoriously difficult to plan around.

Stan tried to control his enthusiasm the next morning as he woofed down breakfast at the hotel and supervised the loading of the trucks. The department head had chastised him by phone the previous night for even opening the box, and for doing as little as brushing off most of the dirt. Stan had expected that response, and he was willing to take the criticism. He hadn't spent twelve years of his life swatting mosquitoes just to take a back seat while some senior faculty member flew down here to do the honors. This was his research. These were his kids. They all deserved their moment in the sun. Yesterday, he had taken it.

Today, however, they would back off and show professional restraint, as they concentrated on photographing and measuring and recording data while they all waited for more expertise before anything further was disturbed.

There was lightness in Stan's step as he helped unload the two trucks and made his way to the cave's small entrance. "You first, Dr. Drexler," Nelson said politely. Stan wasn't even all the way in when he noticed mud tracks he was sure neither he nor his students had made. *No, come on,* he thought. *Surely we did not have intruders last night of all times.*

He looked around quickly. Everything else they had found over the last few days was completely undisturbed. Only the ornate box and its half disintegrated bit of cloth covering were completely gone, as if they had never existed.

You have got to be kidding, Stan muttered to himself. *Locals? For christsakes, did one of my students tell somebody?* Then he had a second thought. *Was there any chance at all that any of the five students could read hieroglyphics from this region that well?*

Because Dr. Stan Drexler of course could. He had studied nothing but for the last twelve years. And even though there was a fair amount of local variation and he had only gotten a quick glance at it, there are certain words that anyone who has ever loved archeology knows, at least in the culture where they have expertise. "Treasure" is one of those words. Even higher on the list is any phrase that translates roughly as "the greatest treasure ever."

Raul wanted to take her to the hospital in Matamoros the next morning. The contractions had come and gone all through the night. Now Ixchel was sweating hard and periodically moaning in pain. She agreed, but insisted on calling her mother in Houston first. They found a pay phone and amassed all their coins.

Inez answered the phone in her husband's room. "Hours maybe," she whispered to her daughter as she looked at her barely conscious husband through tear-filled eyes. "Maybe not even that long they say."

No, Ixchel thought. *Could this timing be worse? Yet I cannot possibly leave my mother to face this alone. I should have come days sooner. I had no idea he was dying so quickly.* So Ixchel didn't even mention labor to her mother, but asked instead that she plead with the dying man to hold on for a few hours more. Ixchel would be there in eight. Maybe less if Raul would drive fast.

The man at the border peered in through the window at the highly pregnant woman tightly clutching a pillow while she breathed deeply and tears streamed out of her eyes.

"I think you need to take her back to Mexico buddy where she can have that baby."

Raul shook his head. "I am trying. She will not go." And Raul tried to explain about the dying father in Houston, but the border guard was busy trying to explain about the illegalities of entering the U.S. specifically to give birth. Pretty soon both men were raising their voices at each other, insisting that this was important and that the other was simply not listening. Meanwhile an increasingly agitated Ixchel began to try to get her husband's attention. The third time her husband brushed her off, she gave up and instinctively squatted on the seat of the car, her entire mind now focused on the hard work her body was doing. As the argument between the two men escalated into actual shouting, Ixchel let out a shriek of her own that stopped all discussion. Raul turned to Ixchel as she let loose a yell that changed into something between a grunt and a moan. She repeated the sound again while the two baffled men saw a mass of red liquid hit the cloth upholstery. A panic-filled Raul reached over and managed to catch his baby before it landed on his front seat.

"Oh good Lord," the border guard said in disgust. He had never seen a birth and hoped that he never did again.

"Now can we please try to get to her father before he dies?" the exasperated Raul asked as he raised his blood covered hands to show the guard the healthy screaming baby boy. "Allow a dying man to meet his first grandson?"

"Get her checked out at a clinic first on the way." The border guard shook his head in disbelief as he waved the couple, no as he waved the family, on through.

Chapter 4. April 2009

Alex Zeitman liked to think of himself as a sensible guy who didn't make bone-headed decisions that resulted in all manner of grief. As a high school teacher he watched young men and women do just that day in and day out, and he watched their indignation and surprise as smoking weed in the bathroom, or failing to show up most days for class, or copying a friend's paper almost word for word, yielded suspension, flunking, legal trouble or worse.

Consequences. There are consequences to all behavior. He tried hard to tell his students that. Good, bad, stupid, well-intentioned and just plain not-well-thought-out actions all yielded results. Sometimes those consequences turned out to be far more significant than one would think they should be. Like today.

Alex was shivering and dripping wet, thinking that one well-intentioned, but incredibly stupid idea of his may have the consequence of destroying his whole life, and he had only himself to blame. A hundred yards away, the canoe he had just been thrown out of remained trapped against a mound of branches and debris as the high, fast water of a cresting river swollen by massive rains pushed the craft hard against a wall of logs and twigs. Standing on the shore next to him was Ken, the shop teacher at his school and an outdoor enthusiast. Ken's initial nonchalant reassurance that had all was well had begun to change into a look of silent worry. Ken's wife Sara was searching in Ken's pack for a dry jacket to offer Alex. They all knew that Alex's wife Lola was somewhere out there still under water, and as she failed to surface Ken seemed to be measuring the seconds while Alex fought a growing sense of panic. Paddling back upstream in this current was going to be barely possible, but as Ken eyed the canoe that he and Sara had safely guided over to shore, Alex suspected that Ken was thinking of it.

Lola loved canoeing. Loved white water. Loved outdoor adventure. Alex, who had little use for any of the above, had only been trying to do something nice for his wife. After almost twenty-five years of marriage, two careers and three kids, their lives had long since settled into a routine of hard work and responsibility. Recently he could tell that Lola was restless for the things she had loved as a young woman. That made sense. Alex wanted to see her happy. When he found out that Ken and Sara wanted another couple to join them on this outing, it had seemed like such a great idea. A gift to his wife.

But of course busy lives meant not much flexibility in picking the weekend to go. A week of rains that drenched the entire south-central portion of the nation was an inconvenience to be ignored. The fact that Alex, with his six-foot-two, two-hundred-and-twenty-pound body, was and always had been awkward in a canoe was a minor problem. As was the fact that Lola's skills were rusty. Two minutes on this wild river had shown them that they were in over their heads. So they had made the decision to call it a day and to make their way just a little further down river to an easier pullout point. That had seemed totally reasonable. They were adults after all.

And now, where the fuck was Lola? Alex wanted to scream the question as he saw a grim-faced Ken start to pull his own canoe out into the water. A former river guide, Ken was the only one of the three of them with the skills to even begin to try to rescue Lola. But if she was somehow pinned under their canoe, Alex could not even image how Ken could possibly get her free.

Plus, Lola hated being under water. She couldn't handle not being able to breath. Alex knew how claustrophobic his otherwise daring wife was, and Alex had watched her frustration as she tried on two different occasions to learn to scuba and couldn't make herself breath calmly when submerged. Oh God. By now she'd almost certainly gulped giant swallows of icy water into her lungs.

And then there she was. Alert, wide brown eyes and dark reddish-brown hair almost the color of the logs popped up about eighty yards away, just downstream of the logjam that Ken had called a "strainer." All three of them shouted to her before the current sucked her back under. Alex felt his own breathing return, just knowing that she was alive. Seconds later she popped up again, downstream of a second clump of branches, but this time she was coughing out water hard. Alex looked closer. Good Lord. She didn't have her life jacket on.

Ken seemed not to have noticed that fact, as he started

moving, relieved, along the shore hoping to intercept Lola somewhere downstream. She was in the middle of the river now, moving fast, and she appeared to be coughing too hard to even try to make her way to shore. *Oh hell,* Alex thought, *I know that she can barely swim.* He looked around for anything he could grab quickly.

"Alex, get back here!" Sara yelled it as she saw Alex start to wade out into the fast cold water, a canoe paddle in his hand.

"Alex, no!" Ken joined in as well from his position downstream.

But all Alex could think of was that is he was going to have to pay for his decisions, he was damn well going to make sure that he took every reasonable action he could to make this come out right.

Then he noticed how wide the river really was. How far to the center Lola was and how fast she was moving. How slow his own progress in the deep cold water was going to be. And he realized that he'd never make it to her in time. She'd flail on past, still dozens of feet away from him, and none of them would have any way of reaching her before cold and fatigue completely overtook her.

And then it happened. The roar of the water and the sound of Ken and Sara's shouts faded into a muffled background, and all Alex heard was the sound of his own heart pounding. The beat of it remained steady and firm as the water began to move more slowly. As did Lola. Alex had the odd sensation of walking out onto a basketball court, willing his body to move to the rhythm of the game, of this game. His feet felt light but firm as they moved with power along the rocky riverbed. His hands were strong and capable as they lifted the paddle out towards Lola. He was moving at a normal pace to him, but he was already in chest-deep, and only feet from her now. She looked puzzled but grateful, and Alex heard his own voice boom slowly "Lola! Grab the paddle!"

He thrust it into her hands, and as the current slowly twisted her body downstream, her fingers just barely curled around the white blade. Alex pushed the paddle more firmly into her hands. Her grip tightened as she realized that this ordeal could actually be over. Then Alex used the paddle to pull her in closer, finally reaching out to grab her shirt and drag her in towards shore. She collapsed at the waters edge, still coughing hard and shivering uncontrollably.

Sara rushed to her, and Ken hurried back to them, as Alex himself sunk down into the pebbled sand, now shaking with cold. Slowly, Lola's coughing picked up speed, as did Ken and Sara's movements and speech, and then everything moved with his heartbeat again, happening at the pace it should.

"I had no idea you could move that fast," Ken chided Alex with a relieved grin as he joined the group.

"We yelled at him not to go out into that water," Sara was shaking her head to Lola. "But thank heavens he did, huh?"

Lola was smiling. She pulled herself upright and stumbled towards Alex to give him a long hug. "How did you ever make it out there to me?" she asked.

"I wasn't willing to accept any other alternative," he said simply.

"That's good," she laughed. "I'm glad."

As the rest of the day centered around getting off of the river and getting the Zeitmans dry and warm, and all of them back on the road headed home towards Texas, Alex kept having one thought.

I had no idea. I don't know why it never occurred to me. But it didn't. I had absolutely no idea that time would slow down like that for me anywhere but on a basketball court.

Stan Drexler liked to think of himself as a sensible man who didn't overreact. For over two decades he had plodded through a career in academia that had turned out to be far less glamorous than he had hoped, while a couple of failed relationships attested to the difficulties of spending so much time away from home. At least, he liked to tell himself that had been the problem. Maybe he just wasn't good marriage material. At any rate, he was hardly going to let more failures ever be an option.

He had put up with a good bit of kidding over the years regarding his one great discovery, a beautifully carved obsidian box that had disappeared almost immediately after he had found it. He was lucky that he had five students to bear witness to the find or he may have ended up defending his sanity or his ethics. As it was, he had merely looked like a buffoon for the past sixteen years for not stationing his students to guard the find.

Which was why when he was asked to sign for a package that arrived at his office on campus in the spring of 2009, he was in no hurry to open it. The cardboard container was heavy and slightly larger than "the box" and he assumed right away that one of his more caustic colleagues had decided to play a practical joke. Fine. He'd take it home where he could open it in private, and provide less amusement for the joker.

A few days later he reluctantly pulled out his pocketknife and tore off the tape and wrapping, letting it fall onto his couch. Time to get this over with. Yes, inside were cupfuls of Styrofoam pellets and a replica of his one great discovery. Ha ha.

Then Stan looked closer. The detail on this hoax was painstakingly fine. Stan had to wonder why any joker would go to so much trouble. And there was a note, in Spanish.

"Lo siento. Cometí un error. Hace muchos años esta caja fue robado de usted y cuando la compré no sabía. Ahora me doy cuenta que no me pertenece a mí. Por favor, encuéntrele un hogar adecuado."

Stan translated without thinking. "I am sorry. I made a mistake. Many years ago this box was stolen from you and when I bought it I did not know. Now it does not belong with me. Please find it a suitable home. "

A collector with a conscience? Don't be ridiculous, Stan told himself. More likely it was a joke so elaborate that the perpetrator hoped Stan would actually fall for it and make a fool of himself once again.

Reluctantly, he went into the small spare bedroom that he used as a study and pulled out the simple sketch that he made of the box years ago. Done from memory only a few days after its disappearance, his drawing in no way captured the beauty of the carved obsidian, but the shape and general detail were good.

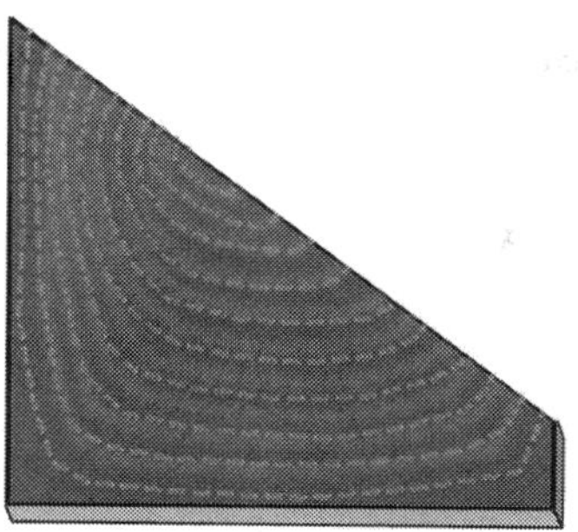

Stan's sketch of the box

This new box had been carefully crafted to have roughly the same almost triangular shape, with arcs of small carved hieroglyphs that made semicircles. He studied its inlaid pieces of colored rocks. The semi-precious stones looked very real. Of course, he and his students had all described the find several times in the literature.

No, I think that one would have had to see the box first hand to duplicate it this well, he thought. But of his students who had been there, there was not one he would consider inclined to indulge in such a cruel hoax.

Stan remembered with chagrin how, in an age before snapping photos of everything everywhere with cell phones and digital cameras, he had not even thought to stop and take one damn photograph of the original box before leaving for the night. Why would he have? At the time there had been no reason to.

Okay, I'll take the bait. He rolled his eyes. He'd take it to the lab in a few weeks and try to get it analyzed and dated. If it actually contained semi-precious stones and was hand-carved then, hoax or not, it was a work of art and ought to have some decent resale value. Maybe he could get the last laugh after all.

Then it occurred to him. Could the "note' possibly still be inside? Surely it wasn't there. Obviously, no one alive could duplicate that page. Even the few words he had been able to quickly translate were known by no one other than him.

He lifted up the heavy lid and peaked. The piece of yellowed paper lay there like it had never been touched. It contained more information than he remembered. Something about two boys and a setting and a rising sun. Had sixteen more years in this field improved his translation skills that much? It looked like it had.

There was no map like he thought he vaguely remembered. Instead, more hieroglyphs. Many more, in the tiniest of script, many of which appeared to be numbers. And at the top was still the outrageous claim that all this information would guide him to… yes, that part was still there. It would guide him to the greatest treasure ever.

Stan sunk into a chair. Now what? Perhaps it was time to overreact.

Part 1. Treasure Hunting for a Good Time
Chapter 5. January 2010

Because there were always a few new kids in each section of physics after the return from the Christmas break, the dynamics of every class tended to change a bit half way through the year. Some were there via simple schedule changes, already known to many of their fellow students, and Alex had to keep an eye on them to ensure that they did not disrupt the already functioning classroom dynamics.

Then there were the transfer students, kids forced by changing circumstances to uproot their lives in the middle of their junior or senior year and place themselves in the hostile unknown environment of a new high school. Alex always wondered two things. One: why in the world were so many sixteen to eighteen year olds so totally lacking in empathy to a stranger? And two: why were those years so terribly defining in one's life, making this difficult adjustment something that would last emotionally well beyond the high school years?

He couldn't answer either question, but he always tried in his own way to make the road a little easier for the totally new faces he found in front of him each January. Which is why he felt so terribly bad as he stammered while looking at the name and then the new face of the very short young Latino in the second row.

Xuha Santos. He had absolutely no idea. So he took a stab at it.

"Zoo hah Santos?" The boy gave a resigned chuckled and Alex knew he had blown it. Three wannabe skinheads in the back of the room snickered loudly.

"My people pronounce the letter x as a *shh* sound," the new boy said in a friendly stage whisper.

"Shh. Your people don't live here," one of the boys in back named Tyler replied in an equally loud stage whisper. Most of the class snickered along. Alex swallowed hard and tried again.

"Shoo hah Santos." The boy made a humorous grimace.

"My people pronounce u and h together with the sound *wah*" he added.

Oh boy, Alex thought, *this is getting difficult.*

"Shhh wah ah. Shwa? Shwa Santos?"

"Present" the boy said happily.

"Right. Welcome to semester two of physics, Xuha." Alex pronounced the name correctly. The sound was familiar. What was it? The name for the "uh" sound in English. Spelled schwa, he thought. Dictionaries used an upside down e to represent it. Surely he could remember that. Schwa.

"I think Zoo-hah fits him much better," another kid from the back laughed.

"Welcome to semester two of physics, zoo-hah," the third kid in the group, Travis, mimicked Alex perfectly in tone and inflection. Alex gave him a fast glare that stopped the twittering laughter all around. The class knew when they were about to push Mr. Z too far and they knew they were getting close.

Although Alex started in on the lesson without further comment, he couldn't help feeling a little sad. Thanks to one inept pronunciation, now no matter what he did point forward this poor kid was going to get called Zoo-hah by everyone. It would be his "real" name before the day was done and there was nothing Alex could do at this point to rectify it.

Sometimes, he thought to himself, *I get damn tired of these kids.* It was not a good start to a new semester.

Last May when Stan walked the box that had shown up in the mail down to the basement lab to be examined by experts on dating Maya artifacts, he still hadn't been sure that it was authentic. By that point, however, he had concluded that it either was real or was such an elaborate and well-contrived replica that it was of interest either way. His department chair had understood quite well why Stan had hesitated for weeks before bringing the box to anyone's attention, and the man had been equally wary about declaring the relic as the real thing.

The examination of the artifact went on for seven long months. Stan waited patiently throughout the rest of 2009 while others dated the rock, examined the carvings and the precious stone inlays, and studied the style of the box. While they analyzed, he had spent July and August in Guatemala as usual, then taught his normal collection of fall semester classes. The wheels of research move slowly. He had headed back to the current excavation in progress a few days after Christmas, as had been his schedule now for over two decades.

None of the other experts, of course, ever expected that the paper that Stan and his students had briefly glimpsed would still be inside the box after it had probably changed hands several times, and Stan was more than happy to let everyone assume that had been the case. It was enough that he stood to be humiliated again if the box itself were a hoax. He hardly needed some other expert translating a document that could somehow turn out to merely make fun of him one more time. So before Stan had turned the relic over to the school he had removed the ancient yellow paper, placed it carefully between two pieces of very clean, very dry glass and put the whole thing in his front hall closet at home. Just until he figured out if the box was real, he assured himself. Then he'd think of a way to bring it forward.

Then a few days ago, just before he was scheduled to return to campus for the spring semester, he had received word that a group of his peers had reached their decision. A nervous Stan Drexler had chosen to fly back to the states a few days early just to hear their verdict in person. Stan had not been disappointed. They declared the artifact to be authentic, although not the work of post-classic Maya. The group believed that the box had been crafted somewhat later, by early colonial Maya, most likely of the Kan Ek Itzen group and probably from the seventeenth century. In other words it was old, but technically not ancient. Many on the panel were kind enough to go over their analysis with him in person and in great detail, and the esteem implied by that courtesy had not been lost on Stan.

And once he had heard their verdict, he realized with some surprise that he had no intention of finding a way to return the document that now resided in his front hall closet. No, he was going to try to finish translating the document himself. And he was going to seek out the treasure it promised.

Not for wealth, of course. Unlike amateur treasure seekers, Stan knew damn well how complex and varied the laws were concerning the category of precious metals and jewels collectively known as "treasure trove" and he knew how quickly anything else was governed by the 1970 UNESCO convention on a nation's rights to its own cultural property. The former often gave full or partial ownership to the government or the landowner, and the latter gave virtually all of a find of archeological significance to the nation in which it was located. Meaning that in the end, whatever he found, it was unlikely that much if any of it would be his. Except for the one thing that mattered.

For while it was true that Doctor Drexler had sort of been vindicated with the return of the box, it was also true that his poor judgment in not protecting the artifact originally would always tarnish his reputation. Unless, of course, he became known point forward as the great Dr. Stan Drexler who found the long hidden Maya whatever it was.

And to think that the decision that had cost him so much had been born of little more than hunger, fatigue and a humane reticence to not ask exhausted kids to put up with a miserable night unnecessarily. Had the comfort and well-being of those five students turned out to be that important? Certainly not. He didn't even think that at the time the students had realized he had been thinking of their welfare. They had hardly turned into five appreciative colleagues.

In fact, three of them, he was pretty sure, had gotten out of the field entirely. He knew that Jake had gone into import/export, moving out to Southern California and turning a background in archeology into a lucrative marketing tool. Stan sort of winced whenever he leafed through magazines for artifact hunters and saw the lurid ads for Jake's business, although he had to admit on some level that the man was certainly doing well for himself. And given that Jake hadn't really been the academic sort, maybe it was best.

Another of the boys, Kyle, had become ill and left school without ever finishing his degree, and soon after that he and Stan had lost touch. Stan had always meant to look Kyle up. For all that the boy had a caustic exterior, he had often been surprisingly helpful in the field and in the end he was the one who had gone most out of his way to defend Stan's decision not to guard the box overnight. Stan had been dismayed to hear a rumor several years ago that Kyle had died from AIDS not long after leaving school. He hoped that it wasn't true.

One of the two girls in the group, Jennifer, had stayed in the area and married upwards. Or at least that was how it had been phrased to him, along with the story that Jennifer had elected to go for the fulltime role of wife and mother. He was told that her husband was some sort of prominent business figure and she was now something of a society item. Well, he could only hope that her academic background provided fodder for more intelligent conversation at social events.

The third boy, Nelson, had actually gone on to become a colleague of sorts. More accurately he was an associate professor at another Southern university with whom Dr. Drexler's school was often in competition for funding, for prestige, and for publication space in the major journals. Of all the five students, Stan thought that Nelson had been most critical, after the fact, of the negligent decision to leave the discovery unguarded. It wasn't that Nelson was a mean kid. But he had clearly been the most serious of the five, the one most determined to be an archeologist himself. Maybe the one most excited about the possibilities of the discovery and the most disappointed by its loss.

After the incident, Nelson had switched almost immediately to another advisor, firmly hitching his wagon to a professor he deemed more responsible, and had little to say to Stan. He and Nelson had met at a few functions over the years and always greeted each other politely and without real warmth. Stan suspected that Nelson still held a buried resentment regarding the whole incident.

The last of the five, the girl named Shelby, stood before him now, her eyes wide. She had been the most enigmatic of the group, as serious about the work as Nelson, yet almost as supportive of Stan's ultimately careless decision as Kyle. She had finished her doctorate with him and also stayed in the greater Atlanta area, but moved out of academia almost immediately afterwards and into the world of curators and museums, and thus mostly out of Stan's circle as well. But now she had heard about the box. Its mysterious return by a guilt-ridden collector was the hottest of topics among collectors of all periods. How many lovers of antiquities suspected that one or two or more items in their collection had been procured by less than ethical means?

Shelby suspected the answer was most. At least that was what she was telling Stan, eyes filled with respect for, and interest in, the unnamed collector with a conscience. Now that the artifact had just been deemed authentic, Shelby was hoping to write an article on this interesting phenomenon and to lead the article off with an interview with her old professor. It could stimulate more introspection among collectors and even possibly jar a few poorly procured items loose to be housed in museums.

Would Dr. Drexler please grant her a real interview? Stan eyed the woman warily. She had to be forty years old now, yet she was still as slight as she had been as a student, and the intervening sixteen years had barely added lines to her face. Her very light brown hair was still worn in an unflattering single long braid down her back. Thanks mostly to her dress and grooming she remained what would once have been called "plain." Most notable of all, though, was that her large grey eyes still had that odd clarity and directness to them that Stan remembered most.

She'd been a good student and a hard worker. Under almost any other circumstances Stan would have been more than happy to be the subject of her interview. But he had made this little decision about hiding the paper inside the box and the paper was something that Shelby had seen. Something Shelby would certainly ask him about. Want to talk about. Speculate about. Could he look into those clear grey eyes and simply lie? Not today, he decided.

"Shelby, it is so great to see you after all of these years and to find out that you've done so well. We should have gotten together sooner. I had no idea you were so close by. I'm very proud of you. Really."

"But…" she laughed.

"But you've just caught me at a bad time. I'm headed back to Guatemala tomorrow to tie up a couple of loose ends because I left so quickly when the decision was announced. I'm really booked solid when I get back, probably for all of February. I'm sure you've got some sort of publication deadline," he said hopefully.

"Not really," she shook her head. "This is an important story. It can wait for you. You let me know when you're settled back in and have got some time to sit down and really talk through this."

"Uhhh, early March?" Stan suggested.

"Perfect," Shelby smiled. "Let's pick a date now."

And so Stan reluctantly picked up his day planner and agreed to an interview the first week of March.

Most professions involve one or more critical balancing acts. Health care providers weigh time spent and emotional involvement with one's patients against seeing more of the sick and maintaining one's own emotional strength. Restaurants struggle to serve good food that doesn't cost too much, doesn't take too long to prepare, and makes enough of a profit to pay the help well and still make money for the owner. And so on.

One of the things that Alex liked about teaching was that his choices almost never involved other people's welfare versus his own money. He simply did the best he could by his students with what he had and that was that. That is not to say that he didn't have quandaries, though. Like the one standing before him now.

Xuha, or Zoohah as he was now commonly known, had turned out to be a bright student, a junior who was more than adequately prepared for the second semester of basic physics. At roughly five feet three inches tall and maybe one hundred and forty pounds, he was stocky, strong, and had a confident easy humor about him in spite of his stature. Alex suspected that the kid had been well liked at his old school.

Alex had heard Xuha's frequent joking around in class and he was impressed that the boy managed to be funny without being mean, and managed to either not hear or not take offense at much of the meanness directed at him. For some reason this good-natured confidence seemed to particularly bother the three aspiring Neo-Nazis who typically sat in the back of the room. Travis, Tanner and Tyler, who had been a general pain in the ass throughout the fall semester, had now made it one of their chief missions to put this happy transplant in his place. The ensuing war of snide remarks turned out to be highly amusing to the other students and too often managed to deter covering adequate material in the one hour and fifteen minutes every other day that was allotted to a science class in a block-scheduled Texas school.

So although Alex privately cheered Xuha on, outwardly he stayed neutral and disapproving of the entire war of words. He had already intervened by separating the three Ts, as everyone called them, seating the three boys at three different corners of the room while putting Xuha at the fourth.

But now his whole neutral stance was being threatened. Xuha was anxious to play a school sport, an activity that Alex encouraged for all of his students. Because the boy worked and needed the job, it had to be a sport that was flexible and less demanding than, say, baseball. Xuha had decided he wanted to make the tennis team, which, under other circumstances, would have been perfect.

Tennis players from Early Gulch High School were pretty much always overmatched and the team would welcome any able-bodied volunteer. Alex knew, because he had coached it for five years before deciding that his days of high school coaching were over and that his own three young children needed his afterschool time far worse than he needed the pittance that high school coaching paid. Frankly, Early Gulch, which sat at the convenient crossroads of two state highways, was attended by mostly lower income rural white kids, with a growing number of lower income rural Latinos, a consistent minority of lower income rural blacks, and a smattering of Asians. It was rare for a student at EGHS to have played tennis competitively or even to have been coached at the sport before joining the team.

So for the past twelve years Alex had helped out by providing free one-on-one tennis lessons to the school's aspiring players, as his schedule permitted. This was much to the relief of the variety of reluctant coaches who followed him, all of whom knew how to handle the paperwork of running a sport but knew little about the playing of tennis.

And Alex liked doing it. It gave him a way to keep his hand in coaching and to do some good for kids without making time commitments that took away from being there for his own children. Some of his protégés had even gone on to do okay, given their original lack of experience. It was win-win, as people liked to say. Until today, when it was suddenly lose-lose.

He could lose by telling Xuha that he would not coach him. Xuha would lose a chance to be a decent player, the team would lose, and Alex would lose because he would be treating one innocent kid poorly for no better reason than that he did not wish to appear to be taking sides. Or he could agree to coach Xuha, and lose in an instant the neutrality he had worked so hard to cultivate in his third period class.

If there was anything Alex hated it was modifying his own behavior as a result of the behavior of jerks. Fine. Let the three Ts add teacher's pet jokes to their repertoire. "I'd be happy to help you out, Xuha." The boy's face lit up as he nodded with enthusiasm.

Although the United States of America began to define and enforce requirements for citizenship early on, it did not pass its first act limiting immigration until almost one hundred years after the nation was founded. This ground-breaking act of 1875 set our nation's first immigration standards by prohibiting convicts and prostitutes from setting up residence here. Fearing they may not have gone far enough, over the next fifteen years congress also voted to exclude lunatics, idiots, paupers, polygamists, and the "diseased."

Ms. Johnson always bought the best brands of frozen pizza, and the kids that came to her modest little house after school almost always got to eat as much as they wanted. It was one of the many reasons Travis, Tyler and Tanner came almost every day. Another was that while they were there Ms. Johnson treated them like adults, not like students, which of course she had to do when she was their teacher in the classroom. After all, she wasn't *that* much older than they were. So, as long as they kept quiet about how much time they spent at a teacher's house, she let them cuss, a little at least. And she definitely let them say anything bad that they wanted to about anyone, even their parents and other students. Sometimes she even encouraged it.

"If you three are going to be the fine Aryan warriors I just know you are going to be, you have to learn to analyze," she said, tossing her long blonde hair out of her eyes. "You need to be *discerning*." She said it slowly like she wanted to make sure that they learned the word. Then added, by way of definition, "You know. To be able to call bullshit bullshit."

Travis and Tanner both smiled. Tyler could tell that they kind of liked it when Ms. Johnson cussed around them.

Some afternoons, she invited more students to come, other boys and even once in a while a girl. Tyler didn't like those afternoons quite as well because Ms. Johnson was always more cautious then. She wouldn't say anything bad about the Blacks or the Mexicans, and she would cut off Tyler and his friends if they tried to do so. Instead her pretty blue eyes would change from passionate to thoughtful as she'd talk a lot about being proud of who you were, respecting your own history and your own people. Sugar-coated stuff. Some of the kids got it and got invited back for the times when Ms. Johnson was less cautious. Others gave Ms. Johnson a funny look when she talked like that, like maybe she was hiding a contagious disease. Those kids never got asked to come have pizza again.

Even though Tyler liked some of the kids that returned often, he thought that the very best afternoons were when it was just the four of them. Ms. Johnson and "her boys" as she called them, the four Ts. They all knew that Ms. Johnson's first name was Tina even though none of them ever dared called her that. But they were permitted to laugh that anyone else who joined their little group would have to have a name that started with "T" too.

"T for what?" Travis asked one afternoon.

Ms. Johnson gave it some thought.

"T for The Master Race," Tyler answered before Ms. Johnson could think of anything. He had a tendency to do that, which he felt kind of bad about, but things just seemed to pop into his head and out of his mouth so quickly.

"Let Ms. J answer, asshole," Tanner glared at him. Tanner always stood up for Ms. Johnson, but as usual she intervened graciously.

"Boys, boys. You have to be strong together. Support each other. Tanner, be glad that Tyler has such a quick mind. It will be useful for our cause. All three of you need to focus more on your academics you know." She smiled as she saw all three of them wince. "Come on, I know that guys like to fight with guns and knives and trust me, you are going to have lots of opportunity to do that once the race wars start. But we have to have more than superior bodies going for us, you know. Let's not forget how important it is that we also learn to make the best possible use of our superior minds."

And then before any of the three could argue with her about minds or bodies, she turned to the back counter and produced a tray of beautiful homemade brownies.

"Eat up," she smiled to end the discussion. "I agree that you need to bulk up, to grow strong. I'm so proud of the way the three of you have committed at such a young age to taking some responsibility for the white race." Pride glowed in Ms. Johnson's pretty, young face. "I just know that my boys here have some very vital role to play in the struggles that are going to lie ahead."

Ever since Alex had hauled his wife out of a cold raging river almost a year ago, there had been something different about her. At first Alex chalked it up to the fact that she had a face-to-face encounter with death. Lola confided in him that the experience had shaken her to her very core.

Then Alex had been aware that his wife's new job had consumed a lot more of her concentration than the old job. A trained geoscientist, she had gone from oil prospecting in the Gulf of Mexico for a big oil company to looking for drilling locations in the Niger Delta for a tiny enterprise. He had watched her become emotionally involved in the little company's success, and in her fellow employees, many of whom were Nigerian themselves. Over months Alex had been subjected to emotional outbursts about Biafra and oil spills and the history of slavery, and he had come to understand that Nigeria had somehow captured a piece of Lola's heart as well as her mind. That was, he admitted to himself, how she generally was.

But by last fall Alex had been sure that there was more was going on. Lola seemed only half present at times, and she often acted like the needs and concerns of her husband and of their fourteen-year-old daughter were trivial compared to something. To what? To a secret lover? To the needs of Africa? To achieving world peace? By the time Lola left in December for a three-week work assignment in Lagos, a tiny piece of Alex had begun to worry that she might never come home.

And when she did arrive back in Houston Christmas afternoon, hollow-eyed and exhausted, he had known that she had crossed some threshold without him. It made him sadder than he could fathom. Not that she had grown, lived, experienced. But that she was choosing to do it alone.

Alex's response to his wife's increasing distance had been to reach out and try to please her, so since Christmas he had been spent time orchestrating his first ever surprise party for Lola. She turned fifty in late January and Alex engineered a plethora of unexpected treats including getting older daughter Ariel to sneak home from college midweek for the event, getting Lola's sister Summer to fly in for a day from Denver, and assembling an assortment of friends and well-wishers at the restaurant for a very special dinner. It went perfectly and Alex was highly pleased with himself for pulling it off, and for the first time in months Lola had seemed genuinely *there* and happy.

But that only lasted a day. The next day son Zane ran into serious problems while traveling, and after hearing the news Lola returned to her preoccupied self. Alex realized that he had to find a time and way to talk to his wife about the growing gulf between them. He just, well, he just wasn't sure how to bring up a subject when he wasn't even sure what the real subject was.

Lola, meanwhile, had spent the last few months trying to imagine how she could possibly have a much needed conversation with Alex. It was tempting to simply put it off forever, but that wasn't fair and she realized that the longer she waited the more awkward and difficult it was going to be. He already suspected that something was wrong. It was hardly right to let the man she loved worry this way.

Finally, the two of them were home alone. Alex was happy on the couch with a beer and bowl of popcorn. No sports team that he held dear was on the television. The game he was watching wasn't even close. There wasn't going to be a better time. Lola took a deep breath and dove in.

"Alex, I've always had a knack for picking up what others are feeling."

"You sure have," he agreed, giving her slightly under a quarter of his attention just to be polite.

"That knack has gotten a lot stronger recently," she added.

"Oh, that's interesting. Is that a bad thing?" he asked trying to be helpful. Curiosity had gained her more of his concentration, but the game still held over half of it.

"I can kind of read your mind, Alex."

"What?" One hundred per cent of Alex looked away from the screen and into Lola's deep brown eyes, as he teetered between a new worry that his wife was going a little crazy and a worse worry that she was telling him the truth.

She smiled reassuringly at him before she spoke. "You want to ask me to tell you exactly what you are thinking right now, don't you? But you're not sure if that's a good idea. It may make me feel like you doubt me, or that you want me to perform like a circus animal." Lola's eyes narrowed a little and then she went on, with almost a mischievous look. "You're thinking this may all be easier if I'm delusional but you have the very strong feeling that I'm not. You think that I probably am really a telepath and knowing your luck I'm probably even a very good one. Yes, it turns out that I am."

Lola took a short breath and went on.

"And now that you think about it, it doesn't even seem all that odd to you. I've always kind of been that way anyway, and sure this means that you have to trust me but you already do that, don't you, so it shouldn't be a big deal. And yes you can see a little cleavage with this t-shirt I'm wearing which is why you like it better that the ones I usually wear, and no I did not know that I have a little something stuck in between my teeth, which, apparently unbeknownst to me I have tendency to have happen especially when I eat popcorn."

Alex held up his hand for silence, while he thought for a few seconds.

"Lola," he said. "If this is true, and I'm not saying that it is, then you've been aware that I knew that something was wrong. You've known that I was worried about you. So why haven't you and I had this conversation weeks ago?"

Lola, to her credit, looked embarrassed. "Because of my party. I didn't want to tell you until it was over."

"What? I don't get it. It was just a dinner. I was trying to make you happy."

"And you did. You did. Please understand Alex. It was so sweet of you and I didn't want to do anything to spoil it. Come on. How can you have a surprise party for a telepath?" She smiled at Alex in a way she had not for months. "I do like leveling with you way more than I like keeping things from you, and yes I love you too."

Okay, Alex thought slowly and deliberately. *I do believe her. And because this doesn't work two ways, we need to lay down some ground rules here.*

"Now you're thinking words at me and that doesn't work nearly as well," Lola said. "I get that you want to establish some dos and don'ts. I'm in total agreement, but first let me save you some aggravation."

And so Lola picked up her laptop and showed Alex the website she had been spending much of her time on for the past six months as she had discovered, and then practiced and learned about, the strange new skill that had been thrust upon her by the combination of a canoe accident and by the needs of a desperate, telepathic Nigerian woman.

"Read some of this please," she asked. "It will put your mind at ease a lot about what I can and can't do, and then once you understand more about it, I will tell you the whole story of how I got sucked into this. I think you'll understand, Alex, that I had to accept a lot of things first myself, before I had any hope of sharing this with you."

And because that did make sense to Alex, he read. And he asked Lola questions. And she reassured him every way she could. And then he read some more.

By the end of January 2010 Alex Zeitman had seen everything Lola wanted to show him, and he had come to terms with the fact that what ever other oddities did or did not exist about him, the facts were that he was a fifty-one-year-old high school physics teacher with three children, a bum knee, and hair that was going from sand-colored straight to white far faster than it should. And, by the way, he also had a wife who could sort of, kind of, detect thoughts or at least feelings in a manner that some people would describe as telepathy. There was nothing the least bit magic about her. She was just wired that way. And, thanks to an unusual combination of circumstances, her skill level had increased dramatically over the past few months.

Well, Alex thought to himself, that explained a lot. And maybe it could turn out to be useful.

"I know what you're thinking," Lola smiled at Alex as she got ready for bed the next night.

"I thought you weren't going to do that?" he said a little irritated.

"I'm not doing that," she announced as she pulled back the covers and crawled in next to him. "It's what you're always thinking when I come to bed. Well, almost always. Sometimes you're preoccupied reading something and sometimes you're already asleep."

"So it doesn't require any special skill to know what's on my mind right now?" Alex asked, warming a little to the playful tone in Lola's voice.

"Not right now." She giggled as he pulled her closer. "Definitely not now."

And Lola could not help thinking how relieved she was that Alex accepted her and wasn't mad.

And Alex could not help thinking how relieved he was that there was nothing really the matter with his wife other than the fact that she was odd, which is something he had known all along.

He saw her smile softly at the feeling he must have communicated. Damn. He pulled back and perched for just a second between apprehension and acceptance, between his desire for privacy and his desire for closeness. Acceptance won. He put his arms around his wife, enjoying the feel and smell of her, thinking that it had never been so clear to him that intimacy came in many ways.

January 1697

Ichik had felt so proud to be trusted with the larger of the two boxes, even though it was a lot heavier than the one that his brother had been asked to carry. But after he had walked for several days the extra weight began to feel like a burden, not a privilege. At one point he even considered just burying the jade box and being done with it. It wasn't like he would have to face his mother and explain what he had done. He knew already that he could never go home again. So, would it not be safer buried somewhere now rather than maybe being stolen from him later?

But his mother had been more than clear. Ancestors were watching. He had been chosen to act on behalf of his own grandfather. He must travel every morning in the direction that the sun rose, and he must make his way through the land of the Itza and past it. He had been told to go where there no longer were small villages and settlements willing to give him shelter and food for a few days. He could take his time but he must avoid the Spaniards at all costs and go to where he had to hunt and forage and turn to his meager rations to survive. He had been trained to do this. He must keep walking until he found strange people who were not his own and who were not the Spanish. He should greet them in peace. Not with fighting. That was good because Ichik knew that he wasn't particularly great at fighting. For the last couple of years he had used his bigger stature to scare off would-be combatants. It had worked well enough but had done little to improve his fighting skills. So greeting in peace was good.

"Make friends," his mother had said. "Make friends like you are so good at doing and keep walking until you reach a body of water so big that you cannot see across it and you cannot go around it. Then stop of course." She had smiled at the obviousness of her instructions. "And then the difficult part will begin."

Ichik tried singing under his breath as he walked, just to pass the time and to take his mind off of how much he missed his mother and his brother and his sister, and how heavy the box felt, and of course to take his mind off of the difficult times ahead, whatever they might be.

Chapter 6. February 2010

In a sports-oriented state like Texas, all varsity sports are also considered high school classes. To make the team, one usually has to take the class, at the detriment, of course, of taking an academic subject. Early Gulch, like many high schools, used a modified block schedule, where students took a total of ten classes. Five met one day and five the next. Schools which do this call them things like A and B days, or red and blue days, or some such, with the idea being that with this schedule less time is wasted in the halls going from room to room and teachers are given more time to really get into their material.

However, because the Texas testing system of 2010 focused on English and math, Alex's school, like many others, had math and English "double blocked." That is, these subjects met each and every day to ensure that students would do as well on the state standardized testing as possible. Science, foreign languages, history and all other subjects met half as often. Except for sports. To the outrage of many an academically oriented parent, sports was also "double blocked" because, well, because the football team just wasn't going to win as many games if they didn't get in every bit as much practice as the UIL would allow. And double blocking sports gave the football team the absolute most practice time permitted. And what you do for one sport, you have to do for all.

So in order to run cross country, or be on the swim team, a student had to give up two classes for the entire year, and still be willing to practice after school till supper. In the process of transferring, Xuha was left with at most one class period he could give up for tennis. And with a family that needed for him to have a job, he could at best make practice after school every other day.

Alex knew that at most schools that would simply mean that he was not allowed on the team. And even at Early Gulch, that would be the consequence in many of the more popular sports. But the tennis team, always eager for decent players, would make an exception if Xuha was good enough. But he had to be good enough. So Alex had his work cut out for him.

For the life of him Stan could not imagine why this interview with his former student was making him so nervous. It was true that until the box had resurfaced he had structured a lot of his time and activities around finding ways not to talk to people about the missing box. But over the last ten months he thought he had come a long way in terms of getting over the odd mix of shame, defensiveness and regret that had marred even the mention of his stolen discovery.

And he had a perfect plan regarding his removal of the single written page. He would state right at the start of the interview that the page had of course not been there when the box was returned to him and no one would expect it to be so. Surely it had been removed by the first owner. Done with that subject.

So, what then? Stan was a slight man with thinning, graying dark hair and heavy glasses. He knew he dressed like a college professor, and he had never considered himself sexy. The subject of archeology had enough appeal, he supposed, that it had brought him a certain number of dates when he was younger and, to his surprise, that had resulted in a couple of serious girlfriends. Yet, Stan had felt each time that once the woman really got to know him, she was, well, kind of bored. Let's face it, he told himself, he probably was a boring person. One who cared more about an ancient society than he did about his own. Frankly he didn't need any more reminders of that fact, and so these days he pretty much avoided women in general. Beautiful women interested him only hypothetically and from afar, like art objects.

It had once surprised him that the field of archeology itself also attracted some of the more beautiful co-eds as majors and even as grad students. Like Jennifer. Stan believed philosophically that professors had no business fraternizing with students, or even ogling them, so in the tank-top-and-shorts-friendly hot climates in which he found himself in close quarters with these girls, his behavior had always been above reproach. He could tell that some had been slightly offended; others had been appreciative to discover that to Dr. Drexler they absolutely were just one of the boys.

But if he was totally honest with himself he had to admit that of all the young women he had taught, Shelby with her decidedly non-flirty clothes and no-nonsense manner was one of the few who had, once or twice, well, made him uncomfortable. It was the way she had looked at him he supposed. Maybe it was the way she really cared about the subjects that he cared about. It was, who knows what? Who cared? She had been a student and had been absolutely off limits and that was that.

The first time that Alex had the dream, it was very short and frightening. He simply existed in space, and he was surrounded by absolute darkness and total silence. He was completely alone. All he knew was that he was there, and that he was getting no other information. It lasted long enough for him to feel a sense of fear, and then he woke up.

Lola was already home from work by the time Alex got done running a long list of errands, and she and Teddie were passionately agreeing with each other when Alex walked through the door. It was good to see. Not only had Lola spent most of the last year preoccupied and distant, but about a year ago fourteen-year-old Teddie had hit adolescence with a vengeance and morphed—it had seemed almost overnight—from a sweet, sensitive child into an inexplicitly angry young woman. No one seemed to bring out the hostility as quickly as her own mother.

"You are going to try to teach another complete beginner how to play tennis, aren't you?" Lola stopped the conversation and laughed to Alex as he walked in the door. Alex stiffened a little, thinking how easily Lola seemed to be able to forget her promise to ignore his thoughts. Then he saw her looking at the bags of sticks, string, and plastic kids' balls sticking out of his shopping bag and chuckled himself. "Sometimes you read my mind without even reading it," he sighed.

"I always have," she said, moving over to greet him with a kiss.

"Offspring in the room," Teddie chirped loudly. And the parents opted for a hug that Teddie pointedly ignored.

"Before mom and I got started talking about my newspaper story, Mom was telling me how Zane got arrested for murder last week, on the day after mom's birthday. Dad! How did I not get told about this?"

Teddie idolized her almost twenty-four year old big brother Zane, and clearly wanted to direct some of her understandable outrage to her father.

"He wasn't charged, dear, or you would certainly have heard about it," Alex offered in his most calming voice. "He was taken into custody in Samoa while traveling on business because he had been seen with people possibly connected with the murder. It took a few hours to sort out what had really happened."

"Zane has started hanging out with murderers? How did I not get told about this?" Teddie rephrased the question.

"Teddie. Over the last week and a half we have had your mother's birthday party, your sister Ariel here visiting from college, and your Aunt Summer here and, well, a lot else going on. Zane was held for a few hours and he's fine. A man he chartered a boat from fled and is wanted for murder, but Zane thinks that man is innocent too. Your brother is back in Chicago now and you should just call him and let him tell you about it."

When Teddie said nothing and glared, Alex added, "We were scared, actually really scared for a few hours, but you were in school at that time and Ariel was traveling back to campus and by the time we had a chance to tell you guys it had turned out there wasn't much to tell."

Alex tried to send Lola the message that he wished she had kept this to herself for a while longer but his wife either didn't pick up the thought or chose to ignore it. Alex suspected that she was ignoring it.

"He got stuck in Samoa in an earthquake the time before. Why does Zane like going to Samoa so much?" Teddie persisted. This time Lola intervened with a subject change.

"You should hear about this great article Teddie is writing for the school paper. I am so proud of her."

"Mom, it's not much of a school paper. You can tell because

I'm only a freshman and I still get to write about anything I want."

"They don't have a lot of kids who want to be on it," Alex explained. It was true. Those that didn't play sports tended towards 4H and rodeo activities, and most of the kids worked minimum wage jobs so they could have cars and spending money. The school paper was probably one of the least popular and least impressive activities at Early Gulch, right after the tennis team. Teddie had been a welcome addition.

"What are you writing about?" Alex persisted.

"Oh. Ms. Johnson the history teacher."

"You are going to interview her? A feature article?"

Teddie shook her head. "Some of the kids told me about how she said her class was not doing any black history month. Our school is mostly white and her students are doing white history month."

Oh no, Alex thought. This had trouble for everyone written all over it. Decades ago Early Gulch had been the proud home of a highly active sect of the Ku Klux Klan. While any sort of overt racism was obviously and clearly prohibited at the school and had been for a long time, Alex and other teachers and administrators were all well aware that the roots of organized racism still ran deep in the area.

"Teddie. Maybe this is one you ought to back off of?"

"Why?" an outraged Teddie and an equally outraged Lola both asked in unison.

What Alex wanted to say was "because I work there and have to deal with the ramifications." And what he wanted to say was "because all you are going to do is stir up hatred and resentment even more by focusing on it." But he knew that either response would result in an argument where he was outnumbered two to one by humans who fought with their words way better than he did. So he implemented a tactical retreat.

"How did you get from talking about Zane getting arrested for murder to talking about a newspaper article about black history month? That's a weird segue."

See, he could use words too. Even if it was just to change the subject back to the lesser of two evils.

Although the United States Congress of the late 1800s applied their new immigration restrictions equally to convicts, prostitutes, lunatics, and idiots of all nationalities and ethnic origins, it is worth noting that they did single out one group of people for special and specific exclusion. In the 1882 Chinese Exclusion Act, the immigration of all Chinese laborers was halted for ten years and courts were specifically forbidden from granting citizenship to anyone who was Chinese. The latter provision was repealed in 1943.

Rising anti-Catholicism also led several groups around this time to pass restrictions at the state level to prevent immigration and nationalization of other undesirables including the Irish and the German Catholics, who had been arriving in droves for decades and threatened to upset the homogeneity of the nation. These two groups may have fared no better than their Chinese brethren except for the fact that enough of them had already arrived and become citizens to make for a formidable voting block. Politicians at the national level recognized this, even if the state governments did not.

Alex and Xuha met at the school tennis courts on Saturday morning. Alex came armed with teaching tools he had used over the years to turn his wife, three children and a trickle of students into reasonable tennis players. He'd used a lot of the same techniques to instruct basketball, volleyball and baseball as well, and he prided himself on being able to get any human who was willing to listen to him and to practice as directed up to a decent level of proficiency in any sport.

The first problem, he found, was that most people claimed they would listen but then they didn't. They sort of stood there looking attentive while hoping that the words would somehow drift into their brains effortlessly. Actually, Alex thought, the students in his physics classes did that a lot as well.

Those that managed to really listen still generally did not remember or practice as well as Alex recommended, or in the ways in which he told them to. So they improved, but not that quickly, not that well. Alex eventually would back off, realizing that the person had accepted all the coaching that they wanted. If they were happy, he should be happy. But he wasn't. He always wanted his students to get better.

And then he started to coach Xuha. The boy tended to joke around a lot on the court, and at first that annoyed Alex. He preferred his students to be more serious. But after a while, when he saw how hard Xuha concentrated on learning in spite of the laughing remarks and the funny faces he made at the tennis balls, Alex decided that it was no more than a style issue. Perhaps the boy had been using humor most of his life to deflect.

By the end of the first session together it was apparent that Xuha was not only listening to Alex, he was also taking the instruction seriously and to heart. The boy, already strong and with decent hand-eye coordination, had picked up the basic rules of the game and enough technique to hold his own on the court with his EGHS teammates. After the second Saturday morning under Alex's tutelage, Xuha had a good chance of beating most of his teammates. And for the first time in many years Alex remembered why he had once thought coaching a sport would be such fun.

Shelby kept telling herself that there was no reason at all for this interview to make her so nervous. Interviewing Stan Drexler was a great idea, she had unique access to him and the ensuing article would be something of an accomplishment. Furthermore, there was hardly a less imposing person in the world than Dr. Drexler. For although he was well informed, diligent and dedicated to his subject, Shelby would hardly consider him worldly or wily. If he had been, this entire missing box fiasco would have gone down very differently so many years ago.

How could the man possibly not have suspected his students right from the beginning? They were the most obvious of potential thieves, and yet he had barely questioned them. Shelby realized sadly that Stan's trust came from the fact that he thought he knew each one of them, and so he had spoken up on their behalf to the school. And clearly, he had also thought he was the only person in the cave that day who could recognize the Kan Ek hieroglyph for treasure. Come on.

His trusting nature was a huge blind spot. Shelby told herself that, if anything, the man was worthy of distain, but as she organized her notes for the interview, she was having trouble working up the requisite amount of disrespect. There was something just a little bit endearing about the man's secure moral compass. His work ethic had once inspired the young Shelby, and to this day she still regretted her own small part in his downfall.

Well, what was done was done. She had managed back then to deflect any awkward questions while she had finished her degree. So there was just no reason to fear his suspicions now. She knew what she needed to do, and it was to simply interview the man, and be done with it. What could be the problem with that?

A week later, Alex picked up the school paper with trepidation. He had forgotten about Teddie's article, and she had not brought it up again. Had she really written it? Had the journalism teacher let it go through? Oh yes. There it was on page two.

"American History Class Takes Unique Approach" by Teddie Zeitman. Okay. Alex began reading. Hmmm. It looked like Teddie had maybe taken the high road here, skirting trouble for everyone by treating Ms. Johnson's approach to Black History Month as an innovation to be commended rather than treating it like the thinly disguised racism that Alex had suspected it was.

"I just believe that we all should get to be proud of our racial heritage," she quoted Ms. Johnson as saying. And then Teddie detailed how each student was expected to prepare a report on their own particular cultural history and what the history of their own people meant to them.

"Maybe this isn't as bad a thing as I thought," Alex started to think as he read. Teddie had interviewed two Latinos who were happy to talk about their own backgrounds. Alex noticed with a start that one was Xuha. Xuha was from Mexico. Apparently part of his ancestry was Maya and he was excited to be preparing his report on that. One African-American girl was going to talk about a book her great grandmother had written. One girl had an Irish ancestor who had become a politician. Good stuff. Okay. We value everyone's history.

And then here was a quote from Tyler. "I consider my people to be Southrons and so my report will be about my people and how in 1861 they formed a proud white Christian nation that was free from the political correctness of the north and the illegal aliens." Whoa. The journalism teacher had let that quote go through? And what was a Southron?

Here was another, from a student Alex did not know, who apparently had some German ancestry and therefore was hoping to focus on the accomplishments of Germany, specifically in the 1920s and 1930s. That sounded dangerous. Another student was planning on detailing the "vast list of achievements of the Northern Europeans and their descendants as opposed to other races." What?

Teddie then included a short paragraph asking Ms. Johnson whether she intended to direct the projects to ensure that no offensive or inappropriate material would be presented. She got a quote back saying juniors in high school were almost adults and need to learn to filter information for themselves. Teddie quoted Ms. Johnson as saying that in the study of history almost every point of view was offensive to someone.

Teddie had clearly done nothing but report the facts, and had even reported them rather carefully. Rather cleverly. And Alex suspected a busy journalism teacher had not given this article the attention that maybe she should have. He also suspected that there were going to be some people who were going to be unhappy with Ms. Johnson's innovative approach. And Teddie had tried her best to get their attention.

The second time that Alex had the dream, it was slightly longer and less frightening. Like the first time, he simply existed in space. But this time, he also had his body. He was sure of it because he realized that he was running. Leisurely. In fact, he was positive that he was running comfortable twelve-minute miles and that he had been doing so for some time. He was loping along on nothing in absolute darkness and he had no plans to stop any time soon. So Alex kept jogging, and then he woke up.

Nelson, the displeased grad student, had turned into Dr. Nelson Nowicki and had long since moved on to studying the cultures and artifacts of Native Americans of the Southeastern United States. He hardly ever thought of the disappointing Stan Drexler and Lake Peten anymore. Hardly ever.

He kissed his wife goodbye, gave his young daughter a hug and his infant son a peck on the head before he headed to his office on campus. He liked to get in early and get some real work done, before students showed up and distracted him. Plus, that early morning time in his office was the closest thing to privacy he ever got these days.

He unlocked the door, turned on his computer, and turned on the hot pot to heat water for a stout cup of the Earl Grey tea he loved. The sooner he could wash the taste of the coffee out of his mouth the better. Why did Lisa insist on making it for him every morning? For that matter, why did everybody always seem to do things that he disliked them doing?

He checked his emails first. Plenty of school-related stuff, mostly from students and some from the university administration. He turned to the news. Thanks to his personal settings, he got any scrap of information that related to the Maya and archeology, and today there was something of note.

The obsidian box that had been mysteriously returned to Dr. Drexler last April had finally been verified as authentic by a team of experts. Nelson's former mentor had his famous box back in his possession. Nelson snorted in disgust. The man certainly didn't deserve that piece of good fortune after so recklessly disregarding the artifact's safety.

Nelson did a few neck rolls and let his eyes rest for a moment while the memories of early 1993 came, and today he let them linger. Nelson wasn't sure why, but after all these years whenever those particular memories came to visit, they always stayed longer than they should.

Was it pathetic, he wondered, to have been so absolutely enamored with a girl that he was willing to do anything to please her? And was it equally wretched to keep remembering years later how very good it felt?

Nelson knew that he absolutely had to get past the place where he kept thinking of her. He needed to stop remembering the insects chirping so loudly that he had wished he could turn down their volume, the better to hear her soft moans. He could forgive himself, if he would just stop remembering the feel of her, the smell of her, the smell of the rainforest around them and the excitement at the sheer audacity of all they were doing together. Of course, all the audacious ideas had been hers. He had been so happy just to have her, just to play along.

Nelson wanted so badly to think of himself as nothing more than a blameless innocent but sometimes, like now when his mind transfixed on the events once again, he had to admit that it all may have been just a little his fault.

Because, of course, after his pleasure had come his harsh, quick lesson on the consequences of reckless behavior. And every time he thought of the sheer joy of that time, he had been forced to also remember the painful facts that had followed. And as he chastised himself without mercy for the little part he played in losing the great find that could have launched his career, he had slowly grown to hate everyone else who had been involved that night.

Some teachers are in the profession because they like having summers off. Some want a schedule that dovetails with that of their children. Others like their subject matter, such as music or art, and want to make a living touching that subject every day even though they don't particularly like young people or like to instruct others. But some, like Alex, really do enjoy teaching teenagers.

Unfortunately, as in many professions, today's teacher also draws extraneous duty that is less fulfilling. For teachers, this often involves additional duty as security guards. Why in the world, someone reasonable may ask, would society expect trained educators to spend part of their time and energy policing hallways and watching for disturbances? Well, it needs to be done and often there is no one else to ask to do it.

Alex had long ago accepted the fact that part of his job was to play mini rent-a-cop before and after classes in the hallways and parking lots of the school where he worked. Furthermore, he accepted graciously that he personally would be assigned, over and over again, to the worst locations. Not because the administration disliked him. Actually they seemed rather glad to have him. No, he got those assignments, like the part of the parking lot most likely to have the drug deals and the edge of the grounds most likely to see fights, and the area around the boys room, because he was a six foot two, two hundred and twenty pound male who had the best chance of intervening physically if that should become necessary. Alex didn't begrudge that fact at all. He figured his gender and size bought him advantages every day in ways he barely realized and it felt good to pay it back a bit by helping to keep his world safer. And, fortunately for him, and for the many smaller, less physical teachers who sometimes drew equally hazardous locations, stepping into a dangerous situation was seldom required. Just being there often prevented it.

But it looked like this day was going to be an exception to that rule. The two boys were circling each other, yelling insults, when Alex arrived on the scene. Predictably, a small crowd of students had already gathered and many were cheering on one boy or the other. School had ended for the day, but most of the students stayed put, yelling out encouragement and words designed to provoke the fight.

Both boys were younger, white and male. Maybe freshmen. Neither moved like they knew much about fighting. Alex hurried towards them and tried to step in between them. "Cut it out guys. Call it a day now and neither one of you gets detention. Let's do this the easy way."

But the two boys kept circling, focused entirely on their anger. Clearly Alex had underestimated how mad they both were. Each seemed so determined to hurt the other that Alex realized that he was just someone in their way. Great.

Before Alex could think of a way to diffuse the situation, one boy jumped to Alex's right and charged towards the other boy, head down, ramming himself as hard as he could into the others stomach. The second boy winced at the impact, and then tried to grab the neck of the first in some sort of wrestling hold.

"Okay, I said enough, you two," Alex pushed his way in between them and tried to pry the second boy's arm loose. The first boy had started to kick, trying to break free. Angry at being thwarted, the second boy let his opponent go with a shove and turned towards Alex instead.

Alex watched fascinated as the boy's leg shot out towards him, moving lightening-fast at first and then moving increasingly more slowly as it came right towards Alex's bad knee. He heard his own heart pound while all movement around him lost its speed. Alex focused on grabbing the boy's slow moving ankle and pulling the astonished young man off balance, sending the boy backwards to land on his own butt. Alex followed him to the ground, grabbing the boy's left wrist and twisting his arm hard behind his back. Then Alex pushed him face first into to the ground, putting his good knee on the boy's back and holding him down while the other boy just watched with his mouth open.

Alex looked up to the see the school's real security guard running his way, followed by two administrators, all of their feet moving faster and faster as everything else around Alex picked up speed until all was normal once again.

"'Dude. I mean, Mr. Z." It was one of the boys in his second period advanced physics class. "You rock. I mean, I never saw on old dude move as fast as you just did. No offense. But that was cool."

"Thanks Leonard," Alex muttered. "No offense taken." He knew he looked calm on the outside, which was good. But on the inside all Alex could do was listen to the speed of his heartbeat and marvel to himself. *Damn. It happened again.*

On the drive home from school that day Alex started to think that it was time to stop ignoring a phenomenon he had once associated entirely with his basketball abilities and to consider just what was going on. He knew something about physics after all. Granted his first career of choice had been athlete, followed by coach. He had fallen into the role of science teacher when an advisor mentioned that if he wanted to coach high school, he was going to have to teach something, and teaching physical education was one of the worst assignments. Alex's next choice had been history. He loved history. He would enjoy teaching that.

But, it turned out, so would a lot of other people. The same advisor had suggested that Alex look into how much additional course work would be required to become certified to teach science or math. If push came to shove, his specialty would be in demand and he would be harder to replace.

That made sense. Alex had been a smart enough kid, motivated more sometimes by his sense of competition than his desire to learn, but he had no trouble learning. He wasn't so fond of life sciences, and math past basic calculus left him scratching his head. But he'd enjoyed the physical sciences and done well in chemistry and physics. In fact, to him one of the more intriguing parts of his own dad's job as a fire fighter had been learning how fires started and spread, and Alex had eagerly absorbed all the stories his dad would tell on the subject.

So twenty-year-old Alex decided that he could, indeed, learn to teach science. Little did he know when he made the decision the extent to which coaching would leave him less and less fulfilled over the years, and how much he would come to enjoy teaching physics.

How could a physics teacher not be curious about the fact that his own perception of the passage of time was getting to be every bit as relative as good old Albert Einstein had said it was? Albert, of course, had focused on particles of light and hypothetical creatures who could run at speeds approaching the seven hundred million miles per hour that light moved at. Even zipping along at a mere seventy million miles per hour, the creatures in Einstein's thought experiments experienced and presumably understood the nature of special relativity because it affected them on a daily basis.

But humans did not achieve such speeds. Time dilation was nothing more than a theory to them, proved by Einstein's logic and a host of exotic lab experiments. Right? Right. Or so Alex had previously thought.

The next morning when he got to his room he found Tina Johnson standing at his door waiting for him.

"Hi Tina." He greeted her warmly even though they had barely met and he suspected that this was not a friendly visit. She glared and followed him into his classroom and closed the door behind her. As she faced him, Alex could see two red blotches of anger on the woman's face.

"You tell your daughter that if she ever pulls a stunt like that again she will regret that she ever set her sorry little liberal ass in this school. Do you understand me?"

"What did Teddie do to warrant such unprofessional anger?" Alex asked coolly.

"She didn't tell me that she was writing an article for the paper." Tina said. "She started hanging out with, flirting with some of the junior boys in my class. Some of my boys. I'd keep an eye on that too, if I was you." Tina gave Alex a meaningful look.

"Anyway, she acts all interested in what their heritage month reports are on so they talk to her of course, and then she asks me about what the class is doing and where I got this idea for heritage month, and so I tell her a little because I think maybe, you know, she really is interested in hearing some truth for once, and the next thing I know I'm being quoted in the school paper, and now I've got three administrators taking turns sitting in all my classes. I told all my students that they could report on anything they wanted any way they wanted because, you see, I don't believe in censorship and just putting out the bullshit version of the story that someone in charge wants you to hear. You get me? That's not being a historian. So I promised my kids that they could look for the truth, the real truth in any part of their heritage that they wanted. Only thanks to your stupid daughter's article now we've got everybody watching what we're doing. So I gotta go back to my kids and say no, tow the line. Don't say anything they won't like. Say the bullshit they want to hear because otherwise we're all in trouble."

Alex just stared at his fellow teacher like she had arrived from another planet. He couldn't think of a single remark worth saying. Tina stared back.

"I can tell that you're one of those whites that's ashamed of who he is. Fine. Have your opinions, but don't come to me for help when the race wars start. And if I were you I'd keep your daughter away from me, and I'd keep her far, far away from my boys. "

Tina turned and walked out and Alex was proud of himself that he had not wasted a single word, not a single breath, on trying to talk to her.

The next day in class, as Alex picked up the special pen to begin writing more equations on the overhead projector, he paused and looked around at the room full of bored faces.

"I'm not going to do this today," he said. "I'm just not." Several students looked at him with new-found interest.

"How many of you have smart phones hidden on you? Don't worry, I'm not going to take them away. Just this once I want you to get them out and use them. Seriously."

Slowly one, two then about fifteen phones came out of hiding. It was amazing, given the general low family incomes of these students. Alex shook his head and paired the remaining seven phoneless students up with partners.

"Pop quiz. No talking except whispers from you guys working together. I want you to find out the full name, in either English or German, of a paper published in nineteen-oh-five by a clerk in a Swiss patent office. I also need the clerk's name, age, and what the radical claim of this paper was. The sooner you hand me your four answers and your cell phone the more points you get. The phones go back to you at the end of class."

Students' fingers began flying over tiny keyboards. Who couldn't use a few easy points in a physics class? There was a little bit of unauthorized collaborating, but Alex let it slide. In the end all 22 students got an A and everyone knew that twenty-six-year-old patent clerk Albert Einstein published "On the Electrodynamics of Moving Bodies" in 1905 asserting that the speed of light is always the same to everyone no matter how fast they themselves are moving.

"That was radical?" Tyler asked incredulously.

Alex smiled. "Still is. And that is what we are going to talk about next week."

February 1697

After all of the build-up from his mother and his older brother, the younger son Balam found the first two months of his journey uneventful and boring. He made his way slowly but surely through thick rainforest and fed himself by hunting, foraging and occasionally finding other Maya friendly enough to take him in for the night and feed him. He saw none of the dreaded Spaniards during that time, and in fact Balam came across little of anything that would cause concern in a boy raised as he had been.

Then, after almost two months, he came to the river. It was bigger than any he had ever seen in his life. First he considered trying to build some sort of small boat to cross it, but that would take forever, and afterward he would just have to abandon his creation on the other side anyway. That seemed like such a waste. He spent an hour eying the moving water. He had certainly swum farther on the lakes at home. The current did not seem terribly swift and the drop-off was not steep. It appeared that maybe he could wade out a good bit of the way. The problem was his pack. He still had a few bits of dried food from his mother, valued now for their scent of home as much as for their contribution to his diet, and they would certainly be spoiled once they were soaked in river water. But his clothes would dry, as would his tools. Finally he decided to do it.

The water was colder and murkier than he expected, and moving faster than it appeared. About waist deep he paused, wondering if perhaps this was a bad idea. Be brave, he told himself. And he pushed off with his feet into the deeper water.

The current in the middle was even stronger, and though he was managing to swim and stay afloat, his now wet pack was heavier than he had expected. It was slowly wriggling its way off to his downstream side and was in danger of working itself loose entirely. He tried to adjust it while swimming but only succeeded in making it worse. Finally it pulled away from his body, and it drug along, attached to him now by only a single cord as it traveled submerged about a foot downstream of him.

Balam kicked with just his legs to stay afloat while he gave the bag a desperate pull back towards him, and the force of the water and his tug tore open one side of the pack. Before Balam could get the pack firmly back in his grasp he saw something fall out and he knew at once what it was. His pack was lighter without the precious box inside of it.

Minutes later, sitting on the far shore, Balam shivered with cold and fear. He, his clothes and his tools had all made the journey safely. He would eat the soggy remnants of the rest of his mother's food that night. But somewhere at the bottom of the river now was the very precious, very important thing that his relatives and the gods themselves had trusted him to carry. Trusted him to deliver. Had anyone in all of history failed so poorly? Balam was glad that no one alive was there to see him cry.

Then Balam made a decision. He would not be a failure. He simply would not. He looked around desperately for all the landmarks he could find. He had his whole life. That was a long time. He would make some sort of grid along the riverbank. Mark it with rocks. Divide it into small pieces. Swim in back and forth in segments, diving down to the bottom of the river at every location until he had checked every single piece of the river bottom. Balam understood that there was only so much space to be covered. It could be done logically. It may take years, but the little rose quartz box he was responsible for absolutely could be found.

Chapter 7. March 2010

Monday, March 1, Shelby arrived at Professor Drexler's office armed for battle. She had on her most business-like clothes, shoes that she did not walk in all that well but which added a full two inches to her height. She had on pearls and carried a briefcase and hoped that everything about her said, "I'm an adult. An important, professional adult. Do not question me or even talk to me like a former student."

The more Shelby had considered the upcoming interview, the more concerned she had become that Dr. Drexler may have changed over the years. Perhaps he had become more suspicious. Shelby decided that the more imposing she was, the less likely it was that this trip down memory lane would inspire Stan Drexler to start second guessing exactly how the box had gone missing to begin with. She was going to do this interview, but she had to keep him focused on the present.

Stan, meanwhile, had practiced not once but twice in front of a mirror delivering his own carefully crafted introduction. Eye contact. Sincerity. Talk a lot about finding the box originally. Keep the conversation off of the details of its resurfacing several months ago. He did not want to get her speculating about the current fate of the document inside. So he thought he had the approach down. Keep her focused on the past.

"Professor Drexler," Shelby entered his office at nine o'clock on the dot and headed straight for the guest chair on the other side of his desk. "May I call you Stan?" She said it like it was barely a question. She had given this opening much thought and decided that it set just the right tone.

She sat a small recording device on his desk. "Standard procedure," she said, once again simply assuming permission. Then more loudly after she hit the record button. "Stan, as a fellow lover of all antiquities and of early art of the Western Hemisphere in particular, I am so happy to have this chance to interview you today Monday, March first, two-thousand and ten."

Stan winced. This wasn't going quite the way he had rehearsed it.

"And I am glad to be speaking with you, Shelby," he replied stiffly. "I, um, I took the liberty of preparing a short introduction to our interview, assuming that if I got a few basic facts out on the table it would make for a more efficient question and answer session. I hope that will be okay."

What? Shelby thought. *This isn't what I had planned.*

Stan ignored her look and went on. "On Monday April twentieth, two-thousand and nine, I received a package through the United States Postal Service with a back address that I would later learn was that of the Smithsonian Institute."

"You don't think it came from the Smithsonian Institute?" she asked.

"No. I do not." He looked a bit annoyed at being interrupted. "I think the sender of the package wished to be anonymous." Stan continued with his script.

"Upon opening it, I discovered that it contained either a replica of or the original artifact that I and a group of students unearthed in Guatemala in February nineteen-ninety-three and that has been lost ever since. If the original, the artifact appeared to have been in no way damaged or altered, and if a replica it appeared to be an excellent imitation. But of course it did not contain the original note—I suppose that you'd call it a note—the piece of well-preserved fig paper which was found in the box in ninety-three and appeared to have been written contemporaneously with the box's burial in the cave where we discovered it. Sadly the original note was never photographed nor translated."

He was careful to make concerned eye contact with Shelby as he went on. "Instead, there was a modern note, written recently in contemporary Spanish, basically saying that a collector had purchased this artifact in good faith and later discovered its ill-gotten origins and wished to return it to me. I'm sure that the ancient note was removed by whoever stole the box to begin with," he muttered it like it was a trivial and obvious point. "And I would guess that the artifact has changed hands several times over the years until, very fortuitously, it landed in the hands of a reputable collector who chose to do the right thing."

He smiled in conclusion. "I am looking forward to seeing the box on display in a museum, and am happy to have final resolution to this rather unfortunate incident." Then, as if he was giving a press conference. "I'll be happy now to answer your questions."

Right. Shelby pulled out her prepared list of questions. Stan responded to each one cordially with whatever prepared response of his matched best. At the end Shelby turned off her recorder and thanked him very much.

And as she walked out of his office, all Stan could think of was "Why do I have the feeling that the interview was total bullshit?"

And as Shelby walked to her car, very businesslike, recorder in hand, all she could think of was "You know, that entire interview was absolute bullshit."

Tina knew that she should not have lost her temper, not spoken so plainly with the physics teacher. She hardly knew the man, although she wasn't particularly impressed with what she had seen. It was just that the little stunt his slut of a daughter had pulled putting that information in the school paper and drawing all that attention to Tina really made her mad. It was hard enough, trying to reach these kids and teach them the truth without bringing all that politically correct censorship down upon her.

And the way that girl had gone about it just infuriated Tina. Flouncing around in her cute little clothes with that girly body of hers, making those wide eyes at Tina's boys just to get them to open up and talk to her. Tina figured that it was time to start protecting her boys better, especially at this important time while their ideas were being formed. They weren't going to like being protected from the likes of Teddie Zeitman, and Tina knew it. But it would be for their own good.

Tina took a deep breath. When she had come to the cause, when she had embraced the knowledge, she had been warned that she had accepted a difficult life. It's hard knowing the truth when so many others insist on turning a blind eye, insist on pretending that all races are equal, were ever intended by our Creator to be equal.

Tina felt sick sometimes when she thought of all the blacks and browns and Chinese and whatnots out there multiplying like rabbits while the whites sat around feeling guilty and talking about why the world wasn't better.

But as a history teacher, Tina believed that she could make a difference. She could recruit able young minds and bodies to the cause, turn them to the light before they ever went the sorry way of the timid, apologetic white male of today.

So of course she had to protect her boys while their ideas were being formed. They needed to grow stronger and surer of themselves. Maybe it would be a good idea to let them feel some tastes of victory to offset the frustration that she knew her new rule was going to cause. And maybe unleashing her boys like that could be useful for the cause, too.

"Dad. I did not flirt with those boys, okay? Ick. They're wannabe skinheads. Look, I was nice to them when I talked to them, probably nicer than I would have usually been. But that's just common sense. Who's going to give you information if you're rude to them? Come on."

Alex had to agree that made sense. He got that Teddie was angry at Ms. Johnson's accusation, but he wondered if she resented being accused of flirting, or resented being accused of flirting with these particular boys. Either way, from Teddie's point of view she had done nothing wrong.

"Shouldn't you have told the boys you were asking about their projects on behalf of the school paper?" Alex prodded gently.

"Oh, *that* would have gotten me a lot of information. Those kids really believe that all school-sponsored activities are part of a liberal propaganda machine, Dad. Seriously paranoid people."

"Well, you've made yourself quite an enemy in Ms. Johnson, dear. I don't think she's a fan of mine either, now."

Teddie winced. It was hard enough being a freshman without always having to worry about how every little thing you did seemed to reflect on your teacher father. It got tiresome.

"You know Dad, I don't think Ms. Johnson is the kind of

friend you want anyway. I hear that she tows the line in front of the administration, but in the classroom when no one is there but students she comes out with some pretty racist things. I mean she always phrases them like discussion questions, so if they get repeated they don't sound that bad, but her class spends a lot of time talking about things that make some of the kids uncomfortable."

"Teddie, I think you're exaggerating. If that were really the case, honey, kids would be speaking up, to their parents, to the department head."

Teddie had her you-adults-just-do-not-understand expression firmly on her face. "Dad, if a kid reports her then she twists it around like they were just having a class discussion and that this kid is saying stuff because he didn't do well on a test or something. And that kid can usually kiss a good grade from her goodbye."

Her dad gave that possibility some thought. "I think the other history teachers would know and be involved if this lady was really crossing a line."

More of the look. "Dad, you need to get out of the science department more. Word is that most of the Early Gulch history department pretty much agrees with everything Ms. Johnson teaches. The others keep their opinions more to themselves, but they don't object. The few that do, like Mr. Hanson who left last year, they're not lasting very long. I think there's some group or organization out there that has all of the history teachers involved."

"Now who sounds paranoid?" her dad kidded.

"You know what they say. Doesn't mean they're not out to get you. I'm sorry I put you on Ms. Johnson's radar. Be careful, Dad. I think she likes hurting people that don't agree with her."

The third time that Alex had the dream, he felt more comfortable. He was still running his leisurely twelve-minute miles like he had been doing for some time. Maybe forever? But he wasn't alone and he realized that he never had been. Creatures with a sort of soft yellow glimmer were around him in every direction. The ones in the far distance were barely visible and looked like lightening bugs. He was surprised that he hadn't noticed them before. A few were closer to him now, ahead of him or behind him, and he could tell that they were glowing beings of some sort, not bugs at all. They were rather beautiful actually, and they were all moving. Then he woke up.

Stan had picked up the phone to call Shelby three, or four, or okay maybe it was five times in the couple of weeks after their interview. Every time he put the phone back down without dialing, and each time for the same reason. Namely, there was no good reason to call her. She had offered amid the pleasantries to email him a copy of her article before it was published. She had said it would be weeks. He had not received the email.

He had, to all appearances, gotten away with deceiving the one person he thought it may be difficult to deceive. So why did he want to talk to her again? It took a while, but finally it occurred to Stan that he was disappointed at having been successful. He had, on some deep level, wanted her to catch him in his lie.

Why? Guilt? He didn't need more professional censure or trouble with the school's administration. A second incident of any sort could well end his career. Was that what he really wanted? No, Stan was sure he did not.

No, he realized, what he wanted was a co-conspirator. Another able brain willing to help him unravel the mysteries of the document he had stashed in his closet and now had been struggling to translate, continuing in small doses to add more accuracy and nuance as he worked. It was lonely working alone. Silly man. He had wanted Shelby to find the truth with those penetrating eyes of hers and then had wanted her to offer to abandon her own ethics and help him. What was wrong with him? What kind of professor wanted that from a student? What kind of scumbag wanted that from any other human? Stan put down the phone for the fifth and final time, disgusted with himself.

He still wasn't sure why the woman had been every bit as cautious, even perhaps as non-forthcoming with him as he had been with her. But that was her business. He had chosen his path, had solidified it every single time he had said that the document had not been in the box. He had absolutely finalized his path when he told Shelby that. It was done now and the best he could do was to keep others, innocent others like Shelby, from joining him in his lie.

Alex had most of his physics class talking about young Albert Einstein and why an absolute speed of light mattered. He couldn't go as far as saying the entire class was enthused about the subject, but at least most of them were paying attention, at least for now. Only Tanner, Tyler and Travis were hanging back, almost refusing to participate.

Finally, Alex asked the three of them to stay for a few minutes after class.

"What's the problem, guys? You have something against Albert Einstein?"

"We found out he's Jewish," Travis said evenly.

"Yeah. We thought he was German." Tanner added.

"They offered to make him president of Israel," Tyler said as though that explained it all.

"So? Why do you have a problem learning about the theories of a Jewish physicist? Of which, by the way, there are quite a few. You do know that, right?"

"There's so many of them because they work to keep the rest of us out of intellectual fields, so they can run the world secretly," Travis said.

Alex looked hard at the three boys. They were serious.

"Where are you guys getting this stuff?"

"You wouldn't understand," Tyler said.

Alex persisted. "Have any of you ever actually met anyone who is Jewish?"

"You don't usually meet them. They like to stay hidden," Tanner replied with certainty. "Ms. Johnson says that's part of why they are so dangerous. She says—" and with a sharp look from both Travis and Tyler, he closed his mouth instantly and turned red.

"We have our sources," Travis said with finality. "We may have to sit in your class and listen, but we don't have to like it." Then to his two friends, "Come on. You can't give the truth to someone who isn't ready to hear it." And as the three boys walked off Alex started to wonder if maybe Teddie hadn't been right.

In 1903 Congress passed a new law forbidding epileptics, the insane, beggars and anarchists from immigrating to the United States. In 1907 Japanese became the first national group to be allowed to immigrate here only in restricted numbers.

Americans were becoming concerned about immigration. It was one thing to have the previously unwelcome Irish and German Catholics coming over in droves. But back in the good old 1880s at least three-quarters of those immigrating to the U.S. came from northern and western Europe. By the first ten years of the nineteen-hundreds, almost three-quarters of the immigrants were now coming from what a congressional study referred to as the "inferior" and "less desirable" regions of southern and eastern Europe. In other words, the majority of immigrants were now Italians, Slavs and Jews. The Anglo-Saxons began pressuring Congress to do something.

Native Americans had no interest in the debate. It would seem reasonable to assume that all Europeans remained equally undesirable to them.

Alex had been ecstatic when the freshman English teacher who also managed this year's tennis team deemed Xuha exceptional enough, by EGHS standards, to join the team with a modified practice schedule. Alex had long since worked his way through the basics of tennis with the boy and taught Xuha a variety of simple drills that he could practice against a wall by himself when time permitted. Apparently the boy had been practicing them a lot. Once Xuha made the team, Alex expected to end the Saturday practices, and was surprised and delighted when Xuha asked if they could continue.

With the main goal of making the team achieved, Saturday mornings became a little more relaxed. They still met early in the morning, but they moved the sessions to an older and seldom used public court at the back of a park in town. Sometimes Alex and Xuha would just play a match, and discuss it afterwards while they shared the iced tea that Alex would bring. Alex had learned long ago to tread lightly on personal matters with students. So he let Xuha finally bring up the reason he had landed at EGHS mid-year.

"My foster parents moved up here for work. I was sixteen when we moved. I turned seventeen last month, and I could have moved in with a friend's family I suppose and stayed put, and maybe I should have, but these folks have been so good to me and they count on me so I came along."

"They count on you?" Alex asked. In his world, children generally counted on parents, not the other way around. But, as Alex learned over iced tea, Xuha's adopted family included two parents who both worked two minimum-wage jobs. The dad now primarily worked for a cousin's yard care company during the day and picked up janitorial work at night. The mom did housecleaning with a relative of hers during the day and picked up janitorial work with the same company as her husband, often on the same schedule. Their old jobs in Houston had both fizzled out last fall as the economy barely sputtered along, and now they were happy to have relatives helping them out so that they could try to make a new life outside of the city.

Xuha watched their four children nights and evenings, with special instructions to keep their oldest, a ten-year-old son, away from gangs and out of trouble. Xuha worked part time at a fast food place to buy his own clothes, keep gas in a clunker of a car, buy lunches and have spending money, and he had to be home around his foster parents' schedule. Alex thought of his own family and suddenly each of them seemed to have led terribly easy, terribly spoiled lives.

"Your real parents?" he asked hesitantly.

"Never knew my dad," Xuha shook his head. "But I'm told he was not only there when I was born, but he delivered me." To Alex's surprised look he added, "I was an emergency birth in a car. Not my style to come into this world in a normal fashion, huh?" Alex could see the raw emotion behind the bravado.

"You knew your mother?" he asked gently.

"Oh yes. She came to the United States because my grandfather was here for cancer treatments. They were from Mexico City. Nice established family. Had some money, at least before my grandfather got ill. The treatments didn't help and my grandfather died here in Houston hours after I was born. I'm told I was rushed to his deathbed. His first, his only, grandchild. He cried when he saw me and then he died." Xuha laughed. "How's that for a start in life? Making someone cry."

"You knew your grandmother then?"

"She raised me until I was almost six. Sort of."

"Sort of?" Alex asked. He hoped he wasn't treading too far into personal ground.

"Well, she never was very strong after my grandfather died. Sad. Sick a lot. Always crying. Lot of crying in my history, huh? But she wouldn't go back to Mexico right away because they buried my grandfather here and she wanted to spend time by his grave. I'm told that my mother agreed to stay with her until she was done grieving, and my grandmother kept promising that she'd be ready to go in just a month or two more but she never was."

"Your dad didn't stay too?"

"He couldn't. He had to get back to work. My grandmother told me that he got angry with my mother when she didn't come home after a while and my parents fought on the phone and then my mom got hit by a car."

"No."

"Yes. Buella said I was three, three and a half. I don't remember my mother. But after she died all my grandmother did was cry every day and night and I do remember all those tears. She blamed herself for everything. I used to heat canned things up for dinner and try to get her to eat. I guess I was almost six when she died. Just died in her bed."

Alex looked at Xuha and watched the boy make a clown's sad face that mocked his own sorrow. "Then I was the one who cried. I thought it was my fault that she died, you see. That if I'd known how to cook she'd have eaten and gotten strong and gotten out of bed and then fed us both." He added a comic eye roll. "A child's logic, huh? If I could have cooked better I'd have had someone to feed me." Alex didn't laugh.

"Your foster mother found you then?"

"Yeah. She was a neighbor, and according to her she was kind of keeping an eye on me already. Newly married, really pregnant with her first child. When Buella died she and her husband took me in and fed me and never fought once about my being there. They raised and treated me like their own, as best they could. Most of what I know about my real parents comes from things my grandmother said, but she told Maria, my foster mom, the same stories. So I believe them."

"Wow Xuha." Alex wasn't sure what else to say when an odd question occurred to him. "So you were born in the U.S.? You're a citizen?"

"I think so. I have a birth certificate. From the hospital in Houston where my grandfather died."

"Where does it say you were born?"

"En route to hospital."

"Well that should count," Alex mused.

"Why do you ask?" Xuha seemed a little defensive now.

"Oh, it's nothing. I guess because I am helping out some friends of my son. There are some complicated nationality and immigration issues involved and he knows that I've dealt with some of this before. So it was on my mind. It just seems that you've had enough trouble in your young life, and for some reason the animosity towards undocumented immigrants has grown exponentially in our region over the last couple of years. It's pretty sad. I'm just glad to know that you're okay in that regard."

Xuha didn't say anything for several seconds. Alex took the cue and sipped his own tea in silence.

"I don't think that Maria and Diego have the same luxury," Xuha said finally.

"No, I was guessing that they didn't. Let's keep that between us. Your foster parents sound like wonderful people working very hard to raise a family and do what's right. I'd hate to see any trouble come their way."

Ms. Johnson had put out the very best pizza, the meat-eaters special. She had plenty of cokes iced down and had made a fresh pan of brownies. Tanner and Travis were happy as pigs in slop, but Tyler was a little wary. Ms. Johnson usually went all out like this only when she wanted to ask something of them. He was saving his enthusiasm for the food until he heard today's request.

"Boys, I need you to be soldiers," Ms. Johnson finally said.

"You want us to join the army? I thought you said that the whole military is now run by a bunch of bullshit liberals," Travis said.

"It's gonna be run by a bunch of fag bullshit liberals the way its going," Tanner chimed in, looking at Ms. Johnson for approval.

Ms. Johnson shook her head. "Come on boys. I've told you, the fags aren't the problem. They may be disgusting, but they are not the ones that are going to kill you and your families someday. Let 'em join the military. Who cares? We are going to have our own army to protect us when the day comes, and good thing, because we can't count on this army, huh?"

She laughed and her boys laughed too. "No, I need you to start preparing to be soldiers for the white race. Like any good soldier, there needs to be some training. A little more gym time for starters."

"Oh come on," Tanner whined. He was the biggest of the three, and carried easily twenty pounds more than he needed. Not surprisingly he was the one who hated working out the most.

"I'm just saying you'll be glad if you do. And so will those you are protecting, you know? Like really glad and grateful."

"You mean girls, don't you?" Tyler asked.

"I do. But here is the difficult part. When a soldier is in training, really getting ready for a big mission, he knows that it's no time for girls. He focuses. Does what a man needs to do." She noticed the look of skepticism on the boys' faces. "It's okay. It's time you three started thinking of yourself as men. Men training for a mission. That means I want you to back off of the girls for a while.

Stay aloof. Stay mysterious. Get where you need to be on this journey and I promise you that you will be rewarded with more grateful adoring girls than you could ever imagine."

Travis grimaced. He liked going out with girls, when he could get one to go out with him, that was. Not that he was having a lot of success in that arena lately.

"I'm not saying you need to stay away from girls for very long," Ms. Johnson added. "Just a while, until we get a good focus going here. You train hard and I'll give the word when this part of your training is up. Not long, I promise. Okay?"

"Sure," Tanner agreed right away. Hell, he wasn't seeing a girl anyway.

"Yeah, okay," Travis added. He'd had some hopes for the weekend, but he could back off for a while. It was good to keep Ms. Johnson happy.

"Tyler?" Ms. Johnson prodded. She had known Tyler would be her most reticent on this issue. In fact, Tyler was precisely Ms. Johnson's reason for introducing this edict. She'd seen Teddie Zeitman making eyes at Tyler to get the information for her story. She'd seen Tyler making eyes back. Real eyes, smitten eyes. Ms. Johnson understood how one pretty girl filled with a lot of we-are-all-equal-in-this-world bullshit could undo a powerful amount of the teaching that Ms. Johnson had done over the last several months.

Right now, at this moment, she figured that there wasn't a Jew, immigrant or person of any color that posed more of a threat to her little band of trainees than cute little Teddie Zeitman. "Tyler? Are you ready to be a soldier? Ready to be a man who takes responsibility and commits?"

"Yes Ms. J," Tyler said with resignation. He knew he couldn't fight this. Better to hope that Ms. Johnson would change her mind quickly, like she did about a lot of their training.

"Excellent. Then part two of this discussion, gentle*men,*" Ms. Johnson smiled, "is that we need to start doing a much better job of honing your fighting skills. The only way to get better is to fight. I mean real fights."

"Seriously … like we really get to punch spics and—"

"We get kicked out of school when we fight," Tyler interrupted.

"Well, then we are just going to have to find some ways to get you in fights off of school grounds. I think it's time we pick two or three of your least desirable fellow students and give them a taste of what the white race can do. Any nominees?"

As she had hoped and expected, the boys moved on easily from the unpleasant prohibition on dating to the much more fun idea of picking on a few undesirables. With sense, they nominated smaller boys with few friends or family members to protect them. Her boys understood without being told that this was supposed to be an exercise in teaching a lesson, not starting a war. As the boys laughed and threw out names, Ms. Johnson waited patiently for the name she knew she would hear sooner or later, the pet of that physics teacher who now had half the junior class learning about some Jew.

"Hey, how about Zoohah?"

"Yeah. Now *there* is a boy who needs a lesson in appropriate humility. How does a kid that short get to be so sure of himself?"

"Yeah."

Ms. Johnson smiled. There was more than one way to bring down a self-righteous teacher and his do-good daughter.

"Yeah," she agreed. "He'd be a very good choice." She loved her boys.

This year it was Ariel and her friends who descended on the Zeitman house for spring break. As seniors in college they now all had that coveted twenty-one-year-old ID, and that sophistication that underclassmen lacked in selecting a destination.

The four girls had managed to two get cabins on a cruise ship out of Galveston, and of course Ariel had offered free lodging coming and going. Ariel's trip had been both her birthday and her Christmas present and Alex still thought it was extravagant, but this was one arena in which he had learned to voice his opinions once and then let it drop. Clearly he was out of touch with what had become normal for middle class kids.

Lola was ecstatic. She always loved to meet and entertain her children's friends, and she had been working for a week on a grocery list to make sure the group had a great time while on the premises. Alex was more neutral. It happened to be his spring break too, and even though he loved Ariel dearly, this visit meant that not only would he and Lola not be going anywhere, but for several days of his vacation he would be expected to wear a shirt, not occupy the couch fulltime, put up with noise and strangers and assist in keeping the place tidy. Not a total win in his book.

Yet, he was a reasonable man and he loved his family, so he made an effort to greet each of Ariel's three friends warmly, ask the polite questions and show an interest in each girl. Laura, a fellow math and computer science major, had been to the Zeitmans twice before now and she was almost honorary family. Both she and Ariel were in the five year master's program and would graduate together a year from this spring. Heather, who he had never met, was studying some sort of fashion marketing. Alex quickly determined that he and Heather just didn't have much to say to each other. He got the impression she had been included because the girls needed a fourth.

The last girl, Megan, was a lively petite young lady who loved to share her enthusiasm with anyone who would listen. Alex was a good listener. So over the course of the few shared meals and encounters Alex learned about the exceptional anthropology department at the girls' university, and particularly about the wonderful archeological work that the school sponsored around the world.

As with most such endeavors, the department had focused on excavations in a few regions, driven largely by the expertise and interest of its professors. Megan, an anthropology major, had been accepted for a six-week session in Guatemala after her graduation in May.

Alex was half paying attention to Megan's stories of the last stand of Maya civilization on some lake she was going to visit, when the girl mentioned her admiration for the work of Dr. Drexler. Alex smiled. "I knew a Drexler once. Heard he went on to become some sort of archeologist. What's this guy's first name?"

Megan thought. "Stan? I think." She picked up her smart phone and started tapping. "Yeah. Stan Drexler. Says in his bio that he's from Texas! He's kind of famous. You really know him?"

"No," Alex mused, "I probably don't know him anymore. But decades ago I went to high school with a Stan Drexler. Kind of a little guy. Quiet. Smart. Not a lot of social skills. We didn't hang in the same circles really."

Megan passed him her phone. "Is that the guy?"

Alex put on his glasses and studied the little picture. "Yeah, I think it probably is. What do you know? Small world."

"Want me to tell him you say hi?" she chirped.

"I don't know, Megan. I doubt he remembers me. High school was a long time ago for us you know."

"People never forget high school," Megan said.

Yeah, Alex thought. *That was true. And that was probably why a hello from Alex Zeitman to Stan Drexler wasn't such a hot idea even thirty-three years later.*

"If you happen to think of it. No big deal."

Jennifer Havens never used the title "doctor" that she had earned the right to years ago when she finished her PhD in archeology. She was certainly Mrs. Havens in every way, she thought, as she sipped on a cup of tea and browsed around on the internet. But she still did cache anything that related to the Maya and archeology, the subject of her dissertation, and she noticed that her folder contained some news.

Well, well. The obsidian box that had been mysteriously returned had finally been verified as authentic by a team of experts. So Dr. Drexler finally had his famous box back in his possession. The artifact must represent so many things to others, she thought, but to her it mostly brought back memories of sitting naked in the moonlight by a small stream in Guatemala. And memories of the really good sex that always followed.

Back then, Jennifer slept with a lot of men. She enjoyed sex, pure and simple. She loved how men responded to her beauty. She savored their adoration. And she especially enjoyed the thrill of sex in a forbidden location or at an inappropriate time. The very best mix had always been an awe struck man who could not believe his good fortune, bewitched by her beauty into a dangerous tryst he would never have considered in his wildest dreams. She always had loved making men take risks to have her.

That was the main reason why those six weeks in Guatemala back in 1993 had been such fun. Timid, sexually unadventurous Nelson, banging her in trees, in the back of the school's vehicles, in the caves where they were excavating. His initial discomfort always overtaken by his passion. It had been so exquisite.

Today, Jennifer recognized that she had found all the treasure that she had ever sought. She had all the money she wanted. She was married to a perfectly reasonable man who gave her everything she desired and who, as an unexpected bonus, had turned out to be considerably more fun than she had expected. He had provided well for her and for their two young teenaged children. At forty-one she was well preserved. Life was good.

She wondered idly whether Jake or Kyle was better in the sack. Back then she hadn't bothered to find out. Skill didn't really matter all that much, though, did it? Almost any man could be taught pretty quickly how to satisfy a woman.

Then she wondered idly if one of them would still be attracted to her? Not that she wanted to act on that attraction. But maybe there could be some fun in finding out?

Ariel had given her dad a warm thank you before she left and Alex found himself glad that he had been as gracious to his guests as he had. Then after the girls had left, Lola approached him with one of those smiles she got when she thought she had an idea he would really like.

"So it wasn't much of a spring break for you this year, was it?"

Alex gave her a hard look. "No special skill needed to pick that one up?"

"You gave a very gracious and loving performance," she

responded. "But can we at least agree that based on knowing you as well as I do I would have been aware of your desire for a little more fun yourself even without picking up a single vibration from you?"

"Okay. So what do you have in mind to make me happy?"

She giggled. "We do have a twenty-fifth anniversary coming up this summer. Do you remember six years ago when I got to go to that modern carbonates class in Belize?"

"Yeah? Seemed like the sorriest excuse for a geological field trip that I ever heard of. Snorkeling around looking at reefs so you could find oil better? Right. Every bit as bad as Zane getting sent to Fiji by a pharmaceutical company."

"I know, I know. But I loved Belize and told you how much I wanted to go back. With you. Remember?"

"I do. And I'd love to go. But it doesn't seem like such a good time dear. Now that she's in that master's program we've got another year of college for Ariel that we hadn't planned on." Alex felt compelled to be the voice of common sense.

"I know. But we also won't have another twenty-fifth anniversary. Ever. Anyway, I was looking around online and I found a terrific deal. Can't we at least consider it?"

"Of course, we can and should. You know how much I love a good deal." Then, because he wanted to see her smile come back: "If you can figure out a way to swing it, and find a workable solution for Teddie while we're gone, then I am the happiest of travel companions. You know that."

Then he added. "Where exactly is Belize?"

"South of the Yucatan. Central America, next to Guatemala. But a very different history and culture from either place. Very Caribbean."

"Okay. There may be cheaper getaways out there, you know, but if that's really where you want to go, then keep looking at those online deals and see what you can do."

The smile was back. And it was hard to tell who was making whom happy.

Shelby had counted. She had picked up the phone exactly six

times to call Stan and every single time she had put the phone back. This was not a situation she had expected to ever find herself in.

True, back in 1993, she had made a less than admirable decision. Not a bad one, not an awful one. She hadn't stolen anything or even done anything wrong. But she had kept her mouth shut, and she still wasn't proud of why. The best she could figure was that after a lifetime of being, well, just the sort of girl who would tell on people, for once she had wanted the cool kids to like her. Or at least not to hate her. At twenty-four, of course, Shelby told herself that she should have outgrown memories of junior high and high school, but somehow the feel of being less than worthy persisted into adulthood. Guys like Jake and Kyle with all their clowning around and deprecating humor took her right back to the lunchroom. Right back to being made fun of. So she had done a dumb thing and protected them just so they would think she was okay.

The worst of it was, she didn't even know for sure if Jake and Kyle had done anything wrong either. Maybe she had agonized for years over protecting two boys who would have been annoyed at her accusation, but could have proven themselves innocent. She didn't even know for sure.

When she read about the box being returned to Professor Drexler, it had dawned on her that not only would interviewing him be something of a career advancer, but it also might give her a shot at finally finding out more of the truth. The interview with Stan could provide her with clues to maybe piece the whole thing together at last. And then, if appropriate, she could consider how to rectify any wrong she had once committed just so two cute, cocky guys wouldn't think even less of her.

It was a fine idea. Only Stan the guileless seemed to have changed. He had been wary and cautious, and Shelby was pretty sure he now had a secret or two of his own. Damn. Why did things like this just seem to get more difficult to straighten out with time?

The seventh time, Shelby hit dial. She'd had it. It was time to tell her old professor everything she knew and get this mess rectified before it got any worse.

March 1697

Nimah and her daughter Naylay stayed busy after the boys left, preparing food and moving supplies to the cave. Busy was good because it helped fill the horrible sense of loss they both felt, and it helped stave off their fear of what was to come.

Naylay loved the little stream that ran near the cave, and sometimes when she forgot for a while about her brothers she played on the rocks below the small waterfall, talking to little pretend creatures that the girl imagined. At those times, Nimah would let her be. She was still a child after all and deserved some happiness.

But events moved fast after Balam and Ichik left. In early March, a couple of hundred more soldiers of the others arrived in Tayasal. This would have been frightening enough, but they brought with them thousands of the Xiu Maya, cutting down the forest as they came, and once they arrived at Lake Peten they began quickly building a fort along the shore of the lake.

As Nimah watched the giant guns roll in on wheels, she finished moving the rest of her essential household goods to the cave. She watched as the soldiers reassembled a big heavy boat filled with weapons that the many Xiu Maya had dragged through the jungle in pieces. She knew no good would come of such a vessel.

Thankfully she and Naylay were well hidden in the cave on that horrible day when the soldiers came into the city, killing and burning and smashing all that they could find. Later Nimah would learn that, just as her father had predicted, the Spanish had set the entire library on fire and burned it to the ground, destroying every single precious manuscript that had been preserved in it, including his own writings. They broke hundreds of beautiful works of art into pieces, leaving not one carving, not one statue standing by the end of that horrible day.

Hundreds of Maya died trying to protect their homes and the precious symbols of their gods. When asked why conquest was not enough for them, why they had to destroy everything they conquered, the Spanish answered proudly that they were eradicating "the lies of the devil" and therefore were doing the work of the Lord.

.

Chapter 8. April 2010

This time Stan and Shelby met in a bar that Shelby had selected. She wore one of her less functional pair of jeans and a top that was slightly more fitted, slightly more feminine than her usual choice. She was getting rid of the professional woman. She thought about undoing the braid too but decided that was going too far. She did add a bit of mascara and a touch of bronzer at the last minute and hoped that for once she looked more or less like a normal woman out for a drink.

Stan had been surprised by the call, surprised by the invitation. Shelby said they needed to talk in a more informal setting. He hoped that meant without a recorder turned on. He chose a pair of jeans instead of slacks, and a cotton pullover without a collar. Sure, he could do informal too, he thought, as he ran a comb through his thinning dark hair. He considered wearing a pair of sandals, but decided that was going too far. He opted for one of his more well worn pairs of loafers. Casual, but still him.

She ordered a glass of white wine. He had an imported beer. They talked about the bar, how Atlanta had changed over the years, new buildings on campus and improvements in the area's museums. They ordered a second round.

Finally, Shelby realized that this wasn't going to happen of its own accord. She took a deep breath and looked Stan hard in the eye. "We went back to the cave that night." He knew right away what she was talking about, and he felt like a sword of ice had just been driven into him.

"You what? Who?" Then, getting several looks from the folks seated up at the bar, he lowered his voice. "How could you? I would have trusted you kids with my life. My God. You stole the greatest find of my career!"

"We didn't. I mean we didn't steal it as far as I know." Shelby looked down at the floor. "I should have told you this story a long time ago."

Stan had become very calm, so calm that he surprised himself. It almost felt like someone else was saying the words for him. "Why don't you tell me the story now, Shelby?"

She nodded. "Both Kyle and I were pretty knowledgeable at the time when it came to Kan Ek hieroglyphs. If you remember, we were both doing projects in that field. I was standing closer and I was pretty sure I saw the hieroglyphs for gold and great and treasure on that yellow paper inside the box. Kyle, who was farther away, thought he saw treasure too, but he wasn't sure until you said you couldn't read the document at all. You're a pretty bad liar, Dr. Drexler. We could all tell that you were covering up something."

Stan noticed that they had slipped backwards in time with the telling, back to the student-professor relationship.

"As soon as you said that," she went on, "Kyle was positive that you had read something. Remember how you went up to your room right after dinner that night to make phone calls home? Well, Nelson headed off to his room too. He always did whatever you did back then. And then Jennifer went upstairs because I think she got tired of Jake and Kyle both hitting on her. Anyway, Jake and Kyle and I were left in the bar and got to talking and I guess I kind of verified what Kyle saw because I was trying to impress them. Then the two boys decided that you were planning to hide the manuscript somehow and try to find the treasure yourself, cheat the school and all your colleagues out of the information. They said that wasn't right."

"Of course I wasn't going to do that," Stan interjected.

"Well, they decided, and they convinced me, that it was our duty to go back and photograph the thing. Not disturb it, not take it, just make sure we had a record of it. Just in case. It seemed pretty reasonable."

"Okay," Stan agreed. "I can see how you kids may have gotten to that point. I did lie about being able to read it, as apparently you guessed, but I did it just because I didn't want to generate a lot of crazy speculation, have you kids calling home telling people we'd found a map to some sort of enormous buried treasure. Hell, I didn't want half the town outside the cave the next morning. You know…"

"I do," she said. "That's what I told them. But it didn't seem like there was any harm in getting a photograph."

"So you got one?"

"I didn't get anything," she said morosely. "You had the keys to the big four wheel drive vehicle, and Jake had the keys to the little truck. Two seats. I'd have been happy to ride in back but the boys decided that they would just go, and I should stand watch in the bar just in case you or Nelson or Jennifer came back down. I was supposed to tell you some story about how they'd gone out so you wouldn't miss the truck or get suspicious."

She paused and looked embarrassed. "I told them I wasn't comfortable sitting in the bar by myself that late at night for very long and they laughed and told me not to worry because in my case I'd be just fine."

Those clear eyes looked straight into Stan's now. "Isn't it funny that of all the things that happened that night, that feeling of embarrassment is the one thing I remember most?"

Stan couldn't even fathom what would constitute a good response. So he asked instead, "What happened when they returned?"

"Well, they were gone almost an hour, enough time to drive to the site and drive back. When they got back they were shook. Told me they got to the cave and the box was gone. They were clearly upset and it didn't look like they were acting, and they said they got no photos, no nothing. They said that they looked around outside, couldn't find any obvious clues in the dark, and came back to the hotel."

"They swore me to secrecy about the whole thing, saying that they didn't think you'd normally doubt any of us but if you heard about what they'd tried to do then you might start to wonder. So it was really important that the three of us go get some sleep and pretend very hard like this never happened, and tomorrow we had to put on the acting performances of our lives."

Shelby looked just miserable. "And I did. I did, Dr. Drexler, and I know that I should have told you but I was in this totally down place and I didn't want to give these boys one more reason to think less of me. So I convinced myself that their drive back to the cave was a harmless unrelated event that I could keep secret just to make everything simpler."

Stan sighed. "I wish you had spoken up."

"I know. It may not have helped but at least you'd have been operating with more information. At the very least you'd have known when the box disappeared." She downed the rest of her second glass of wine.

"Did you ever wonder why I stopped interacting with you much in the department and finished my dissertation just as fast as I could? Why you didn't hear from me for fifteen years after I got my degree?" she asked. "I live ten miles from the university."

"I understand now," Stan said. He wanted to say hurtful things to her, things that would make her feel even worse for withholding such information and for so long. But he couldn't bring himself to do it.

Stan was determined now to make his own confession, and he hoped that afterwards Shelby might be as forgiving to him as he was trying to be to her.

He motioned the waitress to bring another round of drinks.

Tyler was waiting for Teddie when she came out of her freshman social science class. He could see her trying to step away from him, and he figured she probably thought that he was going to give her a hard time about the newspaper article. He gave her his friendliest smile. "Hi."

"Hi," she said, wary.

"Look, I just wanted to tell you that I wasn't mad at you or anything. I mean, Ms. Johnson thought you were trying to make trouble for her when you wrote that story, but the way I see it you were just curious and asking questions. It's good to ask questions."

Teddie gave him a baffled look and Tyler couldn't help noticing her skin again. It was true that Teddie had dark hair, but it kind of naturally fell into curls that made Tyler think of Scarlett in the movie *Gone with the Wind*. And her brown eyes were set into the most delicate, almost translucent white skin that Tyler thought he had ever seen. Teddie had skin that almost glowed like moonlight. Sometimes when he thought about her he secretly called her Snow

White because that was how she seemed to him—pure and delicate—like how he imagined newly fallen snow must look.

"I think sometimes when people sense there is a truth but they are afraid to ask about it, they sort make excuses to ask questions. You know, like you did," Tyler said.

"I wasn't making excuses Tyler." Teddie had gone from baffled back to wary.

"I know. I mean, I understand. I mean, if you want more answers or to know more information or if you just kind of want to talk about things any time well then, you know, I wanted to make sure you knew that you could come back and talk to me more. That's all." And Tyler told himself firmly, *I'm not trying to date her. I am trying to recruit her. Ms. Johnson can't possibly object to that.*

"Okay," Teddie said cautiously. Then, because she realized that he was trying to be friendly, she added, "Look, I'm glad you're not mad, Tyler. I just like to write about what's really going on. I figure if you're part of something, you don't mind talking about it."

"Exactly," Tyler said, picking up enthusiasm. "We shouldn't have to hide our white pride any more than someone has to hide their gay pride or black pride or, you know, right? So like, maybe I can do an interview with you or something for the last newspaper of the school year?" Tyler was walking faster to keep up with her and warming to the idea. The last paper of the year would be good because it generally came out right before the start of summer, which would minimize any fallout from the article. Plus it would give him one, maybe two or three more reasons to meet with Teddie. Reasons even Ms. Johnson would like.

"Yeah, Tyler. That may make a good story. Let me get back to you on timing."

"You do that. I'm pretty much available." And then because he didn't want to end on such a pathetic note, he gestured back to the class Teddie had just left.

"What a useless subject, huh? I couldn't wait to get done with it."

"World Geography? Useless?" Teddie said. She decided to keep it to herself that she actually found the rest of the world interesting.

Over the past few months Lola learned more about her peculiar gift and how to filter and tone down the barrage of information that flooded the mind of a full telepath like the one she had become. Her adventures of the past year had brought her close to two Nigerian telepaths. Somadina, a young Igbo woman who worked in her village with the Dibia, the local medicine men, laughingly called herself a witch doctor. In fact she was a nurse's aid in training, a new wife and young mother, and one of the most amazing women Lola had ever met. Lola and Somadina had formed an unexpected link about a year ago and in many ways had grown their abilities together.

Olumiji, on the other hand, was a highly experienced and adept telepath who was one of the leaders of an organization called x^0. This group kept to the shadows, seeking out the ever-increasing number of humans developing telepathy, and working to educate and train them, to see that their gifts were used for good. A Yoruban from the Lagos area, Olumiji had intervened to help Lola and Somadina, and continued to train and assist both women.

His brother, Jumoke, was an engineer in the Lagos office of the small oil company for which Lola worked. Jumoke was a telepath himself, but complicated the situation and the relationship with his brother with his own firm belief that the idea of telepathy was nonsense and that his brother was a kook.

Families. You've got to love 'em, Lola thought. And she felt Olumiji lightly knocking on the mental door he had helped train her to erect.

Hey there. Good to hear from you. With her greeting came her permission to enter. It had taken her a while to learn that such a request for communication wasn't threatening, wasn't invasive. In fact it was remarkably like having a friend discover that you were online and send you a chat message. You could tell them you were busy. You could ignore them. Or you could talk to them. Your choice. Lola found it funny the extent to which modern social networking had aided her acceptance and understanding of mental links between humans.

Today, Olumiji had caught that she was thinking of him. That was a common occurrence, even among humans with poorly developed gifts. It happened often that one family member or friend would think of another, and suddenly that other would feel motivated to call or contact the first. "I was just thinking about you!" Lola knew that a lot of telephone conversations started with those words.

So she had been thinking of Olumiji and there he was. However, he wanted to do more than say hi.

Lola, I got a sense of you making some exotic travel plans. Belize. Can I know more?

Of course. She sent a rush of feeling that conveyed how happy she was that she had finally been able to tell Alex about her surprising gifts and how adept she had become with them, and how happy she was that he seemed to believe, to accept and even to understand. Olumiji was one of the very few with whom she could almost have word to word contact, but it was still so much easier to just send her feelings.

You and Somadina are incredibly lucky to have found the men you did, he thought. *It bodes well for humans in general, I think, that non-gifted partners can be so supportive. This is a very positive development.*

Well, it's certainly positive for me, she laughed. Then she went on to convey the sense of a celebration, an important wedding anniversary, and a desire to mark the occasion with a special trip.

Why Belize?

I went there once for business, sort of. A field trip. I loved it and thought Alex would too. We both enjoy remote. Why the curiosity?

My sister is there. In Dangriga.

I flew into Dangriga!

She's there with a non-profit doing a sort of community service stint. She's got almost another year and she's more than a little homesick. If you actually go through Dangriga I thought maybe you could just say hi, be a little distraction, you know?

I do and I'd be glad to. Is she…

Not at all. Don't know if I've ever met anyone less receptive.

Jumoke and I are several years older and it must have been tough growing up with the two of us.

Lola started to feel the beginning of the headache that prolonged conversations like this still gave her. Olumiji felt her feel it, and sent his feelings of apology.

I'll send you an email Lola with details. So sorry, so glad you and Alex are well. Take care, friend.

And then he was gone.

In 1917 Congress passed landmark legislation limiting immigration of those over sixteen years old to people who could read in at least one language. The unabashed purpose of the law was to keep out the riff raff, particularly that riff raff coming in from Italy and Poland, which tended to have much lower literacy rates. Congress also added an eight-dollar head tax to discourage the poor.

The oddest part of the new law however, was the implementation of the Asiatic barred zone. This part of the law specified a massive region of the world stretching from Turkey and Saudi Arabia eastward through India, Southeast Asia, Indonesia and on into the Pacific. People from anywhere inside this huge swath of the earth, except for those from the U.S. territories of Guam and the Philippines, were specifically prohibited from migrating to the United States. At all. Any of them. The Asiatic barred zone amendment passed without debate and was not removed until 1952.

"So you believed Jake and Kyle?" Stan fumbled for an opening.

"Yeah, that night I totally believed them. They were so upset about the box being gone," Shelby said.

"But later you got suspicious?" he pushed further.

"The next day. I'm not much of an actress, so when we all got to the cave that next morning I just basically kept quiet and looked distressed, which didn't exactly require role-playing. But the two of them? Something seemed different. They sort of kept looking at each other and, I don't know, something about it was off.

"They seemed guilty?" Stan persisted.

"Maybe," Shelby hesitated. "Maybe more like nervous. But it was nothing more than a suspicion, and I made a bad decision then and there to squelch it and leave well enough alone. I finished my work with you as quickly as I could, interacted with you and them as little as possible, and got the hell off of campus."

And that much was true, Stan thought. Shelby had worked hard and never criticized him, but she had changed after that particular trip. She'd pretty much stopped looking him in the eye in that direct way, and yes, he had noticed it too. But of course Stan had attributed it to Shelby's likely loss of respect for him. He'd basically blamed himself.

"Then why in the world would you make a point of looking me up now?" he asked, genuinely curious.

She looked him right in the eye, just like she had so many years ago. "Because I was really hoping that against all odds the document inside had come back also. I wanted to see if my quick translation was anything close to real, or if it was just a foolish mistake made out of excitement, wishful thinking and inexperience. But of course, it didn't come back," Shelby said matter-of-factly.

Of course, Stan thought. *Of course. Okay, openings didn't get any better.*

"Shelby. About that…"

The fourth time that Alex had the dream, one of the creatures gliding along behind him began to catch up with him. As it grew closer its soft yellow glimmer provided a warm glow in the otherwise massive darkness. He? She? It had a faintly human, androgynous appearance, with a face that looked almost angelic. Not threatening, at any rate. Alex decided to go with "she."

He was startled when she spoke.

"Without us, you are absolutely alone in the universe," she said softly, pleasantly. "Limited to only knowing your own body and that which your body can physically touch. We are absolutely your only way of knowing anything at all beyond your own nerve endings. Good thing we exist." She gave him a friendly smile as she passed him and moved on off into the distance.

Then he woke up.

Xuha and Mr. Zeitman generally met on Saturday morning at a public court in town that was more convenient for both of them than the school courts. They each got there about nine and worked out for a couple of hours. On this Saturday Xuha came a little early hoping to hit the wall and warm up before he had to begin the harder warm-ups Mr. Z gave him. Xuha liked to be at the top of his form for these sessions.

He was over by the wall, pulling out the racquet that Mr. Zeitman had insisted Xuha take once the teacher saw how bad Xuha's own racquet was. Xuha hadn't wanted to tell the man that he got interested in tennis after he found the old racquet in a dumpster. Somehow that just didn't seem like the sort of thing one shared. So he had reluctantly accepted the better, newer racquet and learned to play with it.

When two guys in ski masks stepped out from behind the wall, Xuha's first reaction wasn't fear as much as it was puzzlement.

"What's going on guys? You get lost on the way to the slopes?" Xuha laughed. But they stepped forward in a menacing fashion and Xuha got the point pretty quickly. He could fight. He didn't like to, but he could, and it looked like today he would. At least there were only two of them.

Alex had to park his car further away than usual and as he approached the courts from a distance he saw three boys fighting. Oh not again. He looked closer as he picked up his pace. Two were trying to come in close and get a shorter, stockier boy to the ground, but the short stocky boy was having none of it. The boy, it had to be Xuha. He was using his legs and arms to keep the other two at a distance, moving all four limbs with a speed that surprised Alex.

It appeared to surprise his assailants too. Finally Xuha got a good kick into the groin of one, and spun to sock the other hard on the left side of his nose. Both crumpled in pain. Xuha stopped, hands on his hip, struggling to catch his breath. Then Xuha looked up and saw Alex approaching just as Alex saw a third thug, armed with a crow bar, emerge from behind the wall. Alex started to yell but thug three didn't hesitative. He swung the steel bar as hard as he could into Xuha's right collarbone before Xuha could turn around. Alex thought he heard bone crack, then Xuha doubled over on the ground in pain.

Thug three grabbed his two cohorts by their shirts, pulled them to their feet and shoved them towards the other side of wall.

Alex was torn. He wanted to chase the kids in the worst way and find out who they were. But there were three of them, one with a crow bar, and this was a fight he was likely to lose.

Meanwhile Xuha needed medical attention. Reluctantly, Alex let the three scumbags run off to whatever rock they crawled out from, and turned to help the boy who had truly become his protégé. Alex saw the pain in Xuha's eyes and feared the worst. All this practice. All this effort. And now the boy probably wouldn't get to play out his first season. It seemed so oddly depressing, so completely unfair.

As Alex helped Xuha to his car, he thought quietly to himself that he hadn't ever felt this angry and defeated. No, that wasn't entirely true. He hadn't felt this angry and defeated since he sat in a stupid hospital room in 1981 watching the Grammy Awards and mourning the end of his basketball career. But at least that time the pain had been accidental.

"I knew that you were hiding something." Shelby was actually laughing after Stan told her.

"I thought you might be more, I don't know, disappointed in me," Stan mused. "I always tried too hard to do what was right and then I go and do something so stupid because I was afraid someone had figured out a new clever way to make fun of me."

"I guess I'm more amused at the both of us," she said. "Behaving badly just because we don't want to be laughed at. And it's not like we're good at bad behavior. I've been guilt ridden for going on two decades thinking I may have helped someone steal something. You compromise your ideals once and you can't even keep it a secret. How do you know I won't turn you and your document in?"

"Will you?" But he was sure already that she wouldn't. So he asked, "How do you want to play this, Shelby?"

"Seriously?" she had a little girl's eagerness in her response.

"Seriously. We're partners in crime now, or at least partners in a couple of small lies. We can tell on each other and make each others' professional lives awkward, or we can team up and resolve to be worthy of each other's trust point forward."

"I'm way happier with the trust thing," she said.

"Good. Because I have been working on this translation myself, but I'm stumped in so many places. A second opinion would be truly helpful. We've got some serious interpreting to do." Stan realized that he was grinning like a fool for the first time since… geez, since when? Since 1981, when he'd held a letter in his hand saying he'd gotten into the grad school of his dreams.

Jake Perkins only tucked the letters PhD after his name when he thought it would increase sales. He knew that there was little that was scholarly about him, but he had always had a natural knack for using appearances to his advantage, even back when he had been mucking around in Guatemala.

Funny how those mucking years had stayed with him in ways he would never have guessed. Today, they'd given him two very unexpected messages. The first was from an Atlanta socialite who he had once been in grad school with but had not heard from in years. Pretty Jenny. She'd found him through social networking and hoped he was well. What was he up to these days? Jake decided to hold off on answering her for a while.

The second message came on a disposable cell phone that Jake kept for the sole purpose of receiving occasional messages from only one person. He had seen plenty of crime dramas, after all, and understood all too well how a person's regular cell phone or landline could be used against them. Not that he was paranoid. But it was better to be careful.

He kept the phone in the bottom drawer of the desk in his office in the largest of his three import/export showrooms in Los Angeles, and he tried to remember to give it a quick glance at least once a day when he wasn't traveling, although most days there was of course no message. Just as there wasn't supposed to be. Today, he barely looked at it, feeling so certain that there would be nothing that he almost did not see the something that was there.

"Pursing plan b hpfl lead acapulco v prmising."

Oh for God's sake. Acapulco? Jake put his head in his hands, thinking that a resort place like that had to be freaking expensive and at this point totally unnecessary. Jake, after all, was paying the bills here. This was bullshit.

He almost never responded to texts on this phone, preferring just to get the updates and to leave well enough alone. But today's news was unacceptable.

"Hell no," he typed back. "Not authorized. Not needed. Have good plan in place. Just lie low." He didn't know why he bothered to type it. The person receiving it had never really followed Jake's instructions before, so why would he start now?

Tina was not pleased.

"I told you boys—no physical injuries to your selves or to him that will attract attention. There were three of you. Get him on the ground. Kick him in the stomach, in the crotch and the legs. Hurt him enough to let him know he isn't welcome here and then get yourself out of there. What was so hard about that?" Her exasperation could not have been more obvious.

Tanner sat with his head tilted back, holding a bag of frozen corn against his broken nose.

"That swollen thing is going to make it clear to everyone that you were in a fight, Tanner. You're almost a foot taller and sixty pounds heavier. How did you let him get you in the face like that?"

Tanner shook his head morosely. "The little fucker is way faster than he looks."

"Tanner. Not that word."

"Sorry ma'am."

"And you were hardly a lot of help to anyone, lying on the ground clutching your balls," she said derisively to Tyler. She shook her head in disbelief.

But when she turned to Travis, it was apparent that he was the target of most of her real anger.

"I put you in charge of this mission. Three warriors. Yet you decide to hang back and let your buddies do all the work, and then come out armed to do real medical harm. You cracked his collarbone, you idiot. You think that isn't going to attract attention? Get people looking for who did this? This was supposed to be a stealth operation. Instill a little fear and respect. Period."

"I thought, I thought it was better if we had a contingency plan. The element of surprise, in case he, like, you know, he turned out to be tougher than he looked. And he did. Plus I wanted to put him out of commission for a while." Travis was defensive and still angry himself. "Tennis is a sport for girls and wimps, but I still don't like the way he's putting his stunted brown body out there all over our school's courts."

"Yeah," Tanner joined in. "It's a sport for white girls and our white wimps," he laughed.

"Yeah, well, thanks to your brilliant plan, we've not only got Xuha's parents certainly looking for who did this, but we also have Xuha's tennis coach, personal trainer and all around do-gooder Mr. Zeitman involved." Tina glared back. "Get out of here. Go home. I don't have anything to feed you boys today."

"I wouldn't worry about his parents," Tyler remarked quietly as they gathered up their stuff to leave. "I heard that they're not his real parents, they just take care of him. I don't think there is anything legal about the arrangement, and I also don't think they are here legally. They won't cause any trouble."

"Okay, Tyler, that is useful," Tina said. "If we know we can count on these people not to make a fuss, then maybe this kid Xuha becomes worth making an example out of again. Guardians who can't risk looking out for him? After all this dies down, we may just push a little harder." Tina was smiling now. "How sure are we that Xuha himself is here legally?"

Tyler shrugged.

"I think I'll do some research of my own," Tina said. "This may take a while, but I really don't like what that nasty little spic did to my boys. Come back over Monday after school." Ms. Johnson sounded a little more forgiving. "I'll have some groceries by then."

Nelson read the short interview with disgust. Shelby had treated Stan Drexler like some sort of wronged hero who had finally been vindicated, and had used the piece to basically advocate for a campaign to educate private collectors about the degree to which stolen artifacts are sold to the unsuspecting.

Nelson did not think most buyers were unsuspecting. He did not think that a private collector ever gave up an artifact anonymously after discovering its ill-gotten origins, and he doubted that anyone had in this case.

Then he hesitated. Everyone did things for a reason. So who had sent Stan the box and why? If this wasn't the work of a remorseful collector, then maybe its return wasn't actually good fortune for Stan at all.

That possibility made Nelson feel just a little bit better. Dr. Drexler had been in charge, dammit, didn't the man deserve the full consequences of his poor judgment? Of course he did.

Alex was used to listening to Lola fret about items in the news, and had long ago accepted that she took world events to heart in a way he simply didn't. But tonight she was especially distraught. A drilling rig called the Deepwater Horizon had just exploded in the Gulf of Mexico, apparently killing eleven workers and leaving undetermined amounts of oil spewing out into the sea.

"Geez, those poor men. Their poor families. You know, I've stood out there on the rotary floor, feet away from these guys. Alex, those roughnecks are amazing." She thought for a second. "I could have been out there."

"But you weren't there," Alex said calmly. He knew that Lola's fervor was only partly fueled by her concern about the injuries and deaths. Nigeria had a horrible history of largely ignored oil spills, and Lola was passionate about her industry's need to operate without such destructive mistakes.

"These are my people," she said sadly. "Most of them want to do things right. But they just fucked-up big time."

"Don't get ahead of yourself here," Alex tried to comfort her. "They'll probably have it plugged back up by tomorrow and everything will be fine. ' Your people' do use a lot of great technology."

But Lola only gave him a dubious look as the phone rang and Alex answered it reluctantly.

"Alex? Alex Zeitman?"

"Yes, this is Alex," he replied to the vaguely familiar voice.

"Stan Drexler here. One of my best undergrads just spent her spring break at your house and she insisted I call you. Hard to believe we graduated from high school together thirty-three years ago, isn't it?"

Alex let his irritation at the interruption fall away. Goofy, naïve, eager Stan Drexler had never been a friend, but as Alex had made his way through his teen years he had come to appreciate things about the guy. It was nice to hear that life had apparently treated the man well.

"I've got that student Megan here in my office right now along with your daughter Ariel," Stan added. "I was finishing up for the day when the girls dropped by."

Okay, that explained how Stan got the home phone number.

"Your daughter is a delightful young lady, Alex. She tells me you are back in high school these days, educating our future Nobel Prize winners in physics."

Alex had to laugh at that. "Not too many candidates for that in my classes. But yes, Ariel is great and I'm glad she and Megan got you to call me. And it's good to hear that you're a real professor Stan. You always did love that ancient history. I'm glad you ended up studying it."

As the two men fell into a short but easy conversation, each seemed to forget the extent to which they had once treated each other with a certain amount of distain.

How funny, Alex thought as he hung up the phone. *You never forget high school. But sometimes, years later, you do get the chance to pretend that it was better than it really was.*

April 1697

As Ichik's mother had predicted, the other Itza and even the Kowoj had offered Ichik food and shelter as he passed through their territories. The Chinamita people were more wary, but in this day and age when they shared a common enemy in the Spanish, even they at least let him pass through undisturbed.

After just over three months of carefully making his way through the dense vegetation towards the rising sun, Ichik felt a change in the terrain. He had climbed in elevation for much of the first two months, and descended for most the past several weeks. Now the ground was becoming marshy, and the insects almost unbearable. He climbed a tree for the second time that day to get a better view. And then he saw it.

The giant lake that his mother had spoken of and called the edge of the earth was before him. Along it were houses, built up high on pieces of wood so that they almost looked like they floated in the air. Ichik had never seen such a thing, but he supposed that the builders had done this in order to keep their floors dry. Sensible enough.

Surrounding the houses were giant piles of trees, cut down for what purpose Ichik could not imagine. It was far more wood than any group this size would need for building or for cooking. Clearly tree cutting was the main activity in this village. Strange. Ichik watched the settlement for a while and thought.

Nimah had told her son that this would be the most difficult part of his journey. He had been entrusted with the task of not only getting to this place, but also the task of meeting these people once he got here. Befriending them, becoming accepted by them, living with them. His mother had been quite specific. He was to become one of them, whoever they were. Whatever they were. He was to marry. He was to have children. His children were to be of these people.

But his mother could not have predicted this dilemma, for Ichik could clearly see plenty of people walking around. They posed an unexpected problem.

Half of them had the palest white skin he had ever seen, with hair that was yellow and orange and tan. They were not Itza and they were not Spanish. What were they?

And the other half of them had the darkest skin Ichik had ever seen, almost black, with black hair that curled in ways Ichik did not know hair could. They were not Itza and they were not Spanish either. What were they?

Watching from a distance, Ichik could see that the two groups hardly spoke to each other. They barely interacted. This was indeed a problem. His mother had told him he must become one with those that he met at the end of his journey.

But which of these two people had she meant? Did it matter?

Ichik settled in on the large branch on which he was seated and leaned against the tree trunk, picking leisurely at his teeth with a small twig. There was no hurry, he decided. He knew well how to live off of the land. He would watch these two groups for a while. Finally, when he was ready, he would pick the right one to join.

Chapter 9. May 2010

Something about turning fifteen made Teddie feel stronger. Everyday she was becoming more of a woman and less of a child. She felt her confidence most when she dealt with other kids. She felt it least when she found herself in conflict with adults.

She was learning that many of those conflicts could be avoided with a sweet smile and the appearance of cooperation. Yet, she had no idea how to handle the situation when Ms. Johnson appeared outside her World Geography class and asked the teacher if she could please speak to Teddie Zeitman for a moment. The teacher agreed of course. Teddie nervously complied.

In the hall, Ms. Johnson was waiting for her far enough down the hallway for a private conversion to be possible. Teddie could tell how angry the woman was just from her tight nervous body language.

"I don't know what sort of game you think you are playing young lady, but let me assure you that you do not want to engage in it with me."

"I'm not playing any games ma'am," Teddie said it as politely as she could.

"And what exactly do you call contacting one of my students about getting a second interview about my teaching and my class?"

"I didn't contact anyone," Teddie said surprised. *Oh wait,* she thought. *Tyler had mentioned a second interview to her.*

"Tyler Dodd tells me that you not only contacted him, but that you were rather insistent that he talk to you. He said that he finally had no choice. You do understand that harassing another student is grounds for suspension, don't you?"

"I did not harass anyone Ms. Johnson, honest." Teddie felt the panic rising inside her. "I…" She was about to add that she didn't even particularly *want* to talk to Tyler Dodd when it occurred to her that perhaps that was the wrong approach. Little lies were certainly justified when dealing with creepy dangerous people.

"Tyler's kind of cute, ma'am." Teddie tried to look sweet and harmless. "But if I misunderstood and I'm bothering him of course I'll leave him alone. The article, well," she did her best to look embarrassed, "it was just an excuse. The paper never runs an article on the same thing twice in a row."

Ms. Johnson looked a little bit relieved. "I have a special relationship with some of my students, Teddie. A few of them don't have much of a home life, you know, and I try to look out for them a little more than a teacher normally might. Just trying to do the right thing. I am very sure that Tyler would be happier if you never bothered him again. If you are willing not to cause the boy any more problems, then I think we can consider this little harassment issue over."

Teddie felt herself shudder and hoped it did not show.

"Of course Ms. Johnson. Sorry for the trouble I caused, Ms. Johnson."

As Tina Johnson walked back to her classroom, Tina thought to herself that the conversation had gone rather well. As Teddie walked back into her World Geography class, Teddie thought to herself that Ms. Johnson qualified as an absolute creep. Whatever else was or was not true, Teddie was positive that Tyler Dodd liked her and had sought her out to talk to her. Why he had told Ms. Johnson otherwise was a mystery, and why the woman was intervening on the boy's behalf was stranger still.

Teddie spent the rest of the class period trying to devise ways in which she could loosen Ms. Johnson's grasp on a student she didn't particularly like but was starting to feel just a little sorry for.

Two weeks after he sent his cease and desist message, Jake Perkins got his response. He had been traveling for the past ten days on business and had left the disposable cell phone in its home in the bottom drawer of his office desk. Back now, he gave it its quick daily glance and saw "in Acapulco had to go vry important u don't get it this is it"

Pretty much what Jake had expected. They were always just on the verge of getting answers, or at least so close that Jake would have to fund the most recent harebrained scheme. Over and over. Jake was more than tired of this arrangement. He had thought that there was an agreement in place this time that there would be no more travel, no more expenses, for a while. Jake thought that they had decided to take a new approach. Apparently not. Shit. Jake figured at this point he had three choices.

One. He could keep funneling funds from his successful business into this stupid venture. Two. He could say, "screw it," stop paying the bills and of course risk losing out on a piece of the greatest treasure ever, on the off chance that this time this lead was different. What were the odds?

Three. For once, he could forget about how busy he always was. Make an excuse to his wife and his employees and hope that the two would not compare notes. Then, he could get on a plane, go to Acapulco and find out what the fuck was going on.

Today, door number three sounded highly appealing. Jack pulled up his calendar and gave it a thorough look and then turned to his computer to book a flight.

On impulse, he paused first to send a belated but friendly response to Jennifer's post of two weeks ago. She had, after all, played a part in this whole nonsense too. Perhaps she knew more than Jake realized. Perhaps she could and would be helpful. It certainly wouldn't hurt to have another ally. "Jennifer you little cupcake" he started typing. "How fine to hear from you."

Alex had been relieved to learn that the fracture in Xuha's right collarbone was small and healing well. He genuinely liked the boy, both in class and on the court, and he couldn't lose the feeling that somehow he had been part of the reason that Xuha was targeted in the first place. Even though the attack had put an end to the boy's tennis season, after a few weeks Xuha asked him if they could go back to practice sessions.

"I don't think that's a good idea," Alex hesitated.

"I've been practicing hitting the ball with my left hand. Just very lightly. It's helping me to concentrate on my technique." Xuha seemed determined.

"Okay. Sure." How could you argue with that kind of dedication. It reminded Alex of himself at seventeen, spending hours on a basketball court, practicing a single shot over and over until he could feel the ball slowly leave his fingers, feel it move along its desired trajectory, feel it drop into the basket while he followed its deliberate progress with his mind and body and soul. How could one explain a fascination with something so trivial, so basic? Maybe the fascination had been with getting this one simple thing absolutely perfect. Alex did not know. But he recognized the same dynamic when Xuha picked up a racquet, and so he was happy to help the boy.

Taking a break on the court, the conversation eventually returned to Xuha and his family.

"Xuha isn't a common Mexican name," Alex remarked. "Aztec? Mayan? Do you know much about your heritage?"

"I little. I know that I'm part Spanish, part native Mexican, with my father's side from Mexico City and my mother's people from the area around Acapulco, even though they moved to Mexico City too when my mother was a baby. My first name is Mayan, as was my mother's name and her father's too. It's a tradition in my family. One child is given a first name from this group of ancestors and along with it comes this solemn responsibility. I was my mother's only child and so it came to me, along with a note from my mother. It's what I have of her."

"Responsibility?" Now Alex was curious. "Responsibility for what?"

"Oh, it's nothing. Just a dumb family tradition." Xuha looked embarrassed. Alex tried to think of a response that would put the conversation back on to a better track.

"So does this tradition go on forever?" he tried, and felt gratified when Xuha smiled in relief.

"No. It has an end. My line of people is required to do this thing until it's a good time not to do it."

That's an interesting concept, Alex thought.

Stan and Shelby sat close together at a worktable in the basement of the university's anthropology department, magnifying glasses in hand. Stan had arranged this work session, suggesting to the department head that not only would Shelby's expertise be useful, but perhaps the visit would shake loose helpful memories from her from the day of the original discovery.

Stan's standing in the department had slowly but surely gone up as the box had been authenticated, and the department head had agreed to make the artifact available to the former student for her study.

Shelby had been examining the lid itself now for almost an hour. It was covered in legitimate Mayan hieroglyphs, many of which she could read for herself. They were meticulously carved into the obsidian and were arranged not in rows or columns but rather in concentric half circles. Yet while most of them could be translated individually, they made absolutely no sense when read together one after another.

The sides, on the other hand, were decorated in what could appear to be hieroglyphs to an untrained eye but were merely stylistic designs—attractive but without obvious meaning. Shelby looked at the shape of the box itself. Only one corner made a right angle. If you called that corner the lower right, then the right side of the box was a maybe fifteen inches long. The lid was not hinged, but designed with the same odd dimensions to fit snuggly on top of the box and be lifted off.

She smiled gratefully at Stan. "After all these years, you can't imagine what it means to me to finally get to touch it."

"I do understand, actually. I felt the same way myself."

Shelby thought for a few seconds. "The exact dimensions have of course been measured?"

"Of course. To a tiny fraction of an inch."

"Have you had anyone in your math department look at it?"

"What on earth for?" Stan asked.

"I'm not sure. But the Maya were such a mathematical people, I can't believe they would design something as odd as this without the shape itself having some sort of meaning."

Stan considered. "I'm not sure I want to take such an elementary question to these guys with advanced calculus on their brains."

Shelby nodded her understanding. "What I'm talking about

is more like simple geometry. You don't know any high school geometry teachers by chance, do you?"

"No, but now that you mention it I recently had a conversation with somebody I went to high school with. He's a physics teacher, but back when we were both in geometry together this guy was a real whiz at it."

"I thought you were the smartest kid in your high school class," she teased.

"I was," he said matter-of-factly. "Alex was a jock, and a popular one too. As a freshman in high school it annoyed me to no end that he was actually in an advanced math class with me, and that was made much worse when I discovered that he was better at an academic subject than I was."

"So you parted as mortal enemies?" Shelby asked.

"No, it got way more complicated than that, but suffice to say that there are no hard feelings, and as it turns out his daughter even attends this university."

"No kidding. A student of yours?"

"Not really. She took an intro class with me, she's doing that specialized math computer economics major in the five-year master's program. But thanks to her I know how to reach her dad. I'll give him a call back and see if he feels like looking into an old Maya geometry problem while he's off for the summer."

"Can't hurt," Shelby agreed.

They parted with plans to meet at Stan's the following week to discuss what they both obliquely referred to as the "other piece of information."

After her outburst at the boys following their attack on Xuha, Ms. Johnson seemed almost sorry for the way she had talked to them. After-school treats became consistently more lavish, and she returned to her habit of praising the boys. Tyler waited for the punch line. It turned out that there were two of them, and the first one was good.

Ms. Johnson had been talking a lot lately about how important it was that the white race retain its superiority not only in the realm of physical prowess but also in the realm of mental achievement. "It's what always has set us apart from the more agrarian, simpler races," she explained.

"We invented music and math and science. We ignited the Renaissance. We solved the mysteries of nature. We can't let that slip away or be forgotten. Especially now with all the Asians acting like they own that. We can't let them have it. They simply lack the capacity for creativity and for invention that is bred into the Aryan mind. The world needs us to remain leaders in math and science."

Tanner looked particularly uncomfortable. He'd flunked math his freshman year and he hated science.

"You boys aren't stupid. You can learn anything you have to. I want to make sure that all three of you are taking AP physics next year."

"That's crazy." Travis spoke up. "Tanner here can't pass advanced physics."

"'He can if you help him. Really help him," Ms. Johnson persisted. "You boys need to do this for yourselves and for me. To prove them wrong when they say people like us are stupid or uneducated. We need to show them otherwise."

Tyler considered this a lucky break. He'd wanted to take advanced physics so bad just because Teddie tended to hang around her dad's classroom a lot, and he had been afraid he'd never see her otherwise. Tyler had fully expected that Ms. Johnson would veto the class.

The second edict was less of a problem for Tanner and Travis and more of one for Tyler.

"This summer, I'd like you boys to do a little traveling with me. I think it's time that you met more of the Confederate nation that you belong to, and that some of that nation got to know you. You boys and boys like you are the very future we are hoping for."

"There is, like, a Confederate capital that we are going to go visit?" Tanner asked.

"No Tanner, the Confederacy no longer has a physical capital. Its essence lives on in our hearts. But people who believe what you and I do have rallies and get together, share what we know and provide support for each other."

Tanner and Travis were smiling. "You mean we're going to get to go on a road trip," Travis said.

"Yes, and I want all three of you to come." She looked directly at Tyler as he looked away.

They all knew that Tanner and Travis could pretty much come and go as they pleased. Tanner lived with his dad, who traveled a lot for his job and who drank a fair amount when he was home. Travis lived with his elderly grandmother, who generally didn't even know if Travis was home or not.

But Tyler had parents who often insisted on knowing where he was. They were accepting of, but not wildly enthused, about his friendship with Travis and Tanner, and they remained cautious of all the time he spent after school at Ms. Johnson's house. Tyler did not think there was any way they would let him go on a road trip with her.

"Tyler, it's time for you to start to demonstrate a real commitment to the cause. I expect you to find a way to be able to join us."

Tyler gulped. Junior high and freshman year had been hell after he and his folks had moved here. His life had been so much easier after he'd found Travis and Tanner. He had friends to sit with. No one hassled him. He had somewhere to go after school. He could of course walk away from that, but into what?

"I'll find a way," he assured Ms. Johnson.

"I thought you would," she smiled sweetly.

After World War I, Americans feared that the labor pool would overflow with European refugees, and in 1921, for the first time, Congress imposed numerical controls on immigration. A fixed number of people were allowed to immigrate from each country in Europe, and this number was tied to how many U.S. citizens were here already from that country. This meant that countries such as England, Ireland and Germany had quotas so big that they were never filled, while the small quotas from the less desirable countries filled up fast and applicants were turned away. The result was that the preponderance of citizens with northern and western European ancestry was maintained.

However, there was a loophole for the very determined. Any number of people were still allowed to immigrate into the United States from other North American countries, provided they had lived in that North American country for at least a year. So, in the early 1920s, a number of Italians and Slavs moved to Mexico. From there, they were able to legally immigrate into the U.S. as more desirable Mexicans.

The school year was winding down and the Texas summer heat had arrived. Both Alex and his students were filled with a mix of apathy and longing for the year to be over. For years now Alex had taught five sections of regular physics and the only section of AP physics at Early Gulch. He still marveled at how every year and every class was different. The truth was that this 2009–2010 school year had produced a disappointing crop of advanced physics students. The kids were individually bright enough, but most, if not all, were clearly just in class to fill out their science requirements, memorizing material that they thought they would never use and about which they could have cared less.

Alex wondered how much of that was his own fault. Maybe he had been doing the same thing for too long. Was it getting stale? In truth, the student who showed up for a high school physics class was seldom enthused. But maybe he needed to be working harder these days to capitalize on what little enthusiasm existed.

On the other hand, in spite of some of the behavior problems in his regular physics classes, the students this past year had tended to be more engaged than usual. Even his most potentially unruly class, third period with the three T-heads, as they now called themselves, rose to the standard of intelligent discussion on occasion. Alex wondered how many of his eighty or so first-year physics students would go on to take the more advanced class next year.

This bunch would be a fine group for trying something a little new, something designed to grab the interest of an eighteen year old. What would he have cared about at eighteen? Besides sports and girls? Alex started toying with ideas.

Stan was surprised at how nervous he felt at Shelby's impending visit. His bizarre fantasies ranged from those of her showing up with the police or fellow curators to bust him for his theft, to equally bizarre fantasies of her melting into his arms and wanting him sexually after she viewed the stolen document. He was a rational man and he realized that neither scenario made sense. Finally he put his nervous energy into making the little condo particularly tidy. He went ahead and chilled the good white wine he had bought after noticing that was what she had drunk the other night. No pressure, but it was good to have it on hand.

Shelby smiled at him when he opened the door. "This is where I cross the threshold," she said as she walked in. He knew what she meant. "You can still walk away," he replied, but of course at this point he had to desperately hope that she wouldn't.

"Nope. After a lot of soul searching I see no reason at all why the world would be better served by having this information in the hands of your university. In fact, I can come up with a lot of scenarios in which that is a worse case. Let's solve this mystery Stan. Then we will worry about what to do about it."

He nodded with relief. "A glass of wine?"

"Absolutely." Okay. Stan poured himself one too.

Stan had placed the ancient paper between two pieces of glass to protect it. It had been cut into exactly the same shape as the box, but in this case the letters ran in neat, easy-to-follow rows. Stan laid the glass down on the carpet where it could be examined most easily and safely.

Shelby sat on the floor next to it, sipped her wine quietly and studied it for a while.

"Kind of like a newspaper article," she mused.

"How so?" This analogy had not occurred to Stan.

"You know. Grab 'em with a headline."

"Okay. I see that. Something that basically translates as 'Here are the instructions on how to find the greatest treasure ever' is a damn good way to get a reader's attention."

"Perfectly legible and clear, too. The author had no interest in being subtle here," she said.

"So do you think it's a hoax? Or something else? I don't know, like maybe the equivalent of finding a Publisher's Clearing House ad from another culture."

"Well, maybe, but this first part of the actual text pretty much seems to be a political rant. The writer abhors the Spanish invaders and is pretty unhappy as well with the Maya who have been working with them. Times are awful. People are ugly, hateful and intolerant. Compassion and understanding are in short supply. It goes on for a while."

"Yeah," Stan said. "That's pretty much what I got out of it too. Whoever wrote this was good and pissed. So go on."

Shelby sipped more wine and studied the text for a while. "It's written by a woman. That's interesting. She describes herself as the daughter of a great man. Maybe a king? So she's a princess? Her father has the treasure. Had the treasure. Has hidden the treasure? Has hidden it so well that it cannot possibly be found without these instructions. She is very adamant about that."

"Which is good, I suppose, for inducing one to try to find it. Nice to be reassured that it may not have been found two centuries ago. Not sure that word translates as 'king' though. He's someone important however. So go on."

"He has trusted her and her offspring to be the guardians of this message. No, of *these messages*. There are more of them?"

Again Stan nodded. "That's more or less what I got again." Stan watched Shelby, who was now stretched out on his rug prone, while she struggled with the meaning of the next part of the message.

"There's three of these boxes! It says very plainly that you need all three to make sense of the rest of the message."

"Yes!" Stan was grinning now. "That's how it reads to me. Three boxes."

"Okay," Shelby was wriggling in the floor now in excitement. "She gave the larger of the other two to her oldest son and sent him to the east. She told him to walk until there were no Maya and no Spaniards and to become one with the people he found, to marry and have many children there. Pretty specific. She wants at least one of these boxes completely out of her world and passed on to another whole culture."

"I read it as boy, not son, but I think you may be right," Stan said. "She sent her son."

"A pretty unusual move for a Maya. They were not terribly big on sharing information with outsiders," Shelby mused.

"They didn't have a lot of good options once the Spanish arrived," Stan said. "Plus, this writer seems frustrated with other clans and very determined to protect this information."

"Wait," Shelby said. "She sent a third box off to the west with her other son and told him the same thing. Oh come on. There is no way these other two boxes are still both around and can be found."

Stan was eying her thoughtfully. "We could start checking excavation sites due east and due west of this one. Who knows how far the boys got? We don't normally look for hidden objects, rather artifacts left behind. But having a line to look along and knowing we were searching for something similar, well, maybe..."

"Maybe," Shelby agreed. "What's all the rest of this?" She picked up the magnifying glass. "The writing becomes very tiny."

"That's the part I really wanted your opinion on most."

"It's numbers. Lots and lots of numbers. Are they random?"

"They're not sequential if that is what you mean. But of course there must be some meaning to the order. Believe me, you have no idea how long I have stared at these digits. The first problem, of course, is that the Maya had place values like we do. You know, forty is not the same as zero four."

"Right," Shelby agreed. "Only they stacked their digits up and down instead of running them left to right and they worked in base twenty instead of base ten."

"Sort of," Stan said. "My biggest problem is that I'm have trouble telling where one number ends and the next begins. After all this time I am only sure of two things. There are one-thousand seven-hundred and twenty-eight individual digits listed here, and a lot of them are zeroes. Beyond that, I've yet to find a pattern."

"Is there something significant about one-thousand seven-hundred and twenty-eight?" Shelby wondered.

"Not that's obvious to me. It's twelve cubed, which is kind of cool. It's also thirty-six columns by forty-eight-rows, which is what we have here, but so what?"

"Well it's all pretty clearly an elaborate code of some sort. Why would someone go to all of this trouble?"

Stan reached into his front hall closet with a smile, and pulled out a second, smaller set of glass panels.

"Turns out there was a second page hidden under the first. She apparently wanted to add an afterthought. She literally answers your question."

Shelby eagerly moved closer to the second document and then read aloud.

"I do this because," she began and laughed to Stan. "I do this because this treasure is too great to be found by the greedy and callous." She turned to Stan in an aside, "I think 'greedy and callous' is a good translation." He nodded and Shelby kept reading. "This treasure is too great to be found by the greedy and callous people of today. I do not want them to have it. They will pass away."

"And not soon enough in this lady's opinion it sounds like," Shelby said. Then she read on.

"I do this because this treasure is too great to be lost forever. The kind? compassionate? caring? ones whom I believe with all my heart will live here someday, no matter what their ancestry, must have this treasure as my gift, as my father's gift, to them. May it not be found till then."

"Whew," Shelby said sitting up and shaking her head. "That gives me goose bumps." Stan had moved over next to her to read the final and moving passage again himself. Oddly, he had yet to tire of reading it. Shelby turned and she looked straight into Stan's eyes. "Do you think we are worthy of being the compassionate ones?"

Stan put his arm around her shoulders by way of comfort and she put hers around his waist by way of accepting that comfort and then she was kissing him and of course he was kissing back.

Stan realized that at least one of his bizarre fantasies wasn't nearly as bizarre as it had sounded. And no question, it had been the one that was the vastly better scenario of the two.

The fifth time that Alex had the dream, he was starting to get annoyed. He didn't mind the jogging; it was pleasant enough. In real life, he realized, he hardly jogged at all any more and when he did he grew tired ever more easily. It was discouraging, this getting old. But here he felt like he could run forever, and that was good.

No, he found himself annoyed with the creature's assertion that if not for her and her kind he would be all alone in the universe. That wasn't true. He had people. Lola, Zane, Ariel, Teddie. Friends, co-workers, students. He was most definitely not alone. What was with these creatures?

"You don't like our claim that you depend on us for every bit of information outside of yourself?" one of them asked pleasantly as she came up from behind him.

"No, I don't. This is a stupid dream and I'm getting tired of it and I most definitely am not alone in the universe."

She smiled. "Do you know what I am?"

Alex shrugged, "An angel? An alien? Creatures from a book I read long ago and thought I'd forgotten?"

"Good heavens no," the being actually laughed with a soft tinkling sort of sound. "Nothing like that. I'm a particle of light, Alex. Or a light wave if you prefer. I'm both."

Great, Alex thought. *I'm dreaming about light waves.*

"Think about it, Alex," she continued in a friendly tone. "We, at all of our frequencies from the big radio waves you listen to the tiniest waves that sunburn your skin, are your only way of getting information that comes from a distance away from your body."

"That's not true," Alex said. "I can smell things with out any help from you at all."

"You don't smell anything unless the air carries a tiny particle of the substance into your nose. That's touching your body. It doesn't count."

"Okay," Alex persisted. "I can certainly hear things from a

distance without any electromagnetic information involved what-so-ever."

The creature actually rolled her eyes and sighed. "Technically, hearing is no more than your ear sensing a pressure wave delivered to you by the air. Without air touching your ear it doesn't work at all. It's still touch."

"But I do get information at a distance," Alex persisted.

"It doesn't count. Pressure waves are incredibly slow and you have to be immersed in a medium of some sort." The light creature tossed her head in irritation and moved on out of range. Alex woke up.

Holy shit, he muttered. *It is time for this school year to end. Now I'm dreaming about arguing with light waves…*

When Lola saw that she had an email from Foluke Adewuyi her first thought was that her spam filter was working poorly. Then she laughed and felt a little foolish. Foluke was her friends' younger sister. Lola wasn't proud of the fact, but the truth was that she had enough trouble remembering and pronouncing her Nigerian friends multisyllabic first names, and so she seldom attempted their last names. She simply had not recognized Adewuyi as the family name.

It turned out that Foluke was indeed writing from Dangriga, Belize, and while she did not sound wildly enthused about a day with strangers, she apparently was humoring her brother and making herself available to show the Zeitmans around during their upcoming visit. Lola knew Olumiji well enough to suspect that he had presented this to his sister as a favor to him as well. Each, under the guise of helping him out, would gain something.

Lola's thoughts had not been on Olumiji for more than a minute when she felt Somadina seeking her attention.

Hey you. Lola visualized the giant bowl of strawberry ice cream sitting next to Texas roses on a red-checkered tablecloth, the image that somehow the two women had come to associate with Lola offering a greeting from her world. Somadina responded with the image of red lilies, and a platter of fruits and nuts on a red brocade cloth that, to them both, signified a greeting from hers.

Call me, Somadina sent.

Dialing now. And the two old friends spent a happy dozen or so minutes getting caught up with the accuracy that only words could provide.

"So what's new with Somadina?" Alex asked as Lola finally came to bed.

"How'd you know?"

"She's your buddy dear. The one girlfriend you've got to whom you can tell anything. Your voice goes up with excitement when you two talk."

At Lola's surprised look, he added, "I think it's great. You ought to look into visiting her someday."

"I'd like that a lot, but her big news is that she's pregnant again, and very happy about it. So maybe I'll think about a visit after she has the baby and things settle down a little for her."

Lola paused, knowing that the next piece of news would change the tone of the conversation. "Look, I also heard from Olumiji."

"Oh that's nice." Alex said it as he rolled over as if he were going to go to sleep. He knew that he should say something more but he couldn't think of what. He recognized that he had trouble being as warm about Lola's friendship with the x^0 leader. It wasn't that he was jealous, really. He wasn't by nature possessive of Lola, and neither Lola's love for him nor her loyalty to him was in doubt. But it was hard for Alex not to feel excluded from this particular friendship, and somehow it wasn't quite the same as being excluded from a relationship between two girlfriends.

Furthermore, Alex admitted to himself, Olumiji was one of the very few men who had ever made him feel, well, less than capable in every arena. Alex was adept at so many things, mental and physical, so he was used to being thought of as competent. But no way in hell could he read minds. He didn't even come close.

He didn't think he begrudged Lola the skill. She'd always been adept at things of her own. He didn't even think that he begrudged the entire x^0 organization what it could do. But something about this one super-telepath having a friendship with his wife, well,

Alex just couldn't work up a lot of enthusiasm about it. But he was trying.

"His sister is in Belize, in a town we could easily pass though as part of our trip. He was hoping we might say hi and let her show us around a bit."

"Maybe," was the best Alex could do. "Let's see how our plans work out."

Lola felt the tight little bundle of guilt, resentment and frustration that the mention of Olumiji's name caused and let it be. She'd been told once that having both her gift and a happy life would require all the maturity, compassion and good sense of which she was capable. How true that had turned out to be.

Kyle had been impossible to find. Jennifer wondered if the rumors she had heard about an illness had maybe been true after all. She hadn't really believed them up until now because it was so like Kyle to get fed up with the whole grad school bit and use something like that to make his exit. Clean and easy.

Then again, it would be just like Kyle to be living off of the grid somewhere, growing medical marijuana in California or fleecing clients on Wall Street under a new name. Hard to predict what direction someone like Kyle had gone.

Once again Jennifer studied Jake's response to her. Unlike Kyle, he had been totally easy to find, with ads for his import business plastered all over the internet. Multiple showrooms. He looked highly successful. Maybe a little pudgier and balder, so she guessed that he probably lacked the time and energy to care well for his body. He was no longer much of a stud. Interesting. There were links to a pretty enough wife and a couple of healthy looking teenaged kids. He seemed to have fallen into a very normal life. Interesting too.

Jennifer wrote back. "Coming out to LA this summer for a charity I work with. It would be fun to get caught up. Want to meet for dinner?"

She smiled and hit send. As an afterthought, she went to her favorite search engine and typed in "charities," "headquarters" and

"Los Angeles." Surely there was at least one suitable one out there that would be delighted to have her patronage.

Alex was surprised when Stan called him again only a few weeks later.

"Hey, I know this is out of the blue, but I clearly remember you once having a better feel for geometric shapes than anyone I ever met. Any chance that you might find it fun to just take a stab at looking at the shape of an artifact I've got here to see if anything about it jumps out at you?"

So Alex heard about the oddly designed stone box from his old classmate, and agreed to take a hard look at its exact dimensions.

"I'll send diagrams and photographs and anything at all that I can think of," Stan promised.

"Really, just a sketch with measurements will be okay. I doubt that there is any hidden meaning there, but sure, I'll look for one.

Stan chuckled, then paused as if we wanted to say more. "Thanks Alex."

"Happy to do it."

But in spite of Alex's request to keep it simple, a large manila envelope showed up a few days later with pictures and sketches and all the details one could want and more.

He cares a lot about solving this, Alex thought to himself. *I wonder why.*

May 1697

Most, if not all, cultures encourage persistence. Balam's was no exception. The idea of spending his life diving into a river seeking a precious possession he had lost seemed only noble and right. But after watching three moons wax and wane with no success, Balam was lonely and hungry for cooked food, not to mention more tired of being wet than he would ever have thought possible.

He was seriously considering options that ranged from merely taking a few days off and perhaps hunting for something better than the edible plants, few fish and rare bird eggs that he had been eating, to taking a few years off and coming back to the spot as a stronger grown man, perhaps even, by then, bringing friends or sons of his own to help him. With many diving into the river at once, surely the odds of finding the little stone box would be so much better? Balam knew he was warming to the latter plan.

Funny. Almost no culture has fables or sayings telling folks that there really is a time to quit, a sensible point at which to walk away. Balam had begun to think that was because everybody already knew that particular truth in their hearts. No one needed a clever saying or poem to remind them that sometimes the best thing you can do is to give up.

In the end, Balam made a deal with himself and all that he held sacred. He had started the search on a full moon. He would finish it on one. The next one. And if he then left without the box, which he probably would, then he would solemnly promise to return to this spot with his own sons to continue the search, and if necessary he would instruct his sons to do the same with theirs. Every generation would keep searching until the box was found. Surely that would suffice to fulfill his obligation.

Giving up has an effect. Sometimes it is not a particularly good one, but sometimes it is. After the decision was made, Balam still dove every day, but now he allowed himself to swim around and play a little as well. He relaxed in the water. He took more time to forage food and he ate a little better. A few days before the full moon he felt so strong that he stayed in the river after the sunset, comfortable in the light of the nearly full moon already high enough to be above the trees.

A school of small fish swam by, too little to be of use for eating, and he laughed as their passing tickled his leg. Then he jumped. A bigger fish chasing the school had startled him. As he moved towards shore his toe hit a large rock. Without thinking, Balam went under to retrieve it, expecting one more stone, and instead finding the prized rose-colored agate box.

The spot was well outside of his search area by several arm lengths. Balam stood in waist-deep water clutching the box and shivered. Whether it had been put in his hands because the gods were pleased with him or thrust back into his possession by his frustrated ancestors, he could not know. But he was certain now that he was meant to care for it and to do all that his ancestors had instructed.

Chapter 10. June 2010

"You absolutely promise that your grandmother is gonna say I'm staying there for the weekend?" Tyler asked Travis for the third time that morning.

"Geez, man, stop worrying about it. I told her like twenty times. Even she ought to be able to remember after that."

Tanner, in the front seat of Ms. Johnson's 2001 Chevy four-door Silverado and Travis in the back, were excited and happy. The truck bed held the camping gear for the boys and Ms. Johnson, and several gallon jugs full of lemonade. Tanner and Travis each held a large sheet cake on their laps.

"Us women have to do our part," she explained as she handed the last of the cakes to Tyler to hold. Then to Tanner, who was eying the cake he was holding hungrily. "Make sure you get some of this ginger bread one here, once we get there. It's the best."

But as they got closer to the East Texas town hosting the rally, Ms. Johnson became more pensive.

"There is gonna be a lot of different groups here, you guys, you gotta know that. It's Klan organized, but you got all kinds of freelance sects invited. You're gonna have the CI, that's the Christian Identity people and, well, a lot of young riff raff into all the tattoos and music, and I understand that you guys are gonna want to hang with that group a little."

She hesitated like she was unsure of how much to tell them. "It's supposed to be a rally to bring us all together, to celebrate white identity and the important things we all agree on, and that's why I wanted to bring you, so you could kind of get a feel for, like, all the facets of the movement."

The boys nodded. They were cool with that. It was Ms. Johnson who seemed to be having the second thoughts.

"What I'm trying to say is I want you guys to stay out of trouble. There're some pretty wide gaps between the CI folks and black metal fans, you know? We got bible preachers on one end and devil worshippers on the other. Sure, go listen to music, have some fun. But you three need to stay together and check in with me every so often." They all three nodded agreeably.

"So you really don't remember the names of *any* of the bands that are going to be there?" Travis was incredulous.

"They all pretty much sounded the same to me, Travis. Either German words I couldn't pronounce or things with blood, war or Satan in the name." Ms. Johnson rolled her eyes.

"One last thing, boys. No liquor and no drugs. I mean it. I don't know what some of those biker types are going to bring in and they can't catch everything at the gate. And absolutely no girls. I mean that even more. That's how most fights get started at these things and I just can't take the chance of any of you getting hurt."

"Oh come on," Tanner bellowed in sorrow at the last part of this edict. He had figured he had the best chance of getting laid here that he'd ever had anywhere.

"Tanner. My car, my gear, my food, my rules. I'll be checking on you."

Then, at his dejected look, "Come on. You're gonna love the music, love the people, love the feel of being with all whites and never once having to pretend that it doesn't feel good. And the last night the Klan is gonna put on a fire show that will amaze you. You'll see."

On a Friday night two weeks after he booked the flight, Jake Perkins arrived at Juan N. Álvarez International Airport in Acapulco, with both his family and his business associates appropriately unaware of where he had gone. He looked for a cab to take him to the hotel and was pleasantly surprised to find himself traveling north to the less expensive traditional part of town popular with middle-class Mexicans. Okay. At least he wasn't paying to put his partner up at some glitzy, overpriced high-rise room with a balcony.

Kyle was waiting for him in the modest lobby bar, well tanned, relaxed, his straight coal-black hair worn long enough now to pull back dramatically into a ponytail. He was sipping a beer. The life and look of a well-sponsored treasure hunter appeared to suit him well.

"Whatever you found had damn well better be worth the

aggravation you caused me," Jake grumbled. "We had a plan."

"No," Kyle said slowly. "You had a plan. I, meanwhile, have slowly and methodically been covering ground to the east and to the west of Lake Peten for seventeen years now, and I have finally found our very first bona fide lead." Kyle looked proud of himself. Jake rolled his eyes.

"Okay," Kyle said. "We've had a few false starts that did not pan out. I admit that. Some of the approaches I took early on were ill advised. But that was years ago, before I got a good handle on how to go after this. Today, I promise you, we are exactly where we want to be."

"You're going to tell me why?"

"No. I'm going to do better than that. Monday morning, I'm going to show you." As Jake started to sputter an objection, Kyle lowered his hands slowly as though to hush him. "It's not going anywhere and trust me it will be worth the wait. Drink your beer Jake. Relax. It's happy hour and for once in your life you've got all the time in the world. Try to enjoy it."

Stan and Shelby met a couple of nights a week now, to pore over the document, share ideas, and, well, you know. The ideas weren't coming so fast these days but the "you know" was going extremely well.

Alex had gotten back with some geometrical information, sketched out and mailed to Stan. Shelby studied it. "So we have something here called a right trapezoid. That means that, geometry-wise, it is just a two by twelve rectangle stuck under a right triangle."

"Apparently," Stan said.

"And our right triangle is special" she added, glancing at Alex's scrawled notes.

"It is. It's a three-four-five right triangle. You remember how you square the two sides, add them together and take the square root and that gives you the length of the diagonal side?"

"Uh no, not really. But I don't see how it matters. We don't use the same units of measurement that the Maya did."

"Units don't matter." Stan said. "It's a proportion thing. These aren't inches or centimeters. Alex just took measurements and computed their ratios. The point is that someone took some pains to make the proportions of this box special."

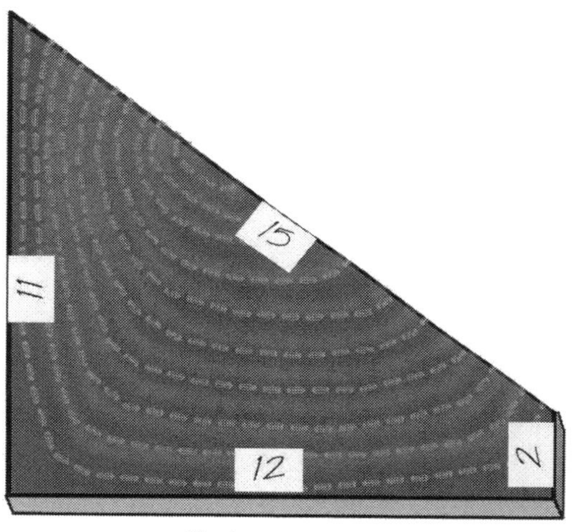

Alex's response

"Why?"

"Maybe it's something religious or personal, but I think it's for the same reason that we'd do it if we were, say, burying such a thing in a time capsule or shooting it out into space. It's a way to say 'Hey, I'm intelligent too' to whomever finds it. It adds credibility."

Shelby nodded. "Okay. I buy that. You know, I've been thinking a lot about the hieroglyphs on the box themselves. These were chiseled in with great care and meant to last." Shelby said.

"I agree."

"Yet there's more here than a nonsensical string of concepts or words. There are spaces, inserted at unpredictable intervals. I think that those are there to make the code harder to break."

"Yeah I sort of assumed the same thing," Stan said.

"More than that, if you look at the actual meanings, my guess is that the maker of the box bothered to chisel words that are never used when one finally decodes the thing. I mean there are words in there that refer to food and cooking and concepts that are just clearly not going to be part of the final message."

"You don't suppose that this great treasure is, I don't know, the best recipe ever for corn tortillas?" Stan was joking. Mostly.

"I hope not," Shelby laughed, "but besides the more obvious problems of the treasure having been already looted or its turning out to exist somewhere we can't access, we have got to accept that it could be, well, allegorical. It could have been a lock of a beloved's hair. We could even be the butt of an ancient joke of some kind."

Stan winced at the last possibility. Then, after a few seconds of thought: "I don't cook much and I didn't so much notice the culinary words but now that you bring it up it sounds to me like, at the very least, the person who designed this interspersed a favorite recipe as filler."

Shelby nodded. "One more way of making the code harder to crack if all you have is the document and the large box." She thought for a minute, troubled now by how her reference to an ancient joke had bothered him.

"You know, the Maya culture was generally hard working, and not overly playful," Shelby said. "We're not talking about a group of people inclined to waste a lot of time for giggles. Whatever this is, I think we can rule out gag gift as an option."

"You're right," he agreed with relief. "But just about anything else is possible. That's what is going to make this so interesting to finally solve."

Tyler wasn't sure what exactly he had expected at the rally, but it wasn't this. Most of it seemed like a cross between a crafts fair and a church picnic. The Christians had sort of carved out a spot for themselves, and their area had the best free food and the highest density of babies. Lots of babies, lots of moms, lots of little kids running around everywhere. Lots of homemade goods for sale. It looked like a quilt festival.

The Klan had placed itself in a central location and appeared to be policing the crowd and handling newcomers. Tyler had noticed that one was only admitted by invitation, and that he, Travis and

Tanner had clearly been permitted in as Ms. J's guests. He did not see a single person who looked like any of his or her ancestors had been other than northern European.

Various other groups had set up booths outside of the Klan's core. There were several selling survival products ranging from non-hybrid seeds to grow food indefinitely while the racial wars were in progress to special cases designed for safely storing and quickly accessing multiple large guns under one's mattress. Several gun dealers had flyers offering discounts to rally attendees.

One booth was recruiting the racially aware to move to a new Aryan homeland in the Northwest. Another sought to sign up Catholics who sought "racial integrity." A third purported to seek donations for the white South Africans who were described as now living "under siege."

Ms. Johnson soon got distracted greeting old friends, and the three boys wandered off, eying the posters and pamphlets and displays. Travis bought himself a ball cap that said "1488" and explained to Tanner that the 88 not only stood for Heil Hitler, which of course Tanner knew, but that it also referred to the name of a book written by a white American patriot, and also referred to 88 key words from *Mein Kampf*.

"You know, it has multiple levels," Travis explained with just a touch of condescension.

Tyler bought himself a black t-shirt with the fourteen words themselves written on the front in bold white print: "We must secure the existence of our people and a future for White Children." The front was okay but he really liked the back of the shirt better. It had an alternative to the fourteen words in a more cursive hand: *"Because the beauty of the White Aryan woman must not perish from the earth,"* and there was just a touch of glitter added to the white script. But the best part was that above the words was a sketch of a gorgeous young girl's face, and Tyler thought that she looked just a little bit like Teddie. He'd paid thirty-five whole dollars for the shirt but the truth was that he would have paid a hundred if he'd had to.

"Stop staring at that shirt," Travis chided him, and because Tyler was worried that Travis suspected why Tyler was so fascinated by the drawing he quickly stuffed the shirt into his backpack. "Let's go check out the really interesting action." And so the three boys wandered off towards the more distant and isolated skinhead section, which was pretty much where they knew that they were going to spend their time all along.

Ariel and Zane's visits to Texas overlapped briefly in June and it was nice to have the whole family together. Alex was glad that Zane still made an effort to come back to visit, even though his vacation time was limited now and travel was expensive. He and his son had always been fond of each other, but Alex had to admit that when Zane was growing up, the two of them weren't particularly close. Alex supposed that it was natural to want one's son to be like oneself. Maybe not sensible to want it. But natural.

Zane had turned out instead to be very much his own person, and now that the process was nearly complete, Alex wondered if he didn't perhaps love the son he actually had more than he would ever have loved a basketball-playing clone of himself.

He heard Zane out on the porch talking to Lola, something about finding English class boring. Okay. There was one thing that he had in common with the boy.

"Can I join you guys?" he asked, walking out onto the porch. For once Lola looked genuinely glad to be interrupted.

"Dad. I'm just talking to Mom about how different I am."

Oh dear, Alex thought. Just when he was feeling so content. Why did Zane's being gay have to come up today? He knew that they should probably have more conversations about it, but, the truth was that Alex struggled to be as comfortable with the subject as the rest of his family was. Lola took one look at him and started to laugh and Alex wondered why.

"We're talking about this, Dad," Zane said evenly. And Alex watched wordlessly as his son's facial features tweaked and moved and twisted in ways he could not possibly move the muscles on his own face. *That's very impressive,* Alex thought. He was envious of Zane's incredible muscle control.

Then he noticed that Zane had not been just wiggling his

eyebrows and his ears. In spite of the thick male eyebrows and Zane's hint of facial hair, Zane's face was now very close to that of Lola's, down to the deep brown of her eyes. Not that there wasn't a resemblance to begin with of course, but…

"Holy shit." In a world that just seemed to keep getting weirder, Alex didn't know what else to say.

"Yeah," Zane said, letting his muscles relax back into the familiar comfort of Zane Zeitman. He grinned. "It's way more effective with a wig. It's amazing how much we judge appearance by hair, which of course I can't alter. I can do this though."

His parents both watched with their mouths slightly open as Zane's face turned rapidly from his normal pale tan to a bright, almost rash red, then, as it changed more slowly to a very deep brown, then on to a pale grey, and then finally back to the normal tan beige of Zane.

Alex was busy trying to figure out how that was even physically possible, while Lola seemed much more concerned about why Zane hadn't told them he could do this sooner. It appeared the young Zane had spent a good bit of his adolescence scared that if he spoke up about what he could do, then his parents would turn him over to nasty government researchers who would lock him away in a lab. *Good lord. So that had been bothering his son all these years?*

"You spent way too much time reading science fiction when you were younger," Alex mumbled. Lola gave him a look that clearly said, "Handle this well." Alex ignored her.

"I'm still not comfortable having this known outside the family." Zane was serious.

"Don't worry," Alex reassured him. "We'll keep this one to ourselves."

Lola persisted with the analysis. "So instead of being a freak yourself, you want to enter a field where you can protect the freaks of the world. All of them."

"You got it, mom. I'd like to help make a world where children who grow up different don't grow up so afraid. Period."

"Wait, Zane's changing jobs?" Out the front door came Ariel carrying a fresh beer for her dad and Alex wondered how she had known. He looked behind his fiery haired daughter and saw Teddie trailing along.

"Zane's going back to school dear," Lola told him. It looked like he had missed an important piece of the earlier conversation. Alex winced. He knew that Ariel's decision to go with a five-year master's program had already stretched them way too thin.

"Zane, I don't know if we can help you much."

His son just laughed. "It's okay, dad, you don't have to help me. Have I got a story to tell you."

"There's more?" Alex asked, noticing that Zane seemed exceptionally pleased with himself.

"Yup." And Zane proudly told his family about how he had helped the dying head of the pharmaceutical company he had worked for this past year, and in return had apparently earned enough appreciation that the man had put aside money to now pay for Zane's schooling.

Alex shook his head in astonishment, genuinely proud. And as they sat on the porch sipping drinks, watching the pale peach colors in the sky fade, Alex thought to himself that this was one of those nice evenings, one of those precious family times, that he hoped he would always remember.

"So when are you going to get married and do your Aryan duty, dear, and make a half dozen or so beautiful little white babies?" Tina's friend Jolene said it kindly, but it still irritated Tina.

"Soon as I find myself a single white male who lives by the family values he preaches," Tina said sharply. "Until then, this little baby is *my* partner," and she patted her shoulder bag.

"You're packing?" Jolene asked in surprise.

"I'm exercising my constitutional rights," Tina said. "I don't go anywhere without my honey here."

"Surely they don't let you bring a gun to school?" Jolene asked.

"Surely they knew better than to ask what I keep in my purse," Tina retorted. "They get metal detectors, I get a new job. I'm serious. As to the other, find me a fellow patriot that doesn't act like an asshole and I'm all his."

"God made you to be subservient, Tina," Jolene chided gently.

"Yeah, well, you and me never did see eye to eye on that one," Tina responded. "I think God made me to fight for my race alongside my man. I just seem to be having trouble finding the right warrior to join."

"So what's your plan?" Jolene persisted, casting a glace towards the three high school boys Tina had brought with her. "Trying to grow your own?"

"Hush, lady," Tina laughed, a little embarrassed. "Those are juveniles over there, and I'm just doing my civic duty educating those boys."

"You're less than eight years older than them, sweetie."

"Yeah, well, once they get out of high school we'll have to see what happens. That's a year away and until then I am one very careful concerned adult. Nothing more."

"Yeah," Jolene gave her friend a little wink. "I can tell."

At first Jake embraced his role of busy, frustrated financier, but by Saturday night the sun, heat and margaritas had worked their magic and left him in no particular hurry. By Sunday he and Kyle were sitting in a bar drinking beers with lime and laughing like it was old times. When he woke up Monday he was more than a little sad that he had to traipse off to a courthouse with Kyle and then board a plane to go home. He made the mistake of saying so.

"I lured you down here for a couple of reasons, my man," Kyle confessed as they walked slowly, drinking coffee and eating pastries as they moved. "That was one of them. How'd you get to be so uptight?" The question only brought back a surge of frustration, however, and Jake decided to let it pass. Sensing that his friend's silence was best left alone, Kyle changed the subject.

"I figured that maybe we were being too cautious with our search. That's because the child our princess sent this direction was the one she talks about as being only ten years old. I'm thinking of my own ten-year-old nephew and I don't seeing him making it ten miles from home. But this kid is considered almost an adult in his world. He's trained to live off of the land. And he probably takes a family obligation much more seriously than you and I can imagine."

Kyle stopped to drain the last of his coffee before he went on. "It says that his mother told him to walk all the way to the sea. If you're going more or less west from Lake Peten, and you've got to be going off course here and there because there are rivers and lakes and even small mountain ranges to cross, anyway, thanks to the curve in southern Mexico you don't hit the sea for a very long time. Not until you get all the way to Acapulco."

"Was Acapulco even here in the late sixteen hundreds?"

Kyle shook his head. Sometimes it was amazing how little history Jake knew.

"Cortez established it as a port back in fifteen-thirty, mi amigo, and had a road built between it and Mexico City in fifteen-thirty-one. By sixteen-ninety, this place had been a thriving town for over one-hundred and fifty years. That's older than Denver is now. And for over a century it had been the Spanish center of trade with the Philippines."

"Okay, okay. So a resourceful but non-Spanish-speaking Maya boy shows up here under instructions to make a new home. What does he do? Find work? Steal?"

"Probably both," Kyle said. By now they were at the courthouse, with Kyle requesting in his perfect Spanish the records he'd been looking at recently. As he and Jake moved to a worktable, Kyle laid a very old book in front of Jake.

"What's this?"

"A list of criminals executed here between seventeen-fifty and eighteen-hundred."

"We don't know the name of our boy."

"We don't. But we do know that in seventeen-fifty-two a thirty-one-year-old male Mestizo described as half Spanish and half Indian was put to death for a string of crimes that he may or may not have committed.

"He's too young," Jake said. Kyle ignored him.

"The man's last name is given as 'de Lago de Peten.'"

"Of Lake Peten?"

"Yeah. Now, given everything you know about the history and geography of this region, how many Maya people do you think moved from Lake Peten to Acapulco to live in a Spanish port city in the early seventeen-hundreds?"

"Okay. You have a point. But he's still too young."

"Of course he is. He's Mestizo. Half Spanish. He's the child of our princess's son."

Now Jake was starting to smile. "Sure. The criminal is born in seventeen-twenty-one. That makes his dad thirty-something when he's born. Old for back then, but not too old to still be fathering children. There must be brothers and sisters. Are there still Lago de Petens living here?"

"No, there are not." Kyle was looking very pleased with himself. "But one of the things you have got to love about the Catholic Church is the way that they kept such good records of births, marriages and deaths. And once you have an actual name to use to start the search…"

"Do you want me to stay? To help you?"

"No need. It may surprise you to learn that I've spent more time here and in churches than in the bars, and I've pretty much got the local de Lago de Peten family tree through the seventeen-hundreds. There was a big earthquake here in seventeen-seventy-six, and records were poorly kept for a few years after and a couple of the lines go cold. I'm guessing deaths in the earthquake. Anyway, I'm up to a marriage in eighteen-o-five and working away."

Jake shook his head in disbelief. "We could actually do this."

"With this information, there's a shot. Of course, even if we find the living heirs, we don't know which one if any has the artifact. It could have been given to a secret mistress, lost in a poker game, even just plain thrown away as junk any time along the way."

"Probably not the latter," Jake said. "If it looks like its larger cousin, it's too pretty for someone to have thrown it away, and I suspect that was by design."

"I agree," Kyle said, "but don't forget that we probably aren't going to get very far without box number three. And even with it, all we have is a set of instructions and a whole new set of problems."

"Hell, you've got a way of bringing a guy down," Jake said. "Keep up the work. I'd be very excited to find myself dealing with these new problems. It would be a nice change of pace."

Except for forays into the other areas for food, the three boys from Early Gulch spent most of the three days listening to the parade of metal bands, interspersed with blaring recorded music when no one was performing live. White power music distributors were there, handing out fliers and concert schedules, and selling CDs and fanzines. The boys were already fans of the dark black metal sounds and the sometimes more lyrical white power skinhead music, but they discovered fascist experimental music and even country and folk musicians who shared their cause, if not their musical tastes. Most of the performers were fairly local, but there were a few big names that the boys had heard of and even a few foreign bands that had made the trek. Who would have thought that a Ukraine National Socialist black metal band would find its way to East Texas and be such a hit?

Tanner snuck in a little beer one night courtesy of a generous neighbor, and Tyler managed to spend the rest of the money he had brought on a knife that no one should have sold to a seventeen year old, but otherwise the boys pretty well followed Tina's guidelines for good conduct. In the end they agreed that given the restrictions on their behavior, it was probably the best three days imaginable. So it was more with regret than anticipation that they made their way on Sunday night back to the central area for the Klan's closing ceremony.

There had of course been speakers on every topic imaginable for the last three days, and Ms. Johnson had encouraged the boys to attend at least a couple of the lectures. But the music had just been so good—it never seemed to make sense to leave it and listen to some old guy talk. Ms. Johnson had seemed a little disappointed that they had not showed more interest in the content of the rally, so as they gathered for the finale Travis went to some pains to show her the fanzines and literature handed out where the bands had been performing. She nodded as she read. "I guess you all have been learning too," she admitted.

A man was addressing the crowd as they gathered and found places to sit.

"It's been a great three days, right?" When only a smattering of people yelled "right" back to him, he gave a laughing, "I can't hear you." "Right," the crowd shrieked back.

The speaker continued to work the crowd in a manner used over the entire breadth of the political spectrum. "Before we get to the show itself, I thought we all could use a little humor. Those of you who know me personally know that I'm no fan of the profession of psychiatry, seeing as how they are all nothing more than one of many fronts for ZOG. But long before ZOG, before the Zionists occupied our government and made it their puppet regime, there were some psychiatrists that made real sense. Seriously." The crowd perked up, anticipating a good punch line from this well known hater of a profession so predominantly Jewish.

The speaker began reading. "In eighteen-fifty-one a prominent Southern physician, Samuel Cartwright, writing in the New Orleans Medical and Surgical Journal, said he'd identified two new types of insanity among slaves. One was drapetomania, which was to be diagnosed whenever a Negro sought to run away. He reasoned that slave owners stirred this mental illness by being too kind to 'their negroes ... treating them as equals,' which confused the poor slaves because God had made them to be 'submissive knee benders,' even giving them a super flexible knee joint for this purpose."

The speaker paused for the laughter he knew would follow. Once the crowd settled down he went on. "The other mental disorder he'd discovered was dysaesthesia aethiopis, which was characterized by idleness and improper respect for the master's property. Cartwright advised that light beatings and hard labor reliably cured this mental illness, as such medicine could turn an 'arrant rascal' into a 'good negro that can hoe or plow.' "

Tyler could feel the kinship and the joy in the crowds amused reaction, and he thought to himself how this world here was so much more interesting, so much more alive than the boring bland life his parents seemed to lead. Hell, even his parents seemed bored with their jobs, their home and each other. How could they possibly expect him to want to follow in their footsteps?

He looked up to see the giant cross soaked in kerosene that was now being pulled upright with a series of pulleys. Men dressed in white hoods stood around it. Others, in assorted costumes and uniforms, were joining them, representing various other factions and sects attending the rally. They marched in solemnly together, sending a message of unity and common purpose. All traces of laughter were gone as they took their places around the cross, contemplating the unacceptable horror of the absolute annihilation of the white race.

Tyler watched fascinated as the massive cross was lit. No race should be eradicated. Certainly not his own. As he watched it burn, he pledged to himself to live a life worthy of these people and of their noble fight.

As more immigrants began to arrive in the 1920s from the rest of the Western Hemisphere, it began to occur to the United States that border patrol might be a good idea. In 1924, forty-five people were hired to keep watch on the eight-thousand miles of U.S. land and sea borders.

At that time 150,000 people per year were allowed by law to immigrate into the U.S. Of course, those from Persia, Arabia, India, China, Southeast Asia, and most Pacific Islands were not allowed in at all. By law, eighty-five percent of those who were allowed in had to come from what were basically Anglo-Saxon nations.

Then in 1929 the U.S. economy collapsed, and for the first time more people began leaving the United States than entering it. In 1932, approximately three times as many people moved out as moved in.

Alex and Xuha continued their tennis workouts into the summer, with Xuha growing stronger each week, as he became a better left-handed player. Finally, after two and a half months, he felt confident enough to try a few gingerly hits right handed.

"I think I will always practice left-handed too. It seems to me the flexibility could be a real asset on the court. For injury, to give my arm a rest or even for just for throwing off an opponent."

Alex agreed. "If I were you I'd focus particularly hard on serving with both hands. That's where you'll get the most impact I think."

And so the two of them worked on serves, first right handed and then left handed, comparing the advantages of each against various hypothetical opponents as they worked. They finally quit when the June sun rose high enough for the Texas summer heat to take over the morning completely.

"That day you got attacked. You still have no idea who they were or why they attacked you?" Alex wondered aloud as they both gulped water and gathered up their gear.

Xuha shook his head. "I mean, I can guess. It's pretty obvious around school who might be inclined to do that. But they didn't say anything to me and no one has threatened me since. I try to stay out of trouble."

"You do," Alex agreed. "But given the way you fought the first two attackers off, I'd guess you've been in a fight or two before. I have to admit, I had no idea you could move that fast, and I work with you physically."

Xuha grinned. "I don't like to fight, but I can if I have to. I know this is going to sound kind of odd, and I'm not sure that I'm explaining it all that well. But if it's a situation where I really have to, or really want to make my body do something, you know, hit a ball or hit a person, it's like everything almost slows down a little for me. So then I can do it. Does that make any sense?"

Alex just looked at him strangely.

"I tried to tell this once to another boy I played soccer with. He was like really scary good and he was trying to help me, give me tips and stuff, and I was afraid he was going to think I was crazy, you know?" Xuha made a crazy face. By now Alex had gotten used to the boy's odd facial humor and he just ignored it.

"But this soccer player didn't think I was crazy at all. He said that's exactly what happened to him sometimes on the soccer field."

Now Xuha really had Alex's attention.

"He told me he wished he could control it, you know, like make a kiss with a pretty girl last longer, but it didn't seem to work that way. It just happened when it needed to and he said that he thought that maybe all great athletes could do that sort of thing when they played, even if they didn't quite realize they were doing it."

"That's a very interesting theory Xuha. Do you think that maybe some people become so good at a sport because they can do that? Or maybe they get really good first and then this technique follows?"

Xuha shrugged. "I've heard some people describe something like it right before a car crash or other kind of emergency. You said you used to be quite a basketball player, Mr. Z? So, did you ever have this happen to you?"

Alex smiled. "Maybe a little. I think I have an idea at least of what it is you're talking about."

"Okay. So anyway, that's what happened to me during that fight you saw. Like I didn't ask for it or anything or tell my body to do it, but these guys just started moving a little slower, you know, slower to me and it made it easier to defend myself."

"I wish that could have somehow protected you from the idiot behind you whom you couldn't see."

"Me too," Xuha said. "For that kind of protection I have to go to my alternate plan."

"What's that?"

"Don't piss people off and stay out of fights."

The sixth time that Alex had the dream, he felt like throwing up.

Not from the jogging, which he seemed to be doing effortlessly. Rather, from the information that the softly glowing light creatures were starting to bring him.

The first passed him and conveyed to Alex that far behind him a man was kneeling helpless in front of another, his hands raised in entreaty. Begging. The standing man held a large rock high over the kneeling man's head. The next glowing creature showed Alex the standing man having lowered the rock just a fraction of an inch. With the next creature came the knowledge that the rock was even lower and that the kneeling man was starting to cry. To plead louder.

And slowly, so very slowly, as each glowing creature passed Alex, Alex saw the scene progress as if he were seeing the individual picture frames in a movie pass before his eyes. Very slowly the rock came down. Very slowly the rock crushed into the kneeling man's skull. Very slowly blood spurted out and gore and a mess that had once been a living human being very, very slowly crumpled to the ground. And Alex felt ill.

"Why did you show me something so awful in such slow motion?"

"We didn't choose to do that." The light creature looked almost offended. "For you, it happened in such slow motion."

"What do you mean, for me?"

"For you. Because you were moving away from the two men so very fast. Half as fast as we ourselves travel. It kept taking us a while to catch up to you and to give you the next piece of information about what was going on. Events only happen for you at the speed at which you see them happening."

"That's ridiculous," Alex said. "Things happen at the speed at which they really happen."

The light creature looked at him almost sadly. "Alex. You know better. There is no 'really.'"

The weekend before Stan left for his semi-annual trip to Guatemala he and Shelby went out to a nice restaurant. Stan still felt awkward about these things but he insisted on picking up the tab. Shelby was becoming more than his partner and colleague. She was kind of his girlfriend and Stan was aware that his six- to ten-week absences had been a problem with past relationships.

Shelby's only issue, however, seemed to be that she wished she was going herself. They had agreed that she would keep a key to

Stan's place, both so she could keep watch over it and so she could study the document at her leisure. Stan was well aware of the trust he was placing in her and it appeared to be on her mind as well.

"I don't know what I was thinking," she muttered as the waiter wheeled away the lavish desert cart.

"About passing on desert?" Stan asked.

"No. When I didn't tell you about Kyle and Jake driving back to the cave. You know, if they could have gotten a hold of the keys to the big truck, I would have insisted on going with them. Then, well, who knows what my part in this might have turned into?"

"You still think they might really have stolen it? I think I was a better judge of character than that, Shelby. Kyle was kind of cynical and not so sure of what he wanted in life and Jake was kind of, well he was Jake. But I just didn't see cold bloodedness in either."

"I didn't either really, but when I was watching them the next day in the cave, I don't know, something struck me as off about their performance in front of you. Maybe I should try to make contact with them while you are gone. You know, just say hi?"

Stan was confused. "You can't contact Kyle. He's dead. Died of complications due to AIDS was the word around campus."

Shelby shrugged. "After he left school sick with something, I never heard about him being hospitalized, never got word of a funeral, you know? It was just one of those circulating rumors that nobody could confirm or deny but sort of came up whenever anybody asked, 'Whatever happened to Kyle?'"

"So you think he's alive?"

"Possibly. He could have dropped out of the whole field of archeology in guilt. Or in disinterest. Or he could be working with Jake. Or be dead. I suspect Jake knows."

"People look up old friends all the time," Stan smiled. Then he stopped. "Wait a minute. Maybe I didn't have the keys to the big truck."

"You did. I don't remember much about that next morning, but I do remember you pulling them out of your pocket, because that truck made such a difference to how my night went."

"Let me rephrase. About half the time Jennifer would leave

something in the truck that she needed. Toiletries. Personal feminine items. Her damned hairbrush. She was always getting the keys from me just before I headed up to bed to go fetch something, and I got tired of her disturbing me to return them. So we got in this habit of her just shoving them back under my door on her way back to her room."

"You sure she wasn't taking your truck out partying? Running around?" Shelby laughed.

"You would have known. You shared a room with her."

"I usually came up to bed before her. She would hang out and come up later. I didn't think too much about it. We were just different. Was your gas gauge ever down in the morning?"

"Never so much so that it caught my attention, but I have to admit that unless I needed to fill, I wasn't really watching it that closely. And it's not like I felt like I had to go out and check on the trucks. There was lots of noise coming and going at that hotel." Stan looked surprised at the realization. "She could have been going out. Partying with the locals."

"You don't think Jennifer stole the artifact, do you?" Shelby was startled by this new idea. Then she shook her head. "I can't imagine it. She and I got along well enough, considering our studies were the only thing we had in common. It's not that she had outstanding ethics or anything, but she was decent enough, and frankly I can't imagine her even wanting to steal something like that."

"I agree," Stan said. "Why don't you look her up too, Shelby? You know that I'm finally going back to the cave for the first time in decades, and I'm going to be asking more questions than usual around town this time to see if I can dredge up any new clues. Maybe you can dredge up a few of your own and when I get back we'll have more pieces of the modern day puzzle to factor into this mess too."

"Hurry back." The nice thing was that Shelby said it with affection and sincerity, but without a bit of self-pity.

The call from Ariel came at nearly the end of June. She had

been back on campus for two weeks now, doing an informal internship with one of her professors, and it had not been going particularly well. The woman was disorganized and seemed to have little for Ariel to do. Even though his daughter was receiving both a little course credit and pay, Alex could tell how frustrated she was. She had already complained a week earlier that she had spent an entire day taking staples out of copies of old papers, punching holes in them and putting them in binders instead. Alex felt bad that the opportunity had turned out so poorly.

This time though, he recognized the excitement in his daughter's voice. "Dad. I'm going to Guatemala. Tomorrow."

"You're what? For an economics professor?"

"No. Don't be ridiculous. Megan's leaving tomorrow with Dr. Drexler and one of the students, the other girl, she had her appendix burst this afternoon. She's going to be okay but there is no way she's going anywhere. I can share Megan's room and I can help out, and I get some credit and a little pay."

"Ariel, you don't know anything about archeology."

His daughter seemed undaunted. "I took a class. And they can't find anyone else this fast and my passport's good and Dr. Drexler says seeing as I'm your daughter and you are actually helping him with his work right now, he'll make an exception and take me along. He says that he could really use an extra person and doesn't want to have to deal with finding a replacement once he's already in the field. So thank you, thank you dad for knowing this guy."

"Don't you already have an internship? In your own field?" Alex asked.

"Yeah. I resigned from it today, and I've never seen someone look more relieved than Dr. Perez did. She truly did not know what to do with me. She told me to have a great summer and we'd work the rest out later."

"Well, Ariel, then I guess this is great. You know that your mother and I are going to be in Belize next month. Maybe we can see you?"

"Sounds good, dad. I think that Belize is close to Guatemala.

Give mom my love. You guys check your email. I'll be in touch."

And then she was gone. Shouldn't she get some shots first? Did she have the right gear? Sometimes Alex marveled at the speed with which his mercurial daughter charged into the unknown.

June 1697

Nimah and her daughter Naylay hid and lived in the cave with the box for almost three months before Nimah dared go back into town. She had heard the screams and seen the flames, and that was more than enough to keep her away. When she finally made her way to her aunt's house she was relieved and happy to find both aunt and uncle alive and their home intact.

"We are doing what we have to," her uncle explained sadly. "We are practical. Our gods do not want us to die. We can claim to worship theirs if it buys us life and freedom. They are only words. The strangers cannot know or change what we believe in our hearts."

"No one should be forced to pretend to worship the God of another!" Nimah responded hotly. "What sort of evil God would even want his followers to do that?"

"Nimah," her aunt said quietly. "You have three children of your own and no husband now. My dear dead sister would want me to ask this of you. Please think of your children, of her grandchildren, before you risk all of your lives for nothing."

"I only have a daughter now," she replied sadly.

"No!" her uncle barked. "Did those monsters kill your sons?"

"I hope not," Nimah said softy, "but I'll never know. I can tell you two now, because the need for secrecy has passed. My father asked me to send my two boys away once the strangers came."

Her aunt and uncle gave each other a knowing look

"Did your father involve you in protecting his family's secrets?"

"He did," she told them. "He said that of all his children, he trusted me to be clever and to find a way to get the job done. And I did."

"I was afraid something like this would happen when your

mother married into that family," her aunt sighed. "Will you and Naylay be okay?"

Nimah smiled reassuringly. "We will be fine. I've plenty of provisions in a well hidden cave, and we will come to visit you often when it seems safe."

"And your boys?" her uncle asked.

"My sons trained and prepared all their lives for their journeys. They will do what they need to do."

"Your father asked a lot of you," her uncle remarked.

"I know," she said. "He had good reason to do so."

Chapter 11. July 2010

Airline bookings fascinated Alex. As the family member who was off work in the summers, he was the resident expert at finding cheap flights and successfully bidding for nice hotel rooms at a fraction of their listed cost. However, even frugal Alex, who always liked to save a few bucks, had his limits.

He and Lola had two choices traveling to Belize. They could board a flight in Houston and fly directly to Belize City. Travel time two hours and thirty minutes.

Or, they could save thirty dollars per person by flying to Dallas, laying over for an hour and a half, flying to Miami, spending the night at the airport in Miami, and then taking a two and a half hour flight early the next morning from Miami to Belize City. Total travel time eighteen hours.

What fascinated Alex most about this scenario was how it just made no sense for anyone. The airlines would in reality spend far more money slinging them and their luggage around. No sane human would choose to spend a night in an airport, and any hotel would cost them more than the total sixty dollars saved. It was an option that was beyond stupid. At yet, some variation of this had shown up as the first twelve flight options on three separate search engines. This was why Alex really, truly did not want computers to run the world.

In fact, Alex thought as he boarded the plane in Houston, the prospect of the upcoming eight days in a world with limited electronics sounded just fine, in spite of the fact that Alex wasn't much for sitting on the beach for hours. His genes had evolved to make the most of misty days and a sun that stayed low in the sky, and his aging back and ongoing knee issues made a beach chair uncomfortable after less than an hour. No, the beach was for Lola. He would have his fun snorkeling with her, and maybe going for a dive or two on a couple of days while she soaked up the sun. He'd talk her into hitting tennis balls a few times in the early morning before it got too hot and she'd talk him into a couple of fancy overpriced meals out that would invariably take way longer than eating dinner ever should, and they'd do a little sightseeing and shopping together even though neither was all that big on either but you just sort of had to do a little of that when you traveled. After twenty-five years they knew how to vacation together, and had evolved a rhythm that worked well enough for both of them. It was nice, comfortable, fun. Alex supposed it was called love.

The last few of days of their journey however, looked like they would be considerably weirder. Lola had argued that they should see more of the country than just a beach resort. Alex had to agree with that. So now they would be spending a couple of nights at a lodge near Maya ruins up in the southwest Belize highlands known as the Maya Mountains. This turned out to be remarkably close to Flores Guatemala where daughter Ariel, friend Megan and Alex's old classmate Stan were all happily digging away. Stan turned out to be willing to gas up his four-wheel drive vehicle and bring the two girls over a hundred or so miles of winding roads for an evening visit and night at the lodge. Okay. That would be weird but interesting.

Then Lola had persisted with her plan to visit her friend's sister, so now the journey would end in Dangriga with a day of sightseeing and dinner with an unknown Nigerian woman. That part would just be weird.

When Jennifer made a myriad of excuses to her family and friends about the trip out to LA in early July, she wasn't really sure herself what it was that she was after. While trying on a variety of travel outfits in front of her full-length mirror, looking for that perfect and important first impression, she finally admitted that she was basically looking for reassurance that sixteen years of life had not diminished her desirability. Okay, she was in fact looking forward to seeing Jake's eyes widen in surprised appreciation when he first saw her. You could only get that particular satisfaction, you know, from a man who had lusted after you once years ago and had not seen you since.

And once she got that satisfaction? Today she had an affectionate relationship that she valued, and causing her man worry was not her way. She honestly wasn't sure how deep her need for reassurance went, but she rather hoped that it didn't go as far as seducing Jake completely.

Of course, Jennifer knew without question that she would have done exactly that years ago. Back in a world with no attachments of her own, she had simply believed in fun. Other adults were adults. If they didn't like their own choices, it wasn't her problem.

Only one tryst in her past gave her pause. Not because of the sex itself, which had been fabulous and which she still didn't regret in the least. No, the pause came from the unintended consequences she had set in motion with her behavior.

Maybe, she thought, maybe the very best option with Jake would be to turn him into her confessor, after all these years, to lay out the whole story of that one night gone horribly awry. Then she could see if he still wanted to have her. If he did, now that would be reassurance. She smiled to herself. The idea had promise.

The authentication of the obsidian box forced a change in Stan's excavation plans for the summer. For the past several years he and his students had focused on the area north of Lake Peten, setting up their home base in one of the small hotels on that side of the lake. However, this summer, he returned to the Flores area of years ago to examine the caves due east of the town for anything that might now help place the box in context. In a sense, Stan's excavation team had "gone home."

At one time Stan's semi-annual digs had as many as twelve graduate students accompanying him, at least on a summer dig. The winter trip, while shorter, drier and more pleasant temperature wise, always involved fewer students. It required a willingness to leave home right after Christmas and, even more problematic, entailed the additional hassle of having to obtain permission to not return to school until the second week of class. Many of his kids not only took classes but also helped teach them, and, like Stan, they were forced to secure short-term subs.

Stan had to admit, at least to himself, that over recent years the popularity of his work had declined among students. Not that there weren't many still drawn by the allure of ancient worlds, but this last decade or so seemed to have produced a more practical breed. More student loans and a declining economy, he supposed, had forced young people to take a harder look at exactly how they were going to make a living with their degrees. The business school was having to beat applicants off with a stick, while he had been forced to open his digs to incoming grad students like Megan and, in an unprecedented move to fill a last minute slot, to a non-major like Ariel Zeitman.

Fortunately, Ariel turned out to be low maintenance, hard working and hardy. Megan had vouched for that already, of course, but all-the-better when it had turned out to be true. And now the same young lady was offering him two more opportunities, neither of which was to be sneezed at.

One, in exchange for a few hours of driving, he was going to get to not only thank Alex Zeitman in person for figuring out that his box contained a special right triangle, but he could also ask the man in person for his discrete and considerably more in-depth assistance. The guy had, after all, been a terrific code cracker as a kid, showing off in class by solving cryptograms in seconds just for fun. Quiet, scrawny fourteen-year-old Stan had watched him solve those puzzles with a mixture of amazement and pure envy.

Which lead Stan to the second opportunity. After thirty-four years, Stan thought that it was time to act like a grown up and clear the air about what had actually happened between them during his senior year of high school. Come on. If two guys weren't adults by the time that they turned fifty-two years old, they never would be. And that would be just too sad.

The beach and snorkeling part of the trip turned out much as Alex expected. He wasn't certified and only managed to get himself on one introductory dive, once again vowing to pursue certification once he got home. What a shame that Lola's underwater claustrophobia kept her from joining him. The reefs at depth had been gorgeous.

The shallow portions of the reefs visible from the near

surface, however, had been another story. They snorkeled together a few times, but each time were disappointed at how sickly the coral appeared. They were even more dismayed to hear later from the guides how reefs the world over appeared to be suffering these days. Climate change? An overdose of gasoline traces from boats and sunscreen traces from tourists? Alex marveled quietly at what a delicate balance the earth maintained, and how easily well meaning curious humans in large numbers could upset that balance.

They left the beaches of Belize with slightly more pigment in their skins, plenty of jewelry and clothing items for the kids, many a fine meal in their stomachs and a happy feeling of relaxation. A good vacation. As the van from their lodge left the lowlands the next morning and entered the mountainous area of western Belize, Alex thought that the vacation portion of this trip had pretty much ended. So he was surprised by the breathtaking beauty.

The lodge itself was nestled in between two small waterfalls and surrounded by tropical forest. Even just standing in the parking lot Alex could see wild orchids growing and brightly colored parrots flitting about. It was a fantasy set in a version of paradise.

"Why don't you tell the world that this place is this gorgeous?" Lola was exclaiming. "Many tourists are a mixed blessing," the driver smiled back at her. *Of course,* Alex thought. *We bring money, something the region sorely needs. But we also bring us.*

The lodge that Lola had selected advertised its allegiance to sustainable ecotourism. In the past Alex had honestly paid very little attention to that concept. But now, looking at the array of spectacular plant life in front of him, and remembering the clear struggle for life on the reefs only a few days ago, he was proud and happy that Lola had persuaded him to spend the extra to be staying at a facility that at least gave some conscious thought to the problem.

Lola talked him into a short hike to see some of the closest ruins. She had only a minimum interest in the history, Alex knew, but she liked the hiking. He could do without the walking around for no good reason, but he had a certain fascination for history. So they passed the afternoon pleasantly. Finally as they walked back Lola asked.

"You know that I can pick up some tension every time Stan Drexler's name comes up. I am trying to stay out of it but given that we're having dinner with the man tonight, you want to at least tell me who shitted on whom?"

"Do I seem like I feel guilty to you?" Alex asked. He was a little curious about just how accurate Lola's abilities were.

"They are very accurate if I know the person well and if I allow the abilities to be so, which I usually do not," she replied. "However, if you want to play games with me, in your case I am happy to play them back."

Alex felt a little embarrassed. "You should be embarrassed," Lola said.

"I get that you kind of did something wrong," she continued. "Not awful. You cheated. Cheated on a paper? Alex… that's horrible! You got caught? By Stan? No, that's not quite right. You two were locked in mortal combat for something. At least you saw it as mortal combat. A competition. You never liked to lose. So you bent the rules, but in the end you didn't want to win that way. So you conceded rather than win on a questionable call. Am I close?"

"You're exactly right. At least, you got every bit of the essential feelings involved, without getting very many of the facts."

"That's pretty much how what I can do works," she shrugged. "Was there plagiarism involved?"

"Just kind of," Alex said. "You may be astounded to learn that writing English papers was never my strong suit or my favorite activity even though I generally managed well enough. Anyway, my high school wasn't very big and frankly wasn't very high achieving. As the two smart kids in the class, Stan and I were vying for valedictorian when this girl transferred in at the end of our junior year. Her dad was the new assistant principal and so it was no surprise that all her courses transferred in perfectly, and thanks to a technicality I can't remember, she nudged both Stan and I out of first. So we kind of ignored her and fought for second place."

"A rivalry thing?"

"I suppose. I didn't really have the good sense back then to know that I had already won in almost every other arena. I was six two, and a star on a sports team. I was honestly kind of shy with girls but I had plenty of them flirting with me, and nobody ever gave me any shit. At the time I was too naive to know how charmed a life I led."

"So you didn't have the normal high school experience," Lola affirmed.

"No, I really didn't. But I hated to lose and so I fought Stan Drexler tooth and nail for class salutatorian. Senior year, when I had a big basketball tournament the same weekend I had a big English paper due, I took some shortcuts. I didn't copy word for word, but I got a hold of a couple of old papers and sort of mashed them together. It was creative, but outside the acceptable guidelines, I'm sure."

"And Stan caught you somehow?" Lola asked.

"No, I caught me. I got the A in the class. A few weeks later I got word that I had a full basketball scholarship at a nice college. Stan had some sort of debate tournament that weekend himself, got a B on his paper and an A-minus in the class. A few weeks after that I heard through the grapevine that Stan Drexler's hopes of going to UT had been crushed. He'd get admitted, but he had to make valedictorian or salutatorian to get a free ride and that's the only possible way he could go. Folks weren't so big on education in the little town I grew up in, Lola, and his certainly weren't. Anyway, I'd bumped him out and ended his dreams. He was going to try to work for his dad for a few years, save some money, maybe pick up a few classes at the nearest community college and see what he could do."

"And then you were ashamed of yourself," Lola said.

"I felt stupid for not realizing that he was playing for much higher stakes than I was."

"So you turned yourself in?" she asked.

"Sort of," he answered. "The trick was convincing an English teacher that I hadn't outright cheated enough to flunk the class and lose my own scholarship, but rather that I deserved something more like a B."

"You convinced her?"

Alex laughed. "That old lady was smarter than she looked.

She revised her grades, she somehow justified it to the administration without raising a fuss, and Stan finished as salutatorian. Hardly anyone ever said a word. He went on to have the life he was meant to have, I guess. I hope."

"So why are you so reluctant to see this man?"

"The whole thing is embarrassing," Alex muttered. "Sometimes it would be nice if the past would just go away."

Lola laughed. "You know what William Faulkner said. 'The past is never dead. It's not even past.'"

"Faulkner?" Alex said. "Really? I think he's one of the people that I wrote that paper about…"

Jennifer made a point of checking in with the LA-based charity she had recently adopted as her own, and then returned to her room to get ready to meet Jake in the lobby bar for a drink. She had finally decided that her tight black jeans and a plunging neckline looked sophisticated yet alluring. She needed to make sure that he arrived first. Making an entrance was essential.

Fifteen minutes after the agreed upon time, Jake looked up to see her walking in, and his expression was everything Jennifer could have hoped for. Oh yes. This had been worth the trip.

Fifteen minutes later both their drinks and their descriptions of their current lives were being finished. Fifteen minutes after that they had drunk a second round and had pretty much exhausted every thing they had to say to each other about every current events topic that they could think of. Fifteen more minutes and they were both laughing and flirting as the conversation had inevitably settled on the past.

Jennifer inquired as to whether Jake had ever, well, found a local girlfriend during the two sessions he had spent excavating with Dr. Drexler.

"Not much in the way of opportunity, actually. Umm, a couple of sweet young ladies on the hotel staff but it never got very far and," he laughed at himself, "that's probably a good thing. Very different culture. I could have ended up married or dead."

He noticed the look she was giving him.

"No, you didn't?" Jake said. "Seriously? With a local boy?""

"Well, yes, a couple of times. But I had to be so careful. Couldn't afford to have some guy bragging and stories getting back to the school and me getting sent home in disgrace. So I mostly had to make do with what we brought with us." She gave a sly smile.

"You did not boink Dr. Drexler?"

"I did not. I had scruples."

"You were doing the deed with Kyle? My roommate. And I never knew it?"

Jake seemed to find this very funny.

"No," she said simply.

"Then who?" Jake looked genuinely puzzled and Jennifer was a little offended.

"Come now. There was another lad with us the winter of ninety-three."

Jake thought a second. "Nelson? You actually had sex with Nelson??"

"I had a lot of sex with Nelson," she said evenly.

"What on earth for?" he asked.

And Jennifer thought to herself that this part wasn't going quite like she had hoped.

Ariel was talkative and full of stories and Alex could tell that the time in Guatemala had worked out surprisingly well for her. He had managed to greet Stan warmly enough and accept the man's thanks for the minor geometry work he had done. As the little group settled into a nice meal at the lodge, the awkwardness dissipated. Until Stan turned to Alex and said softly, "I suppose you think that I've been furious with you all these years for trying to get an A by cheating in class." Ariel's eyebrows shot up in surprise. "We never really spoke after Mrs. Jacobs changed your grade, but I just thought that it was time to finally tell you that there were no hard feelings," Stan added.

"That's good, Stan." Alex said it simply and without emotion. He did not want a discussion.

"I also thought I should tell you that Mrs. Jacobs told me

what you did. Turning yourself in. She told me she wanted the whole incident kept very quiet and I could best help with that if I understood what had happened and didn't make a big fuss."

"Well, that is interesting," Alex was smiling a little bit now. "I had no idea you knew. I figured you probably still hated me for trying to cheat you out of something. In the end, uh, I just didn't want to win a game on an unfair call."

"That's what I figured," Stan said. "That February, after you talked to Mrs. Jacobs, how well do you remember it?"

"Are you crazy? That was the best time of my life." Alex caught Lola's look. "Well, at least for back then."

"Yeah," Stan said, oblivious to the others. "After that, you were on fire. Your playing went up a notch, you took our little school all the way to state in our division. The power of a clear conscience?"

"Maybe, kind of. I was fully focused then, that's for sure."

"Alex. I just wanted to let you know that a fair number of those signs wishing you well pasted all over the halls that you probably assumed were from the pep club—well, a lot of them were made by me. This is a little embarrassing but after what you did, I realized that you weren't a jerk and I became one of your biggest fans. It's kind of stupid, but at fifty-two years old I just wanted to tell you that."

Ariel was fascinated at seeing this new side of her dad. Lola was trying to hide a smile.

"I didn't know that Stan, but I'm glad you told me. I was pretty damn self-absorbed back then, especially through the end of basketball season. When I finally came up for air it was like I'd missed a couple months of my life. At which point I did notice that a kid I'd competed with for years had failed to cause me any trouble at all in spite of the fact that I almost cheated him out of his own dreams. Even I recognized that was pretty damn admirable."

"You're welcome." Now Stan said it simply, figuring it was time to end the discussion.

"I also noticed that boy was headed to state himself, in a speech tournament. Remember that big sign that went up outside that cafeteria cheering you on?"

"Yeah. I thought it was a joke at first. Nobody ever made signs for me. Then kids started signing it, wishing me luck. The day before I left for the tournament it was covered in signatures. It was one of my greatest memories of high school."

"I made the sign," Alex said. "I'm sorry it looked like a joke but that was only because I was really bad at doing things like that. I'd never made a sign for anyone before. Anyway, it looked so pitiful that I talked a few girls into writing on it so it would look better and once they did that, it sort of just caught on."

Both men started laughing, and Ariel heard her mother mutter something.

"What?" Ariel asked her mother.

"Nothing dear. I just said, 'It's not even past.' Faulkner. Long story."

It took yet another round of drinks for Jake to grasp the concept that Nelson would "do things for her." Then, whatever sort of things he decided they must have been, he became a bit more accepting of the concept of "pretty Jenny" getting it on with Nelson the dweeb.

"He got the only single room because he was Dr. Drexler's favorite," Jake mused. "We knocked on his door a couple of times at night when we needed something and he didn't answer. Told us later that he slept with earplugs. That sounded so like him. Were you really in there the whole time?"

"Hardly ever. I had my own roommate chaperone, remember? But that wasn't our thing, anyway. We liked doing it in the dirt in the rainforest."

"With all those bugs and critters around?" Jake looked impressed.

"You want to know what our best night ever was?" Jennifer gave an inviting look.

"Hell yes." *Frankly,* Jake thought, *some walks down memory lane were more interesting than others.*

So Jake heard all about how when Jennifer first saw the beautiful box she absolutely knew that she and Nelson had to have sex in front of it. How she had insisted that he remove it from the cave against his strongest professional scruples and take it out into the big, bug-filled jungle where they could cavort like ancient Maya next to it, or at least like Jennifer imagined ancient Maya had cavorted.

Funny, she confessed to him, after that ultimate act of making Nelson defy both Dr. Drexler and all of his training about leaving an artifact intact, he had little else to offer her. Which was just as well because after the box disappeared old Nelson had gone into major guilt mode and hardly spoke to Jennifer or to anyone else.

"Wait," Jake said. "What am I missing here? After you two danced the funky chicken in front of an archeological find, what did you do with the damn artifact?"

"Nothing," Jennifer said with all sincerity. "We put it back in the cave as close to the way we found it as we possibly could. Nelson was feeling guilty about moving it, but he was going to be fine by the next day. I could tell. I was even going to bang him a few more times just to be polite. And then we show up the next morning and the damn thing is gone again. Poor Dr. Drexler's reputation is completely destroyed. We all look like idiots of the first degree. Nelson goes into this lifelong funk trying to convince himself that it was in no way his fault. And honestly, it wasn't. We put it back around ten o'clock that night and I don't know where it went."

Jake sighed. *What the hell,* he thought. *A little confession was good for the soul.*

"Kyle and I took the other truck and went back to the cave that night too."

Jennifer's eyes got very wide. "No. You two weren't…"

"Good grief, no. We just wanted to photograph the document inside. We probably got there around nine-thirty and I don't have to tell you that the box was gone when we got there. We panicked, we went right back to the hotel and we swore to each other not to tell a soul."

"Well now, weren't we both once a couple of rather poorly behaved students?" she said.

"Weren't we, though…" Jake reached under the table and

laughed as he put his hand on the inside of Jennifer's thigh.

"Are we going to be a couple of poorly behaved adults now?" she said coyly.

Jake paused. He didn't cheat on Gail, he never had. But this was a girl he had lusted after years ago and now she was right here making eyes at him. Jake thought that maybe it could be considered more of a do-over from his past than an out-and-out cheat.

But Jennifer was shaking her head. "I think I've got the same situation as you do," she volunteered.

"He's a good guy?" Jake asked.

"Very good," Jennifer said, as Jake withdrew his hand and nodded.

"Mine too. A fine lady, that is. Do you think it's sad that after all these years when the opportunity presents itself for us, we both decline?" Jake asked.

"I think that everything has a season," Jennifer said. "And this isn't ours. That's okay."

She fumbled around reaching for her purse. "I still enjoyed this meeting very much you know. And it was great to share stories about that terribly weird night with somebody who was there."

As she hugged him goodbye fondly and headed to the elevator bank to go back to her room alone, Jake mentally agreed. He'd enjoyed hearing about Jennifer and Nelson, and somehow it was reassuring to learn that two other students had acted even worse and gotten to the artifact first. Funny. If that was all that had happened that night, he'd actually be feeling pretty damn good right now.

The problem was that the biggest reason he had put his hand on the inside of Jennifer's thigh had been that he was trying to change the subject. Trying to change it quickly and effectively, and he had been at a loss to think of any technique that would work better.

He knew that it was just too important that he not keep talking, especially after so much drinking. Sharing that first story with her had been okay. But he could not possibly risk letting her find out how much weirder that night seventeen years ago had really gotten.

Before the meal was over, it became clear to Alex that Stan had a second reason for wanting to talk with him. Under the pretext of sharing more old times, Stan suggested the two of them move to the bar. Lola, Ariel and Megan tactfully decided to head upstairs.

"Do you think cheating is ever justified?" Stan asked.

"I know my wife doesn't think so," he laughed. "And in general I agree. But situations can be tricky. There are times, well, when all the choices one is given aren't great. Then one does the best one can."

"I've got myself in one of those," Stan blurted out. "I'm not proud of it either, but in the course of figuring out whether I was part of a hoax or not, I withheld some information from my university. Now, as you already know, I'm trying to solve something, and it turns out that it involves this thing that I withheld. No harm done to anyone, but now that I've got it, Alex, I'm looking for a shot at something that was in my grasp once long ago and was taken from me. I'm trying to get that chance back."

"I don't hold that against you Stan," Alex said, puzzled. Why did the man want his approval?

"It's a little more complicated than that," Stan added. "It's pretty important that none of my students know about this. That means of course Megan and, by association, your daughter Ariel."

"It's your business Stan." Alex shrugged. "I'm not about to go out of my way to pass along information to my daughter on something in which I have no real involvement."

"Well, that's the problem," Stan said. "I was hoping you might more get involved."

"Oh… Why?"

"I'm doing more than trying to understand the geometry of an oddly shaped box. I'm trying to crack a code intentionally devised by a very clever Maya that involves a total of three of these boxes and a document I have stashed in my front hall closet."

"Your closet?" Alex asked.

"Yeah."

Alex had to laugh. "The clues are in your closet? And you want my help?"

"Exactly. You used to be very good at this kind of thing," Stan said.

"Yeah, but I don't know the first thing about the Mayan alphabet, Stan, or about their hieroglyphs or whatever they used," Alex said.

"You don't have to," Stan reassured him. "I'm not asking for your help with that. What I normally have going for me is that the writer did not intentionally try to put the message into a code."

"And you think that the author of what you are trying to read did?"

"I know that she did. She more or less says so. And that's the part that could use your eyes. You've already been helpful but I need you to look at this document purely from a code cracking point of view."

"What sort of thing are we trying to solve?" Alex asked.

"I guess you'd have to say it's sort of a treasure hunt." Stan smiled. "A treasure hunt did seem like the sort of thing that you'd like."

"You're offering to make me rich beyond my wildest dreams?" Alex asked skeptically.

"Unlikely. Assuming I can find a way to have this document show up later without causing suspicion and keep myself out of trouble, the best I stand to get out of this is probably the satisfaction of figuring this damn thing out. In the very best case, I end up being known in the end as the guy who solved it, not just the guy who had it taken from him to begin with."

"And you're offering me the satisfaction of helping to solve it," Alex said.

"That's it."

Well now wasn't this interesting? Alex thought.

In one night the person perhaps most likely to hate him in the whole world had not only turned out to be a fan, but was now interested in becoming a collaborator.

"Nobody in my family has to know what I'm working on,"

Alex said. "Get me all the information you have and I'll see what I can come up with."

"I'll give you the general outline of the situation now, and then when I get back in August I'll start sending material to you."

And so the two very different men leaned in over the bar to sketch on a cocktail napkin and start to compare ideas.

Jennifer returned home happy. The idea of sex with Jake had turned out to be secondary to the fun of getting Jake's own confession and the knowledge that she and Nelson had not been the only two people hiding a little professional secret for so many years. Interesting. Who'd have thought?

She was surprised to find an email waiting for her from the one student who appeared to have stayed put that night. Thoughtful, dependable Shelby. Now there was a woman who was never going to get in trouble for anything. They had parted on friendly enough terms, promised to get together often, and then had barely interacted in years. And now suddenly Shelby wanted to have lunch. Interesting also.

Some people have faces that naturally tend towards a smile. Others, towards boredom or sorrow or annoyance. Kyle thought that he had been born with a face that wanted to smirk. Even as a little kid it seemed that he had to work at looking genuine. It was frustrating.

Maybe it was part of the reason that somewhere during his early years his pair of psychiatrist parents had embraced his studious older sister as the one with promise, and written him off as the family fuck-up. They hadn't used that word of course. "More prone to get into trouble." "More likely to question authority." The euphemisms were endless but he got the point. His sister Caitlin was a perfect little angel. He was not.

And so he became the sarcastic, difficult to reach adolescent they had feared. As a young adult he'd avoided real trouble and serious intervention from them, but emotionally he had increasingly gone his own way. Their descriptions of him, always offered frequently and publically, moved away from describing rebellion and more towards phrases like "a loner who has difficulty making emotional ties."

Granted, the smirk had served some uses over the years. A surprising number of girls turned out to like sarcastic boys. He garnered plenty of laughs with his acerbic comments, even though people occasionally assumed irony when it hadn't even been intended. No matter. Irony seemed to be rather well liked.

His junior year in college Kyle finally stumbled on a subject that fascinated him, even though his parents quickly and loudly proclaimed it as useless. He supposed that initially that had made him like anthropology even more. However, in 1993, as he watched his advisor Stan Drexler, twenty-four-year-old Kyle considered for the first time in two decades that maybe for once his parents had been right.

Did he really want a life like Dr. Drexler's? Lecturing, writing papers, digging up pottery shards? Kyle had been in a bit of quandary about his future when he and his one good buddy Jake had made the life-altering decision to sneak back into a cave. That choice had somehow set into motion a chain of events that would lead to a life Kyle had never imagined for himself. And yet, it had turned out to be a life that he loved.

Coming down with mono had been his second stroke of luck. It allowed him to easily take a leave of absence from school, move south of the border, turn his perfect Spanish into everyday Mexican and to hone his abilities as a budding detective. That's when he had decided that he was simply not going back.

He had come up with the AIDS rumor himself. It was perfect because people loved it. Had the sarcastic boy turned to infected prostitutes? Embraced male lovers? Sunk into drug use with needles? It had all the elements of a messy fate dealt out to a sardonic outcast. He knew that the rumor would spread quickly and stick.

He wasn't really hiding, of course, because he knew perfectly well that he could still be found. Rather, he was betting that no one from his past really wanted to find him that bad and that this story would discourage the casual attempt. His family, meanwhile, had been told that he'd fallen in love with both a Mexican girl and her world. He called seldom and came home even less and everyone seemed happy with that.

All the more time to devout to his project. Because the one thing that Kyle knew above all else was that no matter what anyone else in this world thought, he was most emphatically not a fuck-up. He was smart, well-organized, disciplined when he chose to be, hardworking if the situation warranted it, and way more determined than any human being on earth suspected.

And now, he had figured out how to follow the right branch of the tree. He had been thinking about the young Mestizo who had been hung. Only one de Lago de Peten of the right age to be his father had been recorded as dying in the local church. The father's name was Balam. "Jaguar" in the Mayan tongue.

And the key had been found when Kyle noticed that one child of each generation after Balam had clearly been given a Mayan name. It wasn't the man who was hung. It wasn't always a boy. It wasn't always the oldest. Occasionally this heir, as Kyle thought of the Mayan-named child, occasionally this new heir was not even the child of the one carrying the name. Occasionally it was a niece or of a nephew, even sometimes when the name carrier had children of their own.

Kyle wondered what had been used to determine who became the heir. Personality? Perhaps the child's nahual, or animal spirit? Whatever it was, it appeared that one and only one heir was appointed in each generation. Until the earthquake of 1776.

The earthquake had made tracing the family difficult. It looked like the heirs from two generations, a woman named Oyama and a male child named Chac had both died. But an older sister to Oyama survived, for Kyle found records of her burial decades later. Oyama was too old to have more children after the earthquake, but eventually one of her granddaughters was named Raxka, the Mayan word for lightening. And Raxka produced Muluc. And so it went.

Thus, Kyle traced the heir, and he hoped the heirloom, all the way to the birth of Ixchel Rojas, in a small town near Acapulco in

1969. And there the trail went dead. But just for now. Because Ixchel Rojas had to have gone somewhere, and no one had any idea just how determined Kyle-who-was-not-a-fuck-up could be.

Olumiji's sister was a thin, soft-spoken Nigerian woman in her late twenties. She greeted the Zeitmans warmly but apologetically. "My two big brothers are much too protective of me," she said before they had barely exchanged pleasantries. "I fear they've sent you here to check on me for no real reason. I'm a little homesick but doing fine."

"Well then, we just get to see Dangriga for a day and no harm done," Lola said.

"Maybe harm done," Foluke laughed. "Unless you have the time to go out to some of the caves, which are beautiful, Dangriga really doesn't have much to offer." And Foluke was right. The town boasted about ten thousand friendly people, a few meager hotels and restaurants, and not much else. Foluke took them out to tour a hot pepper sauce factory and to see the work of a local artist whose colorful portraits captured the everyday lives around him. Both were nice, but neither something they would have come all this way for.

As Foluke escorted them around, she told them about the Garifuna people who made up much of the inhabitants of southern Belize. "The origins are a little murky," she explained, "because record keeping was so poor. But the most accepted theory is that a shipload of African slaves, from what is now Nigeria and probably in the sixteen-seventies, became shipwrecked on a small island in the Caribbean. They made their way to and ended up living for a century or so on St. Vincent Island, both fighting with and intermarrying the indigenous people there. As Europeans developed an interest in St. Vincent in the late seventeen-hundreds and wanted it for their own, the Garifuna people were transported none-to-gently to an island off of Honduras, where they made their way to the Caribbean coasts of Guatemala, Belize and Honduras. And here they have thrived ever since."

"A resilient and resourceful people," Alex remarked.

"Indeed they are. As a group, they are exceedingly poor by

the world's standards, but rich in friendliness and in hope. Did you know that both Los Angeles and New York in your own country have sizable Garifuna populations?"

"I didn't." Lola was surprised. "How is Garifuna food?"

"It can be hard for a visitor to tell. Dangriga isn't exactly known for its culinary establishments," Foluke laughed, "and most of the restaurants here are Chinese. Belize itself is an incredible ethnic mix. But I think I can find you something authentic to try if you're really up for it."

A short time later Alex was marveling over how absolutely delicious fish boiled in coconut milk and served with mashed plantain could really be.

"It's the garlic and basil that makes it so flavorful," Foluke explained. "Otherwise it's pretty bland and mushy."

"Foluke, can I ask you an odd question?" Alex said. "Actually, a few odd questions?"

Lola perked up, clearly both curious and cautious. Alex gave her a look back that said, "Relax."

"I'm helping an old classmate of mine. He's an anthropologist working just west of here in the area around Flores, Guatemala."

"Did you know that whole border between Guatemala and Belize is under dispute and has been for over seventy years?" Foluke volunteered.

"How big an area is disputed?" Lola asked.

"Guatemala claims about half of Belize."

"No. Seriously?"

Foluke shrugged. "I don't think the people who live on either side of the border even give it much thought any more. Arguments can be made either way and they are still probably decades away from getting the issue resolved, if ever. So the people just go on."

"Amazing." Alex shook his head. "Look, my friend Stan is trying to piece together what might have happened to a Mayan boy sent off by his family to hide when the Spanish invaded Tayasal in sixteen-ninety-seven."

"This is a real boy? I mean, he really existed?" Foluke asked.

"We think he did. He was young, maybe twelve years old, but that was kind of considered a teenager in his time. We think that he was told to go east and walk until he ran into the ocean." At Lola's questioning look, Alex nodded. "Yes, this is part of the puzzle Stan asked me to work on." Alex pulled a map out.

"Look. Dangriga is due east of Flores. Do you have any idea what somebody would have run into here in sixteen-ninety-seven?"

"I don't know," Foluke said. "Wait, I kind of do. Belize was big on exporting mahogany, but that didn't start until the late seventeen-hundreds. Before that, British pirates and assorted—I don't know—hooligans moved in along the coast, mostly attacking Spanish ships. When the looting was lean they supplemented their booty by cutting down a tree called logwood, which was used to make dye for clothes. Doesn't seem like a big deal today, but in sixteen-fifty there weren't so many dependable ways to make your clothes any color but grey. After a while, they became less pirates and more tree-cutters and settlers."

"So there were no Maya along the coast then?"

"Not by then," Foluke seemed certain. "I was told that they all moved inland once the Europeans came. The Baymen, that's what the first English loggers were called, they used slaves to help with the logging. It was a skill and being able to do it well afforded a slave a slightly better life."

"So a twelve year old wandering down to this coast would probably have walked into a logging camp. Do you think they would have killed him?"

Foluke shrugged. "My guess? I think they would have put him to work."

In 1939, the United States denied entry to twenty-thousand Jewish children fleeing Nazi Germany, even though families had already been found here to care for each and every child. The reason for denying these children asylum? Admitting them would have forced us to exceed our set total quota for immigrants for that year, and the rationale in Congress, where the granting of the exception was refused, was that we couldn't just go around bending the rules every time it was convenient.

We did, however, find it in our hearts to bend the rules and negotiate a temporary worker program with Mexico at about the same time. This exception was probably not granted out of humanitarian concern for the Mexican worker, but rather was born of the fact that once we entered the war we were having trouble filling jobs here at home, and we did need to do something about that.

We also rewrote the rules concerning China, as those rules had become rather embarrassing now that China was one of our allies. United now with the Chinese in a common animosity towards the Japanese, we allowed a small number of Chinese to legally immigrate to the United States for the first time since 1882 and lifted the ban that specifically forbade any Chinese immigrant from ever becoming a U.S. citizen.

Tina came home from the rally inspired and pleased. She knew that she had taken quite a risk traveling there with three students, but if these boys graduated from high school as racially aware young men able and willing to spread the word to their receptive friends, then Tina knew that she would have managed to make an honest difference in the struggles that the white race faced.

As for her own future with the boys? Well, originally she had not had a plan. Of course not. She was their teacher. Not some creep.

But once they were eighteen, and out of school, she would just have to see what developed. Travis was an alpha. He'd want some pretty young thing to order around, and he and Tina had never had that sort of chemistry between them. Tanner was a better possibility. Big, strong, not all that smart. He followed Travis blindly but could also use a little direction from the right woman. Travis might like it if Tanner was taking directions from a woman who was already part of the family, so to speak. It could work.

Unfortunately, though, Tina wasn't all that attracted to Tanner. She could probably have him eventually, but big and dumb just wasn't her type. No, the truth was that she'd always had a fond spot for the most difficult member of her threesome. The least committed, and the most questioning.

Tyler came from an educated family. They kind of had had airs about them. Like, Tyler's mother refused to put sugar in the family's iced tea. How snooty was that? Tyler added twice as much sugar at Tina's house of course, but the whole different upbringing thing gave the boy a certain charm. Recruiting people like him into the movement was so important.

Tina smiled wistfully. Could the open-mindedness of Tyler's parents extend one day to accepting a girlfriend eight years older than their son? And maybe even to listening to what that girlfriend believed? She figured she could happily spend the rest of her life transitioning from little, stringy-haired Tina crying to her daddy about being called white trash to being the sophisticated voice of the educated white pride movement, while her young smart husband watched her with his adoring eyes.

Thankfully Alex didn't have the dream again until after he got home.

This time, the light beings were all coming at him from the direction in which he was heading.

"Please. Not another slow motion death," he said to the first when she reached him.

"Alex," she said in the sort of overly patient voice that Lola sometimes used with the children when they were small. "I *always* bring you information at exactly the same speed. No matter what. You need to believe that. You're the one that changes speed, not me."

And she let him see a toddler playing in a kitchen. Alex caught a glimpse of a woman headed out of the room. Her doorbell had rung. It would take only a second to answer it. It was only feet away.

The next light creature showed the little boy looking up at the stove. A pot of boiling water intrigued him. The handle hung out where he could grasp it. But luckily the stove was clear across the room and the little boy wobbled slowly.

"For God sake get back in your kitchen," Alex yelled to the

unknown woman. The next light creature arrived and the little boy was already a quarter of the way across the room. How had that kid moved so quickly?

I've got to get there. I've got to keep that kid from pulling that boiling water down on top of himself, Alex thought. He picked up his pace, running harder, running faster.

And all that happened was that the light beings coming at him started to reach him more rapidly. The boy was halfway to the stove in even less time. As Alex picked up speed he learned more quickly that the boy was three quarters of the way there, and then the boy was at the stove. The boy was moving now like a fast-forwarded video image. As Alex tried to run even faster the boy's arm flew up to reach for the handle of the pot, and then, in an unimaginably short instant the boy had the handle in his hand. Even though Alex wasn't nearly close yet he lunged towards the little boy with all his might.

The woman flew into the room moving every bit as fast as the little boy and scooped him up, crying and hugging him. Alex slowed down in exhaustion, and the woman and small boy began to move more slowly too.

"Now they slow down," Alex muttered miserably.

"Nope. They've been moving at the same pace all along," the light creature said. "But the faster you ran towards them, the more quickly we could get to you with the information about what was happening. You just got updates from us faster and faster."

"So the little boy wasn't really moving that quickly towards the stove at all?"

"Alex," the light creature said. "How many times do I have to tell you? There is no 'really.'"

When Alex finally got back out on the court with Xuha he was amazed at how well the boy had healed. Alex himself played poorly, still stiff from the time spent traveling and still a little groggy from the most recent of the odd dreams that he was having.

When they broke for rest and water, Alex said, "I've been trying to think of sort of a theme for my advanced physics class this year. You know, instead of the same old boring chapter-by-chapter approach, I thought we could come at the entire subject matter from a different point of view, something that would give you kids a chance to think a little more for yourselves and explore some ideas on your own. What do you think?"

Xuha nodded. "I think that letting kids explore and think for themselves is always the best way to teach, if you can get kids to do that."

"Yeah, it doesn't always work as well in practice as one would think. But this should be a pretty good group on the whole," Alex said.

"What were you thinking of for a theme?" Xuha asked.

"Time."

"Could be interesting," Xuha seemed agreeable but not overly impressed.

"Actually, I thought we'd spend the first semester trying to build a time machine," Alex said.

"Build a time machine?" Xuha's surprised face was only half intentional for humor and half quite real. "Can we do that?"

"If you mean can we succeed at doing that, the answer is that I highly doubt it. But maybe if we ignore that fact and try anyway, then we can learn some physics trying."

July 1697

After three months of living in hiding, watching both groups, the older boy Ichik, who had gone east, could still see advantages to joining either. The pale people appeared to have slightly better homes and more things, and some of them appeared to be in charge, often ordering each other and the more richly colored people around. However, the pale people clearly had a shortage of women, and this was a serious problem for Ichik given his mother's instructions.

In the end, after all of his analysis, he decided to simply walk out into the clearing at a time when plenty of each were around, and see who wanted him.

As he stepped out from between the trees, hands empty and

held up in a universal sign of peace, no one paid him much attention. He stepped out further, moving hesitantly towards the pale people, when the pale white-haired old man sitting nearest to him barked and gestured towards the other group. Ichik took it as instructions for him to go with the other people.

Ichik was puzzled. How had the old man decided?

The richly toned people with the curly hair seemed equally puzzled. They were quite sure that this boy who had walked out of the forest wasn't one of them. Yet the old man continued to bark works and gesture, louder and harsher, and Ichik thought, *Fine.*

A few of the very dark women were serving food to the children and Ichik smelled cooking for the first time in months. He moved towards them and looked at the pot hungrily. One of the women turned to one of the men questioningly. The man was tall and strong and had skin darker than the darkest tree trunk Ichik had ever seen. He walked up to Ichik and looked him over. He felt the muscles in Ichik's arms and then used the tips of his fingers to expertly find the muscles in his back. The man nodded and said a word to the woman that Ichik quickly memorized as "yes."

Yes, feed him. Yes, he is strong. Yes, he will help us with our work. But the woman hesitated. Ichik looked into the pot and saw that not all that much food remained. Of course. Food for him was food taken away from one of her own.

"You must be good at this part," his own mother Nimah had told him. "I know that you can be." And so Ichik did what he needed to do.

He looked the woman in the eye and he smiled. With warmth. With pleading. With promise on his face that he would be an asset and worth the food he took. She looked hard into his eyes, hesitated a minute, and then she ladled a helping into a small, crude pottery bowl. As she handed it to him she gave him the slightest of smiles back. And Ichik knew that he had found a home.

Chapter 12. August 2010

One of the unexpected fun things about the trip to Guatemala for Ariel was getting to know Kisa, the woman in charge of housekeeping who sometimes also cared for the hotel room that Ariel shared with Megan. On the nights when the other students fell into a discussion about archeology, Ariel often retired to her room to read and found herself visiting instead with Kisa, who usually dropped off towels or soap in the evenings and was curious about Ariel's world and happy to share information about her own.

Until that summer, Ariel had known embarrassingly little about Maya culture and was amazed to discover that over five million people today considered themselves to be Maya. Kisa spoke her own dialect of Mayan as her first language, but like Ariel she spoke conversational Spanish, and they began their encounters by simply exchanging their knowledge of words. Toalla. Jabón. Champú. Secador de pelo. Ariel guessed that Kisa was in her late twenties, and once they got to know each other a little she seemed particularly curious about the American students and what they were doing.

"The older man, the professor. He used to come here often and then did not come for many years. Do you know why he has come back?" Kisa asked during one of their conversations. Ariel marveled at how much easier it was to pick up the individual words when they were not run together by a native speaker.

She did her best to answer in her own broken Spanish. She had been told that the man had been working for the last several years on the other side of the lake.

"And always he brings different young people with him. Why don't the same ones ever come back?"

Ariel explained that some did come two or three times, but all were students who eventually graduated and moved on.

"Does the professor know what happens to the students when they move on?" Kisa asked.

"I think he probably stays in touch with most of them. Why? Are you looking for someone?" Ariel asked.

Kisa looked down shyly for just a second. "No. I just wanted to know if maybe some of them would come back eventually. As professors themselves."

"I suppose that could happen. Is there anyone you'd like me to ask about?"

Kisa shook her head no, but of course Ariel was sure there must have been. Why else does anyone ask such a question?

Before school started Tina took the boys to a second, smaller one-day rally that featured little more than Southern crafts, copious amounts of fried food and a lot of speeches. It was all Klan and Klan affiliates, and lacked the edgy music and skinhead style that the teens particularly enjoyed at the first rally. And frankly, most of the speakers were boring.

The boys did like the cross burning at the end, though, and on the way home Ms. Johnson suggested that once they turned eighteen they should seriously consider joining. True, most of today's members were older and more family oriented, but joining wouldn't preclude the boys one bit from following their own tastes too, and the Klan needed fresh young warriors like them to keep it vital.

They all told Ms. Johnson that they would consider it. Why not? It was good to keep Ms. J happy.

Then it occurred to Tyler that he finally might have the bargaining chip that he had been looking for. He was, after all, the first of the three to turn eighteen. And Ms. Johnson really wanted the credit for bringing them into the fold. Tyler could tell that.

As Ms. Johnson dropped all three boys off at Travis's grandmother's house, Tyler let the other two boys head inside and lingered behind to talk to Ms. Johnson alone.

She rolled down the car window and looked at him surprised, but like she was happy to see him stay behind for a private exchange.

"Ms. J, my birthday is in October."

"'It is Tyler, isn't it."

That will make me almost an adult. Kind of an adult, won't it?"

"Yes Tyler, in many ways turning eighteen makes you an adult."

"Well, I'd like to join the Klan. Join it right away then if I could, in October. But only if you are ready to think of me as an adult then and treat me as one."

Ms. Johnson shook her head. "I appreciate that sentiment Tyler, I really do. I think I know where you may be going with this." She chuckled softly. "And trust me dear boy, wanting to think of you as an adult is important to me too. But you are still a student at the high school where I teach, and still a former student of mine," Ms. Johnson looked down coyly. "Things have to wait, to unfold in due time."

"I don't see why," Tyler persisted, a little irritated at the response. "What does all that matter? I just want to be considered enough of an adult to bring a girl into our group. To have a girlfriend. Frankly I don't see why I have to wait for that any longer."

"What in the world are you talking about?" Ms. Johnson's voice turned a little shrill.

"Uh, Teddie of course. You know, Teddie Zeitman. She's perfect, Ms. J, and I like her so much. She has this beautiful almost alabaster skin just like the one man was talking about at the rally. And she has a smart mind so I know that she could be made to understand the predicament of the white race if I could just talk to her for a while. She'd be perfect for our group. Her name even starts with a 'T.' We could be the five Ts instead of the four." Tyler knew that in his enthusiasm he was running on. "She'd fit in fine, I know she would and the other guys and you would grow to like her and please Ms. Johnson. Let me start bringing Teddie along after school and I'll be the best new Klan member they've ever had. I promise. Maybe I'll even talk Teddie into joining too once she's old enough, and maybe even someday her and I will be one of those families making quilts and selling jam with cute little white babies running around and…"

Finally Tyler noticed the tight line of Ms. Johnson's mouth and the anger in her eyes. "What's wrong? I thought you people *wanted* me to find an Aryan beauty and make lots of babies."

"Do not ever, ever mention that little witch to me again," Ms. Johnson said quietly. "Do not ever, ever consider bringing her to my house. Join the Klan or not. Your choice, your loss. This discussion is closed."

And with that Ms. Johnson hit the accelerator hard and peeled out of Travis's grandmother's dirt driveway. Tyler watched her go, baffled.

Ixchel Maria Rojas, daughter of Yochi and Inez Rojas, was baptized in the local parish but never made her first communion there. Knowing what he did of the culture in the area at the time, Kyle was certain that if Ixchel lived to second grade she made her first communion somewhere. He tried every parish in a fifty-mile radius. No Ixchel receiving the Blessed Sacrament for the first time. And no Ixchel Maria Rojas having a tragic untimely death.

That left one possibility. The family must have moved away in the early seventies. *Think,* he told himself. This isn't hopeless. Why would they move? Where would they go?

Families often moved to where other family members lived. But Yochi and Inez both came from family that had lived in the Acapulco area now for generations. Kyle considered whether maybe they had migrated to the United States, losing themselves in the mass of agricultural workers who crossed the border. He hoped not. He'd never sort that out.

So Kyle tried to learn more about the family. He sought out school rosters and employment records. And discovered that Yochi was well educated and had worked locally as a secondary math teacher. Inez, more typical of her time and gender, appeared to have been a housewife, but only had one child which was unusual for a Catholic woman of her generation. Medical issues? At any rate, while the family wasn't part of the wealthy, certainly, it did look like they had a hold on a secure existence here. Such people were unlikely to leave home for the dangerous uncertainty of life as undocumented workers. It was much more likely that they had moved because the man had gotten a better job. Where do you usually get a better job? In a bigger city. And the biggest city in all of Mexico was only two-hundred miles to the northeast.

Kyle sent a text. "Fllwing trail to Mexic C. More later."

Ten-million people had called Mexico City home back in 1970, and almost all of them were Roman Catholic. That made for a lot of parishes. But somewhere in there a little girl named Ixchel Maria Rojas had left a record. Kyle was sure of it. It could be found.

August was arguably the very worst month to live in Texas. It was generally as hot as July if not hotter, and everyone was considerably more tired of it. People who spent much time at all outdoors were characterized by attitudes ranging between lethargy and ill tempered. September was almost as bad as August, because the extreme heat was even less welcome by then, but September at least held the promise of a short break or two before its end. August, on the other hand, promised nothing but misery to those setting foot anywhere outdoors that did not involve a lake, a pool or a water park.

This particular August, however, Alex was largely oblivious. On one table he had a stack of books ranging from the scientific to the fanciful, all on the subject of time travel. On another table he now had life-size replicas of both the Maya artifact and of the document from inside. Both projects caused him concern.

On the one hand, word had just made it around that the principal at Early Gulch had been unexpectedly reassigned to another school, and that a new principal was taking over. This wasn't great news for Alex. He had the respect of the old principal and knew that he would have been allowed the leeway to approach the first semester of this advanced physics class the way he wanted as long as he assured the administration that he would cover all the required material before he was done. But he knew nothing of this new lady coming in, and she knew nothing of him. It was unfortunate timing.

Meanwhile, Stan had translated for Alex the introduction of the document and its story of the two sons and the two other boxes. He had shared his theory that the second part of the document, with its list of numbers, was probably a key to reading the apparently random hieroglyphs circling the tops of the boxes themselves. That made sense.

Stan had also provided Alex with the basics of reading Mayan numbers. The digits themselves reminded Alex of Braille and Morse code and the first nineteen numbers were so intuitive that anyone could figure them out. For bigger numbers the largely base twenty number system got more complicated because the Maya had

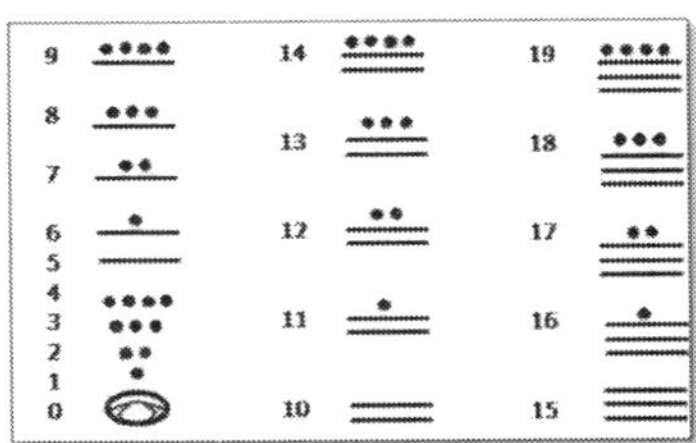

elected to make only their second digit base eighteen, probably to better tie in with their yearly calendar. But if one knew the rules, any number no matter how large could be written in Mayan.

Alex decided that the box must have been shaped so oddly because it was in essence one piece of a three-piece puzzle. The other two boxes were likely trapezoids also, and he was guessing that they could be placed together to form a square, or perhaps a rectangle with some sort of mathematically meaningful proportions. It seemed to him that the Maya liked mathematically meaningful proportions. One of the many cool things about them.

The most obvious approach would be to find a way to tie the long list of numbers to the arcs of hieroglyphs. Maybe put them in pairs and assume that each pair referred to a certain circle and to a place along that circle. Like, the fourth circle from the center, at two o'clock. If Alex could find some way to estimate the shapes and sizes of the other two boxes then he could try to locate the specific words referred to by each pair of numbers. He could leave blanks for the ones that fell on the other two boxes and then Stan could start to translate the ones that fell on the box he did have.

This wouldn't get them the whole message of course, but it

would get over a third of it, assuming that they had the biggest box in hand, and part of a message was way better than none at all. Then as the other two boxes were found, one could then just read off the rest of the message like a code for kids on the back of a cereal box.

Alex was pretty damn proud of himself until he actually tried to do it. Where did the circle start? And what was he to do with the spaces? And because the digits were listed in long columns with no breaks, Alex wasn't sure how to tell an eleven from a one and a one. Alex decided that the person who had designed this little enigma had one clever mind. Unfortunately, she might have designed something so ingenious that the rest of the world could never figure it out.

Jennifer was mildly curious about Shelby's overture of renewed friendship, and the two of them agreed to meet for what they both said was a long overdue lunch. Jennifer arrived early, preferring to watch Shelby enter the restaurant, and she noted that Shelby's style had not improved over the years. Baggy ill-fitting khakis, a bland, loose knit top, comfortable flats and my god she still wore that horribly unflattering braid.

"Shelby! You haven't changed a bit!" Jennifer stood up as the woman came closer and they exchanged a hug. "I really mean it."

"Thanks," Shelby smiled. Then, eying Jennifer's clearly expensive and perfectly put together clothes, shoes, and jewelry Shelby smiled. "I guess you haven't either."

"So I've been meaning to call you for years. What prompted you?"

Shelby had already decided to keep her involvement with Stan to herself for now, and to get straight to the point. It seemed an extreme tactic, but she knew that a direct wavelength had never been Jennifer's natural frequency. So Shelby looked straight into Jennifer's eyes.

"It seems to me that any blame for that Guatemala fiasco has long since run out. And I absolutely don't care at all what you did with whom. Jennifer, I am trying to piece together a puzzle for reasons that will never impact you. Please. Who was it you were fucking that winter in nineteen-ninety-three when the artifact disappeared."

"Oh dear," Jennifer almost looked embarrassed. "What in the world makes you think I was having sex with anyone?"

Shelby paused for just a moment. Jennifer looked thoughtful and didn't say anything.

"I have a good sense of smell," Shelby finally said. "It was hot and humid and we didn't do a lot of laundry. We both left our clothes out all over the room."

"You sniffed my underwear?" Jennifer looked genuinely horrified.

"Good lord, no," Shelby laughed at the thought. "I mostly kicked it under the bed. But some of your clothes reeked of sex. It does have a smell you know."

"Oh. And to think I went to some effort to make sure my shirts were buttoned right and the hair on the back of my head was combed."

"Yes, I noticed that," Shelby said. "I was too shy to say anything back then or maybe I just didn't want to hear the details. I don't know. But at this point I'm betting that whatever was going on is part of what went down that night."

Jennifer gave another little smile and said nothing as the waitress approached the table. After she left with drink orders, Shelby changed tactics again.

"Okay. I'll tell you about the part I played," Shelby said, "and maybe that will make you more comfortable." And for the second time Jennifer heard the story of Kyle and Jake taking off in the truck and leaving Shelby in the bar and the box that wasn't where it was supposed to be at 9:30 at night. Jennifer said nothing as Shelby talked.

Finally, she sipped the lemonade that the waitress had just put on the table and said, "Well, that is interesting. And kind of comical. So okay. No harm with a couple of girls exchanging stories almost two decades later, huh?"

Thus Shelby became the second person in two weeks to be treated to the tantalizing details of Nelson and Jennifer playing like they were on the Discovery Channel for six weeks while Jennifer thought of increasingly bizarre and reckless scenarios to keep their sex interesting.

In the telling of the tale, Jennifer realized how much easier it was to tell a secret the second time around. In the hearing of the tale, Shelby came across some intimate scenarios she had honestly never considered. And finally, at the end of the tale, Jennifer told Shelby of the final act of cavorting in front of the artifact, made all the more pleasurable by coaxing Nelson into moving it, and of its careful, no-harm-done return to the cave later that night. And of course of Nelson's disgust with her, with Dr. Drexler and with the whole world the next morning.

"Nelson always was such a little prick," Shelby remarked. "I understand that you two had some fun but please tell me that you never did it with him again?"

"I didn't particularly want to," Jennifer said. "But no, he would barely look at me after that. He changed advisors when we got back and I don't think he ever spoke more than was absolutely necessary to me or to Dr. Drexler again. It's too bad. We really didn't harm a thing."

"The two stories are pretty funny when you put them together," Shelby agreed. "Thanks for telling me, Jen. I appreciate it. It does, of course, leave unanswered the main question."

"I know," Jennifer said. "So who was it that finally took the box and did not put it back?"

"I'd like to find out."

Jennifer gave Shelby a questioning look, then surprised Shelby with her reply. "Call me if I can help. I do still like solving puzzles too, you know, and I always did feel bad for Dr. Drexler. He was a dweeb too, but a decent guy. He didn't deserve what happened to him."

"You know that I won't hesitate to call if I can use a capable seductress who knows something about archeology," Shelby grinned, doing her best to deflect the discussion away from Stan.

Jennifer hesitated and looked more serious. "Shelby, I did kind of mislead you about a couple things. The first was only because I didn't want to cause trouble for Jake. When I was out in LA last month I looked him up and we had a few drinks. A few too many to be specific. Hadn't seen him since grad school and of course we got to talking about the night the box went missing and he basically told me the same story you just did. I swore to him I wouldn't tell anyone but, well, that promise seems kind of silly in your case. I mean you already know. I thought it may help you to hear that there wasn't any more to it. His version ended just like yours."

Shelby wanted to be annoyed but she recognized Jennifer's conflict. It was probably good that Jennifer did not give up confidences so easily. So she asked cautiously, "What else did you mislead me about?"

Jennifer sighed like it was a much bigger issue. Oh dear.

"I'm telling you the second one because I'd forgotten how much I liked you. My saying that you're looking just the same, well, it's not such a good thing, Shelby. That braid is getting less flattering with the years. Would you have any interest in a trip to a hair salon with me?"

"Nope," Shelby laughed with relief. "I know damn well that you never liked my braid, and I could see the disapproval in your eyes when I walked up. But the thing is, I like it. It's okay. We both get to have our own styles."

"I guess we do." Jennifer didn't quite get why anyone would want to have Shelby's style, but she left it at that. "Give me a call sometime, even if you don't need my help. This was fun." And Shelby thought that Jennifer sounded just a little surprised that it had been.

When the dream came again, Alex was relieved to find himself just jogging along, with no light creatures anywhere near him. They formed little blobs of soft golden glow off in the distance. He jogged easily without interruption.

Finally, as one began to gain on him from behind, she asked pleasantly, "What is it that bothers you about all of this?"

"A lot of things," he said. "So let's start with what doesn't.

Something is happening. No problem with that. You all deliver information on what is happening, moving outward from it, traveling at your very fixed speed. No problem with that. But from then on everything is about information delivery."

"What is wrong with information delivery, Alex?" she asked perplexed. "It's what we do."

"I know. But bear with me here. You have to be delivering it to someone. We are talking about the laws of physics here, and yet a human is required. Which is insane. Or, okay, an alert animal or an alpha centurion or a recording device or something is required but my point is that none of what you're saying about time speeding up and slowing down even happens unless you have somebody to give information to."

"The observer. You are bothered by the fact that the laws of physics include, even in some cases require, an observer to be present," she said, sounding a little surprised.

"Exactly," Alex said with relief. "Physics is a science. It should not require me or anyone else looking at it in order for it to work."

"Are you uncomfortable with the fact that your knowledge of physics and your understanding of philosophy are starting to overlap?" she asked gently.

"Yes, a little. I got into teaching physics because I liked the idea of knowing how the universe really works. I wanted to see the blueprints. And now you keep telling me..."

She smiled with sympathy and understanding as she finished his thought: "... that there is no really. There is only what you see, only what you experience, only what you know. You cannot check what you measure back against the right answer because there is no right answer. Nothing gets distorted. What you see is what is. For you. And I can understand how that would be disconcerting."

"Yes," Alex admitted. "And to think that something so philosophically profound came from asking the sensible, science-oriented question of what would happen if light moved at a fixed and measurable speed. Fixed and measurable kinds of questions should not have it's-whatever-you-think-it-is kinds of answers."

"Well I am most certainly fixed and measurable," she laughed, as she started to move out of earshot. "You do understand that the length of something is every bit as variable as time?" she yelled back to him as a last afterthought.

"I do, I do," Alex muttered at her receding figure. "Let's not go there. I'm still trying to wrap my head around the time thing."

That's when Alex woke up so surprised that he sat up in bed.

"What's the matter?" Lola asked, looking around in concern

"Nothing," he said. "Go back to sleep. I seem to be having bad dreams about special relativity."

"Good thing school's about to start again," she muttered back.

There are at least two time-honored tests to determine whether you love someone that are based on having the person go away for a while and then come back.

Test one. Did you miss them? Seems pretty straightforward and most people are quick to tell themselves, "Of course I did." But the fact is kind of missing, and then again kind of not, because you had forgotten how much fun you used to have without them is not the same as outright "missing" and ought to be cause for concern. Not cause for ending the relationship necessarily. But serious food for thought.

Test two. Once they get back, are they as good as you remembered? We're not talking just the obvious here, good to look at, good in bed, stuff like that, although a serious clash with your memories even about those things is probably a cause for concern too. But this is more a matter of asserting that now that the object of all of your pining is actually on your couch with you, do they listen to you or did you just remember that they did? Laugh with you? Play with you? Not put you down in subtle ways that are hard to explain but you feel none-the-less?

Shelby was already quite aware that Stan had passed test number one. She was fine with her own company and she had some fun in his absence, but she clearly was looking forward to his return. A good sign.

And now, sitting on his couch, damn if he wasn't passing test number two also, listening and laughing with her over the story of Jennifer and Nelson. "I must be the most naive guy in the world. I watched all the guys ogle Jennifer day in and day out, of course, but it never once occurred to me something like that was going on."

Then, seeing the shadow of an expression on Shelby's face, he added quickly, "Getting ogled like that is mostly a matter of style, you know, not so much a matter of looks. Any average looking woman or better can fix herself up to get that kind attention if she wants it. Some ladies find it fun. Some don't. Some don't even know any other style and frankly I always put Jennifer in that last category. Nothing the matter with you or your looks for not choosing the show-off-your-boobs-and-butt look, you know."

And then, at a skeptical, nice try look from Shelby, Stan added with mock seriousness, "I'd really be quite glad to show you right now exactly how much I think of your boobs and butt, if it would help." He grinned.

Okay, test number two passed and then some. Sigh. He was better than she remembered.

As one of the few students returning to the school newspaper for a second year, Teddie was surprised to find herself promoted to a position of assistant editor. It would probably be more work, she acknowledged, but she was only a sophomore and pretty proud of the title none-the-less.

The only problem as far as Teddie could see was that the advisor had chosen to make Teddie assistant editor in charge of student life. Sports, clubs, stuff like that. Teddie couldn't think of a more boring beat. Then again, she realized that given her propensity for seeking out controversial subjects, there was a good chance that the advisor had made the assignment on purpose.

Well, it could be worse. She had an assistant, a senior boy who had never written for the paper before but was all set to focus on sports. Marcus, the quarterback of the football team, was clearly only in the class to fill out a requirement to graduate, and all Teddie could figure was that journalism must have been the only qualifying class that would fit into his schedule. She didn't expect much quality or quantity from him, certainly not during football season, but she had to admit that having the quarterback's byline on a few articles about the football team just might double or triple the number of students who actually read the unimpressive little newspaper.

Besides that, Marcus was friendly and cute. As one of the few African Americans at Early Gulch, he had managed to parlay his athletic skill and congenial nature into acceptance by many of his fellow students, and working with Marcus was at least going to be fun.

Teddie scanned the list of changes to student clubs for the upcoming year, thinking she may be able to do a little feature on each of the new ones. Seriously? They now had one devoted specifically to raising hogs? The one for kids involved in raising livestock had not been enough?

Teddie noted with surprise that the club for Latino students had been disbanded. That was odd; it had been one of the more popular and vibrant groups for the past few years. Maybe there was a story.

The biggest surprise on the list, however, was that the wicked witch of the west, as Teddie thought of Ms. Johnson, was now sponsoring a club of her own. It was a Confederate pride club, for "students wishing to rediscover the heroism and beauty of the Old South." Teddie shuddered. The woman already hated her, and yet this was a story she could not possibly ignore. So now what?

Alex looked over the nineteen students who had for one reason or another made the remarkable decision to take advanced physics. For some, the high level course would help a grade point average. For others, the title of the course would look good on a college application. But these kinds of reasons, so common in some high schools, were generally not factors at Early Gulch, and Alex knew it. Statistically, only a fraction of the students here would get any education beyond high school. A larger percentage would join the military, and some might parlay their science background into better training opportunities there.

More likely, the bulk of the teens in this class were decent enough students who were just trying to get their four years of science taken, had survived physics and this class fit their schedule best. Were any of the nineteen actually interested in physics? Alex was hoping one or two were.

He had mentioned to his department head that he was going to lead off with a bit of an unconventional approach but promised that the class would be on track before the semester was out. She had agreed to be open to his methodology, but had cautioned him that the new administration seemed to have taken a sharp turn towards the conservative and that keeping a low profile with anything new would be wise. So Alex had given a lot of thought to how to best approach this.

It had not escaped his attention that the three skinhead wannabes that had made one of his regular physics classes last year fairly unpleasant were all three enrolled in this one. Alex knew better than to judge by appearances, though. At least two of the boys were more than capable of passing the class. He frankly expected cheating from the third one. His tennis protégé Xuha was there as expected. Finally, he noticed that only five of the students were girls, which was too bad for two reasons.

First, a geophysicist wife and computer savvy daughter had both made Alex aware of the need to encourage females in science and math. He was all for it. But it was hard to encourage when you couldn't get the girls in the class in the first place.

Second, and more selfishly, one sexist stereotype remained with him, but dammit, experience kept showing it to be true. Oh the whole, the girls worked harder and behaved better. With many of them around, the boys behaved better too. A class that was three-quarters male tended to be more challenging for classroom management. So this was going to be interesting.

"How many of you have heard of Albert Einstein and special relativity?"

Alex expected one hundred percent had. He sure hoped so.

"Good. For the first part of this semester, we have the rare privilege of being able to use the same type of equipment Albert

Einstein used to develop that theory, and we have been asked to develop an equally radical and potentially significant theory of our own."

Alex noticed with satisfaction that nineteen kids were looking at him with surprise.

"Early Gulch doesn't have lab equipment," one of the boys said derisively. "We can't afford it."

"We do have this equipment on loan to us," Alex replied.

"What are we going to do with it?" This was asked with just a hint of real curiosity.

Alex smiled. He'd been daydreaming about this moment for over a month.

"We are going to build a time machine."

And now nineteen students eyed him like he was totally bonkers.

"And the very first thing we are going to do is to learn about our lab equipment. Starting today."

Thus the 2010 advanced physics class at Early Gulch began to study the concept of Gedanken experiments, or the idea of using one's brain and powers of reasoning to reach conclusions. Perhaps even amazing conclusions.

"We're going to spend the first couple of weeks of this semester learning how to use our equipment better," Alex explained to the sea of skeptical faces. "In keeping with our appreciation of Dr. Einstein, I am going to be quoting him a fair amount in this class and using his quotes to inspire our activities. Today's quote," and Alex grabbed a marker and headed for the whiteboard. He wrote in large letters: "You do not really understand something unless you can explain it to your grandmother."

Alex saw the eyes roll.

"Sunday, September twelfth is Grandparents Day. That's in three weeks. In keeping with the occasion you will need to furnish a grandparent, or another elderly family member or friend who is willing to attend our class one day that week and to have you explain to them one of several famous thought experiments. You must explain it until they think it more or less makes sense to them."

Travis was aghast. "You seriously are going to ask us to explain physics to our grandmas?" It was then that Alex remembered that Travis lived alone with his grandmother and that the school suspected the woman suffered from worsening dementia. He had forgotten about that problem.

"I do have a small pool of smart elderly folks ready to help out those of you who would rather borrow one of them," he offered and several kids looked relieved.

"Now, here are some of your choices. One per person. I've got the Elitzur–Vaidman bomb-tester to figure out which bombs will go off." Several boys looked up in interest. "Schrödinger's cat is either dead or alive hidden in its box. Anybody into cats? Dead cats?" Alex noticed more interest. "Newton's cannonball is good. Maxwell's demon? Twins in space? Quantum pseudo-telepathy?" Alex went on. "I'm allowing some thought experiments that are more philosophical or mathematical because the point here is to understand the process. Take Kavka's toxin to earn a million dollars but only if you can intend to drink something awful that you don't actually have to. Find a way to paint the angel Gabriel's horn. Read over the list, folks, I've got thirty of them here. Do a little research on your own if you want. Get back to me next class with your top three choices."

"So our equipment is nothing more than our brains?" Xuha seemed a little disappointed.

"Yeah, I was hoping for something with lasers," another boy added.

"Learn to use this equipment well and you'll be surprised what can be discovered," Alex replied. "Even about lasers. It's the most versatile equipment that we have for understanding the universe."

Stan and Shelby pretty much just enjoyed themselves for the first week after Stan got back. But by the following weekend they were both getting antsy to get organized on their mutual project.

"Let's review the bidding," Stan said.

"You play bridge?" Shelby asked surprised.

"Actually I do."

"Really. Me too."

Stan fought the impulse to get distracted.

"I want to go back for a minute and think through what we know about what actually happened 'that night.' To review: One. Jennifer has been contacted and you believe her cavorting in front of a sacred object story."

"True."

"Two. Nobody's talked to Nelson. There is some small chance that he kept the keys to the truck and went back out and removed the box a second time that night for reasons we don't understand. Then he would be the one who shoved the keys under my door."

"Yes, but Jennifer would know that. She didn't say anything about it to me."

Stan thought. "She may not have remembered, she may not have thought it was important. But geez why would Nelson be so pissy all these years if he actually took the damn thing?"

"I'll run that key thing by Jennifer," Shelby said. "She's harmless and she'd like to help. I didn't tell her about you and me, you know, but I think she might have had her suspicions and I see no reason to exclude her. I'm willing to put her in the good guy column."

Stan nodded his agreement. "Then there is door number three. Jake. You're going to see him next month when you go out to LA, but no one has talked to him since."

"Not entirely true. Yes, I'll see him. But Jennifer was in LA earlier this summer and she visited with him. They shared some drinks. He basically confirmed my story with no secret return later that night."

"But that's just what he told Jennifer. He could be lying," Stan pointed out. Shelby agreed.

"Option four. Kyle. Dead, missing, AWOL, whatever. We need to find out if Jake knows where he is, and if not I think we need to consider hiring a pro to find him."

"That's expensive you know," Shelby said.

"Yeah, but by default he's our most likely suspect until we do that. After that it's option five, a total stranger. Total stranger used to make no sense to me, but now I suppose given all the comings and goings that night to and from the cave, any number of locals or even some of the other academic types excavating in the general area could have followed somebody and taken it."

Shelby interrupted. "Stan, what's more important here, the past or the present?"

"What do you mean?"

"You know where the artifact is. It's here. I'm just saying that with limited time and resources I think you may have to choose between figuring out what happened back then, which I know you truly want to do, and figuring out what to do now. And now may be more important."

Stan nodded. He got the point. "Now is more important. No question. The only problem is that now is tied to the past, isn't it? So knowing when to let go of the past is always a problem."

"Isn't that the truth," Shelby said. "And not just for archeologists."

Alex stood in the parking lot with his hands full of books and supplies to bring into his classroom. School was out for the day and it was better to carry all this stuff back in now rather than deal with it in the morning when he would inevitably be running late. The heat sizzled off of the asphalt and the glare of the late afternoon sun on the windshields was blinding. He gave the car door a hard push with his knee and then he remembered. His keys were on the car seat. The locks were on. Damn.

Alex dropped the books and thrust his hands into the narrowing opening, trying to get the gradually slowing car door to hit his arms or at least his wrists. He did not want to break a finger. The door didn't stop, but the speed of the door became slower and slower as he thrust forward until finally it barreled into his left lower arm and he felt the pain. Ouch, that was going to cause some bruising, he thought with a wince.

He stood for a few seconds in the blinding bright shimmer of sunlight on metal and glass, and let his heart slow down and the world around him speed back up. As he bent down to pick up the books he had dropped he thought, *I have got to learn more about what the hell is going on with me.*

After the soldiers returned home from World War II, America had a sudden need to find jobs for them. Rosie the Riveter and her sisters were highly encouraged to resume their fulltime housework, and Mexican citizens who had been brought in to fill the labor shortage found themselves far less welcome. Operation Wetback, begun in the early 1950s, deported somewhere between seven- and nine-hundred-thousand Mexicans per year, and it is now thought that number included numerous American citizens of Mexican descent who were not given the chance to prove their citizenship.

Not surprisingly, many changes in immigration law in the 1950s were to keep communists out and to allow refugees from Eastern Europe who were fleeing communism to get in. We wanted the entire world to know that we had become a nation unified against communism.

We were also becoming generally more racially tolerant. The Asia-Pacific barred zone was removed, and up to two-thousand people per year were now allowed to enter the United States from that part of the world. In 1952, President Truman pushed for more diversity by vetoing using our ethnic mix from the 1920 census to set our 1952 immigration quotas. That was too much. Congress overrode his veto.

When Jake heard from Shelby, he still was trying to figure out what to make of the evening with Jennifer. Her confessions about Nelson had been entertaining. And she was a fun gal, uninhibited and full of laughter. Jake thought that maybe he should have gone up to her room, had another drink and seen what happened. But every time he looked at Gail he was glad he hadn't.

And, he reminded himself, there had been another reason why he had deemed it best that the conversation end. What with all the drinking and reminiscing going on, Jake had been deathly afraid that he would accidently spill the beans about the rest of the night. Oh, it had been harmless enough to confess to Jennifer about going back to the cave with Kyle earlier in the evening, and that part was completely true. And finding out that Jennifer and Nelson had taken the box to begin with had been a good laugh for both of them to share.

But under no circumstances could he tell anyone the part about what had happened after he and Kyle returned to the hotel and Shelby had tried to calm them down and they had all made a pact to keep mum forever. Which of course he had now broken, but so what? No, the really weird part he could not talk about had definitely come later that night.

And now Shelby was on her way out to LA on business and wanted to have dinner with him. Holy crap. Was she going to ply him with drinks and try to get answers out of him too?

Alex was surprised to see Linda Weigel leaving the science department head's office in tears. Linda was a sensible woman who handled the other "advanced" science class at Early Gulch High School. Advanced Biology usually had two sections, and Linda often filled both. Alex faced the fact that biology was simply a more accessible topic than physics for many students, and also credited Linda with being an excellent teacher.

Linda looked away from Alex as she left, clearly not wanting to talk about it. Alex gave Rita, the department head, a baffled look.

"If I have to fire that woman it will be one of the worst travesties in the history of this school," Rita seethed. "I just may quit first." She shook her head. "Fortunately you have no cause to refer to evolution in your curriculum, do you?" Rita smiled matter-of-factly.

"No, but I can't possibly teach advanced physics without addressing the big bang theory and the origins of the universe."

"Shit. I forgot about that." Rita never broke the unspoken ban on cussing, even when students were not around, and that let Alex know just how upset the lady must really be.

"What's going on, Rita?"

She sighed deeply. "Our new principal is asking every

department to take a hard look at our course content and make sure it adequately reflects the beliefs and values of the community which we serve."

"Education is about learning, Rita. And learning isn't necessarily about what is valued in the community," Alex said, disturbed.

"I know, I know. And the science department has been singled out as the single worst offender. I've been asked to speak to each teacher individually."

"Great," Alex muttered. "Science does have a way of challenging beliefs, doesn't it?"

"I am told the two can be compatible, and Alex I personally believe that. I have a lot of traditional beliefs myself and yet I have no trouble presenting evidence and theories in hopes of teaching students to think. Anything less than that is not education."

"I couldn't agree more," Alex said. "So are any departments getting commended in this, this change in philosophy?"

"It turns out that our social studies department has, by and large, been doing a fine job of slowly affirming the United State's rightful role as leader of the free world, and downplaying any insignificant incidents in the past that might ever put us in anything but a very positive light."

"There's historical accuracy for you," Alex said wryly.

"Apparently the new principal is particularly delighted with how Ms. Johnson has taken this a step further and attempted to restore regional pride by downplaying the ills of slavery and emphasizing the more positive aspects of the South," Rita added. "Others are now being encouraged to follow her lead."

"So we want to rewrite history *and* ignore science?"

"Alex, my hands are tied. Right now you seem to have landed on their good side by somehow involving grandparents' day with your advanced physics class. I'm not exactly sure how you managed to do that but I'm glad you did. Please try to stay out of trouble." Rita paused. "I don't want to lose you too."

August 1697

Balam's mother had given him the impression that he would reach this large body of water in a few months. But by Balam's count he had walked three months to get to the large river, and now he had walked another three months more. Large mountains now set off to his left and they kept pushing him northward. He fought their guidance, and as the sun lowered in the sky each night he tried to mark west and not curve with the land.

He was stronger, leaner and more capable every day, and also more anxious for this journey to finally end. So he knew that he had walked faster and had traveled further during the second three months, even though the rougher terrain had slowed him down.

The land had, if anything, become more barren and dry, particularly off towards the mountains. If this kept up Balam worried that food and water would get scarce. There was no end to his journey in sight. For the first time it occurred to Balam to doubt his mother and his grandfather. Perhaps there was no giant body of water. Perhaps he would only die of thirst or starve to death trying to reach it.

He had been of this mindset for several days when he came over a ridge and saw it in the distance. It lay stretched out before him, its beautiful blue waters glistening in the sunlight. Water. Lots of it. Just what he had been told to find. Balam screamed out a shout of pure joy.

Then, he admitted to himself, the water finding was not the whole problem. He had been told more specifically to go to the water's edge and to find the people who lived along it. If there were no people, he was to keep walking along the water's edge until he found them.

So Balam made his way to the lonely shore, and allowed himself a refreshing swim and a long drink. He searched for anything that he could eat. Finally, reluctantly, he picked a direction and began to follow the water's edge.

For the next several days he made his way, enjoying the water and abundance of life that it brought. But although he saw a few boats floating far out in the distance, he passed no villages himself.

Then at sunset on the third day he saw something very disturbing. The sun was now setting over the land. The lake was behind him. The body of water was not the great body of water he had been sent to find and he knew it. He had to go on.

Chapter 13. September 2010

Alex didn't generally share much about school with either Lola or Teddie, and for a lot of different reasons. There was consideration. For decades now Lola had worked terribly hard to prove herself in the very male oil business, all the while demanding almost perfection from herself as mother and nurturer-in-chief. Alex figured that she really didn't need to hear about his troubles as well. He tried to be a plus in her life, so he was generally fine, just fine, whether he really was or not.

Then there was confidentiality. None of his own children were gossips, but Alex didn't like putting them in the awkward position of knowing things about the administration, teachers or other students. The less he said around the house the better.

And then there was a bit of selfishness. The truth was that he didn't want to take school home with him; he didn't really want to talk about it. It was overwhelming sometimes, the number of incidents, crises and conflicts that he dealt with in a single day. Tears, fights and angst of raging hormones filled the hallways, and some days the teachers' lounge wasn't a whole lot better.

He had stayed particularly mum about the changes in the administration and the subtle changes he had noticed as well in the teachers. All were being more cautious this year. There was less laughter, and a sense of being watched. The morning pledge of allegiance and particularly the daily pledge to the state of Texas were being given considerably more time and pomp each day. Even more disturbing was that the moment of silent reflection had just this morning become "a moment to reflect, or if you do find it in your heart to pray, then please feel free to pray that someday soon we may be able to say a prayer together aloud."

Alex's one exception to his "don't take work home" policy was when he came up with an idea of which he was particularly proud. Then he allowed himself the joy of a small victory lap. He supposed that was why he shared the Einstein/explain-a-concept-to-your-grandmother story with Lola and Teddie over dinner. Lola was delighted, but Teddie was not.

"Dad, I know some of these kids and I've even met some of

their grandparents. Do you not understand that you could spend every single class for the entire year listening to Jason Brock try to explain Galileo's thought experiment proving that all objects fall at the same rate to his grandmother? And at the end of the year she still would not get it and neither would Jason?"

"You might be underestimating Jason's grandmother, but yes I am prepared to call time after a while."

"But that's humiliating to both of them. And what about people who can't furnish a grandparent?"

"I was going to try to come up with a couple of subs," Alex said.

"I know the perfect one." Lola practically squirmed in her chair with excitement at this idea. "I've been wanting to invite Maurice to visit."

Maurice was an eighty-five-year-old, retired paleontologist from Lola's hometown and one of the small group of humans alive who possessed such a finely honed sense of empathy that he could be considered a telepath, like Lola. In fact, Maurice had in many ways helped Lola learn to use and live with her gift, and Alex knew that they checked in with each other often.

"It would be great to really see him. He could stay in Zane's room for a couple of days, and not only sub but also be a back-up, kind of your plant onstage. He probably knows half of what you've got these kids explaining already, but you set it up so they explain to grandma and to him. Maurice would blend in to the grandparent thing well, and handle it tactfully."

"It's a good idea," Alex agreed. Luckily, Maurice was available and thought so too.

The Civil Rights movement reverberated through the United States in the 1960s as tolerance for Catholics, Jews, and Asians increased along with a greater acceptance of equality for African Americans. In the new quota system of 1965, for the first time in eighty-three years all Eastern Hemisphere nations were now treated exactly the same, regardless of the ethnicity of that nation. However, in a compromise for this open-mindedness, in 1965 a new and substantially smaller limit was placed on the number of immigrants allowed in from all of Latin America.

It took thirteen years for congress to pass a new law that treated Latin America on an even basis with the rest of the world. Unfortunately, those intervening thirteen years left a huge backlog of visa requests from the United State's neighbors to the south.

This 1978 reform applied a flat limit of 20,000 immigrants per year from any nation on Earth. This worked well for most nations. They were smaller, farther away and they lacked a massive backlog. But in the case of Mexico, after thirteen years of extreme restriction, the new law provided far too few visas far too late. Legal entry into the United States now appeared impossible to many Mexicans.

Before Kyle knocked on the door, he pulled his hair back into a fresh ponytail and smoothed down his clothes so he would look as kempt as possible. The keepers of records for a parish were inevitably more receptive to those with better grooming habits. Back when Kyle had been seeking historical records, nominally of his own ancestors, doors had opened more easily. But now that he was tracing a woman who would be in her forties today, roughly Kyle's own age, the keepers of the files were rightfully more wary.

Kyle had tried seeking his sister, his cousin and an older friend's daughter with varying degrees of receptiveness. Finally he began seeking a woman with whom he shared an inheritance and had to locate. There was an odd bit of truth to that, really, and that morsel of candor must have echoed in his voice because by parish number fourteen the cousin with whom he shared rights to some family land had become the story of choice.

Once he was allowed to see old files, he didn't just look for little Ixchel's first communion records. He looked for mom Inez in the rosters of each church's altar society and the membership of the Catholic Daughters of the Americas. He looked for Yochi Rojas as a teacher in the parish school, and as a possible lector in the church.

Kyle, who was most definitely not being a fuck-up at all the whole time he was in Mexico City, looked and read and skimmed until his eyes burned and then he moved on to the next parish. Until he picked up a parish school newsletter one day from 1993 that passed along the very sad news that beloved secondary school mathematics teacher Yochi Rojas had passed away from cancer while undergoing treatment at a cancer center in the United States. The family wanted his former students and fellow teachers to know that his wife Inez had been with Sr. Rojas when he passed, along with their daughter Ixchel, son-in-law Raul and newborn baby grandson Xuha. The family thanked all the parishioners for their kind words of encouragement and many prayers over the last several months.

Alex was understandably reluctant to have students over to his house. Most teachers learn to put up a barrier between their personal lives and school for their own protection and for the sake of their families. The majority of teenagers would cause no problem, but the average teacher deals with hundreds if not thousands of students and parents over the course of a career, and along the way there are bound to be pranksters, a few angry people, and some that are overly needy or demanding. So while Alex generally gave school his all while he was there, he drew a line at his own personal space.

Xuha, however, had become more than a student. Alex enjoyed coaching the boy and admired the zeal with which he faced challenges both mental and physical. He respected the way that Xuha tackled his life's problems with a wisdom beyond his years. What's more, Xuha's interesting observations about making time slow down when he needed to do so made him more than a protégé. In some ways, Xuha was a potential ally in trying to understand a phenomenon.

So when it started to rain heavily only a few minutes after they got on the court, Alex barely hesitated.

"I've got a big garage, Xuha," he offered. "If you want to keep working, we can pull the cars out and spend some time working on serves and form in there."

Xuha grinned his agreement.

Alex kept on old stereo system in his garage where he could play his vast collection of bubblegum music as loud as liked while he worked. After a good hour or so of tossing balls and serving while listening to some of the most buoyantly cadenced music ever written, they headed into the house for iced tea.

Though kept reasonably clean, the Zeitman house had never won any awards for neatness, and Alex directed Xuha towards the seldom used dining room so they would have a place to sit that was tidy and out of the way. *Oh wait,* Alex thought. He had forgotten about Stan's project scattered across the table.

"What's this?" Xuha was already studying the wooden box that Alex had constructed in the exact dimensions of Stan's artifact in hopes that having a physical object to study would give him some additional insight.

"Oh just a project I'm working on for fun with an old high school buddy of mine. I'm not getting very far with it."

Alex noticed that Xuha was eyeing the box with a more than strange expression on this face. *That's right, Xuha claimed some Mayan ancestry,* Alex remembered.

"The hieroglyphs I've pasted on to it are Mayan," Alex confirmed, thinking that was what had caught Xuha's attention. "The friend is a professor of anthropology at my daughter Ariel's college. He made me photocopies of the actual sides of the box and I pasted them on because I'm trying to help him figure out what it all means."

Xuha didn't say anything at first. Then finally he asked. "When your professor friend is done studying the box, what will happen to it? Who will it belong to?"

Alex shrugged. "I suppose it becomes the property of somebody's government. Maybe Guatemala? Anyway I'd bet it ends up in a museum somewhere. Why?"

"Just curious," Xuha said, and then he changed the subject quickly to ask Alex about an upcoming tennis tournament in the area.

"Hey Dad." Teddie was spending less time this year in his classroom Alex noticed, and he figured that was probably a good thing. But she did drop by at least once a day to check on him and share news.

"I have a date to homecoming! You and mom don't care if I go to homecoming, do you?" The second sentence was an afterthought, from a child who could not imagine there would be any objection.

"To the game? To the dance?" Alex was almost as baffled at being asked. The truth was that Ariel and Zane had been so old for so long that he forgot sometimes that a sophomore in high school was supposed to need permission for such.

"I'll go to the game with friends. This is just a date for the dance."

"Okay. But don't kids usually go to the game with their dates too?"

"Yeah." Teddie rolled her eyes. "But that's a little bit of a problem with this guy. He's got a coach that expects him to be out on the football field instead. Unreasonable."

"You are actually going out with a football player?" Alex was surprised. This wasn't Teddie's style.

"We're not going out, dad, we're just friends. He really needs to bring someone to the dance and I want to go, so it works out nice for both of us."

"Okay," Alex said again. "But why does he really have to bring someone to the dance?"

A second eye-roll in under a minute. "Because he's quarterback on the team, dad. It would be so lame for him to show up stag."

"You're going with Marcus?" Alex was slowly figuring out the situation. "Oh, okay. That's nice. He's a good kid. A senior, which I'm not crazy about, but I'll let your mom know that he's okay. Should be no problem."

"Thanks Dad." Teddie gave him a quick hug and headed out the door.

Tyler sat on the hallway floor in front of his locker, feeling more dejected than he had in his life. He had no intention of ever getting up. There was no reason to live.

He had found the perfect woman. He could have accepted it

if she didn't see in him the perfect man. If she wanted someone older, stronger, more mature, it would be understandable. Tyler knew that he had a ways to go. If Teddie did not see the potential in him, that would have made him sad. But only sad.

This was different entirely. If the rumor mill at Early Gulch was to be believed, Teddie was planning to betray everything in which Tyler believed. In flagrant disloyalty to her entire heritage, she was about to give comfort to the enemy. She was about to consort with one of the primary foes of the white race, flagrantly, publically and in front of the entire school.

She would be forever soiled by the very incident. Unfit for Tyler, unfit for the role of Aryan princess that he had so wished for her. She would be trash, and only trash, if she actually went to the homecoming dance with the likes of Marcus. And Tyler didn't know if he could bear that pain.

Ms. Johnson, of course, would be delighted. For some reason Tyler could not fathom, his teacher hated Teddie, and seemed to also hate Mr. Zeitman who was actually one of the more decent teachers around. Now that he thought about it, Tyler realized that Ms. Johnson would probably rant indefinitely about the indecency of a teacher's daughter accompanying one of the few black students at the school to something as prominent and tradition laden as the homecoming dance. He could hear Ms. Johnson's voice in his head asking, "Is there no respect for the values of the past?"

Tyler wasn't sure that he could sit through one such discussion, let alone many. And that meant that he was not only about to lose Teddie forever, he was also about to lose his afterschool home, the one adult who fed him well and often understood him, and eventually his two best friends as well, because he was already sure that Tanner and Travis would choose Ms. J over him in a heartbeat.

He might have sat on the floor like that forever, just as he had planned, if Tanner hadn't come up and interrupted his self-pity with a good hard kick to his left thigh.

"Asshole. School's out. You gonna sit there all night?"

"Let me alone Tanner." Tyler barely flinched at the kick and only muttered his response.

"You want something you fight for it." Tanner persisted. "I'm not stupid. I've seen you watching that Teddie girl. You gotta keep her from going to that dance with that nigger. Lock her up. Beat some sense into her if you have to. Whatever it takes, dude. I'm with you here. I'll lend a hand."

"Tanner. She wants to go with him. She's not gonna be one of us."

"She can be," Tanner persisted. "She doesn't know what she wants. You've got to show her. Do you want her or don't you?"

"I very much want her."

"Okay, man. Let's get a plan. How about you and I try to keep Travis and Ms. J out of this for once and just handle it like real men. What do you say?"

And for the first time since second period Tyler thought life might be worth living after all.

A quick call to Jennifer had convinced Shelby that Nelson absolutely had not kept the keys to the truck the night that the artifact disappeared. Jennifer had put them under Stan's door, just like she always did, and given how the next day had unfolded, Jennifer had reason to remember it well. So Shelby reluctantly crossed Nelson back off of her suspect list and turned back to Jake and his missing friend Kyle. It was time to go to LA and see what some very direct questioning could do.

A week later, Shelby was ordering raspberry lemonade and staring hard at Jake over her glass. She had seen to it that there was nothing the least bit flirtatious about her dress, her manner or her speech. She had come as an emissary seeking answers and she was being as upfront about it as possible.

Pretty clear that suggesting sex won't get me out of this one, Jake thought as he sipped a beer.

"It's time to act like adults and figure out what happened," Shelby declared before the conversation had barely cleared the pleasantries. "We all had our own good reasons for avoiding each other afterwards, and now that we all know them, the time for worrying about all that silly nonsense is over."

"I don't get it." Jake was being honest too. "You and Dr. Drexler and Jennifer, you say you are all working together, and you have the artifact in your possession now. So what does it matter how it got to you."

Shelby swallowed hard. This next part was going to be difficult. "The document inside did not come with it. After close examination of the relic itself, we believe that whatever is written on it is written in code. The words are out of order, include spaces for no reason and we think the real message is mixed in with random words. We believe that the paper document inside held the key to deciphering the already difficult-to-read hieroglyphs."

Jake looked concerned. "I read your interview with Dr. Drexler and you never mentioned the document at all. I wondered about that."

"It gets more complicated," Shelby went on. "Stan, he is Stan now by the way, anyway Stan is pretty sure he read way back when on the document that there were two smaller relics that have to be found also. It makes sense. The three probably fit together like a very easy jigsaw puzzle. Stan has got some friend of his who is really good at geometry problems trying to figure out the dimensions of the other boxes and how many hieroglyphs would be on each, but this guy has come back to us and said the whole thing has been designed so that we pretty much need all three boxes to make any sense out of it. Or at least two of them. And we figure that the document probably also gives more clues to where the other two artifacts are buried. So we really need to know what happened that night."

"You already know it," Jake said gruffly. "We did a kind of stupid thing. And Nelson and Jennifer did a kind of stupid thing. Somebody else must have figured with that many people coming and going from an excavation site in the dark that something interesting had happened. They took a look, they saw the box, they liked the box, they took the box. It's all of our fault, really. If we'd all stayed put and gone to sleep the way we should have, the artifact would have been every bit as safe as Dr. Drexler thought it would be."

And Jake seemed genuinely sad that all of them had not.

"So that leaves me with two questions," Shelby said. "One. Where is Kyle?"

Jake looked nervous for the first time and shrugged.

"Jake, you're a great schmoozer. But a fairly bad out-and-out liar. What happened to Kyle?"

"I'm just trying to protect an old friend," Jake said defensively. "He ran away from life. His parents in particular. Dr. Mom and Dr. Dad are not, I gather, pleasant people to be around. At least not for Kyle. He lives in Mexico and doesn't want to be found. Not by you either."

"Okay. I don't need to find him if you can answer this second question on behalf of both of you."

Jake looked up worried.

"When you came back from the cave that night, you told me the truth. I could tell it back then and I know it for a fact now. But the next morning, when we all got back to the excavation site, something had changed. I could tell by the way you and Kyle were watching each other and kind of coaching each other along on what to say. Something was off. Jake, what happened that night after we talked in the bar and all went to bed?"

It was Jake's turn to look directly at Shelby.

"You are not going to go away until you get an answer, are you?"

She nodded.

"So if I tell you this, you have got to promise me that you will not think I've lost my mind."

"You're worried I'll think you're crazy?"

"Yeah. I am. Kyle ran all the way to Mexico so no one would think that he was."

"Okay. I am sure that you are not insane," Shelby said it with certainty.

"So you know how we came back and we told you how the thing was missing, and then we all had a round of beers and calmed down. We promised each other how we'd never tell anyone that the two of us had driven over there. You went up to bed and Kyle and I had another beer. Then we went to our room and walked in and the damn relic thing was sitting right there on the middle of our dresser."

"What? In your hotel room? Are you nuts?"

Jake shook his head. "You promised me that you would not say that."

Teddie had been trying for a while to decide on how to best to deal with the new "Beauregards and Belles" club formed by the history department to celebrate the "heroism and beauty" of the Old South. Ms. Johnson was listed as the main sponsor, but it was becoming apparent that several of the history teachers were quite involved. An Old South week was already being planned for the spring with a parade and a dance, and a Civil War reenactment of some sort was being organized for January with help from the Fans of the Confederacy.

The principal sent the newspaper a short blurb to run explaining that the reenactment would highlight some of the many accomplishments of the school's namesake, General Jubal Early. The wording went on to commend the new group for stimulating an interest in history.

Teddie had no problem with kids being interested in history. She did, however, have a problem with a club that celebrated a way of life that had required that other human beings serve as slaves. Pure and simple. Teddie was born and raised in the modern South, and she thought the facts were quite apparent. No slavery, no Old South. You could pretend otherwise, but pretending didn't make it so.

Teddie was willing to grant that old Egypt was based on slavery and so was the Maya empire and probably a lot of other cultures that she had never heard about. The fact that other cultures once used slaves didn't make it okay, she thought, it just made the whole issue even sadder. But teaching young people to celebrate such a culture in front of others who were still dealing with the residual problems that remained for them today elevated the issue from sad to insulting. Like the ubiquitous Confederate flags found on the bumper stickers of half the trucks in the school parking lot. It sent a message, and the message wasn't a kind one. It was a message of "We wish that things were still that way." Teddie didn't see how there could ever be healing of the hundred-and-fifty-year-old wounds that even a fifteen-year-old could recognize, as long as so many white Southerners continued to send that message.

On the other hand, the new principal had issued an edict against clubs that were designed primarily for pupils of a particular ethnic group or advocated ethnic solidarity, and this now explained why the very popular Latino club had been disbanded. Could Teddie interview white students and see if any had felt excluded by the Latino club? She doubted that any had, but it was possible. Maybe she could interview a few different ethnic groups and see what they thought of both clubs. Her best friend Michelle was of Vietnamese descent and there were a few Vietnamese students she could ask. And she could find out if any non-whites felt comfortable joining the Beauregards and Belles. Maybe some did.

Or maybe not.

Teddie recognized the changes taking place at her school and figured that she needed to proceed with caution if she wanted to keep her voice at the newspaper. Maybe her best bet would be to just do a section on this year's changes in student organizations and put a just-the-facts article on the disbanding of the one club and the start-up of the other right next to each other. Surely some of her fellow students would recognize irony when they saw it.

Once it looked like Jake had chosen to be more forthcoming, Shelby moved out of cross-examination mode and suggested that they at least get dinner. Chinese sounded good, so they left the little hotel lobby bar and headed down the street. As they walked, Jake filled in more of the gaps.

Yes, the boys had locked their room before leaving. Yes, the document was inside the box, and no, there was no other note or explanation. Of course their first thought had been to run to get Dr. Drexler, but Kyle thought it wouldn't hurt to photograph it and study it for just a little while. After all, they had headed off about two hours ago to do just that. So, fueled by adrenaline, they started to look at it and they both got engrossed and spent longer than they had planned. Much longer, actually. And then they decided that pounding on their advisor's door at three a.m. with this whole story wasn't going to be so cool an idea either. In retrospect, Jake acknowledged, that would have been their best move.

But to a couple of exhausted guys, Jake's alternate plan made more sense at the time and it involved less of a messy explanation. "I offered to go hide it in the back of the little truck right then when no one was around to see me do it," Jake said, adding that he and Kyle decided that they could then just skip breakfast and return it to the cave first thing in the morning and have everything back in place before the second vehicle arrived.

"It made sense, Shelby, it really did. We were going to leave a note on Dr. Drexler's door saying that we had gone over early. We knew he'd be annoyed by that because we weren't supposed to split up, but it sure beat going into everything else that had happened. Clean, simple, and we would plead being overly enthused. How mad could he be?"

"But you were at breakfast that next morning," Shelby said. "I avoided talking to you guys, and I distinctly remember it."

"We sure were," Jake affirmed, "because when we got out to the truck bright and early just a few hours later—"

"The box was gone again," Shelby guessed herself. Jake's expression confirmed it.

"Yup. Thank God there were two of us, because one person would doubt their own sanity at that point."

"You're not crazy. Let's start with that. And I know I didn't take it, and neither did Stan or Jennifer. So either Kyle scammed you, or Nelson got back into this mess somehow, or a stranger got involved and took it out of the truck."

"How did it get into our room in the first place, Shelby? And why?"

Shelby wished that she had an answer for that too.

Maurice drove up to the Zeitman house in his 2006 Lincoln Town Car, a wiry, little man with a thick comb of white hair, a ruddy complexion and a grin a mile wide. Lola and Teddie both ran outside to greet the adopted family member with a hug.

Alex knew that the elderly man had transitioned from grieving spouse to adept telepath while in his seventies, after a lifetime of identifying microscopic bugs in rock fragments from oil wells. Conservative and Christian, he had been forced to adapt his core beliefs to encompass the input he now received every day from countless other souls whom he had once barely noticed or understood. The result, Alex thought, had been to turn Maurice into a human who was more alive and aware than most people ever became.

The next morning Maurice followed Alex over to Early Gulch. He had been well prepared for his role. Every student was to have five minutes or less to explain the essentials of one of many famous thought experiments. Maurice was to grasp and pull out those essentials while involving the real grandparent, if any, as much as possible. It was more staged than Alex would have liked, but probably the best alternative.

As Alex had come to learn, empathy was Maurice's chief gift and as such he was remarkably nonjudgmental about appearances. The class loved him. He encouraged the shy, smiled and joked with the surly, argued adeptly with the intellectual. By the end of class several of the grandmothers were making eyes at him.

Meanwhile, both the class and a presenter's great uncle seemed to have understood the basic idea behind Heisenberg's Microscope rather well, and one of Alex's four girls in the class did an amazing job of explaining Maxwell's Demon and the implication it had for thermodynamics. Her grandmother, a former science teacher herself, had obviously coached the girl considerably about entropy. Not all the other explanations went so well, but none were awful, and any class period that ended with nineteen students having a better understanding of both the uncertainty principle and thermodynamics was a good class indeed.

So Alex was puzzled when after the students all left Maurice seemed bothered and asked if he could have a word with Alex alone. Sure. Next period was his planning period, so Alex followed Maurice out to his car and agreed to go for a short drive. No one sits talking in a car in Texas in September with out cooling down the car first, so they let the air conditioner do its thing as they drove over to a little gas station for a cup of coffee.

"I don't know exactly how much your wife has told you about what we can do," Maurice began.

Alex laughed. "She sent me to your website and had me educate myself. I'm pretty informed."

"Okay." Maurice looked relieved. "Then you know that I usually stay out of people's heads, for my sake as well as theirs, and when things come at me I can't ignore, I just listen and file it away. If I ran to the police with every threat I heard they'd lock me up as a public nuisance. So you have got to take what I am about to tell you with a big grain of salt."

Alex couldn't help guessing. "You heard, or you sensed, something in my class that troubled you?"

Maurice gave a tight little smile. "Almost nothing but. These are teen-agers, Alex, and you've got mostly boys in there. Twelve of them spent a lot of the period fantasizing about some girl. Amazing how much they can learn in the small amount of time that they actually pay attention to you."

"So you're saying that I've got only three boys who mostly listen to me?"

"I didn't say that," Maurice chuckled dryly. "Two of those boys spent most of the class fantasizing about a boy instead."

"Oh."

"Yeah. And the third was mostly asleep."

Alex looked a little dejected.

"Don't take it so hard. These are kids. They like you better than most of their teachers and even though nearly all of them actually dislike physics, they are learning. You're doing what you can and then some. Please, this is another issue."

Alex put his ego aside and let Maurice go on.

"It so happens that one of the boys in the class is deeply

fixated on your daughter Teddie. That's hard for a dad, I know, but you can't prevent that."

"Great." Alex wondered if there were some things that it was better that he just did not know.

"There are," Maurice said, "and I would never have brought this up in a million years to you except that along with the fixation is a very unhealthy outrage. Your daughter has made him very upset. And I wouldn't even tell you that normally," Maurice held up a hand to stop Alex from commenting, "but he seems to be formulating a plan of some sort to 'show her,' and that doesn't sound good."

"Oh my God," Alex muttered.

"Wait now, Alex. People make plans in their heads all the time that they have no intention of carrying out. So I still don't think I would have told you even this, except that it has gone as far as being discussed with another boy. The big kid that sits behind him is also involved and this second kid has a pretty unhealthy sexual obsession with one of his teachers. Young blonde woman. Near as I can tell he thinks if he helps his friend handle the Teddie issue then this teacher is going to be very proud of him and fall willingly into his arms. Instead of the arms of a third kid who appears to be the little group's leader but is totally oblivious to what his two friends are planning."

"Nothing may come of this, of course," Maurice continued, "but under the circumstances, Alex, I hope you understand that I just couldn't not speak up. You need to keep this in perspective, but I think you also need to keep an eye on things."

"Any idea when or where or how this plan happens?"

"Not really. My gift isn't so good for details, you know that. I got something about a football game and a dance and how important it was that Tanner get his usually drunken dad's car that night. You do know that the dad beats Tanner regularly, don't you?"

"I know that the school has tried looking into that," Alex said sadly. Then it finally occurred to him to see this from Maurice's perspective.

"I thought the class went so well. All that stuff coming at

you, it must have been awful for you to be there."

Maurice shrugged. "I can handle it. Kids are noisier than older people, in this way as well. I knew what I was in for when I agreed to do this." He gave Alex a pat on the leg. "It's okay. But I think you probably understand why I don't go out much."

Shelby returned to Atlanta satisfied that she had another worthwhile piece of information, but Stan was less pleased.

"I just feel so stupid. This entire hotel was apparently filled with intrigue that night over this thing and here I was getting a good night's sleep. What the hell was the matter with me?"

Shelby touched him with affection. "Stan, you may have been a little naive, but honestly you had the purest heart in the group; you slept well because you could. I think our next move is to rule out that Nelson or Kyle took the box out of the truck."

"Why rule out? Neither comes across as particularly trustworthy in this whole incident."

"True," Shelby agreed. "But as far as we now know, neither one of them could have put the box in the hotel room to start with. It makes more sense to me that someone put the box in the room for reasons that we don't understand and then took the box out of the truck later that night probably for the same reason."

"This person didn't want the box to go back to the cave," Stan surmised.

"That's all that makes sense. And this same person wanted Jake and Kyle to have the box. Not you. Otherwise why put it in their room?"

"Okay, so who in the world, besides maybe Jake's mother, would want him to have this thing instead of me?"

"I have no idea," Shelby laughed. "And I think we can probably rule out Jake's mother. But if we can figure out who would want that turn of events and why, then I think we figure out exactly what happened that night. And then you can finally put the past to rest, please, and join me in concentrating on the future here. More particularly, on the future that you and I are going to have once we solve this thing."

Before Maurice left two days later to make the drive back to his West Texas home, he had visited with Lola at great length. She enjoyed the chance to spend face to face time with her mentor, even though she watched with concern as Maurice struggled more frequently to remember a phrase or a fact. Finally, he patted her hand gently.

"It goes with the territory, dear," he assured her. "If you're lucky enough to live as long as I have, your memory isn't going to work like it used to. I'm aware of my lapses. And yes I could not keep from learning from you that Alex's mom struggled with serious dementia and her last years were very tough on all of you. It's a horrible disease that I'm well aware of it. Please don't worry. I've got others keeping a close eye on me."

"Well, I'm one of them now, too," Lola said affectionately, patting his hand back and hoping that of all the difficult fates that could await Maurice, this was not going to be one of them.

Maurice also spent some time with Alex, listening with interest about his efforts as an amateur in the field of Mayan cryptology. Alex was completely forthcoming about Stan and his borrowed manuscript, and the hunt for the remaining two boxes. He figured that lying to Maurice was like lying to Lola. Just a waste of time.

Maurice was more hopeful than Alex about being able to locate at least one of the missing two artifacts. "If this young boy made it to the coast of Belize, this relic is now extremely unusual in its current location. You have a contact there, and will have a better one soon. Olumiji is going to visit his sister in a few weeks. If you agree, I can get him involved in trying to locate the box that was sent to the east."

Alex hesitated. Maurice winced.

"What is it?" Alex asked.

"No, I stay out of things like this."

"Your facial expression has put you into in, Maurice."

"I need to work on a better poker face."

"You do. But for now, say your piece."

Maurice clearly was annoyed at himself. "I'm sorry Alex. I don't always ignore as well as I want to. Lola loves you and only you very much and Olumiji is one of my and her best friends. He would be yours as well if you let him, and he would not hurt either of you for the world, you know."

"I know," Alex said.

"And yet. I do understand," Maurice added. "May I involve him in this anyway?"

"You may. Stan needs to find his artifact and if it takes a powerful Nigerian telepath to do it, then it does." Then after a short pause. "Please tell Olumiji that I appreciate it that if he needs more information he is free to call me. You know, on a real phone, because I don't do this other thing."

Jake could not believe that Shelby had gotten him to talk so much. He wanted to berate himself but the truth was that after all these years it felt good to tell someone the story. And Shelby's no-nonsense response had been refreshing.

Of course someone had put the box in his room. It was just a matter of figuring out who and how. Jake thought that life must be so much easier as the kind of person who never got spooked. No secret fears of ghosts or crazy box spirits. Good old sensible Shelby seemed immune to all the hidden dread of phantom artifact protectors that he and Kyle had barely voiced to each other over the years, and her sunny logic had added a bit of bright light to the gloom.

Jake remembered all too clearly how after Dr. Drexler went to the cave that next morning and made his awful discovery, he and his students had searched the area, dug further into the cave, inquired carefully of the locals, and checked in with two other groups of archeologists working in the Lake Peten area. When nothing more was found and nothing more was to be done, they had packed up for the semester and headed home as scheduled, a silent, guilty, dejected group.

Jake thought that he could commend himself on telling Shelby the truth, and nothing but the truth. It looked like Shelby had always suspected that there was more to the events of that night than she knew, and of course she had been right. So now her doubts had been answered and her curiosity had been satisfied.

However, Jake had to remind himself, he had not told her the *whole* truth. She did not need to know that the mystery had not stopped with the rising sun that day. If anything, events had become more confusing and more frightening as the day wore on.

This dream was filled with golden light creatures, above, below and all around Alex. None of them interacted with him, each going about her business. Finally Alex asked one, "Aren't you going to give me any information?"

Alex could have sworn that she looked a little miffed when she replied, "We were told you didn't particularly like being the observer. You think it is silly for observers to have a place in hard science."

Alex decided to ignore the rebuff. "Is my traveling super fast relative to somebody else the only way possible for time to slow down or speed up?"

"Certainly not," she said. "There is the whole extreme gravity, general relativity thing, and there's what you now call string theory with its extra time dimension, and there is—"

Alex cut her off. "Is there any way for time to appear to move slower for me than it normally does without extreme speeds, gravity, or acceleration and at the scale at which I exist as a physical being?"

"Of course," she said. "It appears to move very slowly to you every time Lola drags you to something like a ballet."

"That's psychological. I mean can it happen as a physical phenomenon?"

"You mean can it really, really happen?" she asked with a just a touch of mockery on her face.

Alex rolled his eyes. "I know. Don't you dare say it." And the light creature softened her expression as Alex said it himself, "There is no really. Really."

After Maurice's visit Alex was tempted to just read from the text book and work problems from it for the full hour-and-fifteen-minute class period that was given him every other day for a science class at Early Gulch. Why bother doing anything else? They weren't listening anyway.

But then he looked out at the nineteen upturned faces and realized that they were paying attention, kind of. In their own way. Sometimes. And they were hoping he would entice them to pay attention just a little bit more, by being just a tad more interesting than the subject matter warranted. Okay, Alex thought. He would try.

"Today, we start to build our time machines. You can choose to work independently or in small groups. In the end, you will need to explain not only how your particular machine works, but you will need to answer questions about how it functions within classical mechanics. With electrical and magnetic fields. Whether it is different to go backwards and forwards in time and if so why. How does gravitation affect it? Radiation? What is happening at the subatomic level? The macroscopic level? What happens when an apparent paradox is created? In essence, I want to know how your machine works on every level that the world of physics touches."

Nineteen kids were giving him a look that said, "Yeah, right."

"Fortunately, in the world of science no one is an island. You get to borrow ideas and knowledge from each other. To facilitate that, we are going to do just what real scientists do. At the end of October, we are going to hold the first ever Early Gulch Time Travel symposium and every team and individual worker will present an update on their machine in progress. This will be instead of a test."

There was a look of mild relief on several faces.

"At that point you can copy all the ideas you want from anyone else in the class and redesign your machine as much as you want before you move on. Then, at the end of November we publish the very first Early Gulch Time Travel technical journal, in which each time machine will be featured and described. Once again this is instead of a test. And once again you may modify your machine all you want after the journal comes out. In other words, you may steal all the ideas you want."

"That really doesn't seem fair," one of Alex's more serious students spoke up.

"In a sense it isn't, Jeremy, but it mirrors how real progress in science happens. You discover something, at some point you make it publically available, and the entire base of human knowledge grows. You still get credit for the original idea."

Jeremy nodded.

"By winter break you or your group will have your plans finalized and will answer a series of questions about your machine. That will be your final exam."

"What happens second semester?" Xuha asked.

"We build one and put you in it," Tanner laughed, and then he did a comic imitation of being zapped by electricity. "Bzzzzzzz. Zoo-ha is gonna love time travel."

"Tanner." Alex said it sharply. Then to all of the class. "The best place to start is to build on the ideas of others." He started pulling books, paperbacks, old VHS tapes, and DVDs out of a box. "Science, pseudo science and fiction are all full of ideas about time travel. They range from the scientifically sound but useless, where the gravitational field would kill you before the time travel effects ever started, to the fanciful and ridiculous where someone puts a machine together in his garage and it works. You can check all of these materials out from me. Don't spend too long on any one of them but scan through them to get started."

Slowly the kids came to the front of the room, a few of them snickering to each other at some of the old titles and covers but slowly picking up one thing or another. By the time the bell rang Alex was happy to see every student had checked out at least one thing and most had several.

As Shelby went about her new life, working at the museum by day, and by night spending time with Stan and working on the hieroglyphs in hopes that more clear meanings would help, two things were eating away at her. One was that in spite of her claims of honesty to both Jennifer and Jake, she was withholding serious information from them. It was time to fill Jennifer in on her relationship with Stan. And the document so carefully kept between the sheets of glass in Stan's closest? That was a secret that became worse the longer it was hidden.

Stan had compounded the second problem by sharing the full truth with an old high school friend and in Shelby's experience once the number of people who knew a secret spread to three it was doomed to a short remaining life. Not that this Alex fellow wasn't trustworthy. It was just the way of the world.

That brought Shelby straight to her most pressing issue. Stan had a certain charming naiveté about him, and Shelby could truly understand how he had wanted to study the document first all by himself after this prize had been ripped from his grasp years ago. Now, Stan had some sort of notion that the manuscript could just mysteriously get "mailed" to him like the box had. "Ooops, I forgot to enclose this earlier," the little note would say. Shelby worried that way too many people were going to be watching by then for such a simple idea to work. Shelby figured that if she did love this man, and there was a very good chance that she did, then she better start thinking of better ways to handle this before it damaged his career for a second time.

September 1697

Nimah ground corn by hand, her fingers and wrists made strong by years of using this technique. Outside, her daughter Naylay worked in the garden. Luckily the Spanish had shown little interest in the lives of those who stayed out of the city, and the lone woman and girl had managed to go unnoticed.

This was good because there were almost no circumstances under which Nimah would ever attend the horrible services at the awful church that these people were building. Almost none. Nimah added the almost because she knew in her heart that if she had to eventually pretend to convert to save Naylay's life, then pretend to convert she would. Nimah hoped with all her heart that it would never come to that.

Her father had cautioned her against the very hatred that she was feeling. He had told her that not only would her boys need to learn to change and adapt in order to survive, but she would also. Hate was the way of death. He had said that to her often.

Her father had been so proud of his people. Not of the giant cities and impressive monuments they had once built so long ago. He told her that those kinds of achievements never mattered in the end; they would always pass away. No, her father had been proud of what her people had learned over the centuries. What they knew. And how they had evolved. They had gone from warlike and unforgiving to being creatures of compassion, they had become a culture that was wise. Knowledge and wisdom, her father had said, were hard fought for and difficult to acquire, and thus they were things of which to be rightfully proud.

The Spanish were not wise, Nimah thought bitterly. They were cruel and shortsighted. But her father had addressed that with her also, before his death. "They will not always be that way," he said. "They too will evolve and grow. Their children's children's children will behave better. They will learn to see all humans as people, eventually. Perhaps they will have to deal with oppressors of their own. But," he cautioned with a smile, knowing her so well, "do not wish that for them."

So Nimah tried to calm her anger. She fought her occasional desire to smash her father's box into tiny pieces, so no Spaniard or Spaniard's child might ever discover the treasure that her father had hidden. Such an act would make the loss of her own two sons be totally in vain, of course, and it would go against all that her father had asked of her. So she worked to seek out compassion inside herself and concentrated on protecting the clues to her father's legacy and to not caring whether the humans who eventually discovered it were Maya, Spanish or even others of which she did not even know.

Her father had promised her that descendants of the very people she hated today would like and even love some of her own descendants. He had insisted to her that was the way of the world. From today's warring nations come tomorrow's allies, he said.

And what of those on either side who chose to hang on to the old hatred longer than most, fanning the flames of almost dead rage lest the embers die? They accomplish nothing but bringing more hatred into their own lives and the lives of others, her father had said. And those who were quicker than most to accept the melding and change of humanity? In their adaptation they lived on, bringing a little more love into the world as they did so.

At least, that was what her father had believed. Nimah listened sadly to the stories of how the Spaniards in the town already treated and abused her people, and she thought to herself that she did not see this ending well for a very long time. Her father had been such a hopeful man.

Part 2. z^2 and Possibilities

Chapter 14. October 2010

Alex worried about the situation with Teddie and Tyler for many days before Lola gingerly asked him about it as he exited the shower one morning.

"You're kind of shouting out your concern," she explained, rinsing out a mouthful of toothpaste. "It'd be easier if you'd give me details instead of letting me try to fill in the blanks."

After hearing of Maurice's predicament in even talking to Alex, Lola was sympathetic. She ran a hot flat iron around chunks of her always unruly chestnut hair while she talked. "That was a tough call for him to make, dear. High probability that these two boys never do anything, and that you may actually cause problems by intervening."

"I know." Alex dried off as he answered. "Yet, how exactly do I do nothing and just hope everything turns out okay when Teddie's safety is involved?"

Lola got the quandary, and as Alex pulled on his clothes he realized that it probably was one she dealt with on a daily basis.

"How do you do it?" he asked her, with a budding appreciation for what her gift of telepathy must cost her in terms of peace of mind.

"I always was a worrier," she shrugged, "so I had some coping mechanisms in place already that probably saved my sanity. But in the case of the safety of your child, you don't take foolish risks." She put the hair straightener down and placed her face squarely in front of the small fan she kept in the bathroom just for this purpose. As it blew the heat out of her hair she said, "Could we, like, hire a body guard to follow her around that night? Someone she wouldn't know about and if it all comes to nothing then no harm done? A chunk of money spent, of course… but…"

"You know, that's not a bad approach." Alex was impressed at the sensibleness of it. He buttoned his shirt as another idea occurred to him. "I'm not even sure it'll cost us anything. I know a young man who can handle himself pretty well physically, even though you wouldn't know it to look at him, and he sure as hell can call for help on a cell phone and he's said several times now that he wished he had a way to repay me for all those tennis lessons."

"Xuha? Doesn't he have a date himself?"

"I don't think so. He keeps to himself a lot and he doesn't have much money for going out... let me talk to him." And so while getting dressed for the day a plan for Teddie's safety was born.

Ariel occasionally called Alex on his cell phone late afternoons when school was out, and he appreciated the one-on-one chance to chat. Her time back at the Zeitman house in August after Guatemala had been brief, and now she was finding her graduate level classes more demanding than she had expected. Alex recognized that she was probably even more driven than her mother, and he found himself wishing that his little ball of fire, as he had once called her, would treat herself to more relaxation.

Instead, she had called to tell him that she decided to modify her major and would have to take an extra class spring semester to do it.

"What exactly is this new degree that they are letting you design yourself?" Alex asked, amazed at how much higher education had changed.

"Originally it was a math and computer science hybrid, Dad, but remember how I had a double undergrad major in economics too?"

"Yeah," her dad said. He had marveled that she had found economics so interesting that she had taken the classes for fun.

"Well, get this. If I take this one more class I can do a self-designed major that merges economics into the math and the computers. Dad. Listen. I am going to get to do an independent study project on using computers to trade on a stock exchange!" Alex could hear the excitement in her voice.

"Ariel, I'm not totally up on this stuff, but don't we do that already, dear?"

"Yes dad. Pretty much nothing but. But there's a whole world being developed on the theories and ramifications of using machines that move at the speed of light instead of slow humans to make stock trades and, dad, I am going to get to be one of those experts."

"Ariel, that's terrific," Alex said, and he meant it. You just had to accept that not everybody had the same idea of fun.

"Oh, one more thing dad. I've been doing some thinking about my time at Lake Peten, and I know that this is going to sound kind of goofy, but I struck up a friendship with one of the maids at the hotel."

"Okay." This hardly qualified as goofy, Alex thought.

"Her name was Kisa, and one day we had this kind of odd conversation, and, dad, I think that somebody needs to go talk to her."

"Because?"

"Because she's really tied into that whole mystery box thing that Megan's advisor and you are trying to solve. I just know she is."

"Because?"

"She asked me a lot of questions, dad. It's hard to explain, and it didn't register with me at the time. Just, please, just believe me."

"Honey, why don't you walk over to Stan's office and tell him that he needs to talk to this lady when he heads back down to Guatemala at the end of the year?"

"That wouldn't work out well. I mean, I'm Megan's friend and I don't think I should be telling him that, and besides I got a kind of funny vibe when Kisa asked me about Professor Drexler."

Alex sighed. He hated messes like this. "Okay dear. I'll try to tactfully see if I can convey something to him."

"Thanks dad. Don't forget, okay? I think that it might be important."

"If your daughter has information pertaining to this, I wish she would come talk to me." Stan sounded just a little annoyed and Alex supposed that he didn't blame him.

"Stan, we've got a few mitigating factors here. One, Ariel is busy beyond belief with her classes right now. Two, I think she's kind of going out on a limb with some sort of hunch here, and she's not so comfortable doing that. If it had been cut and dried she'd have come to you right away. This is more of a, I don't know, the more she thought about it the more it seemed like something sort of situation."

"Okay. So it seems like this maid knows something. In retrospect. Fine. I'll talk to the maid myself when I get down there at the end of December."

"Uh, that's the other reason Ariel wanted me to have this conversation with you. She got the impression that the woman had some issues with you." Then Alex had an idea he thought might diffuse the situation a little. "Maybe it's issues with guys in general. Like maybe this lady has had some bad experiences with men. You know, abuse or worse, and she is more comfortable talking to another woman. You can see how that might be the case."

"I suppose I can," Stan acknowledged. "A lot of machismo still in that region. Let me talk to my colleague Shelby. Maybe she can come with me in December and she can be the one to handle this issue."

"Sounds like a great idea," Alex agreed, relieved.

And now that Stan thought about it, having Shelby go with him in December did sound like a great idea.

Tyler and Tanner had the car secured for the big night, and they had made a point of planning to go to the game together, just the two of them, while Travis asked out a girl. Ms. Johnson had been pleased with Travis' choice of a date, and even happier once she had learned that Tanner and Tyler had each elected to not even go to the dance and to just go to the game together for a while.

"Doubt we'll even stay for the whole thing. School events are stupid," Tanner had declared.

Their plan was for Tyler to entice Teddie away from her girlfriends under the pretense of needing to tell her something really badly, and then for Tanner to call Tyler and say he was out at his car and really felt sick and would Tyler please come help him.

"You know Teddie. She'll insist on rushing out to my car with you to help me," Tanner said. "Once we get her to the car, we shove her into the back seat and I take off and you tell her not to panic, you just really need to talk to her and I'll drive you two out to the middle of nowhere."

"Yeah, but then what?" Tyler wasn't exactly sure how this plan gained them anything.

"So then we explain to her all the reasons why it is really important that she take a stand for the white race and dump her date and show up at the dance with you instead. It's like symbolic. She has to do it."

"And if she won't?"

"Then we beat her up a little. She shows up at the dance looking like someone has been seriously unhappy with her behavior and she helps the cause by sending a message to every white bitch out there who would consider deserting her race, right now in its time of greatest need. Either way it's good, Tyler. She sees the light or she sends a warning. Either way we turn your pain into a thing of beauty."

Tyler was angry, but he wasn't so sure he wanted to beat up on Teddie.

"She says no to you, she deserves it, man," Tanner encouraged him. "And we won't do anything really bad. She'll heal. And then she'll have plenty of time to rethink her decision."

"Okay, genius, so what do we do when she goes running to her old man afterwards and tells on us?"

"We call her a liar. Say she's covering up for damage done to her by some, whatever, pick a minority. Ms. J will back us up and give us an alibi, you know she will. Teddie won't want any more trouble with Ms. J and she'll let it drop."

Tyler still looked skeptical.

"Besides, women like tough men," Tanner assured him. "You'll have her respect after this for sure. And that's the most important thing with women. My dad taught me that."

Shelby liked the idea of going to Guatemala in December, too, but thought that Ariel's lead was too important to ignore for almost three months. "Stan, this maid could quit or get fired, turn ill, move away. It makes no sense to take that kind of chance. If she really knows something that could be helpful then we need to talk to her now."

"So are you able and willing to fly to Flores now to talk to her?"

Shelby thought. "No. I can't get away and that's a lot of money. But you know, we do have a volunteer who I would describe as bored, rich and looking for adventure. Why don't we see if Jennifer meant it when she said she would like to help us out?"

Teddie was sort of watching the football game while looking at a photo on another girl's cell phone when Tyler tapped her once on the shoulder.

"That has got to be the most adorable kitten ever," she said to her friend Michelle before she turned around and gave Tyler a leave-me-alone glare. "I wish my folks would let me get a kitten."

"Teddie, I really need to talk to you," he whispered. "Just for a minute, please. It's about Ms. Johnson. She's starting to do some stuff that's, like, weird and I want you to have it for background for your newspaper stuff. No quoting me or anything, but you need to know this and I can't talk to you at school." He looked at her friend pointedly. "Or here."

Teddie rolled her eyes. "Okay, just for a minute." Then to Michelle, "I'll be right back." Michelle looked hard at Tyler. "You want me to like, maybe follow you?" she asked Teddie softly.

"Nah, I'll be right back." Teddie shook her head as she made her way to the edge of the bleachers.

About fifteen rows back, Xuha closed the book he was looking at and stood up and followed Teddie out of the stadium.

"Dad, this is Ariel. I hope you get this message. Um, I'm not sure exactly how to put this, but the more I think about my conversations with Kisa the more I don't think she had a problem with Dr. Drexler as much as she did with the female students that were working with him. I'm not sure why. It's not like she thought that women shouldn't do things or anything like that, but I think something happened, maybe between her and one of the girls on the trip. I know this is getting complicated and I'm really sorry. But make sure that Dr. Drexler doesn't decide to send one of his female students down there. It would be a bad idea. I'm sorry this is so convoluted, Dad, I really am. I love you lots. Bye."

Tyler hadn't exactly thought through what he was going to tell Teddie while he stalled until Tanner made his fake call for help, so he started improvising with the truth.

"She's managed to get most of the history teachers either involved in the Klan or booted out of Early Gulch, you know. You wouldn't think so any more, but the Klan's got people on the school board and in the administration. They're the kind that keeps it quiet, you know, but they're still real happy to see a young person like Ms. J. who is willing to be more vocal and stir things up."

"That's incredible," Teddie was saying, sounding glad that she'd come out to talk with him.

Great, Tyler thought. *Teddie liked him best as a whistle blower on his own people.* He had a bad feeling about her willingness to ditch Marcus and go to the dance with him. He was almost relieved when the Maya-boy who was Teddie's dad's pet student walked up to join them.

Teddie gave Xuha the same irritated look she had given Tyler only minutes ago. Tyler smiled in satisfaction when Teddie said, "Xuha, I'm busy right now. Could this please wait?"

"Not really. Your dad really needs me to get a message to you."

"If my dad needs me he knows how to call my cell phone," she retorted.

Music from a cell phone started and Teddie reached for her purse, giving Xuha an apologetic glance. But it turned out to be Tyler's phone, and he answered it eagerly.

"What? Chest pains, man? Dizzy? You gotta be kidding. Yeah, yeah, I'll come out to the parking lot, sure, I'll be right there."

He gave Teddie his best helpless look. "Something's wrong. Tanner is in bad shape. I gotta go."

When she didn't say anything, he added, "You don't maybe

know a little first aid or anything, do you?"

"I've had the red cross class. I'm certified in CPR," Xuha chirped up with enthusiasm. "Come on. I'll go with you."

Shit, Tyler muttered to himself. *This was not good.*

"Great, because I've got to get back up there," Teddie said. "Michelle is going to be looking for me and I told Marcus I'd be cheering him on." Then realizing that she was sort of blowing both boys off she added as she headed away, "We'll talk more about that other stuff later Tyler. And Xuha, thanks for helping them." And she disappeared back into the crowd.

A baffled Tyler led Xuha out to Tanner's car. Now what? Well, Xuha was kind of small and didn't really have close friends, except for the kids on the tennis team, and they were hardly a force to worry about. He and his fellow Ts had targeted Xuha once last year when Ms. J had decided they should beat someone up just to send a message. Maybe they could salvage the night a little by using Xuha to send a second message.

"My daughter Ariel is not flaky, Stan, she never has been. In fact she is one of the least flaky people I know." This time Alex was trying not to be annoyed as he took time out of his own Friday night to call Stan and have this discussion. It was the first homecoming game he had missed in years, but between the unpleasant changes at his school and his decision not to shadow Teddie himself, staying home had seemed like his best option. Worry and frustration, however, had combined to put him in a foul mood.

"Alex, I'm not trying to accuse Ariel of anything. But I have a former student of mine who was on that trip who has agreed to fly down there on her own dollar and talk to this hotel maid, and now you're asking me to tell her not to go?"

"Ariel told me that the more she thought about her various conversations with the maid the more it seemed like one of your girl students did something to piss this lady off. Ariel thinks in retrospect that the maid kind of held you responsible for the bad behavior and that was her beef with you."

Alex could hear a clear sigh over the telephone line.

"I'm just saying," Stan said evenly, "that it would have been extremely helpful if perhaps your daughter could have realized all of this at once. Are we going to get more piecemeal impressions and memories from her?"

"I hope not Stan. I know that she has an awful lot on her plate now and she doesn't usually act this way at all. She really is trying to help you."

"Yeah, I suppose she is. Okay, I'll tell Jennifer that plans have changed. But would you please check with your daughter and make sure there isn't anything else I should know?"

"I'll try to get every last drop of information from her that I can this time Stan, I promise." Alex hung up the phone. He considered getting a beer, but then decided to hell with keeping his distance from homecoming. He was going to drive over and catch the last half of the game, with or without Lola.

"You don't have to come with me," he said, picking up his wallet and keys off the counter.

"I know," she said as she grabbed her purse and unplugged her cell phone from its charger and followed him out the door.

When Tyler and Xuha came up to the car, Tanner gave Tyler a puzzled look. "What the fuck? You change your taste in homecoming dates?" he muttered.

"Making the best of the situation, asshole," Tyler muttered back. "Let's try an alternate approach with a different messenger." But Xuha had stopped several feet away, choosing to stay in plain sight and not get in between the parked cars.

"Get in the car you illegal little bitch," Tyler said coming towards Xuha. "Or we make you."

Xuha smiled. He was pretty sure that he had taken these two on before, and this time there was no third guy to hit him from behind. All that time on a tennis court had only sharpened his abilities. He took a deep breath while time slowed down.

"You'll have to make me."

"Oh come on Shelby, I was looking forward to this trip!"

Shelby had called Jennifer right away before she got any further into her planning.

"I know Jennifer, and you don't know how much Stan and I appreciated your willingness to do this. Do you have any memory of this lady at all? This friend of Stan's new student Megan seems to think that one of us really angered her. I honestly don't remember interacting with hardly anyone at the hotel. Do you?"

Jennifer shook her head. "No. We were pretty much in our own world, I think, back then. Like we're not now," she had to laugh. "But no, I don't remember anyone from the hotel. How old is this lady now?"

"I'm not sure," Shelby said. "But that's a good point. She could have been a child or teenager. Do you remember doing anything that anyone might have objected to?"

Jennifer laughed. "Remember that you're asking me that question, honey. I did nothing *but* things that people might object to that summer."

And then it occurred to both of them at the same time.

"That's true," Shelby said. "You really did. And you had no idea who was watching."

"No," Jennifer agreed. "I did not."

As soon as Alex turned into the nearly full parking lot at the football stadium, he saw the cop lights from two cars and his heart nearly stopped. Lola inhaled deeply and closed her eyes for a few seconds.

"She's fine," was all Lola said.

Alex exhaled with relief and tried to turn down the path that lead to the revolving lights, but a security official stepped in front of him and waved him away.

"It's Xuha, not Teddie," Lola said quietly.

Alex rolled down the window. "One of my students is hurt down there. He doesn't have anyone else to come help him."

"It's a good thing that you're here then," the guard said, his expression changing as he waved Alex through now instead. "There's a kid down there that needs a friendly face."

Alex drove a few hundred more feet, got out and hurried over to where a couple of police officers and security people were all clustered. Xuha was standing with them, and looked fine. Tyler, however, was holding an ice bag up to his head and crumpled tissue against his bleeding nose. Tanner was on the ground unconscious. At least Alex hoped that he was unconscious.

The security man sitting in the golf cart clicked off his two-way radio and turned to Alex.

"You're here to help this student?" He pointed to Tanner. "We can't reach his dad. We've called an ambulance, we'd like someone who knows him to go to the hospital with him."

"What happened?" Alex was almost afraid to ask the question.

The other security guard came up on his golf cart from behind. Alex recognized him now in the light. He'd been part of Early Gulch for the past two decades, looking out for students and being fair and reasonable. Alex had always liked the man.

"These two yahoos," and he pointed to Tanner on the ground and to Tyler, "they jumped this kid here in plain sight." He pointed to Xuha. "Right out in the open where I could see it clearly, so don't you boys go claiming otherwise."

"Yeah, well he really provoked us," Tyler snarled.

"It was two on one, and I saw it all," the security guard said flatly.

"What happened to Tanner?" Alex asked.

"I hit him over the top of his head with both fists and he just crumpled," Xuha said.

Alex looked skeptical. Xuha was maybe five four. Tanner was at least six two.

"This kid has some real crouching dragon flying tiger kinds of moves," the security man said, giving Xuha an appreciative nod. "He had it handled before I could get over here."

A loud female voice cut off the security guard's comments. "Oh what did one of those people do now?" Tina Johnson came towards the little group with another history teacher in tow. Her voice was filled with loud, obvious concern. She turned to Tyler.

"You kids simply should not have to be defending yourselves from the likes of them. And at a homecoming game of all places." Then to the police and security guards, "Our children deserve better."

"Oh my heavens," she said in a whisper as her eyes turned to Tanner stretched out on the ground. Alex had the bizarre impression that Tina might ask for smelling salts.

"Perhaps you'd be willing to accompany him to the hospital instead of me?" Alex suggested.

"You?" Tina spat out the word almost in outrage. "Of course I'll go instead of you. I'm part of his family and, unlike you, I recognize that fact."

Medical records, even in the 1990s, were kept quite confidential. Tracing Yochi Rojas using the people who had cared for him during his illness would have been quite difficult. Death, on the other hand, is public. In the United States, if you know a person's full name and the year that they died, you can probably find out where.

Most people think of aerospace and oil when they think of Houston, Texas, but Kyle knew that it also boasted a world-class set of health care facilities and that cancer was one of the diseases most targeted. So he was not terribly surprised to discover that Mr. Rojas had passed away in Houston, survived by wife, daughter, son-in-law, grandchild and a local relative described as a cousin. Kyle knew enough of the culture to guess that the cousin may have been related any number of ways, but he was family and he had turned in the obituary and apparently provided a Catholic cemetery plot as well. Family does that.

Had the rest of his relatives then returned home? Kyle suspected that the son-in-law might have, but he had found no further records of Inez or Ixchel Rojas back in their parish in Mexico City. What did Inez Rojas do in her grief? Perhaps she had fallen ill too. It happened with surprising frequency after the loss of a spouse.

So Kyle continued scanning the death records in Houston looking for Inez's fairly untimely demise. He was oddly saddened when he discovered instead that daughter Ixchel had made the news when she was killed by a hit-and-run driver while dashing across a street in 1996. She was trying to catch a bus to get home and had an armload of groceries. The family had melted into oblivion afterwards, making Kyle think that Grandma Inez and toddler Xuha were alone by then and that they didn't want anyone looking too closely into their paperwork.

Kyle kept scanning death notices and obits although he didn't expect to find anything. Grandma now had a three year old in her care and a reason to live. He was sad to see that it wasn't enough. Inez Rojas died in 1999 with no other information provided.

Kyle thought of all of the complaints he had about his own upbringing. Over-analytical parents trying to produce a perfect child. Yes, it was always good to be reminded that others had survived situations far worse.

Or had the little boy survived? He could have ended up in the foster care system, but only if he was literally wandering the streets lost and crying. Much more likely, he had been taken in by other family members, by friends, even by kind strangers. Or unkind strangers. Never were the heights of human decency or the lows of human depravity more apparent than in the various fates awaiting an innocent abandoned child. Kyle found himself fervently hoping that the little boy had found the former, not the latter.

"Where are you Xuha Santos Rojas?" he asked out loud. "Are you still so defenseless? Is it even remotely possible that you are still walking around the United States illegally with a three-hundred-year-old artifact in your possession?"

In 1986 Ronald Reagan's administration attempted immigration reform. Included in the complex package was a one time offer of amnesty for illegal aliens who had lived and worked here continuously for over four years with no criminal record, who were willing to register for the draft, pass basic English and civics tests, and who could and would fill out the paperwork. Unfortunately, filling out the paperwork meant bringing one's illegal status to the attention of the INS, and in spite of efforts to assuage fears that applicants would not be deported when they applied, response to the offer was about a third to a half of what was expected. Simply put, people were scared.

The INS tried to find creative ways to overcome the mistrust, including having their top officials photographed wearing sombreros and placing reminders about the amnesty program into packages of tortillas sold in Texas. Congress let the program expire in 1988 and nothing like it has been offered since.

Alex wasn't quite the fan of online video phone calls that his wife and kids were, although he could see the charm of being able to see the other person's face and the even greater charm that the call was free. Particularly if it was coming from Belize

It did irritate him a little that Olumiji "contacted" Lola directly with the suggestion that Alex turn his video chat software on, but once he saw Olumiji's warm smile and Foluke's familiar face he made the wise decision to move on.

Foluke broke the ice by letting Alex know that she had gone out of her way to learn a little more Belizean history. "Did you know that you Confederates tried to create a new Dixie down here after the Civil War?"

"We did what? Wait. I'm not a Confederate. What are you talking about?"

"After your civil war. About seven thousand of you decided that you refused to be Yankees and left, and then a lot of you came to Belize to recreate the Old South. I've learned about it from a new friend of mine."

"Seriously." Alex was too fascinated to object to being considered a member of the Confederacy. "What happened to these folks?"

"Well, I think a lot of them got tired of the heat and the bugs and went home, but some stayed. Would you like to meet one of their descendants?"

Alex had noticed that Belize boasted the most intertwined ethnic diversity he had ever encountered. The original mix of largely Scottish, Nigerian, Maya and Spanish genes had been combined with those of indentured servants brought by the British from India and with German Mennonites fleeing religious persecution. Then in recent years East Asians and mid-easterners seeking new opportunities had contributed their genes into the mix. Why in the world had refugees from Dixie ever thought this country was a good place for the South to rise again?

Foluke turned her computer screen to show a young man her age with dark caramel-colored skin, a smattering of even darker freckles, reddish brown hair worn large with its natural African kinks, and the bluest eyes Alex had ever seen.

"This is Yochi. He figures about half of his ancestors on both sides, give or take, came from your Confederacy."

Alex didn't know what to say. Olumiji tried to say it for him.

"Once the refugee Confederates actually settled in here, those that stayed found that they had to adapt their original ideas about separation of the races. Within a few generations they were Belizeans, as sure as all others that have come to call this nation home."

"This really is some great information," Alex said. "And I have got to learn more about Confederates in Belize just to counter some of the things that are going on at my school. But right now I'm looking for help on a very different sort of problem."

"So Maurice said. You are seeking a lost artifact to help a friend of yours. I must ask you a question, Alex. Is it a good idea that this artifact be found?"

Alex gave Olumiji an odd look. "That's a very reasonable question. I've been focused on giving aid to an old buddy who is a decent guy and is trying to repair his tarnished professional reputation by finding this. Between helping a friend and solving a puzzle it seemed a no-brainer."

"Do you know what this treasure actually is?"

"No, we don't. It's made to sound like gold or jewels but honestly Stan says it could be art or books or religious artifacts, anything that this group of Maya valued highly. And yes, the scholars of today would value it highly too. Time isn't kind to anything physical, so finding and caring for this treasure sooner rather than later is probably a good idea. If it is something more esoteric like an actual ancient Maya codex that these later Maya hid, then it couldn't be found by a society more anxious to preserve and care for it than today's."

"Yet only three hundred years ago this same society was burning these things?" Olumiji asked.

"Yes, they were. We were. They were." Alex shrugged with confusion. "I don't know how responsible I am for everything that anyone of European descent ever did." *Good lord, am I starting to sound like Tina Johnson?* he wondered to himself.

"I don't take responsibility for every African king who sold his enemies into slavery," Olumiji said gently. "Let's just be responsible for our own acts of unkindness. That is difficult enough."

"Agreed," Alex said, thinking how really hard it was to dislike this guy once you were actually talking to him.

"What you say about time makes sense to me," Olumiji went on. "If something precious from this civilization is deteriorating and we can find it, we should. So Maurice has spoken to me of this boy who headed east with a piece of your puzzle. Foluke and I will do a little traveling together for the next week. What you seek is unusual and if someone has seen it or heard of it, they will likely tell us. And if they do not tell us, I will know."

"That, that would be very helpful," Alex said. *Especially the last part,* he thought, and could have sworn that Olumiji stifled a smile.

"I have given this some thought," Olumiji went on. "If you look at an elevation map you can see that there is small mountain range on the western side of southern Belize"

"I know it," Alex volunteered. "Lola and I visited it right before we met Foluke."

"Yes, well in my observation no one likes to walk over mountains. If the boy walked due east it is true he hit Dangriga, but in doing that he also had to walk over the northern edge of those foothills. Even that would be an effort. I think if we do not find this thing you seek around Dangriga itself, we will head north because likely the boy himself turned slightly north to avoid the mountains. I think this makes sense."

Alex had to agree that it did. He thanked Olumiji and Foluke and bade farewell to Yochi, who just waved and smiled. "He doesn't speak your kind of English so well," Foluke explained. So Alex just waved back.

And as he shut down the software he felt for the first time in a while like maybe he was going to be of some help to Stan.

"I've decided to found a club of my own," Alex told Xuha as he walked around the court, using his spring-loaded device to pick up the dozens of balls now lying around.

"A school club? Will they let you do that?"

"I wasn't thinking of a school club, but now that you mention it, yes, it could be a school club."

"Oh, you were going to form a real club? Like the Knights of Columbus or the Shriners?"

"Well that's what I was thinking originally, yes. My wife, she's fallen into this organization called 'the letter x to the power of zero.'"

"That's one," Xuha said. "I mean, it's the number one."

"I know," Alex said. "And they just call it that. ' One.' They are all very into humans inter-relating and understanding each other."

"It doesn't sound like such a bad club. You say she fell into it?"

"That may not have been the best choice of words. She's gotten very involved in it. Anyway, I found out a few months ago that my son has made some new friends, shall we say outside of his college circle, and one of them is this guy almost my age who heads up a political philosophical think tank thing called 'the letter y to the power of the number one'."

"That's 'y'." Xuha said.

"I know," Alex said, "and they sometimes call it just 'why.' It's all about the individual's search for a happy life, a sort of an 'express yourself and be who you are' kind of group."

"Well, that sound good too," Xuha said.

"It is, it is," Alex said. "I just was feeling sort of like there was a club waiting for me somewhere, and then this morning it occurred to be that there wasn't. I need to start it myself. And now that you mention it, making it a school club would be perfect."

Xuha was grinning in understanding. "So you are going to start a club called 'the letter z to the power of two.' Zee squared. Zee for Zeitman."

It was nice to be understood, Alex thought. "That's my plan. Then when I started hitting balls with you I realized that this club has to be about time. Understanding how time works. Sooner or later I want it to look closely at people like me and you, who, you know, have some sort of special relationship with time. Athletes, martial arts experts, dancers, acrobats, anyone who uses their body and occasionally gets the sense of becoming slightly disconnected from the normal flow of time being experienced by everyone else."

Xuha was nodding in understanding. "Like my kid friend, the really good soccer player."

"Right. There may be, I don't know, concert pianists and rock and roll guitar players who feel the same way, Xuha. Rescue workers. Firemen. My dad was a fireman. I wonder if he ever experienced anything like what we do?"

"Maybe it's hereditary?"

"I have no idea. But if I can launch this club and then handle that sort of question in a way that keeps people from deciding that I'm a kook, maybe I can learn something."

"So what is your club going to start out by doing?"

Alex sighed as he tried to think of where to begin. "I think about time a lot, Xuha. A real lot. Do you realize that every single day you make, I don't know, hundreds of choices. Maybe thousands. Some don't matter at all but other little ones unexpectedly do. Chomp down with the right side of your mouth instead of the left and you pop loose an old crown and you have to go the dentist where there is a robbery in progress and you call nine-one-one and, you get the idea. The ramifications usually aren't that dramatic, of course, but every little decision that does makes a difference, results in time moving forward along one path instead of another. The possibilities grow out geometrically. They actually grow out at a rate of two to the power of, well, any variable you like."

"And you like the letter 'zee'," Xuha said. "So shouldn't you maybe call the club two to the power of zee?"

"Maybe, but it doesn't have the same ring as zee squared. Plus, I kind of like the idea that the whole geometrically exploding possibilities thing is stealth. Hidden in the name, kind of in a code. Do you think that the school will let me start a club about considering multiple timelines and their ramifications?"

Xuha made an exaggerated wince with his face. "Only if you can find a way to tie it into restoring the South to its former glory."

"You know," Alex said, "I think maybe I can."

Alex tried running harder to catch up to the light being ahead of him so that he could ask her a question. But it seemed to take more and more effort just to go even a little bit faster. "I have got to lose some weight," he muttered to himself as an almost herculean push with his leg muscles yielded only the tiniest bit more speed.

Another golden light particle began to approach him from behind. "Pull-eeze," she muttered, "don't even waste your time trying. You can't do it. You can't go as fast as she does."

"Right," Alex said. "I know that. I know that a physical object like myself cannot obtain the speed of light. The harder I try the heavier I get."

"You know a lot, don't you?" she said.

"Well, I think that I do understand the basics of special relativity," he said rather proudly. "I teach the subject you know."

"Hmm. That's nice. Did it ever occur to you that just maybe you don't know everything about it? Maybe you don't even know very much about it? Maybe you only know just a little tiny piece of it and you just think you know it all?"

"Is it my imagination or are you guys getting snottier all the time?" Alex asked.

"We have no personality, Alex. We're light particles. If you're picking up any kind of personality from us, trust me it is coming from you."

"So now you guys are therapists too?" he muttered back.

"Did it ever occur to you that light, the universe and the conscious mind are all inter-related," she said archly.

"No," Alex said flatly. "I prefer my physical universe to stay separate from the social and biological sciences thank you."

"That's nice. I hope that works out well for you," she smiled back over her shoulder as she moved on out of conversational range.

Alex made his appointment directly with the new principal hoping for exactly the sort of pushback that he was now getting. Like many schools, especially high schools, the principal at Early Gulch no longer handled disciplinary problems with students, or the day-to-day running of class schedules, building and grounds maintenance, or school activities. In a modern school these functions generally get handed over to the various assistant principals, allowing the principal time to deal with the school board, with downtown, and with parents and the community, serving as the all important public face of the school.

This particular principal had also chosen to have minimal contact with the teaching staff, preferring to work instead through her department heads. That choice was not so unusual either. But she seemed particularly annoyed with Alex for taking up her time this morning. She looked up from her appointment calendar.

"It says here you made an appointment with me to discuss forming a new club here to talk about the nature of time. Mr. Zeitman. Rita Cooke is allowing you quite a bit of latitude in teaching your advanced physics class. I don't necessarily agree, but I am giving her the latitude to make that decision. Be advised that you have already received all the leeway that you are likely to get from this administration. It's not my role to approve of school clubs, but it is my opinion that we don't need one more of them right now, and certainly not one about as flaky a topic as time. I suggest that your energy would be better spent concentrating on a solid traditional approach to teaching your subject matter."

Alex waited until the woman was totally finished, and then

he waited for a second or two more.

"Did you have anything else you wanted to discuss with me?" she asked by way of dismissal.

"Yes ma'am. I understand that the history department is working towards staging a reenactment of the battle of Cedar Creek this January."

"Yes. Do you have a problem with that Mr. Zeitman?"

"I came to you, ma'am, because I had an idea to help with that effort. You surely appreciate that it can be difficult to get young people enthused about science."

"Science can be a bit dry," the principal admitted. "But frankly I don't see much of a way to tie it into the Civil War."

"I was hoping that Early Gulch could have a slightly grander vision, ma'am, and it seemed to me that grand visions were your department. This club I am proposing isn't so much to discuss time, as it is to talk about alternative histories. How little decisions can affect the world down the road. How things might be today if they had gone different in the past."

Alex could see that he had the principal's attention now.

"You mean like the Civil War."

"Exactly. Most historians recognize that the battle of Cedar Creek was one of the last possible pivotal movements for the Old South. General Early's brilliant surprise attack on the union not only almost won him the battle, but it was only miles away from D.C., where a war-weary north was about to reluctantly re-elect Abe Lincoln. That loss may well have tipped the scales on Lincoln's re-election prospects, leaving a tired north ready to agree to secession. Except of course that Early lost the battle, and many say it is because he halted his troops and let them loot the union camps for food and supplies."

The principal arched an eyebrow. "I had no idea that my physics teachers knew so much about the Civil War."

"History fascinates me," Alex replied levelly. "And I thought that my advanced physics class might engage the students a little by discussing the idea of building a time machine. We can't do it, of course, but we can think about it, and our ideas could be part of this reenactment. Pretend to take everyone back in time. Present a couple of ideas about time travel to everybody there. Be part of the show. Science and social science working together."

She was nodding and smiling. "Then maybe as an audience we could elect to have our time travelers adjust history," she said, eagerness creeping into her voice. "Find a way to keep Jubal Early and his men charging relentlessly after the union soldiers. We could change how the battle goes. Let the spectators know that it may have changed the election. Changed the whole fate of the South."

"That's it," Alex agreed. "All just as a thought experiment, of course. As a way to educate. But it could take this reenactment the school is planning and turn it into something far more exciting."

"I like it. I actually do, Mr. Zeitman. You've involved another whole department, more kids, more parents. More press. Early Gulch uses science to rewrite history more to their liking. All under the guise, of course, of learning. It will get coverage, get the community talking. This could be very good."

"'I thought that my club, zee squared, could take on some of the workload of organizing the 'let's go back in time and change history' part of this. With only the one advanced physics class, I don't want to burden those students with too much of what I have in mind. It's better done by an extracurricular group. We will work with Ms. Johnson's club of course."

"Of course," she was smiling agreeably now. "I had no idea that you were proposing an auxiliary group to one of the already existing clubs. That's quite different. Clearly I'll approve it. You coordinate with Ms. Johnson."

She gave Alex a funny look.

"You don't look particularly familiar. Have I, uh, have I met you at any outside, maybe community or church activities or events? Have I seen you… anywhere?"

"I'm kind of a loner," Alex said. "I don't tend to join things. But I am very enthused about this."

"Well that's good. We certainly need enthusiasm from our teaching staff. I'll tell you, Mr. Zeitman, getting some of these teachers around here to be excited about what they are doing is like pulling teeth. You wouldn't believe it."

I think I would, Alex thought.

Lola, Teddie and Alex were having a rare dinner together at one end of the dining room table while Alex's work on his Maya box replica was shoved to the other side.

"Teddie, I think you're right about Early Gulch somehow having slid into the clutches of the local Klan."

"I know, Dad. I tried to tell you. And homecoming night Tyler was trying to tell me the same thing."

"Wait, you were talking to Tyler that night?"

"Yeah. He called me downstairs to tell me this big deal about how Ms. Johnson has all these important allies. They don't want to speak up, but they help her behind the scenes, and he was just getting started when Tanner called about getting sick and Xuha offered to help Tanner and I so went back up to the game."

"How did Xuha get into your and Tanner's conversation?" Lola asked.

"No idea. He came out of nowhere saying you needed to talk to me. Did you? And then of course he goes out to help Tanner and they jump him. What a couple of scumbags."

Teddie saw her parents exchange a look.

"What? I can tell that you're not telling me something?"

She stopped for a second. "Wait. Tyler wanted me to come out to the car with him. I know he did, because he asked if I knew first aid."

Alex and Lola waited.

"They were going to hurt *me,* weren't they? But why? I thought Tyler liked me…"

"Sometimes that's how a boy responds to rejection," Lola offered gently.

"Oh my God, that is so sick."

Teddie chewed in silence for a few seconds more. "I bet that he was mad that I was going to the dance with Marcus, too. That neo-Nazi. And to think I talked to him. That's incredible. That asshole."

"Teddie," Alex cautioned, "calm down. Do you think that when he needed to make up something to talk to you about, he maybe went ahead and told you the truth?"

"Yeah. I'd guess that's just what he did. Dad, these guys are out of control. They could have hurt Xuha. I don't know how a little guy like him fought the two of them off. We've got to do something."

"Well, it turns out that I agree. And I need your help," Alex said. Lola raised an eyebrow questioningly.

"Teddie, today I met with the principal and offered my assistance with the Civil War reenactment that the history department is planning. We are going to work with them to design an alternate history in which the South is finally allowed to secede."

Alex ignored two remarkably similar faces both with expressions that said, "Are you nuts?"

"The nice thing about getting a whole 'nother department participating is that this is now going to involve a lot more people and it is going to bring in a lot more publicity."

"Bright sunlight is the best disinfectant," Lola said as Alex's plan began to dawn on her.

"What??" Teddie asked.

"The expression means that outside attention can sometimes be the best solution. I am going to try to get Early Gulch and its growing fascination with bringing back Dixie all the attention that I possibly can."

"Do you think that the school paper can help?" Teddie was starting to get interested.

"Oh," Alex smiled. "I am sure that it can. I was wondering if the assistant editor in charge of school clubs and activities might not even be interested in running a contest of sorts?"

"Contests are great."

"How about one for the best essay on the subject of 'How my life would be different if the South had been allowed to secede.'"

"They will never let me print the really good ones," Teddie complained.

"I'm counting on that," Alex said. "And once this whole

thing starts to get some attention, I am betting that there will be folks out there who would love to see the essays that the administration bans."

"Could Teddie get in trouble doing this?" Lola asked.

"I think that after the house cleaning that is going to happen because of this event, Teddie will be just fine and so will I," Alex said. Then he added, "and Early Gulch will be a lot better."

October 1697

For three months now Ichik had worked harder than he ever had in his life. Days were filled with the backbreaking labor of cutting down the massive trees for a purpose he still did not understand. Nights were filled with loneliness as he struggled to learn more words to talk to those around him. Gestures, tone and expressions guided him, and his unflinching helpfulness and smile kept all but the truly cruel at bay.

Both the richly colored and the pale people had their share of such viciousness, of course, just as his own people had. It appeared to Ichik that the phenomenon of finding another's pain entertaining spanned all three cultures quite well. Thankfully, each of these groups also had a few people willing to stand up to outright meanness and to tell a bully to go away. That is how, after a series of rather tough days, he no longer was whipped when he did not understand a command during the day, and he had once again gotten to eat his own dinner at night. As a bonus, he had learned the phrase "leave him alone" in both of the other people's tongues.

On the best of nights there was music and dancing with his new people, and after a couple of months Ichik shyly tried to join in with the small bone whistle he carried in his pack. His new family appeared startled the first time that he brought it out, and all the other noise had stopped as they stared at him in disbelief. But as he played a few tentative notes they had begun to smile, and now Ichik and his whistle were welcome whenever the music started. Those nights he laughed sometimes and even began to feel like maybe he belonged here.

Ichik began to notice that one of the girls tended to stare at him whenever he played, and he started watching her back out of the corner of his eye. Once she noticed his return attention, she bent her head down demurely, but raised her eyes up to him and smiled in a language understood the world over. He gave her an appreciative nod and tried to play better. She began to move to the rhythm of music and smiled more in return. And for the first time that Ichik could remember in his whole life, he thought that carrying out his mother's instructions and doing the bidding of his ancestors might not be the dreaded curse he had always thought it would be.

Chapter 15. November 2010

Jennifer started the email to Nelson six times before she finally got the tone she wanted. This was not a contact from an ex-lover. Not correspondence from a colleague, as she could hardly pretend to be such. They weren't friends and never had been. She was not pleading for assistance. And no she didn't particularly want to see him or get re-acquainted.

She was merely someone he once knew who was seeking information.

Did he or did he not know of anyone from the hotel in 1993 who had been aware of his frequent nightly trips out into the rainforest with Jennifer?

Nelson composed a dozen different answers to Jennifer's painfully short, matter-of fact inquiry before he considered not answering at all. That might be best. Or worst. What if she followed up his lack of response by calling him? Or by coming to see him? Maybe she would follow up an answer from him that way too. Could that be good? How could it possibly be good?

It annoyed him that in the end, he did what he had done with her all along. He followed her lead. His email response was as short and factual as her original message.

Didn't she remember that sometimes he had brought beer and snacks along for the two of them? Not wanting to risk censure or questions from a hotel staff that appeared to all know and like Dr. Drexler, he had always turned to a quiet young girl who cleaned off the tables to ask for his late night picnic supplies. She had asked no questions. He had thought it best to not involve others. He had absolutely no idea what her name was or if she had talked to anyone else about his requests. As far as he could recollect, no one else had known.

Alex ended up giving the class until Monday, November 1, for their initial presentations on their time machine design. He had already moved his other two project deadlines to now coincide with the class' involvement with the history reenactment, and he was trying to shift the class focus to make sure that they would have something to offer what was turning into a big school event.

The class had divided itself into seven teams. Three of those teams seemed to be very pleased about this collaboration with the history department, and each of them appeared to be focusing largely on issues of time travel to the past. On Monday, all three of these teams made their presentations.

The first team, consisting of two rather quiet, diligent boys, was fascinated with military strategy and enamored with the idea of visiting great battles throughout history. Alex listened to them describe all of the world's most pivotal battles in their presentation and thought that it was an amazing amount of work, but far lighter on physics than he would have liked. He was going to guess that there had been a lot of play with little plastic soldier figures in these boys' past.

Three of the four girls had formed another team and their leader was engrossed in fashion. Antebellum dresses, and long flowing dresses in general, took up more of the presentation than they should have. A frustrated Alex had to remind himself that the grown-up equivalent of dressing up dolls was no more frivolous than that of playing with toy soldiers. Both genders clearly needed more guidance on content.

Although he tried to keep each team to three students or less, Alex granted an exception to the third team, which consisted of Travis, Tanner, Tyler and a fourth shy skinhead aspirant who had no where else to go and had begged to be allowed to join them. In the classroom, like everywhere else, one has to pick their battles.

It still bothered Alex that after the homecoming dance both Tyler and Travis had been only briefly suspended from school and forced to do detention, but for reasons Alex could only guess at neither boy was charged with assault like he should have been. Rather than complain, Alex forced himself to swallow his own anger, knowing that if he managed to stay off of everyone's radar then his plans for the reenactment were far more likely to be successful. So he treated the little hooligans with more consideration than they deserved, while they kept to one corner of the room and did a lot of glaring and muttering like they had somehow been wronged. Tyler in particular would barely look at Alex now, and much of his hostility appeared to be consistently directed at Xuha.

None-the-less this group of four did a reasonably credible job of covering historical and fictional approaches to time travel, and they at least discussed the classic paradox problem of a time traveler going back and killing himself as a baby. They presented the two counter possibilities for consideration. One was the well-known butterfly effect wherein the tiniest of changes, such as the movements of a butterfly's wings, could have pronounced consequences. They talked about the alternative, wherein history is so fixed that the universe itself fights any effort at change. The boys seemed to like this scenario, as they described the herculean endeavor of a group of hardened time warriors who took on the universe itself to right the wrongs of the past. Alex knew better to ask what this team thought those wrongs might have been.

At the end of the first group of presentations, Alex was resolved to get more physics back into this project. He gently reminded all his history buffs that they were addressing only half of the problem.

"Who wants to build a machine to go the future?" Tanner asked. "We're all going to end up there anyway." Even Alex had to smile.

"Yeah, plus the way this country is going it's clearly gonna suck," the fourth team member chimed in.

"Now, that's a worthy question," Alex remarked. "Can you ever know if the future is going to turnout poorly? What is poorly? Worse for you personally? Worse for the human race? And if you go forward in time and don't like what you see, can and should you head back and try to make things better? We are getting out of the realm of physics again, but those are questions worth considering."

On Wednesday the presentations took on a different tone. Three of the four teams that presented seemed to be much more focused on traveling to the future. These kids were the ones who had looked most annoyed about the tie-in to the Civil War reenactment, although Alex suspected that a few of them may have guessed that their teacher had made such a deal in order to keep the physics project alive.

The first group up included Xuha, who had teamed up with two other seniors from the tennis team, and Alex was glad to see him finally making friends. This group pulled in information on how, in a purely theoretical sense, there wasn't a mathematical difference in physics between the past and the future, and they shared their own discomfort with the idea of the lack of free will that was implied.

"If you accept the idea that the universe is something that just is, a complete and predetermined entity which includes a time dimension and a timeline on which you happen at this particular instant to be at one point, then you have to ask 'What's the point?' Not, 'What's the point you are at?" the slight girl, who was captain of the tennis team, explained. "I mean, what's the purpose? It's all already finished. It exists. It doesn't matter what you do because what you do is already incorporated." She looked out at Alex and her fellow students for understanding.

"That is one possible problem with the implications of modern physics," Alex nodded.

"That's stupid," Tyler spoke up for the first time in almost two weeks. "If you accept that you can't do anything about anything because what you do has already been decided, then what's been decided is that you're a wus who doesn't do anything. Right? So why not do things you want so that it turns out that doing the things you want is what you did?"

"Tyler's got an excellent point also. Even if free will were only an illusion, you gain nothing by curling up in a ball, saying there's no sense in getting out of bed and then blaming the universe for your condition." Six more hands shot into the air to respond, and Alex let the discussion continue for another half hour. Yes, he would be behind schedule and deviating from his lesson plan once again, and he knew that he was taking dangerous forays into the metaphysical. But yes, it also looked like he had achieved one of those rare moments in the classroom where nineteen other brains were all engaged and thinking about the subject matter. What a shame Maurice had not come to visit this class period.

Next up was the student currently ranked first in the senior class, who had insisted on working by himself. He also appeared to be focused on getting to the future, and he was trying to seriously devise a way to do it. A largely baffled class ended up listening to a brief history of cryogenics, or the science of freezing a living being to be defrosted and revived much later. Daniel wanted to take the idea a step further, actually moving all the subatomic particles that constituted a living being into a sort of stasis mode, slowing them down considerably so that the individual would age almost not at all while time flew by. Eventually bringing the tiniest building blocks of the still hopefully living creature back to normal energy levels would in essence be a one-way time machine.

"I hope that one way time travel counts?" he asked Alex seriously.

"If you've given it that much thought it does," Alex replied, impressed.

A team of three Latino boys who were all best friends, and also some of the better students in the school, went next, and their focus was on alternate universes. Alex was delighted to see string theory finally make it into the discussion. He listened happily while this team posed the question that if one went into the future, would one perhaps have to first pick which of many futures they wanted to travel to?

The last team consisted of three buddies as well, but based on the presentation it was hard to tell where they were going with their project. The team had one really bright kid who had almost no motivation for academics. Alex felt like his two teammates brought less innate ability to learn and an equal lack of motivation. This team mostly made jokes and fooled around at the front of the room. Alex wondered if they were going to be able to complete a project at all. Well, he was three for four during today's class, he figured, and many a day his batting average was not nearly that good.

Stan knew he should be more appreciative of Alex's help, but honestly it didn't seem like much was coming of it. Alex had made sketches of what he thought were the most likely dimensions of the other trapezoids. Apparently there was a way for each of the boxes to contain a 3-4-5 right triangle and for each one to be a multiple of the others. The three boxes would form a perfect square when put together, and all the various rectangles involved were somehow multiples of these same numbers too. Alex had been very excited about it all once he had worked it out, but Stan was less so. Sure it was good information to have, but it didn't help him translate. The code cracking itself had been deemed impossible until at least one more of the two missing boxes was found.

Worse yet, they hadn't even formed a plan for searching for the box off to the west. Much of that area north of Guatemala City was rough terrain, hotly contested for decades between poorly treated Maya, guerillas who often were trying to help them, and land owners and the army supporting them. Drug lords and thieves had joined in the mix, making the beautiful highlands of Guatemala one of the more dangerous places in the Western Hemisphere. If one of the boxes was buried here, it was probably going to stay hidden right where it was for a very long time.

But Alex had expressed confidence that with only one other box he could get a handle on the number of hieroglyphs involved and maybe, finally, begin to break the long list of digits into meaningful pairs of numbers and then make some inferences about the code itself. It wouldn't be an exact process, but he could make better guesses and narrow the possibilities down to where Stan and Shelby could pick those that produced the more sensible messages. And from their best solutions Alex could hone his answers further.

So Stan had become quite hopeful about these friends in Belize in which Alex was putting a lot of faith. Apparently Alex's wife had some sort of work connection with some Nigerian man whose sister now lived in Belize and this brother and sister had ended up spending over two weeks combing the area around Dangriga and northwards looking for anyone who had ever seen anything like this artifact. Unfortunately, they had not actually found the second box. And all they had managed to come back with was a disturbing story.

Alex noticed the change in his advanced physics class as soon as he walked into the room. The barely veiled angry looks coming from the back corner had been replaced by a clear sense of gloating. In fact, the four boys had all moved forward a couple of rows, and instead of sitting hunched over and barely glancing up at Alex, today they all sat with their long legs stretched out, hands behind their heads, smiling. "We own this room now," their very posture seemed to say.

Xuha, on the other hand, looked down and said very little. He seemed to have no physical injury that Alex could discern, but Alex did not think he had ever seen the boy look so sad.

It took a lot of effort to remain professional, as he walked the class through the next part of the project. The paper, now due before winter break, would have many more requirements specifically related to modern physics. It was time to get more serious. Alex outlined each topic that had to be covered in some detail to a classroom that he was certain was paying him very little attention. Hell, he admitted. He was, in fact, paying very little attention to today's subject matter himself.

When the bell finally rang he softly asked Xuha to remain behind. Xuha paused reluctantly. As Tanner walked by he said to Alex, "Careful, don't touch Maya boy here." He gave Xuha a little push. "Ol' Zoo-ha is poisonous now in case you haven't heard." Tanner looked like he was about to say more when Travis grabbed his arm with a look telling him to stop.

"We won, asshole. Don't go getting us in trouble now," Travis mumbled as they walked out of the room.

"Xuha? What's going on?"

"Please Mr. Z. You don't want to get involved."

"Actually, Xuha, I do. What's going on?"

"I think I made a real enemy of Ms. Johnson and her friends when I beat up on Tanner and Tyler, but honestly Mr. Z, I was just defending myself. I wouldn't have hurt them otherwise, I swear."

"I know that, Xuha, and you were also looking out for my daughter, which makes this my business too. I need to know what those boys did to you."

"They did not do anything. Honest. I don't know for sure who caused me trouble, but we're not talking about students here or a world in which you have any power Mr. Z. So I need to keep you out of this. You've been too good to me. I'm sorry."

He said the last words as he walked out the door, looking, if possible, even sadder than when he had come in.

Jennifer and Shelby were having lunch again, something they had done a few times lately and both rather looked forward to. Jennifer had chortled with delight at the lunch when Shelby shared details of her new and considerably more intimate relationship with their former advisor, and she had been more than understanding when Shelby confided that the missing document was in fact hidden in Stan's front hall closest. All in all, Jennifer turned out to be a worthy confident.

Better yet, she was turning into a friend. Each woman enjoyed the chance to leave the world that filled her own days to enter the world of another, ostensibly more glamorous existence. Wealthy socialite. Career woman. It's always fun to learn more about that greener grass on the other side.

Of course, they could have both left each encounter envious and frustrated, but that isn't the way it seemed to go. Neither woman was driven to convince the other that her own life was better. Shelby's long dark blond braid had become a metaphor for their new friendship. They each were entitled to their own style. Their own choices. No reflection on the other.

So they shared stories that the other enjoyed, they both commended and supported the other, and in the end, each left feeling good about her own life too. It was one of those odd friendships that worked.

It was Jennifer who decided in mid-November that they needed to mutually enlist Jake in their efforts. She had heard back from Nelson and had pretty much decided that Nelson's busgirl who had provided him with beer and snacks had to have become the maid that was still angry at Dr. Drexler's old students. Maybe Jake could talk to this woman? Maybe the two of them could set up a video chat with Jake?

Jake ran an import-export business. Maybe he could even find a reason to get down to Flores, and to write it off as a business expense? Shelby recognized that Stan was growing increasingly frustrated with the lack of progress on all fronts, and she was at her wits' end trying to think of ways to help him. Maybe Jake was the key.

The Nigerian brother and sister had only meant to spend a few days looking for the artifact that Lola wanted to find, but they both had some extra time, and once they got involved in the treasure hunt they got rather intrigued. Plus, the dynamic between a much older brother and his younger sister can be strained, particularly if he only remembers her as a little nuisance. Olumiji recognized that letting his grown, very capable little sister now lead him around the country where she lived was something of a renewal process for them both. After a few days, he decided to keep searching while making this time of getting reacquainted with Foluke a priority.

So they had moved out west and north from Dangriga, asking their questions to an ever-widening arc of people as they combed the coastal area of central Belize. And everywhere they had gotten one of two responses.

The first response was expected. No, the person being asked had never heard of or seen such a thing. Foluke usually asked the questions, while Olumiji used his special talents to pick up on everyone within earshot's true response to the inquiry. Sometimes people were curious, other times they were indifferent, but most people had no idea of where the relic might be found.

And then there was the other response. Foluke got it verbally a few times, and Olumiji picked it up many more. "You also? Are you with the other people who are looking for it too?"

After pressing for more details when possible, Olumiji and Foluke pieced together a story. A young man, he looked like he might be from Mexico, had been through this area ten or fifteen years ago, asking everyone the very same questions. He spoke English well, he was polite, he was determined. He offered modest sums of money for relevant information. A few had taken advantage of him, made up stories and taken the cash, and sent him off on various fool's errands. He'd been savvy enough to make no complaint, and keen enough to keep himself from real harm. After a while, he had left Belize relieved of some of his money and otherwise empty handed.

Then a few years ago he had come back. He had brought a few Mexican youth with him this time, presumably hired, and they had not only questioned people more aggressively but also had searched for themselves around any abandoned old town or deserted building. This time the man had offered no money for information, but he had offered an impressive sum of money for anyone who would find and bring the box to him. Many a local would have been quite happy to oblige. But no one actually knew how to find this thing that the man so desperately sought.

He had left an email address with anyone who would take it, and after his departure a fair number of people, particularly kids, had gone hunting for the treasure that they could sell to this man and then become very rich by local standards. A few older locals observed wryly that if any such artifact was available to be found, the determined youth of Belize would have certainly turned it up by now.

When Olumiji called Alex to share the disappointing news, they agreed that the box had either been damaged and destroyed long ago, or that it had left the area, either sold elsewhere or moved along with an owner who had no idea what they were carrying to their new home.

Alex had been in a foul mood for days and Lola was getting concerned. She knew that he was frustrated with the fact that he hadn't been able to solve Stan's puzzle more readily. When she asked if there had been any new progress she just got a dour look for an answer. Olumiji had given her his own abbreviated version of the disappointing results in Belize, of course, and Lola guessed that lack of progress had added to Alex's funk.

However, when Saturday came and went and there was no

practice session with Xuha, Lola surmised that there was more bothering Alex. She tried a gentle question and was told that he did not want to talk about it. She gave it another day. Then she tried a gentle probe into his mind. Well, no surprise. Alex also didn't want to think about it. He was focused on his popcorn and his beer and every other bit of his thoughts were resolutely concentrated on a tennis match on TV. He caught her looking at him.

"Get out and stay out," he said flatly. They both knew what he meant.

"I'm just concerned," she said.

"Don't be," he replied.

So she tried talking to Teddie.

"I'm worried about him too, Mom. I haven't heard a thing about anything going wrong in his class or his getting in trouble with the administration or anything like that. He seems to almost be back in their good graces now that he's pretending to play nice with the Civil War reenactment. I don't think he and Xuha are speaking to each other, but I can't imagine why. I mean, except for being some kind of ninja fighting machine when he gets attacked, Xuha is like the sweetest little guy I've ever known. I don't mean that to be condescending," she added quickly. "I owe this guy big time."

"I can't imagine that he and your dad had an argument. It would be so unlike both of them," Lola said.

"The only other thing I've noticed is that Tyler and his friends are walking around school lately like they own the place. It's weird, mom. You start to act that way and people start to think you do. You know?"

"Yeah, I do know. What's happening with that crazy teacher that spends all the time with those boys?" Lola asked.

"Ms. Johnson? She's pretty much walking around like she owns the place too. Rumor has it that she kind of does, that really important people on the school board and downtown think she's the greatest now."

"She teaches American history? Mostly Juniors?"

"Yeah. And I'm going to do my best to get anybody but her next year."

"I would so much like to meet this lady," Lola said. "Can you think of any possible legitimate reason I might have for making contact with her?"

"Mommmmmm... please, don't make trouble"

"Honey, I swear I won't."

Teddie sighed an exasperated sigh more like old her thirteen-year-old self.

"Okay. She's started a group for moms that meets afterschool. It's through the PTA I think, and it's supposed to be to provide crafts and costumes for the reenactment thing, but I think they basically sit around and talk about how great white people are."

"No."

"Yes. It's not at any easy time for you to get there. I don't think she's exactly targeting moms with professional careers."

"I have some flexibility," Lola remarked. "When is the next meeting?"

Stan reluctantly agreed with Alex's assessment of the fate of the box in Belize, and with that had to face the fact that perhaps the puzzle carved into his beautiful obsidian relic would never be solved. He was running out of ideas.

Shelby kept persisting that maybe the hotel maid in Flores could be of some help, and so finally Stan agreed that asking Jake to make a visit there on all of their behalf couldn't hurt. They decided that it would likely be less awkward if Shelby and Jennifer made the request and left Stan out of it.

Stan, meanwhile, became increasingly determined to find out who else was searching for the box in Belize. So many facts about the night the first box went missing were still a mystery, with the identity of who finally stole the artifact remaining as the biggest missing piece. So, another unknown man snooping around was a huge lead. The two Nigerians had given Alex an impressive amount of detail regarding the two search efforts conducted by this man. Who was he? How did he know about the multiple artifacts?

After some consideration, Stan decided that it was quite likely that this Mexican was the very collector who had returned the relic back to Stan. Years ago this man must have somehow gotten possession of the artifact and must have had someone interpret the document for him. He must have decided back then to try to find the treasure for himself.

But why had he returned the artifact now? Perhaps he had all the information he needed carefully recorded and he had felt that he could afford to do the right thing. But why bother? Then it occurred to Stan. This man, his mystery alter ego, was just as stumped as he was. This man had no way of finding a relic lost in the mountains of western Guatemala either. This man had also struck out in Belize. This man also didn't know what else to do. So he had sent the box back to Stan hoping that Stan might have a better idea.

Stan laughed out loud. It made sense. He was an expert. He had spent his whole career thinking about this damn thing. If anyone could come up with a new idea of how to go about this, it would be Stan Drexler.

The return to him had not been something done out of guilt. It had been done out of hope.

Shelby had a different take on it. She didn't disagree one bit with all of Stan's analysis. It all made sense. One way or another, this box hand landed in the hands of someone who recognized its value, had sought out expert information and had taken on the treasure hunt for himself. Once totally stymied after years of work, he had returned it in the simple hope of finding a lead.

But here is where Shelby's thoughts went a different direction.

"Stan, you have got to be very careful. If you were to find something out, this guy is clearly not going to just sit back and let you waltz away with what he spent years looking for himself. He has put a lot of time and money into this chase. He's got to be watching you. Keeping track of what you are doing. Somehow. That's creepy."

Well, Stan supposed that it kind of was. But given that he wasn't getting anywhere, he figured that he didn't much need to worry. Besides, he told Shelby, that made his next move even more obvious.

"What are you going to do?" There was fear in Shelby's voice.

"Relax," Stan said. "All I am going to do is send the guy an email."

At Shelby's sharp inhalation of breath, he smiled.

"Clearly the man knows who I am, where I work, and how to get a hold of me. All I know about him is the email address he plastered all over Belize. What have I got to lose?"

She gave it some thought, but in the end even worried Shelby could not think if a single thing.

When Lola tossed and turned, trying to fall asleep, she often used her powers to send a greeting to her friend Somadina, who tended to toss in bed in the early morning herself. With a six-hour time difference, their restlessness often coincided, and this odd fact had been a part of what had forged such a strong link between them originally.

Over the last few days Lola had tossed more than usual, worrying about Alex but resolved to respect his very specific request for privacy. Somadina, on the other hand, was entering her ninth month of pregnancy, and solid sleep was becoming increasingly elusive. Although Somadina put on a brave front, Lola now knew that the woman's own mother had died in childbirth long ago. Somadina was understandably both uncomfortable and nervous.

Take my mind off of things. How are you? Somadina conveyed the feelings if not the exact words.

Lola sent back a sense of her own worry, and Somadina sent back a plan to be of help. At first, Lola's reaction was, *absolutely not. You're about to have a baby.*

Just HEAR my reasoning, Somadina responded. And so Lola listened.

It was true, Lola remembered, that distractions were good this late in a pregnancy. And it was true that the two women shared enough of a bond that Somadina could pretend to nap at home in Nigeria while in essence riding along in Lola's head for a while. It wasn't something that the two women, or any two telepaths, usually did, but it was something that the two of them were capable of and had done once before.

While Lola was engaging in conversation and focusing on the room around her, as she would have to, Somadina could focus entirely on this woman whom Lola had come to consider her enemy.

Enemy is kind of a strong word, Lola thought.

I don't think so, Somadina thought back. *I'll make sure I'm not interrupted here. You take me along to this meeting and let me work on your behalf. I'll be able to get far more information than you could and it will help you get to the bottom of what is happening. Let me go with you and let me help.*

Then Lola remembered something else. Somadina was Nigerian. *I don't know what you will find in my enemy's head,* she sent her concern. *I think there is a lot of hate there for anyone who does not share her ancestry. It could be very, very ugly in there.*

Lola felt Somadina's calm reassurance. *I deal with hate and internal ugliness all the time dear friend. I can handle this.* And so Lola and Somadina made plans to go to a PTA meeting together where women were going to, in Teddie's words, sit around and talk about how great white people were.

Jake had evolved a single rule of life over the years that had helped him cope with the pressures of running a successful business, having a family, having a secret fortune-hunting venture on the side, and dealing with the day-to-day craziness of living in Los Angeles. The rule was that just when you thought life couldn't get any weirder, it would. You could count on it. In fact, it was the one thing you could consistently count on.

So here he was, video chatting with Jennifer, whom he had actually declined the chance to finally sleep with, and Shelby, who he had finally confessed all kinds of truth to, and it looked like these two ladies were clearly best buddies these days, and, stranger yet, they were asking him to get on a plane and go to Guatemala to talk to some maid at the hotel they had all stayed at together almost eighteen years ago. Did this define bizarre? Don't say yes, he told himself, or it's only going to get weirder.

Better to be open and helpful.

"Ladies. How about we save me the time, trouble and expense of going down there, and I just ask Kyle to handle this for us?"

"I thought Kyle was in seclusion. Didn't want to be found," Shelby said.

"He doesn't really want to be found by people from his past," Jake corrected. "But he and I stay in touch a little, and I think he would be willing to help us out. He's a good resource. He's not all that far away from Lake Peten and I don't see any reason at all not to involve him. Okay by you ladies?"

Both women shrugged. If Kyle was nearby and could be trusted… well, why not?

Stan wasn't sure what sort of response he expected from the mystery fortune hunter in Mexico, but the truth was that he had expected something. In retrospect, though, he should have realized that this was what would most likely happen. Nothing. A day later and not a word back.

Why hadn't he put a return receipt on it? Then again, what good would that have done? How about he send a second message with "TALK TO ME YOU ASSHOLE" in the subject line? Well, that would surely get things going in a spirit of cooperation, now wouldn't it?

He'd written everything in both Spanish and English. Should he have included another language? The man could speak any one of a couple of dozen Mayan languages and not even know Spanish. It was possible. He could try a second message with more translations.

Would he sound desperate if he sent more messages? Probably. Could he find some computer geek to trace the IP address or whatever it was they traced on crime shows? That might be worth looking into.

Stan's head was spinning with ideas, but for the time being he recognized that maybe he should just sit tight. The previous keeper of the artifact knew all about Stan Drexler. And he also now knew that Stan Drexler knew about him.

So Stan willed his mind to stop churning and stared at the backlit glow of his computer screen.

"Your move," he said softly to his unknown adversary.

When Lola announced at dinner the next evening that she was taking off work to participate in a PTA effort to provide supplies for the big reenactment event, she got a skeptical raised eyebrow from Alex and a resigned sigh from Teddie. But neither tried to talk her out of it.

The next day she gingerly joined the two-dozen or so women sitting at two long tables in the cafeteria and smiled politely. She could see Ms. Johnson trying to place who she was.

She and Somadina had already agreed not to distract each other. Lola would focus on fitting in and getting women to relax so that their thoughts would flow freely, and Somadina would sense and record anything helpful she could learn and email the details in words to Lola later.

"I am so glad that the principal decided to have this learning activity replace the fall play from the theater department," one mother was saying.

"I know. All that theater stuff is always so liberal. You just can tell that those playwrights were all atheists. They hardly ever mention God once in any of their plays."

"And that theater teacher," the woman looked around like she was about to say something just a little bit naughty, "she keeps casting the *Mexicans,*" she whispered the last word loudly, "and even the blacks in roles just like they were white. I mean you can tell the character is supposed to be white."

"I know." Another lady squirmed in her seat, she was so anxious to join in. "She put that Vietnamese boy in a play last year and cast him as my daughter's son. Can you believe that? Eyes don't get more slanty than this kids'. No offense, but it just wasn't right."

Lola tried breathing deeply. At least she was saved from being expected to join in the conversation by Ms. Johnson herself, who had clearly figured out who she was.

"Well, I didn't expect a serious career lady like you to have the time to come over and help us, Mrs. Zeitman." Ms. Johnson was all smiles.

"I make time for this sort of thing when I can," Lola responded just as cheerily. "My husband is trying to get his class to be part of this and I support that effort."

"Well, that's good to see." More fake smiles all around. As the attention went elsewhere Lola perused a sign-up sheet to figure out what she could commit to providing. The discussion segued from the theater department to the more pressing issue of what to actually do with the Hispanic, black and other minority students taking American history who would need to be somehow included in the reenactment.

"There were black soldiers fighting on both sides," a petite blonde woman who had not said much volunteered timidly.

"Oh, let's not bother to go there," another woman said. "We've got so few black kids here, surely we can just give them some kind of background part."

"Along with that Muslim girl who refuses to take that damn thing off of her head."

"Oh yeah. She is definitely stage crew material."

"Yes, but over a third of the kids here are Mexican. What are going to do with all of them?" asked the mother who had been so disapproving at the casting of her daughter's stage son.

"You know, by the time the Civil War ended, over ten-thousand Mexican Americans had served on both sides," offered the woman who had just pointed out that both sides had black soldiers. "In eighteen-sixty-three, they set up entire companies of Mexican-American Californians because they were such good horsemen. Mexican Americans served under Major Salvador Vallejo, defeating a Confederate invasion of New Mexico." Seeing dismay at this piece of information, she hastily added, "Hispanics also served in Confederate units. The tenth Texas Cavalry, the fifty-fifth Alabama Infantry, and the sixth Missouri Infantry."

At this point the whole room was staring at the soft-spoken and very white woman like she had grown three turquoise heads.

She went on undaunted. "Colonel Santos Benavides from Laredo Texas commanded the thirty-third Cavalry. And naval officer David Farragut, the son of a Spaniard, is the person who made history during the Civil War by saying, 'Damn the torpedoes. Full steam ahead.'"

"Right," Ms. Johnson said. "I am sure you read all that in some fascinating Yankee document dear, but you really do have to learn that you can't believe everything you read. Those people will print all kinds of stuff in their attempt to rewrite our history to suit their political correctness. There is no end to how clever they can be. No one faults you for being taken in."

"I teach history at the community college," the woman said coldly. "I specialize in studying the Civil War, and the Lost Cause movement that followed it and perpetuated the myth of the Old South as both noble and horribly wronged." And everyone twittered.

"Well that explains your problem, honey," Ms. Johnson smiled sweetly. "You have been exposed to entirely too much liberal education in your life." She turned away from the woman and towards the rest of the group.

"I say there were no Mexican soldiers in our armies. Who agrees?"

"I do!" Most of the women shouted it out. Lola noticed for the first time that there were two Latina mothers who had come to help and who had been sitting quietly in the background. They were now gathering up their stuff to leave.

As the second one went through the door Ms. Johnson said loudly, "Oops. Guess those two happened to speak more English than I realized."

Everyone laughed.

Everyone except Lola and the college history teacher.

"Do we speak English well enough to leave too?" Lola said to her quietly.

"I left mentally a while ago," the history professor said. "As you may guess, I'm not a big fan of using popular vote to decide what really happened in the past."

Somadina? Can I get out of here yet?
Please do. The thought came back loud and clear.

The 1990s saw a relaxation of immigration policies as the thriving United States felt confident in its ability to absorb diverse cultures. Special favor was now given to nationalities previously limited and to victims of human trafficking and abuse. Policies were implemented to allow relatives and loved ones to live and work in the U.S. during the years it took for their paperwork to be processed.

Then came September 11, 2001. A shocked nation, by turns angry and frightened, shifted its focus to keeping out dangerous elements and preserving its current national identity. In a telling bit of symbolism, the Statue of Liberty was closed for security reasons, and not fully reopened until 2009.

Somadina's father had a newly acquired cell phone that could be used to send email messages. Unfortunately her father had no idea how to use it to do that. Somadina's half-brother Udo, however, was home, and he quickly and easily set up Somadina's email account so that she could help her friend back in Texas without making the drive all the way to an internet café in Abakaliki.

Lola read Somadina's message with gratitude but with growing apprehension.

"Lots of hate. You were right. But lots more fear. Seriously scared women. They are scared of everyone not like them. Your enemy does not trust you or your husband. She flatters herself that you are both being forced to play along because she is so powerful but she assumes you are waiting for a chance to strike. She hates your daughter very much.

"She is extra scared of your husband's student because he is small and brown and fights off her bigger boys. She has convinced herself that he must have evil powers from another religion. She has decided that by destroying him she is doing the work of her god. This is sad. She has talked her friends into arresting his family. They are being sent back to Mexico even though they have not lived in Mexico for a very long time. Your enemy worked to make sure that they had to leave without even saying goodbye to Xuha and this thought brought her great joy every time she looked at you today."

Yikes, Lola thought. She read on.

"She is now working to get your husband's student deported also. She has let this student know that if he turns to anyone for help she will hurt you or your daughter. She is a very cruel woman. I am sorry to give such harsh words. I send them to you with my affection. I hope this information helps."

Lola typed words right away to send back, but at the same time she concentrated hard to send the right emotions with them. She loved how her telepathy could augment her use of technology.

"You have helped so much. I send thanks and affection back." And Lola concentrated for a minute to make sure that indeed the gratitude and the fondness were felt by her friend.

Lola put the information aside until she came to bed that night, and she curled up around Alex's back and wrapped her arms around his chest. She could tell that he was still awake.

"I can't help what I am," she said.

"So you can't choose to stay out of my head?" he asked irritably.

"I can and I have," Lola said, just a little offended at his doubt. "But that doesn't mean I need to stay out of everyone else's."

Alex sighed. "So what is it you want to tell me?"

"They deported Xuha's foster family. While he was at work. He didn't even get to say goodbye."

"No." Anger overtook any irritation Alex felt at Lola for getting involved in his business.

"He's been told that they are looking more closely into his birth certificate, and that if he complains or tries to get help from you or anyone else, then Teddie or maybe even me will somehow suffer the consequences."

"That's insane." Alex was sitting up now. "How could they hurt you? And how the hell did you find out all of this? I didn't think you could get that specific."

"I can't normally. Somadina helped me. She's really good and we work together well. She's pretty close to giving birth, so, well, the whole thing was pretty brave on her part."

"Wow Lola. How sure are you that you're right?"

"As sure as I am that I'm sitting here."

Alex shook his head. Lola finished her original thought.

"I can't help what I am, so you might as well learn to let me use my talents to help you. You look out for me all the time. I know you do. There's nothing wrong with letting me do a little looking out for you too."

"No," Alex smiled, "there isn't. You can go into battle for me anytime dear." And Lola clearly saw an absolutely cheesy picture of her in his head in which she was half dressed in some sort of comic book battle gear that included thigh high boots, a giant sword and some sort of metal bar that only covered about a third of her breasts.

"Good grief Alex, I didn't mean do battle dressed like that."

He grinned. "I was hoping you would pick up that image." He gave her a hopeful look. "Maybe you could do just a little fighting dressed that way?"

As soon as Alex felt the rhythmic motion in his legs he knew that he was about to have the dream again. He tried to will himself awake, but before he could manage, a golden glow began to engulf him from behind as one of the creatures began to gain on him. He thought to himself, *now what?*

"Did you hear the one about the turtle that got attacked by a vicious gang of snails?" she asked in a friendly tone.

"What? No. What are you talking about?"

"So the turtle gets home totally distraught and he calls the police department. The sergeant who answers the phone is very sympathetic and he asks the turtle to tell him what happened."

The creature had caught up to him and met Alex's gaze evenly as she gave him a sly smile. "Do you know what the turtle said?" she asked with just a hint of coyness. When Alex stared at her speechless, she went on.

"He said, 'I'd like to officer, but I can't. It all happened so fast.'"

"Now you guys are telling me jokes?" Alex asked

incredulously, but the creature only gave a little twinkly laugh as she moved off into the distance.

"Go to private email account." Jake's chubby fingertips had never made the adjustment to fast texting, so it took him a couple of minutes to enter the message without errors. Generally he preferred not to take the chance of doing business over email, but this was just going to take too long to explain by text.

In a few hours Kyle got back to him asking what was up. Jake typed a nice long response detailing how he had sort of kind of spent a little time with both Jennifer and Shelby recently, through no fault of his own, and he had planned to tell Kyle about it next time they talked, but now they were trying to get him to go to Flores to follow this lead. Frankly, following it seemed like a good idea, and why didn't Kyle handle it, and in fact, if it turned out to be significant, then Kyle and Jake could decide whether they wanted to share the information back with the ladies or not.

"Good plan. But need to tell you that I left Mexico City two weeks ago and am in Houston area tracing our best lead NOW. Was going to make contact with news of success. It was looking so good but then hit temporary dead end. Very close to solving something here. No where near Guatemala. Try another idea."

Jake read Kyle's response and sighed in exasperation.

"Your Houston lead will wait until you get back." he typed "But if we do not get involved with this Flores maid we may lose opportunity to scoop on that piece of info. Very urgent you get back to Mexico and go on to Flores and handle this. Now."

"Si Senor," came back the message. "Will report back to you from Flores."

Okay, at least he had Kyle's reluctant cooperation. He wasn't completely clear on why everyone was suddenly chasing after this maid but maybe there was something there. And maybe Kyle was honestly on to something with this Acapulco lineage thing. Maybe there was a chance that after all these years it would all come together somehow.

Jake did have to laugh at the fact that Kyle was finally going back to Flores at Jennifer and Shelby's request. Could this get any weirder?

As soon as he thought it, he tried to grab back the words. Yes, yes, of course it could get stranger. Of course it could.

And then it did. He looked more closely and saw that this super secret email account that he used only for communicating with Kyle had another unopened message in his super secret inbox. It didn't look like spam and it wasn't from Kyle, so he opened it. It was from Dr. Stan Drexler asking who he was. Shit. Now what?

November 1697

The youngest son, Balam, had walked through ten full cycles of the moon when he finally reached the ridge that brought him to his destination. The sun had set, and a tiny sliver of a crescent moon and the evening star were both following the sun down into the most beautiful and vast expanse of blue water that Balam had ever seen.

Unfortunately, the civilization that Balam had been increasingly avoiding filled his view as well. Between him and the several giant boats that floated on the water were buildings and wagons and horses and many, many people. Their sounds and smells assaulted his ears and nose as he stood studying the landscape. His mother wanted him to go live with that? To survive in the middle of this stink and turmoil?

Balam sighed. He had almost failed once already. He would find a way to do what had been asked of him, a way to preserve his grandfather's secret, a way to make this noisy crowded place his children's home.

Chapter 16. December 2010

Kyle remembered Kisa as soon as he saw her. She hadn't been one of the maids. She had been a short, shy girl busing tables in the restaurant, and she had never taken her eyes off of him, the infatuation written clearly across her pretty cinnamon-colored face. Her hair had been as thick, black and glossy as his own, and she had looked too young to be working anywhere. He had flirted with her because, well, because he had been a twenty-four-year-old boy and he pretty much flirted with any cute girl he saw back then, especially one who seemed interested in him. Some of those girls had flirted back and after a few days, Kisa had too, in her own hesitant way.

Her innocent fascination with him had been so charming and unexpected that, had she not been so young, and had she not lived on the other side of serious cultural barriers, Kyle probably would have tried to push the situation further. But he hadn't, thank heavens he thought now. He'd only winked at her a few times and called her pretty in the local Mayan dialect, and enjoyed her blushing response.

Now, she was a confident thirty-something woman, still every bit as pretty and in a position of some authority over the rest of the hotel cleaning staff. Her Spanish was much improved. And yet, sitting in her small office at the hotel, the air between them was filled with awkwardness.

"I remember Dr. Drexler and his students very well," she said carefully in Spanish. "When I first started working here he came twice a year every year, and he always paid well and treated others well. We were sorry that after his loss he no longer came back to the hotel. That was our loss too."

She gave Kyle an oddly suspicious look. "When he finally came back here last summer we learned that after seventeen years his discovery had been returned to him. Amazing, don't you think?"

Yes, Kyle could not agree more that the return had been a remarkable bit of good fortune for Dr. Drexler. He tried his best to say it with a straight face. Kisa looked at the floor awkwardly when he did.

Oh hell, Kyle thought. *Enough of this bullshit.*

"Kisa, I think you remember that I was one of those students and I think you know perfectly well that I was with the professor when the box disappeared. Now all of us who were here then are now trying to arrive at the truth of what happened that night. I played a role in the events of which I am not proud, but I am ready to own up to it. I'd like to tell you everything, everything that happened that I know of when Dr. Drexler's artifact disappeared. You should know that it's a story that no one has ever heard completely."

He gave her a knowing look. "And I also remember you. You worked in the restaurant back then and I am hoping that you will have some observations to share as well."

Kisa looked thoughtful for a minute. "You can buy me dinner in that restaurant tonight. We'll talk then."

Oh. "I'd be glad to Kisa." Kyle said it automatically and then he realized that he meant it.

Jake was tired. Tired of the charade, tired of the sneaking around, tired of thinking that he and Kyle were ever somehow going to find some tremendous fortune. The more he thought about it the more it seemed he had wasted good chucks of his life and his energy hunting for a treasure instead of enjoying his life.

And what did he have to show for it? Well, he did have a decent business that provided nicely for him, and that he enjoyed. It had started out as a front for the treasure hunting but in the end, it was a plus all its own. And in spite of his obsession, he still had a decent, even sometimes fun and loving relationship with a woman, and he'd managed not to blow that, in spite of recent temptations. Another plus. Which posed the question: what exactly did he want with a treasure?

Jake supposed that like most professions, archeology tended to select for certain personality traits. A fascination with the ancient and mysterious often included a latent affinity for superstition. It was time, Jake thought, to acknowledge the half-formed and unspoken motivation that had pushed him and Kyle along for almost two decades.

Deep down both he and Kyle had bought into the idea that

this mystery relic was guided by some unseen force and had chosen the two of them. Even though on most levels they recognized that as ridiculous, they had both wanted it to be true. And that fact alone had kept both he and Kyle on track more than once when one of them had felt like quitting. They denied it of course, well-educated men that they were, but neither had ever been able to shake the eerie idea that the treasure had chosen them.

Enough, Jake declared to himself. The artifact had no mind of its own and he knew it. It certainly had no feet. He did not truly believe that any spirit had picked up the box and gone walking around. Another human was involved. Someone in his group, or someone outside of it, had manipulated him and Kyle long ago and it was time to stop the nonsense.

He opened Dr. Drexler's email and stared at it a minute. Kyle would be rightfully mad, but how many times had Kyle acted unilaterally and made Jake deal with the ensuing mess. This was his turn.

"Hi Stan," he started typing in response to Stan's message. "Bet you are going to be very surprised to find out that you emailed me."

Tina Johnson had called in favors and even had to resort to a few veiled threats to get the Cruz family moved quickly to a detention center while their immigration status was sorted out. Unlike many illegal immigrants, they appeared to have no legal relatives to turn to, and so their troubles were compounded by the difficult choice between detention for their young, possibly American children, or putting those children into the foster care system while their case was resolved. The handling of the situation smacked of even less compassion and good sense than was usually shown, and that was exactly what Tina had pushed for.

But watching Xuha's sad demeanor at school barely soothed her anger at the way such a little brown boy had made fools of two of her glorious white warriors at the homecoming game. He still deserved worse. So Tina pulled a few more strings to get a full copy of Xuha's birth certificate. She was disappointed to see Houston,

Texas listed as the place of birth. That was too bad. She had really hoped that the boy would turn out not to be as American as he claimed.

Tina blew the scanned copy up large on her computer screen to look at it more closely, and was surprised to discover that Xuha had been born in a car. At least, the doctor had listed the place of birth as "in route to the hospital." Maybe that bit of news would at least have some entertainment value around the school if it were carefully leaked to the right students with the right sense of humor.

Then Tina dropped the doctor's name into a search engine and was surprised to discover that not only was the doctor not an obstetrician in the Houston area, but she was a respected oncologist and had been for over two decades. Cancer treatment? What was a cancer specialist doing signing a birth certificate?

When Kisa arrived, Kyle admired her graceful poise as she entered the restaurant. He gestured to the most private corner table. They were two adults about to clear the air about all sorts of things, and the entire wait staff could sense that interruption would be unwelcome.

"I thought that you were sweet and gorgeous back then," Kyle began softly.

"Good start." Kisa smiled. "I thought that you were kind of arrogant and full of yourself but horribly handsome and exotic, and I had a little girl's crush on you."

"Probably guilty on all counts. Except exotic. My parents are both from Barcelona, which doesn't strike me as terribly glamorous." Kyle tried to deflect the compliment with a bit of self-deprecation.

"You're Spanish? With a name like Kyle?" For some reason this seemed to irritate Kisa.

"What can I say? My parents both came to the United States when they were young. They embraced intellectualism and rejected their own parents' values. I was required to learn Spanish only for its usefulness, because they were both most definitely not into their heritage. What did you think I was?"

"I don't know. You look kind of Arabic. Maybe Greek or

Turkish."

"I'm first generation Spanish." Now Kyle looked a little defensive as the problem dawned on him. "Kisa, my ancestors were not the ones who came charging over to the New World to wreak havoc, if that's what is bothering you. My people were back eating paella in Europe."

"But they were related to those people. They probably agreed with them. Look, my whole life has been shaped by the fact that the Spanish did awful things to my ancestors, and frankly for most of the past three-hundred years things haven't gotten a whole lot better here. I've learned to accept their local descendants and, hard as that road has been, I try to judge each one of them on their own merits. My own mother made the tough choice to leave the ways of my people and become a Ladino, a Maya who lives with the Spanish, and as I listen to the anguish that caused my other relatives I try not to judge her either. But I've never actually met anyone from Spain before." Her eyes narrowed as she said the word "Spain."

Go figure, Kyle thought. Most girls had been put off to discover that he was the offspring of two psychiatrists. Who knew what would derail a conversation?

"This may be a bad tact here, but I studied a lot of Maya history, Kisa. Your ancestors engaged in human sacrifice, cannibalism and slavery, along with all of their impressive feats."

"Yet mine were not responsible for the inquisition or the crusades," Kisa retorted. She had studied history too.

"We can throw rocks at each other all day if you want. Look, I can't change history and neither can you. You want to hate me, then hate me. I have done nothing to warrant your hatred." *Screw this*. He started to stand up, ready to leave.

"Wait." She reached out and touched his arm hesitantly. "You have to understand that I was raised on very particular stories about the Spanish, the original Spanish who came here. In my family, they were the very worst of all people, and the reason why my life and so many lives before mine had to be dedicated to a cause at the cost of giving up our own dreams. It's, well, this is hard. Not only have I never met a real Spanish person before, but it certainly didn't occur to me that you might be one. I'm angry with myself more than anything. The magnitude of this probably won't make any sense to you, but I am upset because I may have pissed my ancestors off beyond belief."

"How?" Kyle asked.

Kisa looked like she didn't know whether to laugh or to cry. "Because after three-hundred years of my family giving up almost everything they had just to keep a secret safe from the Spanish, I came along and literally gave that secret to you."

"What?" Now Kyle was starting to catch on. "Right. You, the little busgirl who kept making eyes at me. You were the spirit that kept putting the artifact back in my and Jake's possession."

"I spent my childhood helping my family watch that cave," she said. "It was a duty passed along to us from my grandmother, just as she received it from hers. We were all happy once Dr. Drexler began digging there. We knew that he was basically a good man and that sooner or later he would find it. Should find it. Because we were taught that a good time would come for it to be found, and that it would be clear when that time had arrived. And then... those two horrible people in your group did what they did and I had to find a way to keep them from having any part of my family's treasure."

"Horrible people? We might not have been the Red Cross, Kisa, but there wasn't anyone awful in our group."

"Yes. There was that slut that made the mousy guy with the glasses take the box out of the cave. Didn't she know that once it was out it could never go back? And the way they, they... they didn't just misbehave. They had no respect," Kisa said more heatedly.

Oh yes. He'd heard from Jake about Jennifer and Nelson, and about Jenn's free-spirited approach to celebrating life in front of an ancient artifact. It had been innocent fun to Jennifer, but probably the worst of heresy to Kisa.

"You saw them doing that? I'm sorry Kisa, I really am. You were a child and they were insensitive kids. So you worried that the box had fallen into bad hands after all?" Kyle had to laugh. "You didn't have a lot of options because I'm guessing you then saw it as your duty to keep the box from Dr. Drexler too." Kyle said.

She nodded. "We all liked Dr. Drexler so much, but once I saw that he couldn't keep his own students from committing such an atrocity, I had to find somebody else to trust. You seemed so handsome and noble and decent, and I thought if I could just get you and your friend to believe that the box was meant for you and not the others…" Kisa sighed. "I had no trouble getting keys to the different hotel rooms. I knew yours. So yes, I got to the cave that night, took my family's precious possession back out, and put it into your room. Then when you and the other boy put it in the truck like you were going to try to return it to the cave, I was so frustrated with you. I had to sneak it back out of your truck and put it back in your room again. I needed to convince you that the box was meant for only the two of you."

"You did manage that," Kyle acknowledged. "Quite well, actually. I've pretty much spent my entire adult life trying to decipher the clues carved into it and trying to find the other two boxes just so I can piece the whole puzzle together."

"I can't believe that I put it straight into the arms of a Spaniard," she said sadly.

"I can't believe that you managed to derail all my dreams and set me chasing after god-knows-what all because you couldn't bear to see a professor end up with a find he deserved, and his only crime was that two of his students misbehaved. And for what?"

Then he paused. That was a very good question. And sitting with him was the one person in the entire world most qualified to answer it.

"Kisa. For what? What exactly is this damn treasure that your family has looked after for so many generations?"

Kisa made an obvious effort to calm down. Clearly Kyle was not responsible for the behavior of his fellow students or, for that matter, for the worst actions of the nation of Spain. She knew that. He was only responsible for himself, and she had truly screwed around with his life. She needed not to be angry with him, because when she answered his question he was probably going to be angry with her.

Kisa swallowed hard and looked Kyle in the eye, as he

deserved.

"I have no idea for what. No one does. I think for the first few generations people may have known exactly what it was that we were protecting, but it was decided somewhere along the way that the treasure would be safer if less was known about it."

"No. Seriously? Your family has guarded access to something for three-hundred years and you have no idea what the something is?"

"I was assured on my twelfth birthday that it was significant and important and worth the sacrifice. That was enough for me." Her voice was calmer now.

"I know that your culture is different and this may be hard to understand," she went on. "But I trust my ancestors. And now that the first of the boxes has been found, it's important that we find the other two. It is time. You and Jake were supposed to get the job done."

"Well we didn't fail due to lack of trying," Kyle muttered.

"So you two are really out of ideas?" Kisa sounded a little disappointed.

"Not completely. Returning the box to Stan was Jake's last big idea. He reasoned that the guy was smart and highly motivated and that we knew enough about him to keep a close eye on him. I think Stan's made some progress, too. He's involved some old friend in figuring out the code and he's got new people in Belize covering the ground I covered twice already, but maybe they'll turn up something I missed."

"And what's your last big idea?" Kisa asked.

"I think I may really be on the trail of the box that went to the west. I've traced a family with Mayan names all the way to the current generation in Houston, Texas. The trail just went cold before I came here. I was tracking a seventeen year old that disappeared about a year ago. But I have his name and I still think I can find him when I get back, given a little time."

"So what are you doing here talking to me?" she almost smiled.

"Enjoying myself, in spite of our differences." He was

relaxing, starting to smile just a bit himself. "And learning a little truth about the past to help me better sort out the future."

"And gaining a well-informed partner too, I think."

"Perhaps. One who is going to have to explain to me exactly how she managed to move a fairly heavy obsidian box all over creation all by herself in the middle of the night."

"We can go over those details if it will ease your mind, to see how no real spirits were ever involved. You should know that your new partner was pretty resourceful, even back when she was only fourteen years old." Kisa was smiling.

Kyle asked more seriously. "Kisa, what do you think is a reasonable time limit for hate?"

"I don't believe in hate."

"No one does, but we all do. If someone kills my kin, hurts my friends, ruins my life, I may be able to forgive and move on. But if a large group of people does such a thing? Then I almost certainly don't. I call my hatred lots of things. Justified anger. Revenge. Forcing this group to behave better. Even self-defense. But for how long do I get to punish all the people associated with or descended from those who caused the harm?"

"In parts of the world feuds are centuries old," she remarked, "with a staggering list of injustice and cruelty on both sides. Once it gets to that point, forgiveness or even just acceptance between two groups seems impossible."

"That's what I mean. And each fresh insult keeps the fire going. To stop hating appears to dishonor the sacrifices made by those who came before. Who wants to let their ancestors down?"

"So we keep it going and let our children down instead, as we let the circle grow ever wider," Kisa said. "Immediate blood relatives of the perpetrators? Those who look like them? Pray like them? Dress like them? Anyone who shares a city, or a nation, or a continent with them?"

"Exactly. In other words, how would you like to let one Spaniard who thinks that the burning of Tayasal was an abomination buy you dinner and start over?"

"I'd love that." She thought a second. "Do you know who said 'Nationalism is an infantile disease. It is the measles of mankind'?"

Kyle shook his head. "Gandhi? John Lennon?"

Kisa laughed. "Good guesses. Albert Einstein." Her anger and even embarrassment at not recognizing Kyle's heritage was gone. "I think that it's a good time for you and me to grow up."

Ralph was an old friend of Tina's and he was usually happy to help her. After all, they shared a common vision of a better world, and Tina was one of the few ladies in the movement who was not afraid to stand up for her beliefs and to try to make a difference. But lately she had pushed him for several favors, and Ralph knew that he would soon start to attract unwanted attention if he wasn't careful.

"I will get nowhere if I call a doctor's office," Tina pleaded. "I need to know what that doctor was doing filling out a birth certificate. Please Ralph."

"Tina, what's one more of them? Go for the bigger picture. This lone boy isn't worth either of our time," he responded.

Tina sighed. "He is, Ralph. You don't understand. He's not just Mexican. He's descended from one of those native tribes. Inca or something. You know. Pagan. I think he still worships his evil gods because, well, he's done a few things at my school here that are very disturbing. Not natural. I'm not saying I believe in that stuff or anything, but, well, we both know that the devil can latch on to questionable beliefs in ways we don't always understand. Satan is sneaky. We have to be on guard for that. And this boy, he's got a strength and power that just aren't right. I need to get him out of my school, and the sooner the better."

Now it was Ralph's turn to sigh. Once someone brought the devil into the picture, there was just no arguing with them. "Okay Tina. I'll see what I can find out. Maybe this doctor got paid off to fake a birth certificate or something, although I can't imagine how. I'll get back to you when I know more. But after this, I have got to lay low for a while or I become useless to the cause. Understand?"

Tina understood. And Tina also realized that what she had just told Ralph was powerful enough to work well elsewhere. Maybe her pastor would like to know about this boy's unnatural abilities? Some of the mothers in her afterschool group? Her boys weren't particularly religious, which was fine, because Tina wasn't either. But she had a few students who admired her and yet who were of that ilk. Maybe it was time that she had pizza and sodas exclusively for some of the more seriously devout bible quoters, just so she could alert them to the possible danger?

Alex hadn't delivered many lectures this semester in his advanced physics class, given that so much of the curriculum involved the projects on which the students themselves were working. But today was his fifty-second birthday and he was going to treat himself to half an hour or so of saying pretty much what he wanted to. Today he was going to talk about his favorite topic.

"Time. It passes. Will you?"

A few students laughed. Most ignored him, and Xuha looked as sad as ever.

"For a good time call…"

A few more students looked up.

"It's about time," he remarked, then paused.

A couple more looked up, only because there are few things more compelling in a high school class room than the growing possibility that the teacher may be going bonkers right in front of the class. Alex grinned.

"'Time flies like an arrow; fruit flies like a banana.' That was Groucho Marx's line, by the way. My point is that, with the possible exception of love, there is nothing more pervasive in the language and expressions of every culture on earth than time and its passage. It defines every one of our lives. Literally. And yet, you have all hopefully discovered in the past couple of months how very little we actually understand about it."

Alex paused to make sure that most of his listeners were still listening. "I know that you're all working on your time machines, and you need to keep doing so. But today, I'm going to tell you all about the time machine I once built."

Another compelling topic is the teacher talking too much and giving away information to make the assignment easier. More heads perked up.

"It sat in my garage for a long time. You guys really have no idea how much I actually do know about time travel."

Nineteen skeptical faces were clearly weighing the "bonkers" theory against the "giving away the assignment" theory. Mr. Z continued.

"Years ago I perfected the capability to take me into the past. My plan was to go back and abduct my dad before he met my mom and take him to Australia. I'm a curious guy and wanted to understand more about how time worked. I wanted to see if he'd manage to get back to Texas and still create me. You know, how resilient is the universe?"

"Are you nuts?" one student said.

"I don't think so. You see, I realized that I don't live in a universe. I live in one tiny strand of a multiverse. On my strand, my dad never went to Australia. But if I go back in time, I manage to jump over to a timeline in which my dad does get kidnapped. Or more accurately, I jump over to the timeline in which Alex Zeitman happily living in multiverse number 2,678,941 leaves his own timeline and shows up here. I'm in a new universe, you see. I may or may not be successful at kidnapping my dad. He may or may not produce a child. That child may or may not have my exact genes. It won't matter. That child isn't me. I am me. I can kill any child that he produces as a baby. It makes me a murderer, but it doesn't make me disappear. All that happens is that I continue to live in universe 372,445,991 in which a man named Alex Zeitman showed up from another timeline and killed a child which had his exact same genes."

"So let's say I want to go back and kill baby Hitler." Alex said. Tanner's eyes narrowed.

"Do I make my world a better place?"

"No, you don't," Xuha said softly. "Your world goes on without you. You merely disappeared, going off in your time machine. And in your world no one killed Hitler."

"That's right," Alex said. "I haven't done a thing for my world. You can argue about whether I created a whole new and maybe happier universe elsewhere in which Hitler never came to power," Alex watched all four of his Hitler fans' discomfort, "or whether that other universe always existed, but now you're getting into more metaphysical questions about predestination and free will. The point is that I can go backwards in time in my machine, but I can't go back -- on -- my -- own -- time -- line. My own timeline doesn't have me back there mucking around."

"How do you know?" Travis asked.

"That's an excellent question. As long as I never get into that machine then that is true. But let's say I did go back and I did something useful, or maybe even just looked around. I almost certainly changed something and now I'm on a different timeline. And yet I want to come back home."

"You can't come home," one of the team members who had discussed string theory volunteered. "At least, you can't come back to the universe you left. You can only go forward in the new universe you created. It might be almost the same and it might be really different, but you don't know."

"That's right!" Alex shouted it in his enthusiasm. "I don't know. There might be another man almost like me there. The man like me might have headed off in his own time machine and maybe I can take his place and his life will be so similar that I'm happy there. If he got in his time machine then I know at least that he's not coming home. But other than that all I do know is that once I get into my machine and use it, I can never ever get back here."

The class, for once, was silent.

"How many times do you think I've used my time machine?" Alex asked.

"Zero times," the girl who was captain of the tennis team said softly. "Who wants to change the past if it's not your own past that you're changing?"

"Who wants to leave if you can never come home?" another boy asked.

"That's right. Now I'm going to leave you with one last

thought. If I go back and kidnap my father, I create a new timeline. What if this afternoon I go kidnap my father?"

"He's probably gonna be pretty pissed," Tanner said. Kids laughed.

"Undoubtedly. But now I live in a universe where I did that. What if I don't do it?"

"You're dad's less pissed," Tanner added.

"He is. It's a whole different universe. For me at least. Every single thing I do, all day long, picks the kind of universe in which I am going to live point forward. It changes my future. My entire future. The guy I cut off at the light. The kid with one item I let go ahead of me in the checkout line. Every little decision, every minor choice, creates a new timeline in which I live from now on."

"That's bizarre, Mr. Z."

No, it's wonderful. It makes me the most powerful human in my life, because every single day I have the chance to create different universes and at the end of the day I get to live in the one of those that I chose. That's why I call my new club z^2"

"What's z?" asked Jeremy.

"Z is the number of choices that I made that day. Eight choices? Two-hundred and sixty-four? We all probably make way more choices than that every day, don't we?"

"The universe isn't that big. There isn't room for all those places."

"The multiverse is as big as it needs to be, Sean. Infinity is a tough concept."

Then Alex added the punch line he had been building towards. "So last year I took apart my perfectly good time machine and threw all the components in the trash. I decided that rather than waste my energies going back and altering what was nothing more than other people's timelines, I would concentrate on making sure that my own universe became just as pleasant and fine a place as I possibly could make it."

"You can't judge the outcomes of your actions," Travis said defensively.

"A good point. Well-intended behavior does sometimes

cause problems. Here I have to go with statistics, Travis. I make a lot of decisions every day. Statistically, the more they are intended to make this a better timeline, the better off I am. To that end, Xuha, I need to speak with you after class. The rest of you are free to use as much or little of this in your own projects as you see fit. There is no penalty for ignoring my theories. Please work quietly on your projects until the bell rings."

Xuha approached Alex's desk defensively, but with a bit of grudging admiration on his face. "That was quite a good lecture you delivered Mr. Z."

"Thanks," Alex said as he gestured Xuha out into the hall where they could talk privately for a minute. "I meant what I said. About trying every day with every choice I make to create a universe in which I want to live. So, that is why I'm inviting you to come stay at my house over the winter break. Have Christmas with my family."

"I couldn't…"

"Xuha, I know about your foster parents. I am so very sorry. I know that Ms. Johnson is somehow responsible, and I know that she threatened you and said if you asked me for help she'd hurt me too." Then, in response to Xuha's surprised expression, "I have my sources. I am pretty sure that you're managing to pay the rent all on your own, but I don't know how long you can keep that up."

"I'm being evicted at the end of the month," Xuha said sadly. "Somebody tipped off my landlord that a seventeen year old was now living alone on the premises and could cause who knows what kind of trouble."

"All the more reason then. Pack up your stuff and come over. You can stay in my son Zane's room except for the few days when he's home for the holidays."

"Won't this get you in trouble with the school?" Xuha asked.

"Probably," Alex laughed, "but to be honest, things are so skewed from normal this particular year that I'm not going to even think about that now. I choose to create a universe in which you get some help."

"I think maybe you should be more afraid of Ms. Johnson,"

Xuha said.

"I recognize her as a dangerous and totally misguided woman," Alex said evenly. "And I choose to create a universe in which I am not afraid of her or of the hatred for which she stands."

Xuha hesitated.

"Come on," Alex smiled encouragingly. "Let's create a universe in which we win."

In December 2010 there were over a million youngsters living illegally in the U.S. who had been brought in by their parents for a wide variety of reasons and under many circumstances. Most had never really known any other home. About sixty-five thousand of them were planning to graduate from high school the following spring. Most wanted to go on to get jobs, to join the military, or to get more education. Just like the rest of their classmates.

Back in 2001 a bill was introduced in congress that would have allowed them to do so. Bad timing. In 2009 the bill was re-introduced by members of both political parties, and received bi-partisan support as well as endorsements by a host of educators, including teachers associations and all eight Ivy League universities, and by groups as far ranging as the American Association of Catholic Bishops, the AFL-CIO and the PTA. The statistics in favor of allowing those youngsters to contribute to society were overwhelming.

However, by 2010 the DREAM Act, as it became known, had become caught up in a general anti-immigration fervor. The day after his birthday, on December 8, 2010, Alex heard with relief that the legislation had still managed to pass in the House of Representatives. Now it would go to the Senate.

By the end of the next week Kyle was ready to go back to Houston and continue his search. Kisa had shown him around the cave, introduced him to her family, spent time telling him everything she knew about the original three boxes and the ultimate hope of reuniting them to reveal the treasure's location. Kyle came to realize that Kisa's whole family shared a firm belief that the other two boxes had neither been lost nor destroyed but would turn up exactly as they were meant to when the time was right. They also seemed to accept that Kisa had made a wise decision in passing the artifact along to him, and they accepted that Kyle would do his part to locate the missing two artifacts. In fact, they seemed certain of it.

Kyle did not share this last bit of faith, of course, but he kept his concerns to himself. He did agree that Kisa was an equal partner in his efforts point forward. If Jake didn't see the wisdom in a three-way split, then Kyle and Kisa would just split Kyle's share. After all, the treasure was supposed to be huge. Kisa was content with either arrangement.

Over the first week of December, Jake and Stan called each other and talked. What a mess, they agreed. Jake and Shelby talked. What a lot of stupid behavior, they both said. Jake, Stan, Shelby and Jennifer talked. Before the week was done the comedy of errors that had perpetuated itself throughout the last seventeen years was discussed, explained, laughed about, apologized for and ultimately accepted by all.

It was a good time to put it all behind them and move forward, they decided, preferably with all the intelligence and common sense they could muster. With no more need for secrecy, the foursome readily agreed to join forces. Someone suggested bringing in Nelson as well, but no one could think of a good reason to do so. That left just the little matter of telling Kyle, who had been incommunicado at Lake Paten for several days now. Jake had already decided that if Kyle objected to bringing in more partners, then Jake would simply split his own half with Stan, Shelby and Jennifer. After all, the treasure was supposed to be huge. The group was content with either arrangement.

Teddie worded her announcement in the school paper very carefully. It was to be a short essay contest regarding the Civil War, with the best half dozen or so entries to be published in the mid-January edition of the school paper. The best three essays would be awarded modest scholarship money and school privileges. Topics could include how the Civil War shaped the United States, the beliefs of either or both sides in the conflict, significant battles and turning points in the war, or how the life of the essayist and others would be different today if the war had gone differently.

The journalism teacher was delighted. The administration was delighted. And Teddie and her friends quietly spread the word that the essays on "How my life would be different if the South had won the war" were going to be hands-on favorites to win.

"Really give it some thought," Teddie encouraged, reaching out to students least likely to enter the contest. In the interest of time the journalism teacher would pick the six finalists, but the principal herself would select the top three winners. For purposes of accurate record keeping, Teddie received permission to view and record the entries. Essays began arriving before the winter break, and she used her cell phone to photograph every page carefully and to email the images to herself and her dad, and, just be safe, to her Aunt Summer as well.

When Kyle finally sent Jake a text from the airport in Mexico City, he was surprised to get word back asking him to just pick up a phone and call. "Aren't you scared Dr. Drexler might be tapping your phone?" Kyle laughed when Jake answered.

"About that. Kyle, I've done a little soul searching while you were gone this time and, well, we have a new partner or two, and I've got a lot of news to share with you."

This was interesting, Kyle thought. "Yeah, me too," he responded.

"You too what?" Jake sounded baffled and maybe even a little annoyed at having his announcement derailed.

"I've been soul searching about what exactly it is that we are trying to do. I'm bringing in a new partner. And have I got news to share with you."

There was a long silence.

"Jake, could I come to LA and just talk with you?"

"Sure Kyle. That would probably be an excellent idea."

About a week later Ralph called Tina back.

"You do have good instincts," he laughed. "I used my law enforcement credentials to get a background interview with a nurse who has been part of that office since nineteen-ninety-one. Once she was convinced that the 'cold case' I was looking into would in no way at all impact the good doctor whom she idolizes, she was happy to tell me the whole story."

"She remembered it?"

"Oh yeah. This is the kind of thing you don't forget."

"So where was this kid born?"

"Well, we still don't know, but it probably wasn't Houston. His grandpa was a Mexican, came to Houston for cancer treatment all fine and legal, and then the guy's health went south. Wife was with him. Guess he had some means. They had only one child, a daughter, very pregnant, who, when she hears that dad isn't going to make it much longer, she drives up from Mexico City with her husband. Nurse says the daughter kept calling every few hours to tell her mom that she was on her way. Begging her dad to hold on so she could say goodbye. Pretty pathetic story. Anyway, the daughter actually makes it there before the dad croaks, but the real kicker is that she had the kid in the car on the way."

"Unbelievable," Tina says.

"Yeah, these people are like livestock," Ralph agreed. "But the doctor is one of those liberal types and she feels sorry for the family. So she checks the baby and mom over and they're fine and she fills out a birth certificate for the kid and that's how your Mexican ends up with a cancer doctor's signature on his birth certificate."

"But he was born on U.S. soil," Tina said sadly.

"That's the good part. Not necessarily. The nurse said they all marveled later how the kid was at least hours old and they couldn't believe that those folks just kept driving in their car with this new born."

"Hours old?" Tina asked. "His parents were in route to the hospital for hours? How many hours is it from the Mexican border to Houston?"

"I checked. About eight. If you're really certain this kid is a menace at your school, I'll go ahead and see if there is such a thing as border crossing records from that far back. I doubt it, but…"

"This kid has already beat up several innocent students, Ralph. He has got to be stopped. Please. Anything at all you can find out that might even cast doubt on his citizenship would be so helpful."

"I'll do my best Tina."

"I appreciate it. There's a package filled with my best homemade brownies in the mail to you already." She was smiling as she hung up the phone.

Pastor Vernon Farley was unwilling to single out any one individual and preach against him, but he was easily persuaded to devote the next Sunday's sermon to the dangers of older exotic religions, and the importance of knowing how the devil used our natural human curiosity and the allure of the unknown to entice us away from the true God. It wasn't exactly what Tina had hoped for, but it would have to do. Pastor Farley did have one of the very largest congregations in the area, and other preachers often chose to echo his themes. Tina figured that she could let them lay the groundwork for her, and then she could manage to direct their fear specifically to Xuha.

She was relieved that Lola Zeitman wasn't at the next ladies' reenactment support gathering, and that the big-mouthed college professor had dropped out of the group as well. Knowing that too much prodding from any one person eventually meets resistance, Tina persuaded a fellow history teacher to share conversational concerns about how a little kid like Xuha seemed to do so well at tennis, and to do so well in school in spite of his race and poor inner city background. In fact, it was almost like he was protected by, well, like, something evil. Just saying. It was kind of weird.

Tina's friend ran the scenario by several different clumps of the women there. Some looked at her like she was kind of nutty. But two or three of the little groups of women listened attentively and nodded. Tina watched. Those were the ladies she'd talk to later more privately.

Kyle never thought he'd find himself sitting at Jake's kitchen counter visiting with Jake's wife, but here he was, a guest through the holidays. In a couple of weeks there were going to be kids and packages and a big turkey and all the things he had never thought he had missed but right now all sounded pretty damn good.

"I'm a real live friend of yours now," Kyle said, pleased.

"I've told Gail all about our secret little possession and our seventeen-year mission, and while she is a little incredulous I could have been part of something so convoluted," Jake said while Gail nodded with comic exaggeration, "she is happy neither you nor I ended up hurt or in any real trouble along the way. It's good to have you here, Kyle."

And Kyle thought to himself that it was very good to be there.

Before the dust was settled Jake, Kyle, Stan and Shelby agreed to split the value of whatever was found, if it was found and if it had any value. Everyone agreed that Kisa got a share as well. Jennifer declined any financial interest at all, as did Stan's friend Alex. Alex and Jennifer both claimed they'd only gotten involved because solving the puzzle had frankly sounded like a good time.

So by the end of 2010 the business arrangements were made. There was hope now for the other two boxes to be located. Kyle prepared to head back to Houston. Costs needed to be watched, so Alex offered Kyle lodging.

Friday, December 17, school let out for the rest of the calendar year. Xuha packed up all of his worldly possessions, gave one last very sad look around the small and cheaply made apartment that he had shared so happily with the Cruz family, and drove his old car over to Mr. Zeitman's house. Even working as many hours as he could manage he didn't see how he could possibly pay Mr. Zeitman for room and board, and he hated that feeling. Maybe there were chores he could do or something. What a mess.

At least he wouldn't be alone for Christmas, though. Xuha

felt like he was a fairly tough person, but the prospect of two full weeks of being home from school by himself in that place alone, without the people who had become in every way his family, had seemed daunting. The Zeitmans would have their own traditions of course, and they wouldn't be his. But, Xuha admitted, they would be better than nothing at all.

Friday, December 17, Shelby left work with a lightness in her step. She had managed to get off both the last two weeks of 2010 and the first two of 2011 and was headed to Guatemala the next day with Stan. Well, not exactly Guatemala. First they would go to a resort in Belize where they would enjoy a week at the beach, and then they would meet up with Stan's current crop of students at the very same hotel in Guatemala where it had all started seventeen years ago.

She was going to get to excavate again, get to be a real archeologist for three weeks. Thanks to Kyle, and, Shelby supposed, thanks also to the perceptiveness of Alex's daughter, their new partner Kisa was waiting to collaborate with them when they arrived. It promised to be a wonderful month.

Friday, December 17, Dr. Nelson Nowicki left his office with an air of finality. He was tired of being nice, tired of being polite. His whole career, his whole world would have gone so very differently if he had just been part of the group responsible for finding that artifact. That glory should have been his. Or partly his. Dr. Drexler had ruined his life. No, Jennifer had ruined his life. Actually, whatever scumbag had stolen the artifact after he put it back in the cave had ruined his life and the other two had just contributed to his problems.

Well, enough was enough. He'd avoided the Lake Peten Area for seventeen years now, but it was time to act. He'd leave his wife Lisa a letter explaining his absence. He was going to Atlanta. He was going back to campus. He was going to find the damn artifact that was back in Dr. Drexler's unworthy possession.

It wasn't uncommon for the school to have a break-in or two over the holidays when the campus was largely deserted. And

Nelson knew how to break into the anthropology department with minimum chance of getting caught. It was just going to be Dr. Drexler's piece of continuing bad luck that some uneducated vandal was going to smash that relic into a thousand pieces. No glory to be had for anyone. At least that would be fair.

On the evening of December 17, Lola retired early with a headache and asked her family to leave her be. In fact, her headache was caused from the strain Lola felt from Somadina's labor as the young Nigerian woman worked hard to deliver her second child. A telepathic link is not always a blessing. In the quiet, still darkness of her bedroom, Lola worked to sooth herself, and then to provide Somadina with as much support as she could while staying in the background and leaving the emotional heavy lifting to Somadina's capable and loving husband Azuka. Labor went well, and at about four in the morning Houston time Somadina delivered a healthy baby girl. Lola, roiling with the emotions of her friend's relief and joy, burst into tears of gladness.

On the afternoon of December 18, Alex listened with dismay to a news broadcast. In the Senate, the DREAM Act had fallen five votes short of the sixty needed to prevent a filibuster and allow the senators to actually vote on it. Had it only made it on to the floor of the Senate in December of 2010, it would certainly have passed.

Many people of all political persuasions were surprised that a piece of such reasonable legislation could fail to make it to a vote. But Alex wasn't. He had read a lot on the subject, and he knew the history of U.S. immigration policies all too well.

Chapter 17. Christmas 2010

The winter solstice intrigued Alex, as did all ramifications of the movements of Earth's solar system. Such a fascinating work of intricate machinery carried out with precision on a scale so grand that to us tiny humans it wasn't even apparent what was going on.

For the past three months, night had relentlessly strengthened its grasp upon half of the Earth, as the power of darkness grew with every sunset. Alex understood why the ancients of the north had rejoiced at the winter solstice—the battle changed its course, and, slowly, the power of light grew, with each day now lengthening. Their happiness at the triumph of sunlight had reverberated throughout history into a variety of celebrations still enjoyed enthusiastically in modern times, each one embracing the soft golden glow of a waxing winter sun.

Having a daughter born on the solstice had given the day added meaning, of course, and tonight Alex would make a special dinner for his solstice-born daughter Ariel. It was Tuesday December 21, and the birthday girl was off getting a pedicure with her mother and sister, a modern female ritual that made no sense to Alex, but he supposed that it didn't need to. His three favorite ladies were enjoying themselves, and they would pick son Zane up at the airport at the end of their spa treatments, and, if the modern gods of on-time air travel were kind, a fine family dinner and chocolate cake would follow.

The dough was rising for the homemade pizza Ariel loved, and the toppings had already been chopped. The mushrooms and onions were on the stove being lightly sautéed when the phone rang.

"Alex?" Olumiji's soft deep voice with its Nigerian accent was unmistakable. Alex's first reaction was a sinking "oh not this guy again." Then he remembered why he didn't particularly like to talk to this guy, which was that this guy absolutely had heard his first reaction. Damn. And his second one. Damn again.

"Very few people who are not telepaths themselves know what I can do," Olumiji said kindly. "You are put in a very difficult position whenever I call you. I appreciate the strength that it takes to deal with me. My friend Lola is luckier than she knows, I think, to have found a man with your confidence and your wisdom."

"Uh, thanks."

"I called to offer my assistance to you again, Alex. I am making a trip to Rio and will stop over on the way to visit with my sister Foluke. I will have a few days there. I know that we, we struck out as you would say, last time we looked for your artifact, but I thought that perhaps there had been some new developments or ideas, and I wanted to let you know that if I could be of help on this second visit I was willing."

"I wish," Alex said honestly, realizing that Olumiji could have more easily contacted Lola but had elected to speak directly to him. "I appreciate it, I really do. If anything changes I'll let you know, but right now we just don't have any other leads."

And it wasn't until Alex hung up the phone, and walked out onto the Zeitmans' front porch to give an appreciative eye to the earliest sunset of the year, that it occurred to him that he did, indeed, have a better lead.

"Call back. Call back." He thought it as hard as he possibly could, for once hoping that Lola's super-adept telepathic friend would hear his thoughts loud and clear. The phone rang.

"You've figured something out?" Olumiji's voice was surprised.

"You bet I have. Okay, I may not be able to read people's feelings or things like that, but there are some things I absolutely know and one of them is where the damn sun sets."

"It sets in the west." Olumiji did not sound impressed.

"No, not really. It only sets in the exact west on the spring and on the fall equinox."

"Well yes," Olumiji acknowledged. "It varies a little off of due west over the course of a year, but not much, at least not near the equator where I live anyway."

"That's a myth," Alex retorted. "It varies a good bit even exactly at the equator. Over twenty-three degrees, and ever more as your latitude goes up."

"Are you sure?" Olumiji seemed surprised.

"Completely. I've developed a formula that approximates it

for any latitude below the Arctic Circle and I've measured it myself here in Houston and it's over thirty degrees" Alex had the portable phone and had already pulled out a map. "Lake Peten is seventeen degrees north of the equator. This old document says that the boys were sent off at the winter solstice. The kid going west had a long way to go. We don't know much about him. But the kid going easy probably made it to the coast in a couple of months. Except that he wasn't told to walk east. He was told to follow the sunrise when he started and these people were really into things like sunrises. I don't think it was metaphorical. I don't think he took those orders lightly. He headed out walking over twenty five degrees south of east, well off the path we've been looking along. You don't have to cover a lot of distance for nearly thirty degrees off to make a lot of difference."

"Then he walked right over the mountains?"

"Given the direction he started, it's more likely that he found a path around to the south of the mountains."

"So, where does that path put him?"

"Southern Belize." Alex squinted at the map. "You ever heard of a place called Punta Gorda? Fat Point?"

"I have." Alex could hear the smile in Olumiji's voice. "It's where Foluke's friend Yochi is from. Would you like Foluke and me to visit him, and make a few inquiries on your behalf?"

"You bet I would."

Ralph knew that thousands of people legally cross the border between Mexico and the United States every day, and he didn't think that number had been that much less back in 1993. With computer technology far less prevalent and the post-9/11 fear yet to take hold, he figured there was almost no chance that anyone in Brownsville could be of any help to him regarding a single vehicle driving in from Matamoros seventeen years ago. But Brownsville was on the most direct route from Mexico City to Houston. And he did have a lone aunt living down there who would love to see him for the holidays. The kids were with his ex this year. He had no other plans. Best of all, not only would he be helping the cause, but he figured that just making the trip was going to be worth three or four boxes of

Tina's homemade brownies over the next year. He did love those brownies.

On Wednesday, December 22, Ralph didn't expect much in the way of office staff at the small outpost of customs and border protection, and in fact only one lone man was in the little office. It wasn't because of the usual mass exodus at Christmas, however. Ralph was surprised to discover that border crossings went up dramatically as families on both sides of the border traveled to be together for the holidays, and that much of the CBP staff passed on their own travel and worked extra shifts just to see that families on both sides of the border could be together. *One more way we coddle outsiders,* Ralph thought. He snorted in disgust.

The lone older man laughed at Ralph's request for information from 1993 and assured him that zero helpful records had been kept from then. But the guy listened with some interest once Ralph described the quest to figure out on which side of the border a baby had been born.

"We get some nonsense in that regard. Used to get the occasionally very pregnant Mexican lady coming in, maybe to have the baby. Usually she'd have some relative in Brownsville she'd say she was visiting, claiming she was going back home in a day or two. But sometimes we kinda knew. What are you gonna do? Can't keep all pregnant women out of the country."

"That's pathetic," Ralph agreed. "We really need to amend the Constitution to fix this. There is no excuse. How many women do you see doing this?"

"Oh, maybe a couple a year. Most of them cross back and go home just as pregnant as they came, sometimes with their American sisters or friends with them."

Ralph was disappointed to learn that this wasn't a bigger problem.

"Hey, once we actually did have a baby born exactly while crossing the border. I was working here then, but it wasn't my lane. Rick, that's the guy. The lady looked like she was in labor when they drove up and Rick wasn't going to let them in. He got in an argument with the husband and damn if she didn't have that baby right there while the two of them were yelling at each other."

"You've got to kidding."

"No, it really happened. Rick was so disgusted. You got any idea how messy birth is?"

"Yeah, I was present at a couple of my own. Pretty gross. I hope your guy Rick sent those yoyos straight back to Matamoros that instant."

"No, no he didn't," the older man said. "Turns out the girl's dad was dying at some hospital here and she was trying to get to his deathbed and so Rick let them on through. Damnedest thing."

Something connected in Ralph's brain. "Do you remember what year that was?"

"Not really. Late nineties, I think. Maybe early-nineties. It sort of all runs together after a while, you know?"

"Does Rick still work here?"

"Nay. He was an up-and-coming sort. He was over at the big office in Laredo for a while, not sure where he is now."

"Do you know how I could find him?" Ralph asked.

"Sure. His brother Dave still works here. You want Dave's phone number?"

"You bet I would."

Thursday, December 23, Lola was trying to get packages wrapped before the rest of the family got home from their own last-minute shopping, when she felt a gentle tug on her mind. *Not now,* she thought.

Please. For your own sake. I think you want to video chat with me. It was Olumiji's voice and Lola knew that it was never his way to persist without real reason. With a sigh she threw a large towel over her unwrapped presents and headed for the computer.

When Alex and Zane walked in a few minutes later, they heard Lola's voice coming from the study, at least half an octave higher than usual. "It's beautiful. Absolutely gorgeous. No, I have no idea..."

Alex rounded the corner to see Yochi's face on the home computer screen, and his hands holding up a thin pale olive green box in a trapezoid shape. It was maybe the size of a textbook, covered in arcs of meticulously carved tiny hieroglyphs, and decorated with inlaid colored stones. Even to Alex's untrained eye it was clear it had been made by the same hand or hands that had created the black obsidian box of Stan Drexler's.

"Where did you find this?" Alex barked it with more vehemence than he intended.

"It was his great grandmother's jewelry box," Foluke said a little defensively. "Yochi said she got it from her grandmother, who supposedly was one of your Confederate people."

Alex took a breath. "So this thing that people have been scouring Belize for has been sitting on somebody's dresser? Holding earrings?"

"Certainly not," Olumiji chuckled in the background. "This relic has been sitting safely in a small one room museum run by one of Yochi's distant cousins. We are guessing that the lady in question received it as a gift from her husband in the eighteen-seventies. Her legend has it that the jewelry box was her most prized possession and that is why it is here in the museum."

"What sort of museum is this?"

"That's the best part," Olumiji said. "It's a little house that for decades now has served as a small shrine to the memory of the Confederacy."

"Our Confederacy?" Alex was aghast.

"Not really," Foluke chimed in. "Belize's Confederacy. It's a tribute to the toughest of your people who immigrated here. The ones who stayed and survived and blended and finally became part of Belize and contributed their strengths as surely as all of Belize's other immigrants. It's a shrine to Yochi's people."

Alex just stared.

"If you want to call your friend Stan, maybe he can arrange to visit here. No one will let the jewelry box leave, of course, but they have already agreed to let him come examine it if he promises to do so carefully."

"Of course, I'll contact him right away. This, well, this is unexpected."

"Not so much so, Alex. The place we found it is pretty much on a line east twenty-eight degrees south from Lake Peten, right where that line hits the sea."

"I do know where the sun rises and sets," Alex said.

"You certainly do," Olumiji agreed.

"You want me to do what?" Jennifer, who was clearly in the midst of getting ready for some Christmas Eve festivity at her country club, was not happy with the request or the timing. But Shelby held her ground.

"Jennifer, we're on our way to Punta Gorda tomorrow. We've been looking at photos of the second box and the hieroglyphs are of a slightly different size and they're at a little different angle. The key to solving this is the continuity of the message, and Stan thinks this will be difficult-to-impossible to figure out unless we can physically set the two boxes side by side and at the very least photograph them together. The one in Belize isn't going anywhere. And it would take weeks to get permission to bring the Atlanta one here. Please. Christmas Eve is the perfect time. Stan can tell you where he keeps his key card and can talk you through getting into the building. Leave your party, get the box, go back to your party, meet me tomorrow at the airport with it. We'll have it back where it belongs next week before it can possibly be missed. There is no risk to you. I promise."

Jenifer sighed. Why argue? She knew that sooner or later she was going to be persuaded to do it.

Nelson arrived in Atlanta Friday, December 24, with a couple of hours to kill. He'd managed to book a flight and travel under a cheaply acquired fake ID and was still shaking inside from it. He'd wait until early evening, do what he'd come to do, and be home by midnight, with his wife firmly convinced that he'd driven several hours just to provide Christmas cheer to a favorite old uncle in a rest home. It was only a bonus that the favorite uncle really existed and would have no idea whether Nelson had shown up or not, and the overworked apathetic staff at the rest home wouldn't be sure either.

Nelson was further pleased to discover that plan A was all he needed to get in. The lock on the third window to the left of the men's rest room on the first floor still hadn't been fixed after two decades, and Nelson entered the building just as he had as a grad student any time he'd forgotten his key. He moved quietly, listening for sounds of anyone else in the building. Unless habits had changed, by 9 p.m. on Christmas Eve only one lone watchman would be patrolling the four or five buildings on the south end of campus, and odds were very good the watchman would be nowhere near.

He had taken his biggest risk addressing the next issue. Nelson knew exactly where something under study should be kept, given that labs in basements seldom see renovation in the academic world. But to be certain, he had asked a former student of his to confirm the box's location. More specifically, he'd casually asked the young man to send him a quick phone photo of it, claiming a mild curiosity based on his former association, and a last minute desire to use the photo in something holiday related. The kid had complied without apparent suspicion and Nelson could tell just where the photo had been taken.

Only now that he was standing there, sledgehammer in hand, there was no box. Luckily, locking up artifacts wasn't customary in a building that was believed to be already well secured, so Nelson went to work opening every cabinet and drawer big enough to hold the obsidian relic. It wasn't in any of them.

This isn't possible, Nelson thought. *What is it with this artifact and all this disappearing?*

Frantic and a little bit spooked, Nelson started wandering through the musty, cluttered basement, opening cabinets and doors, hunting for where it could have been inexplicably stashed at the last moment. Had he heard something? He stopped moving and listened carefully. The noise stopped when he did.

When no box was found in the basement, he moved to the first floor. It was filled with classrooms and none of the doors were locked here either. None hid what he was seeking. He paused again, more sure this time that he had picked up sounds. He stopped and listened. It almost sounded like someone breathing, a little heavily. There was a hint of a moan. He stood very still, but then the building went quiet. It must just have been the sound of air in the vents. He started to move and could have sworn he heard the noise starting up again.

He made his way to the second floor next, where most of the professors' individual offices were. Emergency exit lights were all that was on and his flashlight was getting weaker. These doors were all locked, of course, but large glass panels let in enough of the fading light from his flashlight for him to make sure, office by office, that the artifact had not been moved at the last minute to any professor's desk.

After checking the last office, Nelson looked around in helpless frustration. Then he heard a clear sharp sound that sounded for all the world like a moan of ecstasy and he froze. Then, just as the faint light on his flashlight began to flicker into nothingness, a small object came flying at him out of the blue. Nelson jumped back and screamed, and then stared down at the floor at what appeared in the gloom to be a human bone. He dropped the sledgehammer and ran like hell to the boys' bathroom and fled through the window so fast that he forgot to close it.

"So you got it with no problem?" a happy Shelby confirmed by phone a few hours later.

"I not only got it sweetheart," a slightly tipsy Jennifer replied, "I had more fun getting that box than I have had in a very long time."

Shelby found that odd, but thought is was probably better not to ask.

"Are you serious? We're having Christmas dinner now, at eleven o'clock in the morning? What about cinnamon rolls and bacon? We always have that Christmas morning!" Teddie, who had just come downstairs, had reverted to her thirteen-year-old voice at this new outrage.

"Have them with your dinner," Ariel offered cheerfully as

she pulled the rolls out of the oven. Lola, working to thaw the lobster tails fast in running warm water, tried to answer more patiently.

"Your dad just found out that he has to be out the door no later than noon, dear, to make a three o'clock flight to Belize. They're going to be putting the two boxes side by side. It's very exciting. Your dad is going to help them crack the code on some ancient secret. Come on, you want him to get to have Christmas dinner with us before he goes, don't you?"

"I don't want him going to Belize today," Teddie muttered. Then, with more indignation. "What's wrong with this family?"

"What do you mean?" Lola asked. "There's nothing wrong with us."

"Last year we didn't even get to eat until almost eight o'clock at night because you were on a plane coming home from Nigeria," Teddie replied sullenly. "Now this. Why can't we be normal for once?"

"Normal is overrated," Zane quipped as he came into the kitchen carrying two cartons of orange juice.

"There is no way I'm going to get potatoes mashed," Alex apologized as he came into the kitchen pouring a second cup of coffee.

"On it," Ariel said, masher in hand.

"Teddie, set the table please. Zane, you can melt butter for the lobster. Xuha, would you mind handling the cranberry sauce?"

Sweetie, you don't have to rush like this," Alex said. "I can grab something at the airport."

"No!" five other voices said in chorus.

"Okay, okay. I love you all too. Give me ten more minutes to finish packing and then let's eat."

The next morning Zane sat quietly in the study reading his email. His mom had taken Teddie and Xuha out for lunch and errand-running, and just-woken Ariel could be heard in the kitchen making herself breakfast. The day was cool and overcast, and a bit of wind was blowing. Zane looked out the window at a noise, expecting to see twigs and branches picked up by a breeze, and instead was surprised to see a half-dozen or so women on the far edge of the Zeitman's front lawn. Stranger yet, the women were holding picket signs. The Zeitman house was set far back on an oversized lot on a quiet suburban cul-de-sac, and frankly Zane could not think of a less likely, or less effective, place for a demonstration.

"Ariel. Come here. You've got to see this."

A minute later Ariel took a long gulp of her coffee as she squinted through the open blinds at the group.

"You've got to be kidding. I know that mom and dad don't always see eye-to-eye with their neighbors, but you think one of them actually did something to get a protest started?" she said.

"I think it's pretty funny if they did," Zane laughed.

"We've got to find out what those signs say," Ariel chirped. "And I want pictures." She came back in a minute with her cell phone and her dad's binoculars. She studied the group for a few minutes through the lenses, and then she turned to Zane.

"Actually, this isn't all that funny. They're protesting Xuha and they've got signs saying some pretty nasty stuff."

"Can I see?" Zane counted eight women and he studied their messages. Most had to do with Xuha being involved in some sort of pagan devil worship. "They drove over here just to do this?" He was incredulous. Then he added, "We've got to get them out of here. This poor kid Xuha has had his whole world fall apart, and he already feels like he's imposing by just being here. We can't let him and Mom and Teddie come home to this nonsense."

Ariel nodded in agreement. "Technically they're pretty much on the curb, Zane. I don't think we can legally chase them off." She thought a minute. "This is when it might be nice to own one of those really nasty big dogs. But we don't. Think I could sneak out the back door to the pound and borrow one?"

"Takes time for a dog to develop a sense of this being his home," Zane remarked. "And there just isn't any way I can turn into a convincing dog. Even if I was that good, it just involves too much hair."

Ariel raised an eyebrow. "Is this the sort of thing you were trying to tell me about the other night? I thought you were just drunk. You seriously can change the way you look?"

"Let's just say that I have a few skills that I've preferred to keep to myself," Zane muttered. "Except for times like when a have a few too many beers with my sister, whom I trust," he added with a rueful smile. He picked up the binoculars and studied the messages.

"All houses should do the work of the Lord," he read aloud. "Yeah, right. Like embarrassing some seventeen-year-old kid with nowhere else to go is doing the work of the Lord."

"I'd almost call that the work of the devil, myself," Ariel said.

"You know, so would I," Zane agreed. "And as a matter of fact, I think I'm going to call it just that. This attitude of hating in the name of God really pisses me off. Would you be willing to help me play a little dress up here?"

"Sure." Zane hardly ever got this mad, and he hardly ever had liked to play dress up. Ariel was more than curious. "You've got some sort of a plan to chase these people off of our lawn?"

"I do, and I need to do this before I calm down and change my mind. Would you be willing to go see if mom still keeps all those Halloween costumes in the upstairs closet?"

"You know that she does. They never throw anything away. What are you looking for?" Ariel asked.

"A black cape, maybe. I don't know. A tail? A pitchfork? Fake horns would be helpful but I think maybe I can do those myself."

"This I have got to see," Ariel said.

"Yeah, well, keep it between us," Zane replied. "And no photos."

Up in his room, Zane found an old pair of black running shorts. Black hiking boots would have to do. He could brave the chill for the amount of time this would take, because the more skin he exposed the more convincing he would be. Ariel couldn't find anything close to a pitchfork, but she produced a fake cat's tail that she pinned onto his shorts and she handed him a cheap black cape.

Zane picked up the scissors. "Here, trim the hair on the top of my head really short. These little horns are going to need all the help they can get to be visible and I'll just hide the haircut by wearing my toke until I leave."

Ariel nodded. "You wear that hat all the time anyway."

She took the scissors and got started. Sure enough, Zane's scalp was slowly sprouting two little dark brown horns.

"That's oddly impressive," Ariel muttered.

"Anything new like this takes so much concentration," he explained. Ariel kept snipping hair and tried not to over react.

But as he headed to the front door, she stopped him. "You know, I don't think that you should walk out of our house like the devil lives here. Maybe go out the back and cut through the neighbor's yard? Come out of the shrubbery half way down?" He agreed as she handed him the potato masher.

"What am I supposed to do with this?"

"You've got to be holding something in your hand, Zane. Make it look menacing. No one is going to look too closely."

And so dressed like the devil and armed with a potato masher, Zane headed out the back door to meet with the members of one of Texas' finest hate groups, for the purpose of conducting a serious discussion about the nature of good and evil.

Debbie Cooke thought it was a kid stepping out of the bushes until she looked more closely. He was skinny like a kid but tall enough to be a man, and in the light of an overcast sky he was clearly red. Sunburnt red and then some, but not all over. He had streaks of brown and black winding over him like some sort of horrible cancerous vein, slowly moving and making thorn-like hooks that were raised off of his skin. He had small horns and a cape, and when he first opened his mouth smoke came out of it. Then he smiled the most evil smile Debbie Cooke had ever seen. She screamed.

"Don't let me scare you," he said in a low, menacing growl clearly meant to terrify. And then he laughed. "I only came to express my appreciation."

"For what?' Dolores Bolton asked sharply. Unlike Debbie, Dolores wasn't afraid of anybody, ever, and the devil himself wasn't about to change that as far as she was concerned.

"For you," the creature replied and gave a hard long evil leer right into Dolores' horrified eyes, while the whites of his eyes went blood red and his irises turned from black to light golden then back to black again.

Eight women stared aghast, each one waiting for the other to start to run.

"I like what you're doing today. Scarring children is one of my favorite things. I love to see people feel horrible. Hate themselves. Hate each other. It feeds me. Makes me grow large."

The creature chuckled as his chest and abdomen grew bigger and he stood taller.

"I just came to say keep up the good work, ladies. Spread my hate. Spread it," he laughed stepping towards Dolores with his arms wide to engulf her in a hug. To Dolores' credit she stood her ground and didn't flinch as he came towards her. She didn't even flinch as his arms started to close around her. She didn't actually flinch until she felt the extreme heat of his touch, and then she shrieked as loud as she could and ran down the street toward her car and never looked back.

Once Dolores ran, they all ran. The creature stood laughing and waving his potato masher as all three cars peeled out of the cul-de-sac.

"I think that went well," Zane remarked to Ariel back in the study.

"You put on a hell of a performance," Ariel acknowledged. "Is this, is this the sort of thing you do a lot of?"

Zane laughed in his own voice now. "Not really. My body seems to respond to the orders of my brain in ways that other people's bodies just don't. To be honest I used to practice it a lot, mostly whenever I was bored in school. Hey, no need to mention this to anyone else, okay?"

"Are you kidding?" Ariel smiled. "I'd prefer people not describe me as 'unhinged.'"

Alex finally arrived as scheduled in the little town of Punta Gorda Sunday afternoon, the day after Christmas. Stan and Foluke both met him after his tiny plane made a gasp-inducing landing on a short dirt runway that Alex had the feeling was going to show up in various bad dreams of his for years to come. A few hours later Shelby arrived with the original obsidian artifact, carrying it by hand in layers of bubble wrap. Excitement crackled like static electricity as the covering was ripped off of the larger relic and the two boxes were placed together for the first time in over three-hundred years.

The beautiful shiny black obsidian and the soft green jade melded their edges together as if they were part of one whole. The

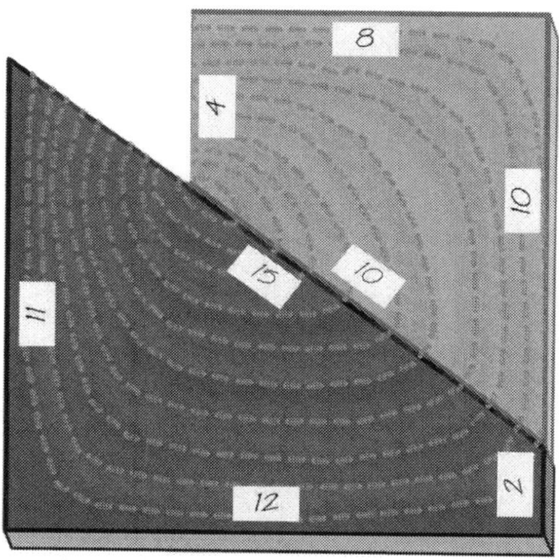

Yochi's box gives a more complete picture

designs along the sides of the two boxes blended together seamlessly. The arcs of text merged perfectly but unfortunately not quite so neatly, changing their curves slightly in subtle ways that could not have been anticipated by examining either box alone.

Alex, Stan and Shelby, who had originally been confident that over the course of a few hours they could make significant headway, had planned to send the larger box back to Atlanta on Monday so it could be in place for university offices reopening on Tuesday. Instead they spent a frustrating evening trying out possibilities, clustered around a cramped card table in the little one-room museum, with the precious parchment Stan had brought in his suitcase laying on the floor where it was safest. Yochi kept the generator going to provide lights and fans, but by midnight all three had headaches from the heat and the frustration, and they had made exactly zero progress deciphering anything. This was turning out to be far more complicated than any of them had expected.

After a call to Jennifer late that night, Jake got involved, and on Monday Kyle was dispatched to Belize to see what he could contribute. While Foluke and Shelby went to meet Kyle's small plane Monday night, Stan stayed back and composed a very short note to the head of the anthropology department explaining how sorry he was that he had broken protocol, taken the relic home to admire over Christmas and had now become quite ill. Not to worry, he and it would be back in the office in a day or too. He and his students would need to postpone their winter departure by a few days, and he would work with the department secretary. Stan thought he remembered that the department head was on vacation in the Caribbean. With any luck the man would not even open the email until after New Year's.

Alex used the time to check in by phone with his family, feeling sad to be missing their time together but also knowing that in his absence he needed to get Lola and Teddie working on setting various events in motion regarding the Civil War reenactment, which was now scheduled for the fast-approaching second Friday in January.

The border patrolman Rick had been transferred to the Houston office years ago as he made his way up the bureaucratic ladder of the U.S. Border Patrol. As his career had hit the inevitable zenith that all careers hit, he had chosen to stay put in the metropolis rather than return to Brownsville. Rick had learned to appreciate city life, what with the art, music, restaurants and even just more variety of thought. He was happy to meet with Ralph and discuss whatever Ralph needed, but he made it fairly clear even on the phone that he had no personal wish to hunt down any one individual, much less the product of the only birth he'd ever witnessed.

"No one is hunting down anybody," Ralph assured him. "I just want to pick your brain on what happened that day," he said, quietly disappointed that the CBP man wasn't more of a kindred spirit. Still, he might remember something that was helpful.

They met on the Monday after Christmas, and as Rick joined him for an after-work beer at a small dive near the CBP office, he told pretty much the same story that Ralph had already heard, although Ralph had to admit that Rick added far more in the way of embellishment. More importantly, though, Rick was sure the year was 1993, and Rick was sure that the couple was headed all the way to Houston where the girl's father was undergoing cancer treatment. But, Rick was also very certain that he had admonished them to stop at a clinic in Brownsville to ensure that mother and baby were alright before proceeding on with an eight-hour drive.

"You basically let this kid become a U.S. citizen." Ralph could not keep the critical tone out of his voice.

"Her father was dying. You're right, she probably refused to stop and get checked. Family means so much in their culture. How many white girls do you know that would do what this girl did?" Rick asked. Ralph eyed him critically.

"Plus, she had a home to return to in Mexico City. She wasn't trying to pull one off on the ol' U.S.A., buddy, so what even makes you think that the boy stayed?"

"We've got a kid at one of the country schools outside of Houston who has this exact history. His arrival into the U.S. fits this timing and description. He's a real troublemaker. Gets in fights—he's knocked one kid unconscious, put him in the hospital. Frankly, one of our thoughts was that maybe if he was here illegally we could just deport him and save the taxpayers some money."

"Well, you can still do that," Rick offered. "Neither I nor the government looks kindly on those who come here without a welcome and then break the laws. The kid has committed assault. He could be charged as an adult and gone tomorrow."

"Not if he's a citizen," Ralph said irritably, almost adding, "Thanks to you."

"He's not. You're not technically in the country until you pass *through* the checkpoint. He was born *at* the checkpoint. If he had no criminal record, well, this whole DREAM Act thing may come back again and help him or some judge might go ahead, call it iffy and let him stay. But if he's breaking laws, trust me you can deport him and no one is going to argue on his behalf."

Now that was finally news that was helpful, Ralph thought. Then he remembered Tina telling him that they hadn't been able to charge Xuha with assault because of the testimony of some liberal-assed security guard who was clearly confused about which kids it was that he was supposed to be protecting.

So we just get him to break a law, Ralph thought. *Tina's clever. Surely she can come up with a way to manage that.*

The Monday after Christmas Lola checked in with her canoeing friends Ken and Sara. Ken not only taught industrial arts at Early Gulch, but he was also one of the sponsors for the rodeo club. Lola knew that he and Alex had thrown around a few ideas about getting some of the more serious rodeo kids to spice up the reenactment. Alex had asked Lola to confirm that Ken was still on for a little extra-curricular rowdiness. "Rowdy is my middle name," he assured her with a laugh.

Next, she used a little basic internet searching to find the female history professor at the community college who had a daughter at Early Gulch. Carolyn Mullen was the petite blonde who had objected to deciding on historical events by using popular vote, and it turned out that Carolyn was more than happy to join Lola for lunch. She perked up right away as Lola began to explain how effective it would be if after local and national eyes were turned upon the school's activities, a local authority like Carolyn would be ready to speak up to put the school's historical errors in perspective. Would Carolyn help?

It turned out that the diminutive history professor was already a committed specialist in debunking the myth of the Southern "Lost Cause" movement that has tried since the late 1860s to downplay the role of slavery in the Civil War. Founded in part by a politically savvy retired General Early, this movement began early on to argue that the South was fighting for a "way of life," as opposed to the historical reality of its fighting at the time for the very specific right to enslave others. Yes, she would be delighted to help.

She also agreed to contact the Southern Poverty Law Center for advice and information. "They track hate groups and their related crimes nationwide and do an excellent job of it," she told Lola. "While we don't exactly have hate crimes happening at the school, at least as far as I know, they may be able to advise us as to whether members of the staff or administration have ties to any of these people. The information could be useful."

Yes, Lola agreed. It certainly could.

Teddie, meanwhile, sought out the drama teacher and the advanced biology teacher at Early Gulch. Both ladies were highly effective educators at their school, and both were now looking for a position elsewhere.

Ms. Cooley, the biology teacher, was hesitant to get involved, hoping to merely cut her losses and move on to a better situation in a less controversial environment. Teddie didn't blame her, and given that she didn't have a specific request for Ms. Cooley other than to keep her eyes open for ways to help, the woman's reticence did not matter so much.

Ms. Shea, the drama teacher, on the other hand, had a key role to play. Luckily, she was still angry at having been instructed to forget about putting on some performance that always seemed to involve questionable politics or morals, and to focus her class time and her own energy towards making the reenactment spectacular. She had been dragging her feet on doing anything to help that effort, but once Teddie enlisted her aid Ms. Shea saw the wisdom in cooperating.

"The more over-the-top this is, the more attention we can get. My dad says the only way to fight what is going on at our school is to make it so public that it can't be denied."

"Over-the-top," Ms. Shea laughed. "I don't think I have ever been asked to stage a production that strides confidently into bad taste. Wish I'd gotten more involved in the theatrics of this sooner, but, you know, maybe it's just as well that no one will have too much time to think about my last minute additions to the dramatic content."

Then she added as an afterthought, "Guess I'll just have to

claim to have 'seen the light' over the holidays before I start to go whole hog with my contributions."

"Maybe you heard a sermon at Christmas that made you really think about your heritage and your way of life?" Teddie suggested. Then she looked at Ms. Shea, whom she really liked. "Could you pull off saying something like that?"

"Sweetie," Ms. Shea said. "I'm a drama teacher. I like to think I could pull off praising Hitler if I wanted to." Then, at Teddie's horrified look, "Don't worry. I don't think I'll have to go nearly that far."

Alex was fascinated by the little one-room museum in which he found himself, and even more fascinated by the stories of thousands of angry rebels who had departed from New Orleans by boat with vows to build a new Dixie in Belize. The hardship of the voyage and the relative lack of amenities in the Central American country had daunted many but not all, and Alex found himself admiring the hardy souls who had adapted, accepted, grown and become part of this fascinating country. And he found it interesting that they had kept their pride in qualities worth admiring. The museum paid homage to courtesy, to friendliness, to the warmth and generosity of the Old South. Alex thought to himself that those were the very qualities that he liked best about his own hometown in East Texas, and that sadly those were the qualities that he saw the least of in the Confederate flag-waiving yahoos in his home of today.

Yochi's pride in his ancestry was strong, even though it made Alex sad that until recently Yochi himself would have been an outcast in most corners of the very South that he so clearly admired. Yochi also was coming to appreciate that Foluke's friends respected his family's property. By Tuesday he reluctantly came to the conclusion that the little museum was ill equipped for four experts to work effectively. Wednesday morning Yochi himself suggested that the group should propose an acceptable plan to his family to take the ornate jade box with them back to the United States where it could be studied under better conditions and then returned in person after a short time.

Foluke volunteered that her brother would personally vouch for the man Alex, although he did not know the others. Yochi thought about that and decided that he would recommend that his family allow the jewelry box to be being taken to Alex's house. Nowhere else would be as good, now that he thought about it. Stan and Shelby could travel to Houston, study to their hearts' content, and return the jewelry box to the museum as soon as they had all the information that they needed.

The group considered options. Kyle and Alex could head out the next day, as Alex would be glad to get home and Kyle had been planning to head over to Houston after the holidays anyway. Stan could postpone his entourage's departure for Guatemala until the following week, in which case he and Shelby could also head to Houston on Thursday as well. There, they could sort out plans for getting back to Atlanta, for returning the larger box to the university, and for the timing of gathering up grad students and getting back to Guatemala, albeit a week late. Did the Zeitmans really have room for this kind of group?

"We'll figure out something," Alex said. "Yochi wants the artifact safe at my house; it can be safe at my house. Trust me, my home has got to be one of the calmest, safest, least disturbed places on the planet."

Chapter 18. New Year's 2011

Alex had learned to tolerate Lola's telepathic abilities, but as the group gathered up their work to head back to the tiny hotel in Punta Gorda, he realized that he could do better. Why not actively use her talents at times to make both of their lives easier? According to what she had told him, all humans project emotions and to some extent also project the thoughts that drive those emotions. In other words, everybody talks. But hardly anyone listens. Some one percent of the population had vague, undeveloped receptive abilities, Lola had said, and some tiny fraction of that, through desire, practice and circumstance, crossed over into being fully adept receivers.

A little over a year ago, Lola had made just such a crossing. Which meant that now he could send information to her, but not get an answer. *Think about it,* Alex laughed to himself. *In some ways isn't that every husband's dream? He can tell his wife things and not have to listen to a word back?*

Alex supposed that was a less than admirable thought… but hey, a man thinks what he thinks, and fortunately Lola's ethics were such that she generally stayed out of his head and let him think in peace. But knowing how much his people-avoiding wife was going to hate the idea of having three unexpected houseguests, and how much better she would deal with it if she had all the warning possible, Alex tried for the first time to actually get Lola's attention. She said images worked well, so he imagined a picture of himself jumping up and down waving a large bright yellow flag. *Look. Look over here. I need to tell you something. This is important. I'm going to totally mess up the rest of your holidays with the kids there and everything by bringing three strangers and two ancient artifacts home with me and I really need you to flow with this.*

Then he remembered. Music was one of the easiest items to transmit and receive. What was a song that Lola liked? That he liked? His subconscious mind found one for him, and he hummed and whistled it over and over as he helped to load up the car. Of course, he'd follow up with a phone call once he got to the better reception at the hotel, but with any luck by then Lola would already know and be in a frame of mind to help him.

Thursday night, December 30, Lola picked them all up at the airport. Largely thanks to Alex's early warning, Lola had found the time to make her peace with the intrusion and had already cleared the dining room table as a workspace and found mattresses for all. The four-some set to work early Friday morning, luxuriating in the comforts of climate control, ample workspace, soft chairs, bright lights, internet access and all the coffee that they cared to consume. "We have become used to our comforts," Shelby laughed, noticing how much easier the work was already.

Alex broke around noon to say goodbye to Xuha who was heading into Houston to celebrate the evening with a friend from his old school. Later he also paused work to bid farewell to his older two children who were headed to the airport to fly back to participate in their own New Year's Eve plans. "Sorry I messed things up, guys. Next year will be normal, I promise," Alex said. Zane nodded to his dad agreeably, but Ariel only gave her dad a funny look.

"Did I say something wrong?" Alex asked.

Ariel just shook her head. "Who knows what next year will bring, dad. We hope for the best, right?" And she gave him a very long hug that even Alex recognized as rather unusual.

"Something I should know?" he asked.

Her very clear, ice blue eyes bored straight into his. "Dad, if you have to choose between going left or going right, go left."

"What??"

"I love you dad." She picked up her bag and was gone.

By that evening enough ideas and permutations had been tried that Stan, Shelby, Kyle and Alex all reached the same conclusion, even though none of them wanted to say it.

Lola left to take Teddie over to spend the night with her closest girlfriend Michelle, promising to stop at the grocery store and pick up an easy meal to make for the group so that they could avoid getting caught up with the crowds of New Year's Eve revelers filling the bars and restaurants. After she left, each of the four would-be code crackers reluctantly added their own opinion into the mix. Each view pretty much boiled down to a single observation. This was hopeless. An intelligent and industrious mind had designed this puzzle with great care to ensure that whatever answers were hidden in the hieroglyphs would remain hidden until all three boxes were reunited. They needed the third box.

They also agreed that Yochi's artifact had been photographed, sketched and diagramed enough ways that it could be returned to its rightful home in Belize, where it should surely stay. And Stan needed to place his artifact back into the safekeeping of his university as soon as possible.

As an added gesture of group goodwill, Kyle added that he and Jake had decided over Christmas that they had simply never placed the paper document back into large obsidian relic before they returned it to Stan, and they were going to accept no arguments to the contrary so Stan no longer needed to worry about his bit of deception. Jake would keep the document for now, but it ultimately would be returned to Kisa as a family heirloom. Given that Kisa, the rightful owner of the box and the document, had placed both in Kyle's possession to begin with, Kyle felt certain that this should tie up all legal loose ends. Stan smiled gratefully.

Finally, the tired group agreed that the night was best spent enjoying themselves, and tomorrow would be best spent coming up with a plan to support Kyle's search for the remaining box while everyone else returned to their normal lives. Lola's arrival with bottles of champagne and ample food was greeted with a loud cheer. Before long, cheese and fruit platters filled the game room and beer and bubbly filled the glasses. Alex insisted on putting "dancing music" on the CD player, which to him meant old Motown and hits from the sixties.

Shelby and Lola were hitting ping-pong balls back and forth while Stan and Kyle were starting a game of darts when Alex cranked up the music to "Ain't No Mountain High Enough". Alex sang the title to Marvin Gaye's song loudly as it began and the rest of the group laughed and sang along.

"Do you think that there's no rivers or valleys and anything else big enough to keep these three boxes apart?" Kyle asked Stan.

"You're letting yourself get too superstitious about this," a tipsy Stan laughed. "Inanimate objects, no matter how old, don't have a sense of being together."

Kyle didn't look convinced. "Whatever. I believe we are at the very least going to witness the reunification of these three ancient puzzle pieces, and we are going to witness it soon." He grabbed his newly refilled champagne glass and raised it high. "To my being able to locate Xuha Santos Rojas!" he declared loudly.

"To that." Stan agreed.

"Here here," Shelby laughed.

Alex saw Lola give him a look of total confusion before his own champagne glass slipped out of his hand and crashed onto the game room floor.

The ensuing discussion became so loud and so heated that no one even noticed as midnight came and went, although each person was dimly aware of the cacophony of fireworks that could be heard going off outside.

Alex talked first. Yes, indeed, Xuha Santos Rojas temporarily lived in this house. He was seventeen. He had been born to a woman traveling to be with her dying father. Alex didn't know Xuha's old address or the name of his previous high school, but he could easily find out. But he probably didn't have to. After the most basic of facts were exchanged, no one in the room doubted that this Xuha and Kyle's mystery Xuha were one and the same.

Kyle tried to lighten the mood by humming music from the "Twilight Zone" but he only got nervous laughter in response.

As the discussion turned to the obvious next step, Alex was adamant and Lola even more so. No, they would not permit anyone to rifle through Xuha's things tonight. He was a guest in their home and had every reason to expect privacy. He'd moved his stuff back into Zane's room before both boys had left earlier in the day, and Zane had closed the door to his room and it would stay that way.

"For Christsakes, Alex, after seventeen years I just want one little goddamned peak!" an inebriated Stan yelled in frustration.

"One day more won't matter," Alex was firm. "Xuha saw the model of your big obsidian box on the table here one day and he stared at it a long time. I thought it was just because of his Maya ancestry, you know, he was curious. But you know what he asked me? He asked me what would happen to your box once everyone got done studying it. When I told him that it would likely end up in a museum somewhere, he looked sad and said no more."

"We know the size of the remaining box," Shelby said softly. "It's not very big. This kid could have been carrying it around as the only memento he has of his mother. Of course he's not going to tell you about it. 'Oh hey Mr. Zeitman I have one just like that.' He's probably done his very best to hide it from you, much as he likes and trusts you."

"That explains why he wouldn't unpack while anyone else was in the room," Lola added.

"He wouldn't?" Alex hadn't known about that.

"We thought it was a little odd. Teddie tried to help him and he really shooed her away. She figured that you had enough to deal with, so she didn't mention it."

"You know, we had another weird conversation." More was coming back to Alex as he thought about it. "He mentioned how some responsibility came to him with his Mayan name. Maybe he knows more about this thing than just that he's carrying it around."

"There will be a lot of answers tomorrow," a sleepy Shelby yawned.

"Okay," Stan acquiesced. "I'm fading too. Let's get some rest and hope that boy gets himself here promptly. Morning will come soon enough and the littlest box isn't going anywhere."

They all agreed.

When the chanting woke Lola a couple of hours later, she thought she was getting input from Somadina, who was probably in some sort of trouble. Lola could feel drunken rage, anger, hate roiling around in the unintelligible words that seemed to have an African sound to them. Then she sat up with a start. Somadina was fine. Somadina was trying to warn her. Lola was in trouble. She shook Alex fiercely.

"It's probably just the cat," he muttered, mostly asleep.

"It's NOT the cat!" she said. "It's coming from the front lawn." Lola stepped into the hallway and could see a bright glow coming in through the front windows. "Oh my god, Alex."

Alex could recognize genuine panic when he heard it and he went from barely awake to completely awake in about two seconds. This was his job. He protected this house. He strode into the front hall and saw through the glass panels on either side of his front door an angry and probably drunk mob of white hooded people on his front lawn, most waving burning torches and chanting something about his house, shelter and Satan. Fuck. Alex couldn't think of a better word.

"Call 911," he barked to Lola, heading back to the bedroom to grab some pants. "Then see if you can make it out the back door and get to a neighbor. Bring back some help if you can. I'm going out there to see what they want."

It was an indication of how serious the situation was that Lola didn't even pause to discuss that plan with him.

He opened the door, and saw that a cross about the size of a grown man had been erected on his front lawn and was being doused in liquid from a metal can. As he opened his mouth to speak, the crowd noticed him, and the chanting was replaced by a plethora of epitaphs.

"Devil worshipper … Race traitor … Hiding the enemy … Friend of Satan…" He caught enough of them to get the idea. Then someone near the front produced a rock grabbed from the landscaping and threw it right at him. Alex ducked as at least a dozen more came his way. Or rather, started to come his way. As the rocks began to slow down in midair Alex smiled in surprise and then in satisfaction. He did all he could do to will them to move more slowly still.

"Pause. Pause. Breathe. Pause." He found that he was chanting it to himself as he tried to keep the world around him almost at a standstill. "Pause. Pause. Breathe. Pause." And as he willed it harder, the rocks went from moving in slow motion to as close to no motion as Alex had ever seen. Looking up, he saw the man with the match about to ignite the cross. He saw another dozen or so hooded figures with rocks in their hands, clearly picked up from the Zeitman's own gardens, ready to throw. Some looked to be aimed at the windows instead of him. And he saw three men off to his far right, headed around to the back of his house where Lola would be coming out of the back door.

Alex didn't know how long this pause would last, or how far he would get before he found himself once again moving in the same time current as everyone else. He had to assume that he would at best be able to stop one thing.

Stop the ignition of the cross? It was on a well-watered, dormant lawn, far from any over hanging tree. Obnoxious, but it would most likely burn itself out without causing harm. So should he follow the three men to his right who might intercept his wife? That seemed like the better choice.

Ariel's odd parting words came back to him like a splash of cold water. Go left. He gave a quick glance to his left. He saw only a lone man going that way with a torch, almost frozen mid-stride as he headed around that side of the Zeitman home. Alex hesitated. What damage could this guy do that the others off to his right could not?

I think I go with Ariel, Alex decided, figuring he could sort the rest out later. He took off to the left in a barefoot run, and had almost caught up with the guy when the world began to move just a little faster. Pause. Pause. Breathe. Pause. Alex tried to will it to move more slowly again. Feet from the man, Alex saw that the man was also carrying a sheet, and was now only a few feet from the propane tank that heated the home and the swimming pool. Right. The recently filled propane tank. The propane tank that was feet from the back deck onto which Lola was very slowly emerging. The tank that was right next to the dining room holding two Mayan artifacts. The tank that was just below Zane's room, which in all probability held the third.

As the man twisted off the cap, his motions sped up a little, and Alex realized with amazement that the man actually intended to put one end of the sheet in the propane tank and to light the other end of it, thinking he could get away fast enough before the tank exploded. The man's movements were starting to approach a pace that was normal. He turned towards his fellow clan members on the front lawn and bellowed in a deep drunken roar, "Going rogue on y'all. Run like hell cuz I'm gonna make the biggest boom yet. WATCH THIS!" As the self-proclaimed rogue stuck one end of the sheet into the tanks small opening and as he moved his torch towards the other loose end of the sheet Alex charged into him hard from the side and knocked him to the ground.

"What the hell," the rogue yelled trying to push Alex off of him, but Alex rolled the man onto his own burning torch. The drunk roared in pain for a second but the fire was quickly suffocated by his own body weight and that of Alex, who was now lying firmly on top of him.

"Where the hell did you come from?" the man said. Before Alex could answer, sirens could be heard in the distance. "Out! Of! Here! Now!" barked a man in the middle of the lawn whose sheet and hooded outfit appeared more ornate and elaborate than the rest, and the crowd began to scatter fast in every direction.

The man under Alex wriggled to get free.

"I don't think you're going anywhere," Alex said. "The rest of your friends can hide behind masks like the cowards they are, but if nothing else the man who was stupid enough to almost blow up my home is going to go down."

"Huh?" the man said, confused.

"That's you, asshole." Alex clarified. "You're the idiot who is going to take the fall for this nonsense."

"They told me that you were letting the devil live at your house," the man muttered angrily. "Joe's wife Dolores said she saw Satan here himself and said it was cuz of that creepy little Mexican kid you let stay here. Said we had to do something or no one was gonna be safe."

"Well, you did something alright," Alex agreed. "And now that you mention it, maybe with you locked up the world will be a little safer."

By the time the police left, Stan, Shelby and Kyle were all downstairs and wide awake, and by the time that everyone calmed back down there was just a hint of light in the southeastern sky. As 2011 dawned its first day, a patrol car sat parked at the entry to the cul-de-sac, a couple of front windows had been duct-taped shut with cardboard, and an ugly scar of burnt grass sat prominently in the center of the Zeitman's lawn. Alex fell into an exhausted sleep and didn't wake until he heard Xuha's voice and a knock on his bedroom door.

"Mr. Z? I'm sorry to wake you. Is everybody okay?" Concern and confusion were apparent in the boy's voice.

"We're fine, Xuha. Everything's okay." And then as his mind began to clear, he remembered that he had a house full of people who couldn't wait to talk to Xuha. He felt protective for the boy. "Help yourself to some cereal Xuha, I'll be out in a minute. I need to talk to you, before anyone else does, okay?"

For the second time in twelve hours he grabbed a pair of pants and willed himself awake. Lola and her purse and car keys were gone, so he was guessing she had left to pick up Teddie and would arrive any minute. The ensuing noise would certainly wake the three houseguests. No time to loose.

As he headed to the bathroom to splash cold water on this face, Alex thought of how he had managed last night for the first time to exert some conscious control over his own perception of the passage of time. But wait. It was more than his perception, no matter what those bitchy light beings said. His body moved with his mind, it covered ground, it got things done at a pace that made sense with how he saw the passage of time at that moment. Everyone else moved at a pace that matched their perception. Alex's mind filled with questions that now went well beyond the obvious ones of how this worked. Could he do this now, by choice, any time? Could he go the other way, make hours fly by on a long plane ride? Could he…

Think about this later, he told himself sternly. And then he willed just a slight slow down, just a little extra time to brush his teeth and grab a clean shirt too, so he could get out to the kitchen before Xuha found himself surrounded by eager treasure hunters who might not fully appreciate the boy's situation.

When Alex got to the kitchen he decided that this was a time that called for being direct.

"I have to talk to you about something important," he told Xuha as he poured himself a cup of coffee. "I know that you have something here with you in this house that means a lot to you, a very lot to you. You keep it hidden because you are afraid that people will try to take it away from you, and once you saw the artifact that I've been studying you've been even more worried about it."

Xuha looked down but said nothing. Alex could see the boys discomfort reflected in every muscle of his tense body.

"It's okay. I would not dream of taking this thing from you, nor will I let anyone else do that. You have my absolute word about that."

Alex could see tight muscles relax slightly.

"Follow me. I have to show you something." It occurred to Alex that this may be one of those cases where a picture was worth a thousand or more words. So he led Xuha to the dining room, where the larger obsidian box now snuggled against the smaller green jade trapezoid, the beautiful carvings on each blending so perfectly that one might almost think they were one irregularly shaped work of art that would have formed a perfect square except for a small missing trapezoid in the upper right corner.

"We don't want to take yours from you. The green box will go back tomorrow to the family that treasures it. We just—"

But Alex never got to finish the thought, because Xuha turned abruptly and left the room. *Shit,* Alex thought. *Maybe that hadn't been the way to handle this after all.*

He was trying to think of the best plan to rectify whatever damage he had done, when Xuha came bounding back down the stairs, with a small light pink object in his hands. Trapezoid shaped and carved out of rose agate, it boasted multiple colored inlays on its sides and was, if possible, more ornate and beautifully done than even the other two. Without saying a word, Xuha solemnly placed it in the space where it was so clearly meant to go.

Alex was not a superstitious man. But for just a second, as the three boxes touched, he could have sworn that he felt a surge of energy, a sense of joy. *Don't be ridiculous,* he told himself, as he marveled at how the three now blended into one simple yet beautiful mosaic. A mosaic that clearly showed a spiral of hieroglyphs emanating outward from the point where the three boxes touched.

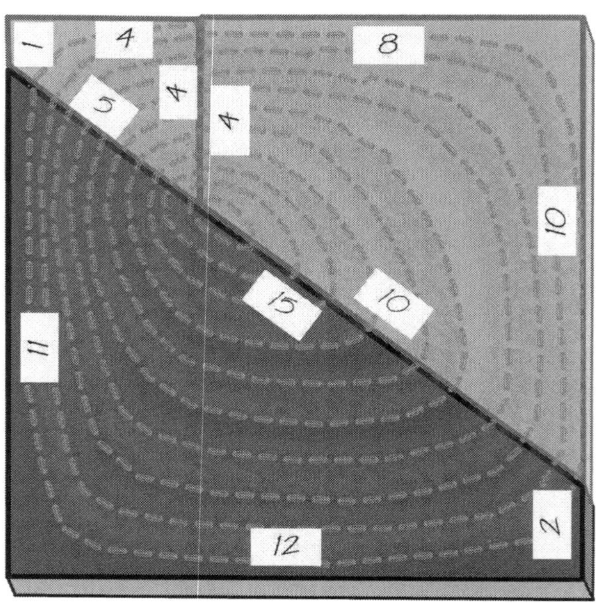

Xuha's box shows the spiral

"They were meant to come together," Xuha said. And he grinned widely. "I was told that some day a good time would come for this box to be back with its brothers, so it could tell its secret. I just didn't think that good time would happen while I was alive."

But Alex was too transfixed to respond. There were no circles and rays. No pairs of numbers. That had been his own faulty reasoning, come from years of working in coordinate systems. These hieroglyphs were written in one continuous line spiraling outward and one could only really see that fact once all three boxes were merged together. Alex fought the desire to grab pen and paper and start working.

"My visitors, they are trying to discover that secret, Xuha. They'd like to see this, to study this. And then I promise that what is yours will be returned to you."

"I know, Mr. Z. I trust you." And Alex thought that perhaps

he had never been paid a higher compliment.

Shelby was the first of the three to wake up, coming downstairs in sweats and a ragged old t-shirt seeking a cup of coffee. She paused at the entrance to the dining room and let out a gasp that Alex and Xuha could hear in the kitchen. She didn't say another word, but headed back upstairs.

Lola and Teddie arrived next, with an incredulous Teddie heading out to the front lawn and demanding information from both of her parents. Alex was trying to calm her down when Shelby could be seen literally pulling a groggy Stan along by the arm to the dining room.

Stan turned to face Xuha, standing in the hallway.

"You may touch it, hold it, study it," Xuha affirmed. "And then I want it back."

"Thank you," Stan said before he turned to admire the creation of beauty that the three boxes made when placed together. "Thank you so much." And he traced the now visible spiral with his hand and then picked up a pad of paper and started to work.

Shelby called Kyle, and Lola took over telling Teddie about the night before, and soon the four would-be code crackers were back at work scribbling, looking things up and comparing ideas, functioning like the high-powered team they had become.

This time, information fell into place as easily as the original designer had intended. Now that it was clear that larger numbers were part of the code, Alex simply broke the string of information into three digit numbers, each of which referred to a hieroglyph on the spiral. Within a few hours they had formulated much of what they sought.

"Well?" a curious Lola asked from the hallway.

"I don't think we're booking any airline tickets to go chase down gold bars buried somewhere," Stan said.

"But you never really thought that would be the case, did you?" Alex asked.

"I guess deep down we all hoped it would," Kyle confessed. "Gold. Jewels. Something dramatic and valuable. Why does one hunt for a treasure? And it really does say 'greatest treasure ever.'"

The disappointment in his voice was clear.

"We still aren't sure what we've got," Shelby offered more explanation to Lola, Teddie and Xuha. "All three boxes include some hieroglyphs we've never seen before and new variations of ones we do know. But we can tell that what we have here is mostly not physical directions on how to find something. I mean, there is a little of that actually, but most of it seems more like directions on how to make something."

"A time machine?" Xuha volunteered with enthusiasm.

Stan shook his head. "It's not mechanical. It's more, well, culinary."

"A recipe?" Lola was incredulous.

"More than anything else that's what it looks like," Stan said. "Most of the words about location turned out to be the filler. Most of the words about cooking turned out to be the ones that got used." There was a sense of general letdown in the room.

"Maybe they didn't lie to you," Teddie suggested hopefully. "You know, think about it. Gold and jewels aren't the greatest treasure of all."

"So what is?" Alex considered.

"Life," Shelby said.

"Air, to a man who is suffocating," Kyle volunteered.

"Water. Food," Stan was thinking aloud.

"Strength," Alex continued. "Health."

"Yeah, health." Shelby liked that answer. "The Maya were masters at herbal medicine. So we're here thinking some of this is about herbs and spices to make the world's greatest stew, but maybe instead it's about herbs to cure something?"

"Totally possible," Stan said, his mood lightening. "Maybe we're sitting on top of a cure for cancer or even just a cure for the common cold?"

"Or it could be the cure for small pox," Xuha worried. "Wiped out massive amounts of Native Americans who had no immunity, and would have been a tremendous treasure three-hundred years ago. Not so helpful today."

"That would be a sad piece of irony," Alex mused.

"We're going to have to learn more about plants and more about herbal medicine I think," Shelby said. "But right now I need a break."

"New year's dinner in half an hour," Lola volunteered. "Hoppin' John, with collard greens and corn bread." She smiled. "An excellent Southern tradition."

Chapter 19. January 2011

Sunday, January 2, the three houseguests left, taking two of the artifacts with them. Neighbors began to drop by to *tsk tsk* sympathetically at the insanity of a Klan rally in their own neighborhood. The two nearest neighbors had both been out. Others could not believe that they had not been awakened, and were so sorry they had not helped. No one mentioned Xuha at all, and Alex wondered how many in his neighborhood understood that the boy was the impetus behind the "insanity."

Monday, January 3, the glass panes were replaced. The police were nice enough to come by to tell Alex that the man that Alex had tackled had been let out on bail, in spite of the fact that he faced serious charges that ranged all the way up to attempted murder. They wanted the Zeitmans to know that the man had disavowed any knowledge of who his masked companions were and that the district attorney had made it clear that he did not believe that for a minute and hoped to bargain the charges down in exchange for more information.

One of the officers took the opportunity to press for more facts about why such a disruption occurred here of all places. The night of the event Alex had speculated that he may have been targeted as a teacher who was not sympathetic to some of his more racist students' views, and Alex and Lola remained silent about their houseguest the second time that they were questioned. Finally, the officer added that he thought it only right to warn Alex that the man who was arrested had declared loudly to anyone who would listen that he planned to sue Alex for the burn damage to his chest. Word from the physician who had treated him in jail was that the burns were rather severe.

"What? He's going to sue you? And he told the police what? That he just ran into a group of like-minded drunks all wearing sheets and hoods just like him and they invited him to come along and burn down our house? That's ridiculous!" Teddie was outraged as her parents filled her in later that evening.

"It's a crazy world, Teddie," Alex agreed, "and tomorrow school starts and we go back to another set of craziness that you and

I are working together to fight. You ready for this?" Teddie calmed down as she nodded. She and her dad had spent a lot of time planning, and in less than two weeks it was going to be show time.

Tuesday morning when classes resumed, Alex let his regular physics classes watch a video about electricity while he concentrated on the role that his time machines would play in the reenactment. The various projects had been combined and retooled into two final time machines, one of which would pretend to travel backwards in time and the other forward. Each group would get ten minutes to describe to the student body and the spectators the imaginary machine they had built, what sort of basic theories drove it, and then what they had chosen to use their machine for. A little science, a little theory and a little tie-in to social studies. It was an added plus that the industrial arts class was collaborating with fine arts to design and build a convincing fake machine for each group to use.

Alex promised to review each presentation before it was made. He emailed his outline to Tina Johnson, to Ms. Shea who had only recently embraced her role of dramatic director, and of course to the entire administration. He wanted no confusion about the fact that he was doing exactly what was expected of him.

Wednesday night Teddie showed her dad the essays that the school paper had received by the deadline. The journalism teacher had picked a fairly nice variety of finalists to run in the school paper, leaning towards non-controversial topics but allowing a reasonable discussion about the causes of the Civil War, the roles played by various minorities, and a range of opinions as to whether the South winning the war would have been a better thing. The two winning "pro" essays praised states' rights and the superiority of the Confederacy in general, and two "con" essays provided well thought-out rebuttals. One gave the more-or-less expected point of view of African Americans, and the other was written by Teddie's own friend Michelle who was of Vietnamese descent. Michelle focused on how other ethnic minorities such as herself would have fared in a modern-day version of the Old South and on the difficulties modern Southern women may have faced compared to their northern sisters.

The journalism teacher had sent her selections on for administration approval and of course for the administration to pick the top three winners. Much to the advisor's surprise, Teddie made no attempt to circumvent the review process.

Tina hadn't seen much of her boys over the holidays, between the demands of her own extended family and theirs. She had been told long ago that no matter how stupid and uninformed one's relatives were, it was best for the cause to show up occasionally for holidays, funerals and weddings, and appear to be what was regarded as normal, lest some bleeding heart cousin finger a racially aware patriot for some meddling group like the FBI. Tina had taken the advice to heart and taught her boys to do the same. It paid to be careful.

With the holidays over, she now had to focus hard on getting this reenactment finalized. Local Confederate groups had provided plenty of material, and Tina had the logistics of the battle of Cedar Creek committed to memory. That useless drama teacher had finally stepped in and was being helpful. Maybe the administration had talked to her.

Tina had been hoping to have her boys and many of the other students who had spent time at her house over the past couple of years be featured in the presentation, in recognition of their willingness to question the mainstream lies. Tina expected Cindy Shea to fight her on that, and to even try her usual stunt of inserting all manner of black and brown skin into roles clearly designed to be performed by whites.

But whoever had talked to the drama teacher must have been persuasive and very clear. The Confederate army was cast as whites only, and Ms. Shea let Tina handpick the officers. The supporting chorus of swooning belles was lily white and appropriately demur, and everyone else was relegated to a service role behind the scenes.

"It's almost like the South really has risen again," Tina giggled to herself.

Olumiji returned the jade box himself, placing it in Yochi's hands along with photographs of how the three boxes had looked when placed together.

"They are very beautiful. When they were put together, did they form a message?" Yochi asked in the mix of Caribbean, African, Spanish and English dialects that made up his native tongue.

"Perhaps," the Nigerian responded. "My friends told me that they thought at first that it was a recipe."

Yochi laughed loudly. "That would be some special dish for people to work so hard to keep that recipe hidden."

"They think now that it maybe forms instructions on how to make some kind of medicine, but it looks like nothing simple or familiar. It might help to have some idea of what this is trying to cure. Is there anything in your history about this, anything you know that could help?"

Yochi shook his head. "I wish there was. I know nothing more about it, only that my family is very glad to have this box returned. Thank you," he added, as he set the ornate green container back in its place.

Tina made time for her boys Thursday after school, because she knew that she had to get them focused on one more important task. Her friend Ralph had been more helpful than she had dared to hope, and given his information she felt sure that if Xuha could possibly be charged with a felony, any felony, he would be removed from her life. At least one little ugly brown thorn in her side would be gone.

She had rather hoped that her small cadre of women protesting on the Zeitman's lawn after Christmas would have succeeded in embarrassing the boy into leaving for parts unknown, but the idiot ladies had been scared off by something they claimed was the devil himself, before Xuha had even seen them. Worse yet, the crazy devil story had managed to rile up some of Tina's younger and more volatile compatriots, leading to an inexcusably drunken disaster in the Zeitman's yard New Year's Eve. Not that Tina didn't rather enjoy the thought of how panicked Mrs. Zeitman and the visitors to the house must have been that night, but given that the Zeitmans were white and had committed no obvious affront to the white race, in the end it was nothing but bad publicity that the movement didn't need.

And now, of course, Tina hardly had time to deal with getting Xuha arrested herself, but surely between them, her boys could find a way. Better yet, maybe they could find a way to make it happen at the reenactment. That of course was in no way necessary, but the more she thought about it the more Tina just liked the idea. Xuha was easy enough to provoke into action if any of the Zeitmans were threatened. It was going to be her big day. Why not add a little icing to the cake. She dressed pretty and put out the boys' favorite pizza.

Stan's fake illness and his late return to campus caused barely a harrumph from his tanned and happy department head, and the department secretary did a wonderful job of delaying travel and contacting students. So it was a fairly content group that set off from the school for Lake Peten a week late, and Shelby was happy to be able to still join them.

Kyle, on the other hand, traveled there on his own a few days later, for the very specific purpose of returning the original fig wood document to its rightful owner and showing her the photographs of the three boxes reunited. She could do with the paper document as she pleased, and perhaps she or her family could shed some light, or just even some better translation, on the message decoded from the three boxes.

Kisa could hardly control her delight when Kyle arrived, demonstrating that after all these years her confidence in him had been warranted. She eagerly studied the photos of the other two boxes, marveling over the workmanship and the detail.

"I wish I could have brought them to you, Kisa," he said, and he meant it. "But the other two are the very precious possessions of others."

"I understand. This will do," she said. Then she studied the photos for a few minutes more. "It was hard to see on just the obsidian box, but when you put them together like this it's more obvious. Look, these are flowers along the sides where the different boxes come together. Plants, but you can best identify them by their flowers. Someone tried to make the inlaid stones the right colors so that there would be no mistaking what flower was what. And see how the box shows a symbol with each plant," she said, squinting hard at the photo. "That symbol is probably used in the text on the top and makes up some of the hieroglyphs that were unknown to you."

"Can you identify the plants?" Kyle asked.

"Some of them quite easily," she laughed. "Two of them are growing like weeds out around the parking lot. But a few of the others, they don't look like anything I've ever seen."

"Maybe those are the ones that had directions on where to find them?"

"Perhaps," she said. "Let me study this for a while, and let me show it to an aunt of mine who is very good with all the local vegetation. After all these years, my family, too, would like to know what this is all about."

"Kisa, I'm sorry there was no treasure, I mean valuable treasure, to be found for you and your kin."

"How do you know?" Kisa asked, puzzled. She smiled. "We haven't finished finding it yet."

Alex had two questions for Ariel when she called to say hello, and she deflected the first easily. After describing the nonsense that occurred on New Year's Eve, Alex asked, "Is there any reason you can think of at all why any group of people, no matter how stupid or how drunk, would have the distinct impression that the devil lives at our house?"

"Dad, you really need to ask Zane about that. But you should know that there weren't a lot of good options and he was just trying to help."

Zane. Great. That meant that it was entirely possible that Dolores Bolton actually had seen the devil on the Zeitman lawn. Second question.

"Ariel, why did you tell me that if I couldn't decide whether to go left or right I should go left?"

"Because I just think it's the correct decision, dad. You know, politically. When in doubt, it's better to go to the left."

"You were talking about politics??"

"Yeah. I thought that you knew that."

"No sweetie I took you kind of literally there. Guess we're lucky you're not a budding young republican."

"Why is that?"

"The house would have blown up and I and your mom may have been killed."

"Oh. Wow."

Carolyn, the local history professor, didn't have any close African-American or Latina friends, and she felt no particular affinity with either group. She was a fifth generation white Texan and a polite, shy woman not prone to adopting causes. However, she did believe in standing up for the truth. Historical accuracy was important. On an intellectual level, she abhorred watching the powerful write those with less influence out of history to satisfy their own vanity, and the recent trends in Texas towards revising history offended her on the deepest level. That is why, she supposed, that she had so uncharacteristically spoken up at that horrible PTA thing and had agreed with the other mom to help with an effort to expose the recent changes at Early Gulch for the blatant racism that they were.

Carolyn prepared a short, easy-to-read press release on the important roles played by many minorities in the Civil War. She prepared another on some of the more horrific facts of slavery to counter some of the recent soft-pedaling that tried to picture slavery as a mutually beneficial arrangement for both landowners and slaves. She prepared a third on how the most significant reason for the Civil War was an attempt by rich landowners to continue a way of life that required slavery, and how any other euphemism for the causes of the Civil War had been nothing more than a pretense both then and now.

Carolyn didn't get how people could act as if a part of history was less awful than it had been, and less wrong than it had been, and how—a century and a half later—they could still be trying to rewrite history to try to make themselves look better. And Carolyn didn't care how people felt about that truth. Facts were facts, and they needed to be faced. History was chock full of morally wrong occurrences. Humans had screwed up left and right throughout time. Why not admit one more screw up and move on?

Immediately after the reenactment, would she be happy to make contact with the media, and to see that her compilation of facts received as much attention as possible as the press sorted out their coverage of what had happened? You bet she would.

The day before the reenactment Alex found himself instinctively avoiding Lola. He knew that she wouldn't be thrilled with the details of what he had planned. Worse yet, as the reality of what he was doing began to sink in, he had to admit that she would have good reason to feel that way. He was taking a risk with the safety of others, and he knew it. That was never something to be done lightly.

He comforted himself with the thought that it was a small gamble for a large gain. And both he and Xuha would be on full alert to make sure that no one got seriously hurt. They did have some formidable skills in that arena. But, yes, there was still a chance of something going horribly wrong and, yes, that did concern him.

Luckily Lola had decided not to take the day off work to attend the event, and had even stopped asking him questions about it. Late that night as he lay in bed, it occurred to Alex to wonder if she knew exactly what he had planned, and for once had decided to keep her own thoughts to herself.

He, Teddie and Xuha left the house extra early the next morning, but when he arrived at school at the first touch of dawn Tina was already standing in the middle of the well lit baseball field with a bullhorn, giving orders to a growing crowd of students, teachers and administrators. Extra bleachers had been brought in to accommodate the many students who were being allowed to attend, and a dozen or so workers were busy assembling the seating. The local group of Confederacy re-enactors was there already, unloading some very impressive cannons. They had brought the large red and white signal flags used by the military of that time, and were distributing replicas of actual Springfield carbines used in the Civil War. Several of the more responsible seniors had been approved to use these single shot rifles to fire harmless black powder as the battle progressed.

As Alex approached Tina, she gave him a quick tight smile as he double-checked with her that the time machines were indeed being used as planned. Yes, she assured him, the first would alter the outcome of the battle. The Confederate soldiers and officers had been briefed, much to their delight, on how to go about avoiding the crucial "fatal halt" that had doomed the real Jubal Early and his soldiers. The rebels would win this time. Then, at the end of the reenactment, the time travelers to the future would find a glorious and noble New South, grown vigorous and strong after being finally allowed to secede by the North in 1865. Learning of this alternate future would be the highlight of the entire reenactment.

Ms. Shea the drama teacher was almost frantic as she handed out costumes and props to half-awake participants, but she paused to acknowledge to Alex that she had worked with the group presenting the second time machine and had made all the preparations to involve them in the activity just in the way that she and Alex had discussed. Cindy Shea looked tenser than Alex had ever seen her, and that served to remind Alex of the risk he was asking others to take.

Teddie checked back in with her dad, armed with her two video cameras and her assurances she had friends who were prepared to get her footage posted online in real time as it became available. Alex could tell that she was nervous, but determined to play her part well. He could not have been more proud of her.

Alex looked at his cheap plastic watch. There wasn't much time left, but he needed to check in with the very last piece, the icing on the cake, so to speak. The one thing that would make sure this went the way he had planned.

Alex hurried over to the freshman hall to check in with the

English teacher who doubled as tennis coach at Early Gulch to make sure that she had not changed her mind about allowing Xuha and several other students to quietly spend the morning holding tennis practice instead of attending the reenactment. The woman had been hesitant to irritate the administration with the request, but Alex had explained to her that most of the ethnic minorities on her team had been denied a role in the reenactment and that the girls had been relegated to the sidelines as well. Over half her team had wanted a part and had complained to Alex when they were given little to none. Maybe just quietly letting this part of the team go practice rather than have them at the reenactment unhappy and potentially causing problems would be a service to everyone involved? She had finally agreed to let them practice on the sly, as long as it was done quietly.

Xuha greeted Alex happily as he made the short walk over to the school's few poorly maintained courts. The courts sat on the other side of a hill from the baseball field that would be hosting the reenactment. Xuha appeared to be not only eager for his important dual roles in the day's events, but he had managed to persuade the entire tennis team to practice with him.

"None of us got very good parts," a slender white boy explained to Alex. "We thought about it and decided that we'd all rather be over here."

"Are you sure about this? None of you have to do this you know."

"Oh, Mr. Z, trust me, we want to do this," a large African-American girl told him heartily. "You don't even want to know what sort of part that woman wanted to give me in the reenactment."

"No," Alex sighed, "I suspect I don't. Okay. Good luck to you guys. Have some fun."

The entire team was grinning.

By ten o'clock the seats in the baseball field were filled with students. Parents and a surprising amount of other spectators filled the folding chairs and blankets that had sprung up everywhere that extra room could be found. Some local news groups had sent people with cameras, and it looked like the Fans of the Confederacy had worked to bring in a fair number of folks, as t-shirts with large Confederate flags on them could be seen everywhere. The principal was clearly pleased with all of the preparations and the impressive turnout.

She stepped up to the small stage that had been erected on top of the pitcher's mound, nervously checked her watch, and then introduced the event with a few vague words about the importance of history and having rightful pride in one's people and region. She commended Tina Johnson, the mistress of ceremonies, for her outstanding work in putting this together, and then introduced Alex with a few additional platitudes about how wonderful it was for once to see science being used to further the support of appropriate social values.

Alex had never been a public speaker, and he knew to keep his part short. In a sentence he explained that one group of his physics students would play a role now and the other later, and he turned the microphone over to his students who explained the general concept of their time machine and prepped the crowd to expect a trip back into history that would change the very course of the battle.

A student explained to the eager crowd that the real battle of Cedar Creek had occurred October 19, 1864. If Confederate General Jubal Early had not had to halt for six hours while his men looted the Union camp, many historians believe that the battle that day would have been his. More importantly, Early and his victorious army would have been ready to march on towards Washington, D.C. where an unpopular Abraham Lincoln was running for re-election against opposition representing the many war-weary northerners ready to let the South secede. In spite of the North's recent victories, this may well have swung the election against Lincoln and then changed the fate of the South. This last part was greeted with hoots of joy from some of the spectators.

And with that the 2011 version of the Battle of Cedar Creek began. The Union camp was set up behind second base, where Union soldiers pretended to eat breakfast and begin their day with no clue of the events ahead. Over the past few months boys had lined up to play the various roles of Confederate officers and soldiers, but it had taken some persuasion to convince the young re-enactors that the battle could not happen unless some of them were willing to play the parts of the Yankees. Gradually Union officers and soldiers had been found, many of them enticed by an extra ten points on the next history test.

Travis, dressed as General Early himself, stood in front of the third base dugout strategizing with some of this officers about the three columns of infantry that had been prepared for the surprise attack. General Gordon's column was already in place, hidden underneath the bleachers ready to sneak single-file along a pretend pig path to take the Union soldiers by surprise. Tyler, proudly dressed as General Gordon, motioned to his men and led the way. The cavalry of General Rosser, played by Tanner, had only a few horses that had been borrowed for the day, but they pretended to be a full cavalry as they led General Gordon's group as far as the horses could go.

There were of course far fewer troops involved, and all but a few of the weapons were plastic, and the cannons only for show. None-the-less, the major components of the battle itself were all represented as the scene unfolded. Tina took over as mistress of ceremonies, explaining to the crowd from the pitcher's mound how the distance had been shrunk down and how the time frame would be condensed, but the basics of the original battle were going to be honored. Except of course, for the fact that this time around General Early just might find a way to keep his troops moving through the Union camp.

The battle began in earnest when the first of the rebels encountered a small group of Union soldiers in a replica of Middletown Cemetery, complete with Styrofoam grave markers gleefully designed by some of the more macabre students taking art class. A fierce fight raged amidst fake gunshots and bayonet clashes as the soldiers, other actors and support from both sides dutiful carried on their roles and Tina continued to update the spectators with commentary about what they were seeing. The acting was minimum, but the costumes and props were great, and those who appeared a bit confused were set straight by Tina, who occasionally grabbed her bullhorn to shout specific directions to the participants and who frequently checked the pages of the careful notes she had stuck into her trusty shoulder bag.

As the battle progressed it was clear that the Confederate soldiers were winning and many of the confused Union soldiers were dispersing into the sidelines. By 11 o'clock the Union camp in center field was completely deserted. Then the first group of time travelers took the stage. While their time machine glowed and cackled with fake energy, these time travelers talked about the arbitrary nature of the direction of time and the purpose to which they were going to use that. When the real Jubal Early and the rest of his men had entered the empty camp, they explained, it appeared that the Confederates had won the battle. So Jubal agreed to a short break, only to have the hungry Confederate soldiers spend hours devouring food and helping themselves to clothing and supplies.

But in the Early Gulch version of history, the would-be physicists wielding the first time machine announced that they had made a harsh decision. They were about to arrive at the camp ahead of the troops, and were going to put all of the food and usable supplies into a giant pile, douse it with kerosene and leave it burning. They then walked out past second base and covered the camp with bright orange tarps while Tina explained that the fire marshal had unfortunately insisted they not actually burn anything.

A few minutes later Travis led his Confederate soldiers into the camp and some of the more expressive of the boys managed to convey outrage that there was not a morsel of food to eat or a scrap of clothing to take. As explained by Tina, the rebel soldiers were now furious at the Yankees for denying them their plunder, and they were going to charge on, their fatigue now overcome by their anger.

Then, much to Tina's surprise, the second group of time travelers appeared unexpectedly on the stage. Tina gave Alex a confused look and he shrugged a giant exaggerated shrug from the sidelines. This group had a wireless microphone of their own and informed an increasingly alarmed Tina and the now totally confused spectators that although their assignment was to travel to the future at the end of the show, they had decided to intervene now instead.

First of all, these time travelers claimed, the team from the other time machine was lying about history. Evidence from General Gordon's notes showed that far less looting had occurred than thought. Some historians said that General Early made a bad military call to rest and then rather than take responsibility for it, he had blamed his men.

"History is not so simple," the student who was their spokesperson declared loudly. "These individual soldiers, many of them no older than us, cannot speak for themselves now, but many did their best in horrible circumstances. We ask that the complexity of history be preserved, especially when it comes to giving a voice to those who had none at the time."

Tina looked confused. She simply hadn't been aware of this controversy. In her circles, General Early was revered for going on to personally found the "Lost Cause" movement, decrying how gallant Southerners had been bullied out of their gracious lifestyle by the North's greater number of troops.

The student was not finished. "Moreover, my group of time travelers does not support the cause of slavery and does not wish to see the South win this battle. Therefore, with or without goods to plunder, we insist that General Early's men must take a break just like they did in the real battle."

Tina looked to Travis to see how General Early was responding to all this and her temper began to rise. Rodeo was a popular activity at Early Gulch and it appeared that the team from the second time machine had somehow enlisted a dozen of the school's best rodeo participants, all Latinos who had been denied parts in the reenactment. They were riding onto the field through a maintenance gate out in center field and they were swinging lassos and carrying a sign proclaiming them to be the First Battalion of Native Cavalry formed in 1863 by U.S. government in California.

Wasn't that the group of Mexican horsemen that the obnoxious history teacher had talked about? Tina thought as several of the swinging lassos came down with expert precision around her

Confederate officers.

The student kept talking. "Several excellent essays were written by students about how much worse their lives would be if the North had permitted the South to secede. These particular articles were banned from the school paper, but you can find them online. Read them and you will understand why we cannot possibly sit on the sidelines."

Tina was done listening. "Get off of this field now," she hissed at the student.

"I'm sorry ma'am, but we can't do that," another student responded solemnly. "You don't get to rewrite history. We're not going to let you."

Then all eight of the time voyagers from machine number two simply walked away from Tina. Two of them began instructing the confused Confederate soldiers to sit down and wait like they had in real life, while the others yelled and motioned to the sidelines to the equally confused Union soldiers and began directing them to join forces between first and second base.

The Confederate officers, all six of whom were now firmly hog-tied, hollered to Tina for help, and Tina yelled at the Union soldiers to ignore the second set of time travelers. Then she screamed at the time travelers to stay out of the battle like they were supposed to. When they ignored her as well, she yelled over at campus security to intervene.

The three security guards sitting behind home plate looked puzzled. They didn't think that they actually ought to be entering a Civil War battle, and so everyone turned to the principal in the stands, who clearly was about to put a stop to the entire nonsense when she looked up and her mouth dropped open.

Coming over the hill off to right field and through the right field gate to join the union forces was the entire tennis team, armed with racquets and pulling a ball machine that was now firing tennis balls straight at the Confederate troops.

"None of us will not be written out of history," Xuha yelled into his own megaphone. "We are here to fight."

Angry at the flying balls, several of the boys in Confederate uniforms charged the tennis team and it only took seconds before racquets and plastic swords and rifles were swatting at each other as a full-fledged melee broke out in right center field. The group of the students in left field who had been relegated to providing refreshments for the troops charged in and began dumping ice water on the fighters, and one of them grabbed a megaphone and announced that they were tired of being on the sidelines too and had formed their own battalion called the fighting restaurant workers.

At that several Southern belles seated in front of the first base dugout shrieked and ran, but Alex noted with satisfaction that several other girls picked up weapons and joined in. Some fought for the South and some for the North, and more than a few just went after the people with the ice water. Alex was pleased to see the young belles fighting.

And most importantly, he was pleased to see Teddie recording away, the crazier the scene she could capture the better. She was fearless now, and she knew exactly what it was she was doing. Several other kids had not been able to resist pulling out their own contraband cell phones, and they were filming away too as students in full Civil War uniforms swung plastic muskets at kids in tennis clothes and white restaurant aprons.

When Alex was positive they had all the footage they would ever need to bring Early Gulch and its historic reenactment all the national attention it deserved, he allowed himself a pleased grin as he walked towards the security guards to ask for help in breaking the battle up before anyone got hurt.

That's when time started to move very, very slowly. The grin left Alex's face as he realized that in spite of his precautions something was in the protracted process of going horribly wrong.

From this day forward, Alex would always remember the order of the events—Teddie turning, slowly moving her camera over her shoulder to capture her friend Xuha holding his racquet up over his head to lead his regiment. Tyler, behind her, looking slowly at Teddie with the recognition on his face of just how thoroughly the girl's loyalties laid elsewhere. Then, the slow beginning of an idea. Alex knew the look, the "get even with the bitch" look.

Alex watched the process of Tyler's hand deliberately reaching into his boot. Slowly, he pulled out a knife that he certainly wasn't allowed to have and gave a defiant look to Xuha. For the first time, Alex realized that although he was watching the events unfold in slow motion, this time his own body was frozen as sluggish and as useless as all the other bodies around him. He perceived the passage of time at one rate, but for the first time ever his body didn't know how to move at the same speed as his perception.

He watched with horror as Tyler's sluggish arm slowly raised the blade into the air, the point of his knife aimed perfectly to slash into the side of Teddie's unsuspecting and beautiful young face. Alex tried to open his mouth fast, to at least yell to Teddie, to warn her, but he barely felt his lips begin to part as the knife began to plunge towards her.

Then Xuha kicked into high gear. Thank God. The boy sped towards Tyler at a speed that astonished even Alex, who couldn't imagine how fast it must appear to the dawdling brains of the rest of the crowd. Xuha charged past Teddie, whose eyes were very slowly starting to widen behind the camera lens, and that's when Alex saw Tina out of the corner of his own eye.

She was off to one side, with her hand in her purse, gazing at Tyler with what Alex could have sworn was love in her eyes. Love? Deep infatuation anyway, and gratitude. Had the woman actually asked Tyler to entice Xuha into violent behavior? Maybe she had. But her expression was turning slowly more apprehensive as Xuha sped towards Tyler, his racquet raised high and now in position to come down hard on Tyler's collarbone, at exactly the same place where Xuha himself had been injured. Alex suspected that Xuha's fury was now only partly about protecting Teddie. Tina must have surmised the same thing as her face went from mildly worried to outright frightened.

And her hand went from inside her purse to slowly raising up into the air, holding the little gun that Teddie had once said the woman bragged about carrying everywhere.

Just when he most needed it to, Alex's body became able to move with the speed that he required. He had to trust Xuha to handle Tyler. Xuha now had to trust him to handle Tina Johnson.

There were almost no circumstances under which 220-pound Alex Zeitman would consider running full force at and tackling a 130-pound woman. But a 130-pound armed woman about to shoot someone he cared for deeply? A gun did have a way of equalizing things. Alex hit Tina hard from the side, just as she took careful aim, and he fell to the ground on top of her, his weight ending her scream in a muffle.

He looked up to see a baffled Teddie jumping back as Tyler grabbed his hand in pain. Events began to pick up speed as Xuha laid down his racquet, having apparently decided at the last instant to go only for the hand holding the knife. Good call Xuha, Alex thought with relief. As the security guard reached them and grabbed the gun out of Tina's hand, Alex rolled off of Tina. He really had to stop falling onto people like this.

"You idiot," Tina shrieked at the guard, reaching for her gun back while trying to sit up with all the dignity that she could muster. "This man just tried to kill me,"

"No, ma'am, he tried to stop you from shooting someone. I saw it all," the flustered guard insisted.

"You can't be sure what really happened," she said indignantly. "He came at me so fast. For all you know, I pulled that gun out to defend myself after he charged at me."

Teddie came towards them with her camera. "I think I got it all on film," she smiled at Ms. Johnson sweetly. Then she turned to her dad. "Isn't it nice to live at a time in history in which we have the instant replay?"

Over the next few days several choice video clips went viral on the internet. The largely female and minority-filled tennis team charging over the hill with the ball machine to fight the Confederacy was viewed only slightly less often than the self-proclaimed restaurant brigade armed with jugs of ice water and apparently taking on both sides. Late-night comedy shows made snide jokes. Alex would have felt bad for turning his school into the butt of so much humor if his actions hadn't also had the desired effect.

Now under close national scrutiny, the Texas school board began looking into the various allegations against the current administration and policies of Early Gulch. Although not everyone on the board was totally unsympathetic to every part of Ms. Johnson's cause, and at least some of them might ordinarily have let some things slide, the attention forced everyone to consider what was best point forward for the image of Texas schools.

Disciplinary action against the students involved was put on hold pending more information. School officials actually thanked Xuha for his role in stopping the attack on Teddie. Carolyn, the college history teacher, did her part publicizing not only the various ways history had been rewritten at Early Gulch, but more importantly how the "Lost Cause" movement had for well over a century shaped the myth of the grievously wronged South.

The essays on "Why I am glad the South did not win the Civil War" not only made their way onto the internet, but they received far more attention and discussion than they ever would have gotten without the reenactment fiasco. Some began to question exactly why the Fans of the Confederacy had become so involved in a high school's activities and why the local school board had turned a blind eye. Statehouse representatives began an investigation into why certain social studies teachers had been let go recently and whether the high school had developed a "social agenda" that was not in keeping with the policies of inclusion mandated by law.

As the drama began to play itself out, both the tennis coach and the newspaper sponsor were deemed innocent of involvement, but Alex Zeitman and Cindy Shea were called on the carpet for the disruptive role they played, and in the end each received a reprimand for knowingly contributing to a chaotic situation that could have resulted in serious injury. Each apologized, but no one with any powers of observation at all would have concluded that either teacher was the least bit sorry.

Tina Johnson, of course, was dismissed immediately for carrying a concealed weapon onto school property and, more to the point, for aiming said weapon at a student she was well known to dislike. She was charged right away with aggravated assault, but a friendly judge was able to quickly reduce her charges to a misdemeanor punishable with a small fine and community service. Alex took some solace from the fact that at least Tina would never teach again.

Tyler faced charges as an adult for assault with a deadly weapon and his future looked bleak until Teddie decided that she did not want to press charges. Alex wasn't happy about that, but Teddie told her dad that the boy faced enough obstacles after being kicked out of school, and that prison time wasn't going to help his situation. She insisted that the situation was complicated, and that she believed that Tyler would make good use of a second chance.

The principal resigned a week later after it came to light that she had strong ties to the local Klan and an interim principal was appointed. He was a small mousy man from a local middle school who loved paperwork and procedure. Under most circumstances the rest of the staff would have probably disliked him from the start. But these were unusual circumstances. Most of the faculty greeted the baffled little man with uncharacteristic warmth and praised his habit of doing things by the book.

Of course, a good many faculty members and even a few administrators remained who had been quietly sympathetic to Tina's cause. Some would choose to move on now that the climate of the school was changing, while others would just become less outspoken about their beliefs. Alex knew that, sadly, there was no quick fix for eradicating hatred. One could punish the overt acts, and could drive the leaders away. But every human holds in his own heart the beliefs that he chooses. Time, innate kindness and good experiences can wear down biases, sometimes. In other cases, it takes another whole generation to let go of the hatred of the past. But only if that next generation isn't specifically taught the same hatreds.

Alex shuddered, thinking about Tina's crusade to pass her particular brands of loathing on to a new generation. Would the many open discussions at the school prompted by the last couple of weeks work to undo a little of what Tina had started? He hoped so.

Alex was jogging along comfortably when one of the light

creatures began to overtake him from behind.

"Haven't seen you in a while," she said in a friendly manner.

"Yeah, well, I've been kind of busy. Say, I have a question for you," he said in an equally friendly fashion.

"Ask away."

"If I change my speed a lot relative to you then I see things happening more quickly or more slowly. But I always see them in the same order, in the same sequence of events, right?"

"Pretty much," she said. "What I mean by that is that the arrow of time technically can go both directions, so that the sequence stays the same but the entire order could be reversed but," she looked at him closely, "you don't care about that do you? Of course not. Time only goes one way for you. So yes, in essence the order is always the same no matter how quickly or slowly the events happen. One, two, three, four. All the changing of speed in the universe cannot alter the order."

"So if a lady sees something she does not like, pulls a gun out of her purse, and then I tackle her to keep her from shooting, and we both fall to the ground, the fact is that she really does pull the gun out before I tackle her?" Alex asked.

"I think you should start spending time with less violent people," the light being said with just a tiny bit of snippiness. She knew what was coming.

"I'll repeat my question. The woman REALLY does pull the gun out before I tackle her?"

"Yes, Alex," the creature sighed. "She really does."

"In other words," and now Alex was grinning broadly, "in other words, there really is a really?"

"Yes Alex," the creature sighed. "In that sense, there is a really."

"Thank you," Alex said.

And he never dreamt about the light creatures again.

Lola had fairly little to say to Alex about the reenactment, although it dominated the local news for several days and Alex was sure that she and Teddie had talked all about it. He let it go for a week. It was one of those beautiful days at the end January that mark the beginning of spring in the South, and Lola was enjoying her Sunday afternoon getting one of her back gardens ready for planting. As she happily played in the dirt he brought her out an iced tea.

"Have you been mad at me for the last week and just hiding it?" he asked.

"Not really," she laughed. "I speak up when I'm mad at you. You ought to know that by now. No, I'm proud of what you accomplished, even though as a mother I just don't feel like I can offer any praise on the subject."

"You think I put Teddie in danger?" he asked.

"You did," she answered, "but the whole situation was dangerous. I get that you were trying to end a bad business at your school and it fortunately ended well. You and Teddie are fine. I'm glad that Xuha is going to be eighteen in a couple of weeks, so you won't have to worry about problems with his living here, and your new principal is at least predictable, with no hidden agenda, so I think you pretty much got life back to normal."

"Speaking of normal," Alex began hesitantly, "what exactly did Teddie say about how I stopped Ms. Johnson?"

"She said you flew like the wind. Apparently you have some super sonic speed abilities left over from your days on a basketball court," Lola said.

"Yeah, I guess I do."

"Do you think that what you can do is outside the range of normal?" Lola asked, and Alex was fairly certain that his frame of mind prompted the question.

"Yeah."

"That's nice," Lola smiled up at him. "I'd hate to find out that I'm married to someone who is normal."

"What I mean is…." and then he stopped. Lola had been cleaning off a stone marker she kept in this little rose garden. The Zeitmans lived far from where Lola's parents were buried and Lola's mother had loved roses. So Lola had made a sort of memorial of her own, planting a mess of roses, adding a couple of statues from her parents' yard, and then placing in the center of the garden this little stone marker that Alex had seen dozens of times and never paid much attention to.

It said, "When someone you love becomes a memory, the memory becomes a treasure." Nice words. Unless you've spent the last year treasure-hunting and all you've ended up with is a garbled recipe that doesn't make much sense but ought to give you something you treasure. Health? Time? Alex and Stan and the others had considered all those. But what if the treasure was memories?

"I think I'll call Zane. Doesn't he have a friend at Penthes—Maven, Raven, somebody who knows a lot about plants and the brain?" Alex said suddenly.

"I think her name is Raven. What's this about dear?"

Alex reached down to help pull his wife up off the ground so that he could give her a hug and a long kiss.

"I think that I may have found it," he said.

"What? Found your heart's desire right in your own back yard?" she giggled.

"That too. But more to the point, I think I may have found the last clue to the greatest treasure of all time. It was sitting right here in your garden."

January 1698

Nimah sat by the little waterfall, dipping her own tired feet into the stream while she watched Naylay laugh and talk with the imaginary creatures she played with all the time. For just a moment Nimah wondered if Naylay's sprites and faeries were real, watching over the twosome that hid in the cave. It was a nice thought.

Of course, long ago her own father had insisted to her that all the things she imagined were real. He had been funny that way, playful and creative, and she supposed that is part of what had made him such an excellent healer. He saw magic everywhere, felt power in every plant and animal around him. Thus he had become her people's most advanced developer of medicines. For with his imagination had also come a keen mind, and knowledge of how of every part of every plant prepared every imaginable way could affect a living body.

Born into a family of healers, he had built on the vast knowledge of those before him. His only sorrows had been the early loss of Nimah's mother, and the fact that his own crowning achievement was developed too late to help the failing memories of many of those he loved.

But he had been able to try it with others. When prepared with great care, exactly as he instructed, over and over again her father's gift had stopped the memory loss that plagued so many of the elders. Even young Nimah had understood the value of this treasure.

"The rest of medicine will catch up," he told her. "Our descendants will live longer and they will need this gift even more. The invaders will come, and they would destroy all record of it, never knowing what they took from this world in the name of their god and in their quest for gold."

And so, as Nimah nursed her father as he died from an illness that even he could not cure, she had promised him to find a way to hide his treasure. Yes, she would preserve every single piece of the complex instructions. Yes, she would do it in a way that would intrigue others, would beg them to solve her mystery. She would set things in motion so that it would take many cycles of years before the puzzle she would design could be solved. Yes, there would be some chance of course that it might be lost forever.

"I don't think it will be," her father had said with his usual optimism when she told him what she planned to do. "Make your boxes particularly beautiful so that people will look after them. And unusual so it will be obvious that they go together. It's a clever idea. I think that when it's a good time for all three boxes to be reunited, then they will be."

As Nimah wiggled her toes in the little stream, she realized that she did believe that someday her father's descendants would have his gift. And when that time finally came, they also would have learned to treat each other with compassion. She let a handful of water run through her fingers. It would be many, many years, surely, but she believed that it could happen. She supposed that is what made her such a hopeful person too.

After

Chapter 20. May 2011

Kisa had prepared a picnic, and she surprised Kyle by insisting that they head over to the beautiful little waterfall outside the cave for their lunch today. As they made the short drive over, Kyle listened to Kisa's stories of how the cave was interwoven into her family's history, having provided shelter and workspace, and, when necessary, a place to hide or to pray or to contemplate over the generations. She was happy that finally she had learned to appreciate the spot just for the beauty it offered, and had even come to appreciate the freedom of no longer being responsible for protecting her ancestors' valuables.

Kyle confessed to Kisa that he felt at home here too and was in no hurry to leave. Kisa was a little surprised by how much that news made her happy.

Now that Kyle was no longer on Jake's payroll, he had begun working as a liaison between Kisa and her family and the company in Chicago that was trying to reconstruct a drug to cure dementia from the still somewhat incomplete directions that Stan and others had pieced together. Alex's hunch had been confirmed and knowing the purpose of the drug had helped a great deal.

Kyle's new boss, Gil, was the man who had run the Penthes drug company now for the last year or so. Stan's old friend Alex and Alex's son both spoke highly of him, and he did appear to be a man of honor. He had paid Kisa and her relatives, the Belizean boy Yochi's family and the Maya high school kid Xuha all a fair sum for the rights to use the information on each of their boxes to try to re-construct this drug from the data available. If such a drug was ultimately found to be effective and approved, all three would receive a small percentage of the sales for the first twenty years. It was possible that Kisa would see some real treasure yet.

Given how convoluted it appeared that the eventual financial arrangements would be, Jake uncharacteristically declined to argue for any part of the eventual booty for himself. He laughed that the business he had founded to fund his treasure-hunting with Kyle had, in fact, turned out to be his treasure. Stan and Shelby had been highly paid as consultants for their work in translating and understanding the pieces of the puzzle, and they probably would get additional well-paid consulting jobs with Penthes for years to come. It wouldn't make them rich, but it was a nice supplement to the work they both already did and enjoyed. Kyle had a strong suspicion that both of their paychecks were now going into one account and that the arrangement would likely be made public and official before too long.

Jennifer also did not request any piece of the prize, stating simply that all she did want was Kisa's forgiveness for any insult she may have unknowingly made due to just being young and fun-loving. She had grown up since and learned more about respecting the customs of others, and she wished no bad feelings.

Kisa had responded with great grace, Kyle thought, saying that she had grown too and become more worldly, and could recognize Jennifer's exuberance and love of life for what it had been. No insult should be taken where none was intended. And thus the two women seemed to have forged an odd respect.

Which, Kyle supposed, should probably have prepared him for exactly why Kisa wanted to have a picnic in this secluded spot. As they began to unload the supplies from the car, she spread out a nice thick blanket. And then she placed another one on top of it. And then a third. As she pulled a fourth blanket out of the car, Kyle laughed.

"Good grief. How many blankets do we need to sit on?" Then he saw Kisa blush. Ah, yes. There was more than one way to eradicate the ghosts of the past, wasn't there? And some ways were clearly more pleasurable than others.

Like the other teachers attending the graduation ceremony, Alex was clad in a disposable, thin black polyester robe and the ridiculous flat hat that some idiot had decided would make graduates the world over look intelligent. It was a stupid costume, but he knew that the school counted on teachers to be there, appropriately dressed, to sit at the end of the rows and provide a certain amount of crowd control to keep the jubilant graduates from getting out of hand. Alex also knew that on some level the kids appreciated the attendance. It added more significance to the day, made them feel like they and this event were important. And Alex was all for that. Normally his school struggled with an almost thirty-percent dropout rate, and any little thing he could do to make a student want to graduate was a good thing.

The class of 2011, however, had turned out differently. There was something raw and real in the months following the disastrous reenactment of the battle of Cedar Creek, and most of the students at the school formerly known as Early Gulch recognized that the insipid and irrelevant world of school had somehow crossed wires with real life. Knowledge, history, truth, science, facts and laws had consequences that mattered. As did actions. Go figure. The dropout rate had at least temporarily plummeted while curiosity and tolerance both seemed to reach new heights.

Teddie and Lola were sitting with the other families, while newly graduated Ariel had stayed home to organize her things for her big trip to start her new job. Alex's stomach twisted a little when he thought about how far away his oldest daughter would be. He looked up into the bleachers and gave Teddie a wistful look. As if Ariel's going away wasn't enough, last month Teddie had surprised them by asking if she could apply for a student exchange program and spend the first semester of her junior year abroad. Armed with best friend Michelle's enthusiasm and Michelle's Vietnamese parents' support, the girls were hoping for an assignment somewhere in Southeast Asia. Alex thought that Lola had reluctantly supported the idea in hopes that Teddie would change her mind, but no mind change seemed to be forthcoming. It was hard to imagine starting the school year without Teddie.

However, next year would also be without Tina Johnson, without the former new principal, and without several others that Alex would not miss in the least. Rumor had it that Tina's friends had already helped her to relocate to a smaller community in Eastern Texas where her current notoriety made her something of a hero in the eyes of many. In spite of the fact that she couldn't get a teaching job in a public school, Alex heard that a small private school in that area had offered her a position for the next school year. He shuddered, thinking how in small pockets the world over hate was still carefully being taught to the next generation.

Then he noticed that both Lola and Teddie were trying to take photos of Xuha, and he had to smile. There was no denying that Xuha had become a welcome addition to their own family. When some in the community had persisted in trying to verify Xuha's citizenship, a border patrol guard from seventeen years ago that Tina had unearthed suddenly developed amnesia about the case. Perhaps the man wanted to do Xuha a favor, or perhaps he just wanted to keep his own life simple and stay far from the limelight cast by the now-infamous reenactment. Either way, without specific testimony to the contrary, it had been ruled that a birth certificate listing Xuha as born on the way to a Houston hospital made him a U.S. citizen. Alex thought that decision was clearly the United States' gain.

Graduating in the top ten percent of his class had guaranteed Xuha admission to any state university, and thanks to the payment from Penthes, Xuha had the means to take advantage of that. He had decided to go the university in El Paso. Alex wished that he wasn't going so far way, but he suspected Xuha would be doing a good bit of volunteer work with the young Mexicans who had recently come across the border, helping those like himself and his now deported foster brother to avoid trouble and to fit into their new home. El Paso was going to be lucky to have him. And, with any luck, Xuha would also be well located for finding and being able to visit the foster family he loved.

As he moved his legs to make his stiffening knee more comfortable, Alex found that his mind wandered during the first couple of speeches. *I ought to do this time travel thing again next year,* he thought. *In fact, I could spend a few weeks the first semester talking about the nature of time in all my classes. Every year. Who knows? If I keep the club going and let the kids build on what's been done before then maybe after a while we'll even come up with some new ideas about time.* Now that did sound like fun.

There were only two speeches that Alex actually listened to, in both cases because they were surprising. Well, to be fair, the first of these was supposed to be odd. The school typically let the valedictorian and salutatorian say a few words, and then selected three other students from the graduating seniors to bring in other points of view. Xuha had been chosen, probably because of his role in so many of the events, and had been given three minutes. Alex's advice to him had been to say something unexpected. Xuha had listened.

"My name is Xuha Santos and I am a time traveler," the boy began. Much of the crowd stopped whispering and listened more closely. "I began my time travels on February twenty-first, nineteen-ninety-three while crossing the border from Mexico, and ever since then I have been moving forward through time. Although occasionally it seems to me that time moves faster or slower than usual," and here he paused to give Alex a meaningful look, "the fact is that I lack the skills to stop time or to turn it around. So I have to keep going forward."

Several faces in the audience began to look less puzzled as they began to understand what he meant. Xuha went on. "Like all time travelers, I wear an imaginary ring. Me, I like to think that it was forged by a clever wizard who was forced to create it against his better judgment. 'Make something which will turn sorrow into joy, and joy into sorrow,' he was ordered. Wasting no true magic on the request, he created a ring that said, 'This too shall pass.' And so it does. For with time travel comes change, change every single second, whether I like it or not.

"I've been asked if I think I was born at a good time." Xuha shrugged comically. "I was born in a car so, technically, no, I guess it wasn't a good time."

He paused for the bit of laughter. "I hope that each of you understands that you are time travelers too. You wear the same ring, and you join me and everyone else in the whole world in a steady forced march of one second per second. For those of you who feel like we have been trapped forever in high school, lately that march has turned into a crawl, and these last nine months have taken forever. For those of you dreading the end of high school fun and the start of more responsibilities, our march turned into a sprint, as the last months flew by.

"But whether any day feels fast or slow to us, we must keep moving. We don't know what kind of world we are marching into. But we do know that if we are alive, we are going into the future. And there, together, we will all find out what happens."

Alex thought that the warm applause that followed Xuha as he took his seat was a fine sign of just how far the school had come in the year and a half since Xuha had arrived.

The second speech that Alex listened to was the very last one, and it wasn't even on the program. But after the diplomas had been handed out, the new principal took the stage to dismiss the crowd, and then he paused and held on to the mike for a second. Looking down, he muttered that he wanted all of the families to know how much he, the school board and administration regretted some of the odd and unfortunate events of the past year.

Alex noticed the man pausing again, as if he were trying to decide whether he should leave it at that or go on. Then the principal looked up, stared directly at Alex and smiled. *What in the world,* Alex wondered.

"I recently joined a school club called z^2," the principal said, more loudly. "Some of you know it for its famous mind experiments with time machines, but I consider myself a member, even though I am the principal, because I like the idea behind it. That is, we are all not only going to the future, whether we like it or not, as a student just pointed out, but that each one of us helps to make that future that we are going to. We do that with our actions, or our lack of them, every single day. So I want to say a few quick words to you right now, because I am personally determined to make the timeline we are all going to live on a better one.

"You see, I feel strongly that blindly admiring a historic figure without knowing much about him is just a bad idea," the principal stated firmly, "and even though our school wasn't so much named for Jubal Early, as it was for a nearby gulch that for whatever reason was named for him, he still became our namesake. And I do not believe that the man deserves that honor. I am going to read you a quote. It will be offensive to many and I apologize for that. But these are Jubal Early's own words, and you should hear them."

"Reason, common sense, true humanity to the black, as well as the safety of the white race, required that the inferior race should be kept in a state of subordination. The conditions of domestic slavery, as it existed in the South, had not only resulted in a great improvement in the moral and physical condition of the negro race, but had furnished a class of laborers as happy and contented as any in the world."

The principal went on. "I abhor those words and I want us all to face the fact that Jubal Early and all of his fellow Confederate officers took up arms against the United States of America. Don't get me wrong, I'm glad that we chose to forgive them because forgiveness is what we needed back then for this nation to heal." The principal took a deep breath before he went on.

"However, I'm glad that they lost their war, because although I was born and raised here in the South, frankly I'm glad that I'm part of this great nation. As an American, and as one who has served his country in the military, I do not understand continuing to honor these men. The Confederate officers were traitors. And they did not become traitors to fight for some noble ideal, and every one of us knows it. We do know exactly what they were fighting for. We need only listen to their own words. No other nation builds statues of and names schools after its traitors, or its leaders that clung to cruel practices of any kind in spite of evolving morals.

"And answering those charges by saying that those in the north hardly treated non-Europeans any better is beside the point. It may be true, but here at this school if you do something wrong you don't escape punishment by pointing out that others did something almost as bad. I hold these men to that same standard.

"And that was why I have asked the school board to rename this school." The muttering of the crowd picked up volume and the principal paused for people to quiet back down. "They didn't like the idea at first, but after I read them the very quote that I just read to you, they agreed to look into an appropriate new name. That process will take a while, so in the meantime, I am," and now the man smiled, "I am hereby declaring the new temporary name of this school to be Hope High School." He shrugged, a little embarrassed. "We have to call it something, and I do like to think that we all hope for a better tomorrow."

Some people sat stunned and a few seemed angry, others looked confused and applauded politely. But over half the crowd rose to their feet and clapped with all the enthusiasm they could show. They all believed that next year, Hope High School was going to have a much better year.

Chapter 21. July 2045

Alex hadn't really wanted to travel to Chicago for the Penthes celebration, but Lola had pushed and pleaded and finally it had been easier to agree to go than to fight with her about it. Yes, of course he was excited to see Teddie and her son, and to meet grandson John's new girlfriend. Yes, it was going to be Zane's big day, as the pharmaceutical company his son had helped shape decades ago was planning to hold a special award dinner this year for Zane. Of course Alex wanted to cheer him on.

But somehow when the rest of the family got together, Alex felt Ariel's absence in ways he didn't normally notice. Sure, she would video call in, her quick smile and bright blue eyes barely diminished by the long hard years and the responsibilities she had carried so well. Alex was more proud of her than he could say. But, as the rest of them laughed and touched and hugged, he would also miss her physical presence almost more than he could bear.

And as the pains in his aging body grew, he had learned to avoid adding emotional pain to the mix as well. Which was why he had simply failed to mention his latest ailments to Lola. Their times together were still good, not yet tinged with the bittersweet tug of thinking this might be the last this or the last that. He wanted to keep it that way for as long as he could. So finally he acquiesced, rather than tell Lola that he was just too sick to travel. When he got home, he promised himself that he would finally get to the doctor and let the inevitable process of unwinding begin. Lola would understand why he had waited.

Once he was actually in Chicago, of course, Alex was glad that he came. He couldn't help but notice that Zane's partner Afi seemed to suffer from almost as many aches and pains as Alex himself, and Alex hoped that the sweet man from the islands of Kiribati was healthier than he seemed.

Zane showed up for the dinner still clueless that he was the guest of honor, although he had dressed better than usual. Alex had to guess that was Afi's doing. Alex decided to sit next to his fourteen-year-old grandson who looked highly uncomfortable in the dress clothes Teddie must have forced on him. Alex could identify.

Fortunately, the boy was almost as big a fan of baseball as his grandfather, and the two of them soon forgot their discomfort with a rousing discussion of who was likely to make it into post-season play. Alex had once held similar conversions with his own grandfather, he realized wistfully. It was nice that not everything had changed.

"I thought we'd do something a little different this year," Gil, the former head of Penthes, stepped up to the mike and began, getting the chatter in the large room to quiet down. "Part of celebrating the story of Penthes, I decided, would be, every once in a while, to step back and celebrate some of the wonderful side stories that this amazing company has spun off."

As the group paid the first tribute to one of Zane's friends, Alex allowed himself the luxury of letting time move just a little more quickly for him than it did for the rest of the guests. Not so quickly that he would miss something, or appear unresponsive or ill himself. But over the years Alex had figured out that he could still behave more or less normally while time moved at about twice its normal rate, and he spent only half as much time being bored. Was he missing out on part of his life when he indulged himself in this little trick? He honestly did not know, but he only bothered to do it when he was pretty certain that whatever it was he missed didn't matter.

Not that he didn't like this friend Toby. The man was great, and Alex wished him well. Alex just wanted to get to the part of the evening that was about Zane. He heard Gil's rapid staccato say, "But today, focusing one's life, one's company or one's culture on wealth preservation is more likely to be considered the waste of good living time that it always was. I like to think that we have Toby and y^1 to thank not only, in part, for this company, but also for the fact that there seem to be a lot of happier, healthier people around these days who are actually enjoying their lives."

As the room laughed and applauded like chipmunks, Alex forced his consciousness to slow down, to experience time at the normal pace. As Toby took the microphone to thank Gil, Alex turned his focus to his son. This was going to be interesting. If anyone in the world hated public speaking more than Alex, it had to be Zane.

Toby sat down to more enthusiastic applause, and the tribute to Zane began. Alex wanted to enjoy this, to savor it, so now he willed time to pass just a little more slowly. Not too much so, or the words and actions all around him would become too distorted, and he himself would appear nervous and fidgety.

Zane made his way to the front of the room and muttered "thank you" while he accepted a plaque, and he added a few vague words about how happy he was that he had in some small way helped. The crowd quieted, straining to hear him. *Going to have to say more than that buddy,* Alex chuckled to himself sympathetically. He watched Zane swallow hard and begin to speak from the heart. The room sensed it and went silent.

"You know, when you are a little kid you have just no idea how your life is going to turn out," he began. "You don't even really know how you want it to turn out. You have no clue what it is you want to be." Then Zane seemed to notice his father smiling. He went on talking, but it was clear to Alex that his son was still struggling to find that one cohesive statement that the crowd so clearly wanted to hear.

Hoping to help, Alex picked up his water glass as though as he was about to make a toast. Zane caught the gesture and figured it out. He'd always been a smart kid. Zane reached for a water glass, picked it up and raised it high.

"To each and every human being getting to joyfully do the dance of life." Zane paused and smiled. "I don't mean just a couple of quiet toe taps, people. I mean twirl-around-in-circles-while-pumping-your-fists-in-the-air dancing. Get your feet moving, because whether you dance with fire or polka bands, with drums, or bagpipes or with a full orchestra, no one can do your particular dance better than you. So dance it with joy."

The applause started and grew until it was thunderous. Alex let time slow way down as he cherished his child's moment of glory and savored his own contribution to it. The sound of the applause took his memory back to that high school graduation in 2011, when a shy new principal had gotten a standing ovation after taking a cue from Alex.

Alex guessed that in his heart he was still that point guard who tended to pass rather than shoot. Decades in the classroom, as a dad, and as a coach, had only strengthened his tendency to be happy knowing that he had contributed to the win. He had in fact taught a Nobel Prize-winner in Physics. More meaningful to him, he had been credited by over a dozen former students in nine separate groundbreaking studies on the nature of time, each of which had its roots in z^2. Yes, he was the guy that knew how to pass the ball, and he got it to the right player at the right time. And Alex liked being that guy.

Later that night, getting ready for bed, Lola reached over and took his hand.

"Now then, it was a good time, wasn't it?" He knew of course that she was talking about the evening and about the whole trip up to Chicago. But he wasn't. He was talking about much more. He was talking about it all.

"Yes," he said sincerely. "It was a very good time."

Chapter 22, March 2064

Zane recognized that today his mom was likely at the end of her life. She'd been approaching it now for months, accepting comfort but refusing any further life-prolonging intervention. The family had spent as much time with her as they were able, but, as so often happens when dying is a very slow process, the living had had to keep on living. He hoped that his mother understood. As he reached to call Teddie again to see what was taking her so long, he saw his mother wince with pain as she stirred.

"Mom? Try to hang on please. I called Teddie and she's on her way, she'll be here in just a few minutes. Please mom. You know Teddie. She'll be so upset if she doesn't make it in time."

It was true. Teddie and his mom had been saying goodbye for months now, Zane was pretty sure, but Teddie would still be upset. And then Zane had another thought. What if his mom asked why Ariel wasn't on her way as well? His mother's memory had been coming and going for weeks, and Zane didn't want to have to start any conversation right now that might upset her. So he improvised. "Ariel is trying too Mom, but it's going to take her longer to get here. Hang on, okay? At least a little longer."

His mom closed her eyes, tired, but with a look of peace on her face, and Zane thought *This is it. This is how every single human story finally ends. Anything else is just a pause. There is no other real ending.* Then reached for her hand and held it gently. And Teddie picked that second to charge through the door.

"Mom. No. Let me say goodbye first." And Lola's eyes opened back up with a start. Then she whispered with sudden urgency. "Where the hell is your dad? I forgot. I need to tell him something." She shifted a little in discomfort.

Zane didn't know what to answer, so he said nothing. Teddie, on the other hand, answered right away. "He's on his way mom. He'll be here any minute." And she turned to Zane and gave him a meaningful look.

"You know that I don't do that any more," Zane muttered under his breath to Teddie as they both moved away from the bed so that their mother could not hear.

"Yeah well it's not exactly like this is a common every day occurrence," Teddie whispered back, gesturing at their mom's bed. "You know. Maybe this could be a one time exception?"

Zane sighed. Teddie was right of course. "Okay. But turn around and don't watch. It's harder if somebody is watching me do it."

"So go into the bathroom and come back out as dad."

"Yeah, okay." That actually was a good idea too.

A few minutes later, a man who was to all appearances an elderly Alex Zeitman walked out of the hospice suite bathroom. Lola's eyes lit up. It was so good to see his face. It had been such a very long time. Where the hell had he been? Lola struggled to recall the thing that had been so important to tell Alex. The thing he just had to know. Dammit, between the medicine and pain she could hardly hold a thought in her head anymore.

Wait. That was it. Holding a thought in her head. Lola recalled those dark, horrible days back in 2046 after Alex had died. After she had said her goodbyes to him, it had seemed like half the life had gone out of her own body as well, and then half her thoughts and memories just seemed to follow.

She remembered Teddie sitting down with her not long after, gently looking her in the eye, telling her that the dementia was taking hold fast. Her best bet remained the Penthes treatment. One of the plants had never been found, of course, and was finally presumed extinct, but the synthesis of its most likely components had improved radically over the decades and the treatment was now far safer and more effective. She should try it.

Lola had agreed without hesitation. It was, after all, the cure that her own family had contributed to finding. Surely it was right for her.

And it had been. For eighteen years now, she had enjoyed the memories of holding her little children, seeing her tiny grandchildren's smiles. She had relived holidays and travels and friendships and successes and more joy than a single soul probably had a right to claim. But, most of all, she had held Alex and their love for each other in her mind and her heart, and that had gotten her through the worst hardships old age had brought.

And she'd never been able to thank Alex.

She reached out to squeeze his hand. Only it was Teddie's hand. She was confused but there was Teddie's face smiling at her while Alex had turned away. Wait, what was Alex doing there anyway? Hadn't he died years ago? But he seemed to be dabbing at his eyes with a tissue.

"It's okay. Uh, dad needs a minute," Teddie said.

Alex turned back to her. "You wanted to tell me something, dear?"

"Just 'thank you.'" For what you did with Stan and Xuha and that whole treasure hunting thing decades ago. If it hadn't been for you, you know, they never would have solved it."

"You weren't so happy with me at the time," Alex smiled. She squeezed his hand.

"I know. That's why I needed to tell you this so badly now."

She paused, gathering what little strength she had.

"Thank you." It looked like she lacked the strength to say more, but after a pause, she added, "for all the memories I got to enjoy after you left. I had to tell you," she said as her eyes fluttered closed, "that they truly were the greatest treasure ever."

(If you liked Alex's adventures, you may also enjoy reading x^0 and y^1, companion novels in this collection. Also, watch for c^3, a fourth novel about another member the Zeitman family that will be available in late 2013.)

Thanks and Links:

I would like to give a special thank you to my husband Kevin Cronin, not only for his encouragement and support but also for his research into the civil war and for his sense of adventure in attending an actual re-enactment of the battle of Cedar Creek. Thanks also go to him for his collaboration on the day-to-day workings of a high school, his expertise on everything from basketball to sun sets, and for his clever design of the shapes of the three boxes. This novel was a joint creative effort between us and could not have been nearly as rich a story without his many contributions.

Thanks also go to friend and Adjunct Associate Math Professor John Ryan for all the information on Maya math, his formula to approximate the solstice location of the rising sun, and his information on hate groups and immigration reform. Thanks to my three children Casey, Shenandoah and Emerald Cronin for their help and encouragement, and to sister June Hanson for her wonderful page by page suggestions and creative help with the cover design. Thanks finally to Joel Handley for once again providing such capable editing.

Although this book is work of fiction, where news items, cultural information, and scientific facts are included, it was my intent to be as accurate as I could. Therefore I would like to express my thanks to the following printed and internet sources for general information and background material used in this book. Any misrepresentation of information from these sources is unintentional and regretted.

Printed Materials:

Immigration Law and Procedure in a Nutshell, 6th edition. David Weissbrodt and Laura Danielson.
ISBN 978-0-314-19944-7.
Inside Organized Racism: Women in the Hate Movement. Kathleen M. Blee.
ISBN 0-520-2174-5

The Myth of the Lost Cause and Civil War History. Edited by Gary W. Gallagher and Alan T. Nolan. ISBN 0-253-33822-0
It's About Time: Understanding Einstein's Relativity. N. David Mermin. ISBN 978-0-691-12201-4
The Shenandoah Valley Campaign of 1864. Edited by Gary W. Gallagher. ISBN 978-0-8078-5956-8
I, Rigoberta Menchu: An Indian Woman in Guatemala, 2nd edition. Rigoberta Menchu. ISBN 978-1-84467-418-3
Physics of the Impossible: A Scientific Exploration into the World of Phasers, Force Fields, Teleportation, and Time Travel. Michio Kaku. ISBN 978-0-385-52069-0
Reminiscences of the Civil War. John Brown Gordon
Popol Vuh: The definitive Edition of the Mayan Book of the Dawn of Life and the Glories of Gods and Kings Translated by Dennis Tedlock. ISBN 978-0-684-81845
They Called Themselves the K.K.K.: The Birth of an American Terrorist Group. Susan Campbell Bartoletti. ISBN 978-0-618-44033-7

The blog for this book can be found at http://www.zsquaredblog.org
Donations from the author's proceeds go to http://www.splcenter.org

The electronic version of this book contains links to the following websites (given here by chapter in order):

Chapter 2
Irene Cara performing "Fame"
http://www.youtube.com/watch?v=nTJHjuhCYos
http://irenecara.com/entry.htm

Chapter 3
http://www.authenticmaya.com/tayasal.htm

Chapter 5
http://treasuretrovegold.blogspot.com/2008/12/basic-treasure-trove-laws.html
http://library.uwb.edu/guides/usimmigration/1875_page_law.html

Chapter 6
http://ocp.hul.harvard.edu/immigration/exclusion.html

http://www.dummies.com/how-to/content/einstein-storms-the-scientific-world.html
http://en.wikipedia.org/wiki/File:Usumacinta.jpg

Chapter 7

Jerry Butler performing "Only the Strong Survive"
https://www.youtube.com/watch?v=Na0_KxRFK-M
http://cbswnewhd.wordpress.com/2011/05/28/going-for-the-gold-jerry-butlers-only-the-strong-survive/

Chapter 8

http://immigration-online.org/362-asiatic-barred-zone.html

Chapter 10

http://www.splcenter.org/get-informed/intelligence-files/ideology/christian-identity
Jimmy Buffett performing "Changes in Latitudes" at a concert in Gulf Shores, Alabama on July 11, 2010 in response to BP's ongoing oil spill in the Gulf of Mexico.
http://www.youtube.com/watch?v=b7JpxavO9NE
http://www.margaritaville.com/
http://academic.udayton.edu/health/01status/mental01.htm

Chapter 11

http://www.globalcoral.org/why_are_coral_reefs_dying.htm
http://www.stanncreek.com/attract_dangriga.html

Chapter 12

Diana Ross and the Supremes performing "Stop! In the Name of Love"
https://www.youtube.com/watch?v=6yPcoS7Y38Q
http://rockhall.com/inductees/the-supremes/

Chapter 13

Vanity Fare performing Hitchin` A Ride
http://www.youtube.com/watch?v=TIwnAs4iwaE
http://www.funtrivia.com/en/subtopics/Hitchin-A-Ride-281124.html
NSYNC performing Bye Bye Bye.
https://www.youtube.com/watch?v=yxf2Q0YoYQQ
http://www.nsync.com/

Chapter 14

Bonnie Tyler performing "Holding Out for a Hero"

https://www.youtube.com/watch?v=OBwS66EBUcY
http://www.bonnietyler.com/
http://www.nytimes.com/1988/03/01/us/amnesty-sale-the-medium-is-the-tortilla.html
http://www.belizemagazine.com/edition03/english/e03_16newrichmond.htm

Chapter 15

http://www.houstonculture.org/hispanic/memorial.html

Chapter 16

http://www.immigrationpolicy.org/issues/DREAM-Act

Chapter 18

Ben E. King performing "Stand by Me"
https://www.youtube.com/watch?v=Vbg7YoXiKn0
http://www.beneking.info/
Marvin Gaye and Tammi Terrell performing "Ain't No Mountain"
http://www.youtube.com/watch?v=H6AdUMHazNo
http://www.marvingayepage.net/

These links are available live at http://www.zsquaredblog.org

About the author:

Sherrie Roth grew up in Western Kansas thinking that there was no place in the universe more fascinating than outer space. After her mother vetoed astronaut as a career ambition, she went on to study journalism and physics in hopes of becoming a science writer.

She published her first science fiction short story in 1979 and then waited a lot of tables while she looked for inspiration for the next story. When it finally came, it declared to her that it had to be whole book, nothing less. One night, while digesting this disturbing piece of news, she drank way too many shots of ouzo with her boyfriend. She woke up thirty-one years later demanding to know what was going on.

The boyfriend, who she had apparently long since married, asked her to calm down and explained that in a fit of practicality she had gone back to school and gotten a degree in geophysics and had spent the last 28 years interpreting seismic data in the oil industry. The good news, according to Mr. Cronin, was that she had found it at least mildly entertaining and ridiculously well-paying. The bad news was that the two of them had still managed to spend almost all of the money.

Apparently she was now Mrs. Cronin, and the further good news was that they had produced three wonderful children whom they loved dearly, even though to be honest that is where a lot of the money had gone. Even better news was that Mr. Cronin turned out to be a warm-hearted, encouraging sort who was happy to see her awake and ready to write. "It's about time," were his exact words.

Sherrie Cronin discovered that over the ensuing decades Sally Ride had already managed to become the first woman in space and apparently had done a fine job of it. No one, however, had written the book that had been in Sherrie's head for decades. The only problem was, the book informed her sternly that it had now grown into a six book series. Sherrie decided that she better start writing it before it got any longer. She's been wide awake ever since, and writing away.

Made in the USA
Charleston, SC
29 August 2013